Christmas 2002 – Xmas m... ... ...
num.)

PENGUIN

THE LAST CHRONI...

Miss Read, or in real life Mrs Dora Saint, was a teacher by profession who started writing after the Second World War, beginning with light essays written for *Punch* and other journals. She has written on educational and country matters, and has worked as a scriptwriter for the BBC. Miss Read is married to a retired schoolmaster and they live in a tiny Berkshire hamlet. She was made an MBE for her services to literature in the 1998 New Year's Honours list.

Miss Read is the author of numerous books, which have gained immense popularity for their humorous and honest depictions of English rural life. She wrote two major series of novels about the villages of Thrush Green and Fairacre, the final titles being *The Year at Thrush Green* (1995) and *A Peaceful Retirement* (1996), the latter marking Miss Read's own retirement. She has also written a cookery book, *Miss Read's Country Cooking*, and two autobiographical works, *A Fortunate Grandchild* and *Time Remembered*, published together in one volume as *Early Days*. Many of her books are published by Penguin, together with twelve omnibus editions. This omnibus concludes the Fairacre series, and *Farewell, Thrush Green*, published by Penguin in 2000, completed the Thrush Green series.

BOOKS BY MISS READ

Novels

Village School

Storm in the Village

Fresh from the Country

Miss Clare Remembers

The Market Square

The Howards of Caxley

News from Thrush Green

Tyler's Row

Farther Afield

No Holly for Miss Quinn

Return to Thrush Green

Village Centenary

Affairs at Thrush Green

At Home in Thrush Green

Mrs Pringle

Changes at Fairacre

Farewell to Fairacre

The Year at Thrush Green

Village Diary

Thrush Green

Winter in Thrush Green

Over the Gate

Village Christmas

Fairacre Festival

Emily Davis

The Christmas Mouse

Battles at Thrush Green

Village Affairs

The White Robin

Gossip from Thrush Green

Summer at Fairacre

The School at Thrush Green

Friends at Thrush Green

Celebrations at Thrush Green

Tales from a Village School

A Peaceful Retirement

Anthologies

Country Bunch

Miss Read's Christmas Book

Omnibuses

FAIRACRE

Chronicles of Fairacre

Further Chronicles of Fairacre

Fairacre Roundabout

Christmas at Fairacre

Fairacre Affairs

The Last Chronicle of Fairacre

THRUSH GREEN

Life at Thrush Green

More Stories from Thrush Green

Tales from Thrush Green

Encounters at Thrush Green

Farewell, Thrush Green

also

The Caxley Chronicles

Non-Fiction

Tiggy

Miss Read's Country Cooking

Early Days

The World of Thrush Green

THE LAST CHRONICLE
OF FAIRACRE

An omnibus volume containing

CHANGES AT FAIRACRE

FAREWELL TO FAIRACRE

A PEACEFUL RETIREMENT

Miss Read

PENGUIN BOOKS

PENGUIN BOOKS

Published by the Penguin Group
Penguin Books Ltd, 80 Strand, London WC2R 0RL, England
Penguin Putnam Inc., 375 Hudson Street, New York, New York 10014, USA
Penguin Books Australia Ltd, 250 Camberwell Road, Camberwell,
Victoria 3124, Australia
Penguin Books Canada Ltd, 10 Alcorn Avenue, Toronto, Ontario, Canada M4V 3B2
Penguin Books India (P) Ltd, 11 Community Centre, Panchsheel Park,
New Delhi – 110 017, India
Penguin Books (NZ) Ltd, Cnr Rosedale and Airborne Roads,
Albany, Auckland, New Zealand
Penguin Books (South Africa) (Pty) Ltd, 24 Sturdee Avenue,
Rosebank 2196, South Africa

Penguin Books Ltd, Registered Offices: 80 Strand, London WC2R 0RL, England

www.penguin.com

First published in one volume as *The Last Chronicle of Fairacre*
by Michael Joseph Ltd 2001
Published by Penguin Books 2002
1

Printed in England by Clays Ltd, St Ives plc

Contents

Introduction

There is something sad about parting from old friends and familiar places and I feel a slight pang when I realize that this omnibus contains the very last of the stories about Fairacre.

I could show you where Miss Clare keeps her biscuit tin and where Mrs Pringle has her spare scrubbing brush. I could take you into Mr Willet's garden and point out the apple tree where a robin nested last year, and I could show you the exact spot under the hedge around Hundred-Acre Field where the best white violets grow.

The first three Fairacre books came out in quick succession, and from readers' letters I found that they liked the fairly small cast of characters, the descriptions of the countryside, the way people reacted to the change of seasons and, of course, the children, particularly Joseph Coggs.

It was what I liked too, and I was fortunate that those early books were published in the 1950s. Village schools were much in the news. Many were closing, to the dismay of those who had attended them. Those people who had gone to the same school which had taught their parents disliked this breaking of tradition. Other readers, I found, had started their schooling in cities and had been evacuated to the country during the 1939–45 war, and their memories of the village schools they attended were fresh and affectionate.

All the Fairacre and Thrush Green books were illustrated by John S. Goodall, except for the very last book, *A Peaceful Retirement*, which came out after his death. The charm and wit of his work added greatly to the readers' enjoyment.

The time has now come to lay down my pen, and this I do with a thankful heart. It has been my good fortune to have had the support of my family, the same outstanding publisher for the whole of my career as a novelist, a bevy of clever artists and the encouragement of readers.

I salute them all as I wave farewell.

Dora Saint (Miss Read)
April 2001

CHANGES AT FAIRACRE

with illustrations by John S. Goodall

To Mary and Eric with love

Contents

PART ONE

FAIRACRE

1 A Visit To Dolly Clare

SPRING came early to Fairacre that year. Half-term was at the end of February and I had seen the school children off the premises, at four o'clock on the Friday, to run home between hedges already beginning to thicken with plump buds.

A few celandine already starred the banks, and in the cottage gardens, and in mine at the school house, the daffodils were beginning to follow the fading snowdrops and early crocuses.

In all my years as head teacher at Fairacre School, I had never before seen such welcome signs of spring at half-term. I could remember the lane deep in snow in earlier Februaries, awash with puddles or glittering with ice. There might perhaps have been a flutter of yellow catkins or a few hardy sticky buds showing on the horse chestnut trees, but this balmy weather was rare and wonderful.

Bob Willet, our school caretaker, church sexton and general factotum in the village, was not quite as euphoric as I was.

'You wants to look further afield,' he told me as the last of the children vanished round the bend of the lane. 'There's blackthorn out already, I see, and you know what that means: a proper sharp spell comin' along. We'll get a frost afore the week's out.'

'Well, I'm going to enjoy this while I can,' I told him. 'Why I might even cut the grass.'

'More fool you then,' said my old friend roundly. 'You

be asking for trouble. Getting above yourself just because the sun's out.'

'I'm going to see Miss Clare during the weekend,' I told him, partly to change the subject.

He brightened up at once. 'Now you give Dolly Clare my love. Amazing old girl, ain't she?'

I agreed that she was, and we parted company amicably.

Dolly Clare, who lived at the next village of Beech Green, knew more about Fairacre School than anyone in the neighbourhood. She had attended it herself as a pupil, and later as a teacher. When I arrived to take up my headship, she was nearing retirement and in charge of the infants' class.

She was a dignified figure, tall, straight-backed, white-haired and extremely gentle. I never heard her raise her voice in anger, and the small children adored her. Her teaching methods were old-fashioned. The children were expected to sit at their desks and to work at them too. There was mighty little roaming aimlessly about the classroom, and if a child had a job to do it was expected to finish it tidily, and with pride in its accomplishment.

By modern-day standards the infants' room was unnaturally quiet, but there was happiness there and complete accord between teacher and pupils. The children trusted Miss Clare. She was fair, she was kind, she looked after them with steadfast affection. They were content to submit to her rule and, in truth, a great many of them were happier here, in the warmth and peace of the schoolroom than in their own homes, so often over-crowded and noisy with upraised and angry voices.

In such a rural community, farming was the major industry. The horse then ruled, and there were carters, farriers, wheelwrights and horse doctors in attendance upon the noble beast, who drew the plough, pulled the carts, provided the family transport and generally governed the ways of the agricultural community.

Families were large and it was nothing unusual to find parents with eight or ten children. In the early days of Miss Clare's teaching the school had almost one hundred pupils. The school leaving age was fourteen, but many left earlier if a job cropped up. It was no wonder that Fairacre School was such a busy and crowded place. Long desks held children in a row, and there was little chance of fidgeting going unnoticed.

By the time I arrived the school took children up to the age of eleven, and after that they went on to the neighbouring village school at Beech Green, where George Annett was the headmaster. Here they stayed until they were fifteen, unless they had qualified for a place at the local grammar school in Caxley, and had departed thither after their eleven-plus examination, knowing that they could stay until eighteen, if need be, possibly going on from there to a university, or perhaps higher education of a technical kind.

From the first, I felt the greatest respect and affection for my colleague, Miss Clare. She was a mine of information about Fairacre and its inhabitants, for she had taught most of them and knew their foibles. She had started life in the local market town of Caxley where she and her older sister Ada began their schooling.

Her father, Francis Clare, had been a thatcher and there was plenty of work to be done. Not only were there a great many thatched cottages and barns in the neighbourhood, but at harvest time the newly-built ricks were thatched, and Francis was in great demand.

At the age of six Dolly and her family moved from Caxley to a small cottage at Beech Green, and there she grew up and still lived. The one love of her life had been killed in the 1914–18 war, and perhaps this accounted, in part, for the warm devotion which generations of young children had enjoyed under her care at Fairacre School. They gave her the comfort and affection which a family of her own would have supplied in happier circumstances, and both Dolly and her charges benefited.

She had shown me soon after we met the contents of an oval gold locket on a gold chain which she wore constantly round her neck. On one side was the photograph of a handsome young man, and facing it a lock of his auburn hair.

Dolly Clare and I worked in perfect accord until her retirement. Since then I had visited her at least once a week in the Beech Green cottage which had been thatched by her father and, more recently, by a man to whom she had given her father's tools when he had died. Frequently she came to stay with me at the school house, and was a welcome visitor to the school itself.

The fact that she out-lived her own generation and knew very little about her sister Ada's children and their progeny, meant that her friends were doubly precious to her. I was honoured to be among them.

A few years earlier she had told me that her cottage and its contents had been left to me on her death, and that I was to be one of the two executors. Such overwhelming generosity stunned me, and made my future secure for I had no real possibility of buying property, and of course the school house went with the post of head teacher. Dolly Clare's wonderful gesture had given me an enormous feeling of gratitude and relief. I knew that I could never repay or thank her adequately.

Later that Friday evening, when I was still relishing the thought of half-term stretching before me, there was a knock at the back door. There stood Bob Willet, holding a

shallow box which contained an assortment of vegetables.

'If you're going to see Dolly Clare could you give her these?'

'Of course. Come in for a minute. The wind's turned, hasn't it?'

'Ah! Gone round east a bit.'

He put the box on the kitchen table, and dusted his hands down his corduroy trousers.

'All from your garden?' I inquired, admiring the bronze onions, the freshly-scrubbed carrots, a snowy caulifower and some outsize potatoes.

'All except the marmalade,' he grinned. 'I never grew that, but Alice had made a batch and thought Dolly'd relish a pot.'

'I'm sure she will. Have a cup of coffee?'

'Don't mind if I do.'

He sat down and looked about him. 'You got a new kettle?'

'The old one sprang a leak.'

'Hand it over, and I'll solder it for you.'

'As a matter of fact, I took it to Caxley.'

Mr Willet clicked his tongue disapprovingly. 'What you want to do that for? Wasting good money.'

'Well, I didn't want to bother you. You do enough for me as it is.'

'Rubbish! I don't do nothin' more'n I do for most folks around here. And they could do most of the jobs themselves, but they're too idle. With you it's different.'

'How?'

'Well, you're a woman, see, and not over-bright about doin' things with your hands.'

'Thanks!'

'No offence meant, Miss Read. I mean, you can do things I can't. Understand forms and that. Write a good letter. Cook a fair dinner – not as good as my wife Alice's, I must allow, but not at all bad. You has your points, but kettle-mending ain't one of 'em.'

He accepted his mug of coffee, and I joined him at the table with my own.

I did not take umbrage at Bob Willet's assessment of my abilities. As he often says: 'Speak the truth and shame the devil!' I faced his strictures with fortitude.

'And how was Dolly when you last saw her?' he inquired, stirring busily.

'As serene as ever, but she is so frail these days. I don't know that she should live alone.'

'She wouldn't want to live any other way. The only person she'd have settled with was her Emily Davis.'

Emily had been a contemporary of Dolly's from the earliest days at Beech Green. Their friendship, begun at that village's school, had survived until Emily's death some years before. The two old friends had planned to live in Dolly's cottage, but their time together was short, for Emily had died, leaving Dolly alone again.

Luckily Dolly had good neighbours who kept an eye on her, and George and Isobel Annett, the teacher at Beech Green school and his wife, lived close by and were as attentive to the old lady as if she were a near relation. Our vicar, the local doctor, and many Fairacre friends called regularly, and she was fortunate enough to have a stalwart and cheerful cleaner who came twice a week to perform her duties, and often simply to visit her friend.

She was a spry young Welsh woman called Mrs John, and had helped me out once in the school house when Mrs Pringle, our dour school cleaner, had let me down. She had two young children, always immaculately turned out, and her house was a model of good housekeeping. She and Miss Clare were fond of each other, and a great deal of Dolly's knitting ended up on the John children's backs.

'Still keeps herself busy, I suppose?' queried Bob Willet, putting aside his empty mug. 'Tell her I'll do a bit of gardenin' for her any time she wants.'

'I will,' I promised.

'Best be getting back. Got the watering to do in the greenhouse, and Mr Mawne's got summat up with one of his window catches. He's another like you. Supposed to be schooled proper but can't do nothin' much in the house.'

'Then it's a good thing we've got you to look after us,' I told him, and watched him stump away down the path.

It was cold and grey the next morning, and Tibby, my elderly cat, was as loth to get up as I was. However, the thought of the freedom from school was cheering enough to get me going, and by the time I was ready to set off to Miss Clare's, the sun was attempting to dispel the heavy clouds.

I had been invited to lunch, and after some protestation on Dolly's part I had agreed if I could do the cooking.

Consequently, I carried in my basket, six eggs and some minced ham ready for the omelette I proposed to make. I had also made an orange jelly and an egg custard – very suitable fare, I considered, for two old ladies – and only hoped that my modest endeavours would have met with Bob Willet's assessment of 'a fair dinner'. I also took some fresh fruit.

With his box of vegetables on the back seat with my basket, I set off for Beech Green. The roads were wet from an overnight shower, and the grass verges were besmeared with dirt thrown there throughout the past winter months by passing traffic.

About a mile along the road I overtook a small figure trudging along with a plastic carrier bag flapping in the breeze. It was one of my pupils, young Joseph Coggs.

I pulled up beside him. 'Where are you off to?'

'Brown's, miss.'

'Want a lift?'

A dazzling smile was the answer, as he clambered into the passenger seat.

Brown's was Beech Green's general store, and I wondered why Joe had been dispatched on a journey of two miles. After all, we had a very good shop in Fairacre.

'And what are you buying from Brown's?'

'Soap powder, miss.'

'Can't you get that at our shop?'

'Not till us have paid the bill.'

'I see.'

We drove along in silence. A pigeon flew dangerously close to the windscreen, and Joe drew in a deep breath.

'Reckon that frightened him,' he said.

'It frightened me too,' I told him. 'Might have smashed the windscreen.'

Joe pondered on this. 'Could you pay for it?'

'The insurance would cover it.'

'How?' asked Joe, mystified.

To my relief, Brown's shop front hove in sight, and I was spared the intricacies of explaining the principles and practice of car insurance to my passenger.

I drew up, and Joe began to open the door. I reached to the back seat and handed him over a banana from my collection of fruit.

'Eat it on the way home,' I said, 'and don't forget to put the skin in the litter bin over there.'

Ever the teacher, I thought, even on holiday!

'Thank you, miss. And for the ride. Me shoe was hurting.'

Poor old Joe, I thought, as I drove away. Shoes that hurt had been his lot for most of his young life, and he would get little sympathy from the rest of the hard-pressed Coggs family.

Dolly Clare was sitting by a bright fire when I arrived, but rose with remarkable agility for such an old lady.

'I've been counting the minutes,' she told me. 'It's so sweet of you to give up your half-term. Company means a lot when you can't get out.'

I looked about the snug sitting-room. As always, it was cheerful with shining furniture and even a few early poly-anthus flowers in a glass vase.

'Emily and I planted them years ago,' she said as I admired them. 'These are the progeny. They do well here, and so do cowslips. I suppose because they are derived from downland flowers. Emily and I picked so many prim-roses when we were children here at Beech Green, but there aren't as many now as there were in the coppices.'

She followed me into the kitchen where I set out my culinary arrangements, and handed over Bob Willet's present.

'The dear thing!' she exclaimed. 'And all so useful. And

homegrown too. I shall write him a note without delay.

Back in the sitting-room I inquired after her health.

'Nothing wrong with me but old age. I have lots of friends who pop in, and Mrs John is vigilant. I only hope I slip away one night like Emily, and don't cause a lot of bother with a long illness.'

It seemed to me that she was even smaller and more frail than when I had last visited her, but she seemed content and happy to talk about times past, and particularly her memories of her friend Emily.

'It's strange, but I think of her more than anyone else. Even my dear Arnold, who would have been a very old man by now, is not as clear in my memory as Emily. I suppose it is because I met her when we were children and one's impressions are so fresh. I have the queerest feeling sometimes that she is actually in the house with me.'

I made a sound of protest. Was she getting fanciful, I thought, getting hallucinations, becoming fearful?

As if she read my mind, she began to laugh.

'It's nothing frightening, I assure you. In fact, just the opposite. I feel Emily's warmth and sympathy, and find it wonderfully comforting. With Arnold, alas, I seem to have lost contact. I remember how dearly we loved each other, but I can't recall his face. For that I have to look here.'

She withdrew the gold oval locket on a long chain and opened it. I knew the portrait well, but studied it afresh before she returned it to be hidden under her blouse.

'And yet, you see, Emily's face is clear as ever to me. What odd tricks the mind plays! I can remember how this cottage looked when I first saw it at the age of six, far more clearly than I can recall places which I've known in the last ten years or so.'

'The brain gets cluttered up,' I said, 'as the years go by. The early impressions are bound to be the sharpest.'

'One of the joys of living in this house for most of my life,' went on Dolly, 'are the pictures I remember of my parents' life here. Times were hard. In those days if you didn't work you didn't eat. It was as simple as that. No cushioning by the state against hardship, and we had a very thin time of it if work was short.'

'How did you manage?'

'We always kept a few chickens, and a pig, of course, as most cottagers did in those days. My mother was a wonderful manager, and could make a shilling go as far as three. We went gleaning too after the harvest, and always had a sack of flour. And neighbours always helped each other in time of sickness and accident.'

'What about parish relief? Wasn't there something called that?'

'Oh, one dreaded "going on the parish"! Mind you, the people in the big houses were usually very generous and sent soup or puddings and such like to needy folk. Somehow we made do until more work came along. In a way, my father was lucky. He was known as a first-class thatcher, and he was in work most of the time. But I can still see my poor mother standing at the kitchen table with a morsel of cold rabbit and onion from the garden wondering whether to make a pie, with far more crust than filling, or to chop it up with hard boiled-eggs and some home-grown lettuce. I think I was about eight at the time, and I remember I persuaded her to make the pie! I didn't like lettuce.'

'She sounds a wonderful woman.'

'We all had to be, and it stood us in good stead in wartime and throughout our lives.'

She began to laugh. 'All this talk of rabbit pie has made me quite hungry. What about us going into the kitchen to see about that delicious omelette?'

So we went.

2   Falling Numbers

DURING half-term I enjoyed the company of another old friend. Amy and I had met at college, taught at neighbouring schools for a while, and kept in touch after her marriage. She lived in a village a few miles south of Caxley, our local market town. She was all that I was not – well-dressed, sociable, much-travelled, lively-minded and, of course, married.

Her husband, James, was a high-powered business man who had an office in the city, and had to spend a good deal of his time visiting European centres of finance, and some in America and Japan. He was energetic, good-tempered and, even in middle-age, devastatingly good-looking. It was not surprising that women were attracted to him and, although he and Amy made a devoted couple, one could not quite accept that *all* his trips were business ones, whatever he said.

I saw Amy frequently, partly because she was alone very often, and also, I flattered myself, because our friendship meant more as the years passed.

She was sitting in her car when I returned from our village shop with some groceries, an unwieldy French loaf swathed in tissue paper and a packet of soap powder which reminded me of Joseph Coggs's errand.

As always, she was elegantly clad. Her tweed suit was of misty blue, and the cloth had been woven in Otterburn, I knew. The matching jumper was of cashmere, and James's sapphire engagement ring added the final touch to Amy's ensemble.

'You should have rung,' I said, opening the door, 'and then I would have changed from this rough old skirt.'

'I don't mind your rough old skirt,' said Amy kindly. 'It's an old friend by now. Incidentally, how long have you had it?'

I stood in the middle of the kitchen and pondered.

Amy removed the loaf, took off the paper and put the bread in the bin.

'Must be getting on for eight years,' I said at last. 'I bought the stuff at Filkins when we toured the Cotswolds one Easter. Remember?'

'Well, it wears very well,' replied Amy. I began to feel pleased. Amy is rather censorious about my appearance.

'It needs cleaning, of course,' she added. 'And hems are up this season.'

'I'll ask Alice Willet to shorten it,' I said meekly, and put the kettle on.

'Well, what news?' I asked over the tea cups.

'Not much. James is as busy as ever, and is doing a Good Deed.'

'Well done James!'

'I hope so, but I can see it is all going to be rather fraught. He came across an old school friend who is down on his luck. Been made redundant, and James is searching for a job in one of his companies that would suit the fellow. But the thing is he's rather a problem.'

'How? Just out of prison? Suffering from something?'

'Not exactly.'

Amy blew a perfect smoke ring, an accomplishment of hers which she knows impresses me inordinately, although I deplore the habit of smoking, as she is well aware.

'He's been terribly depressed because of losing his job, and his wife has left him. Luckily the children are off their hands, but he's one of those chaps who can't do a hand's turn in the house, so he's half-starved and lonely with it.'

I gave an involuntary snort.

'Oh, I know you aren't sympathetic, but not everyone can cope as you do. Even though it is a muddle,' she added unnecessarily, eyeing an untidy pile of washing awaiting the attention of the iron. 'James has invited him to stay for a few days, and I wondered if you would come to dinner next weekend, and cheer him up.'

'Of course I will. You know I always enjoy your meals.'

'It's not just my *meal* I'm inviting you to,' said Amy. 'It's your *support* I need on this particular occasion.'

I promised to do my duty; Amy relaxed, and I did too.

One good thing, this unhappy man was married. He might not be a contented husband at the moment, but at least Amy would not have designs on him as a future husband for me.

Over the years I have been the victim of Amy's machinations. In vain I tell her that I *like* being single. She refuses to believe it, and a procession of males, whom Amy considers suitable partners for an ageing spinster, have been introduced to me. Some I have liked and have remained friends with, some have been harmless and quickly forgotten, and some have been frankly appalling, but I don't hold it against dear old Amy. She was born a match-maker, and will continue her endeavours until death claims her, and I have had ample experience now in evading the state of matrimony. We both play the game like old hands, but I must confess that I find it rather trying at times. This new acquaintance should not give me any trouble.

'What's his name?' I asked.

'James calls him "Basher".'

'Well,' I expostulated, 'I can't call him *that*!'

'I suppose not. It may be Michael or Malcolm. Something beginning with 'M'. I'll find out before you come.'

(As it happened, he turned out to be 'Brian'.)

'By the way,' said Amy, 'I came across Lucy Colgate the other day.'

Lucy had been at college with us, and I had always detested her. Amy was more tolerant.

'I thought she had married,' I said.

'She has, but I can never remember her married name. She was buying fish in Sevenoaks.'

'And what were you doing in Sevenoaks?'

'James had a board meeting, and I went along for the ride. I was doing some shopping when I bumped into Lucy. We had coffee together.'

'And how was she?'

'As tiresome as ever. Intent on impressing one with her worldliness and high spirits.'

'Well, that sounds like Lucy! Do you remember how she used to boast about climbing over the cycle sheds to get in after hours at college? She always wanted to be the Madcap of the Fourth. What is it these days?'

'Oh, homosexuals and abortions and various diseases which used to be happily unmentionable, but now people like Lucy feel obliged to parade even when having morning coffee. I think she imagines that she is shocking people like us. "Opening Our Eyes to Life As It Is," you know.'

'It's time she grew up,' I agreed, 'but she never will. Poor old Lucy! I suppose she still feels a dare-devil under all those wrinkles.'

'No need to be catty. It doesn't suit you,' said Amy primly. She put down her cigarette and then surveyed me closely. 'Nevertheless, we have certainly weathered the years better than Lucy Colgate,' she announced with great satisfaction.

And we both dissolved into laughter.

* * *

Half-term ended with a night of heavy rain. It drummed on the school house roof, and splashed and gurgled into the two rainwater butts.

I sloshed through puddles in the playground and met Mrs Pringle in the lobby. As usual she was taking the wet weather as a personal affront.

'Love's labour lost trying to keep these floors clean in this weather,' she grumbled. 'There's a puddle the size of a football pitch outside the Post Office, and half our lot are playing "Splashem" in it.'

'Splashem' is a simple Fairacre game which involves waiting by a sizeable puddle until some innocent victim appears. The far-from-innocent instigators of the game then jump heavily into the water sending up a shower which drenches their victim. At the same time, the triumphant shout of 'Splashem' is raised. Everyone involved gets wet feet and the unlucky innocent gets soaking clothing as well. It is a game which only a few enjoy, and I have been as ferocious as the outraged parents in trying to stop it. On the whole, the playground is free from it, but on the journey to and from school the malefactors still indulge.

'I'll give them all a wigging,' I promised Mrs Pringle.

'What they wants,' said she, 'is a good hiding. It's a great pity you teachers have got so soft with 'em all. As bad as the Caxley magistrates. I see as Arthur Coggs got something called a *conditional discharge* for fighting in the market place. Nothing but a *let off*, when he deserved a *flogging*.'

'Well, we can't go back to flogging and the stocks and hanging,' I said. 'We've got to put up with justice as it is.'

'More's the pity,' replied Mrs Pringle, bending down to pick a leaf from the floor. She was puce in the face when she straightened up, and her corsets creaked under the strain.

'I'm not the woman I was,' she said with some satisfaction. She must have noticed my expression of alarm. 'First thing in the morning my bronchials are a torment. Nearly coughs my heart up, I does. Fred says I should give up this job, and I reckon he's right.'

I have heard this tale so often from Mrs Pringle's lips, as well as second-hand comments from Fred, her husband, that I have grown quite callous.

'No one,' I told her, 'wants you to work when you aren't fit. If you really find the job too much then you must give in your notice.'

'And leave my stoves to be polished – or *half* polished more like – by some other woman as don't know blacklead from furniture polish? No! I'll struggle on as best I can, till I drop.'

At that, she preceded me into the classroom for a final flick round with the duster.

As I expected, she was limping heavily. Mrs Pringle's bad leg, which 'flares up' regularly, is a good indicator of that lady's disposition.

Today, after my trenchant comments, the leg was even more combustible than usual.

Ernest rushed into the lobby, leaving wet footprints, but luckily Mrs Pringle was busy taking umbrage out of sight.

'Can I ring the bell, miss?'

'Carry on, Ernest,' I said.

School had started again.

At mid-morning a neighbour of Bob Willet's appeared, bringing bad news.

She was the mother of three of my pupils as well as an older child at Beech Green school. The family, the Thompsons, were comparative newcomers to the village, and generally approved.

The father was employed by the local electricity board and went daily to Caxley. Mrs Thompson helped in the village shop in the mornings while the children were at school, but she gave this up during the school holidays.

'She's a good little mother,' Alice Willet had told me, and this was high praise indeed.

The children were well cared for, not overbright, but well-mannered and happy. I was very fond of them and they had settled cheerfully among the others.

I had heard rumours and, as I had feared, Mrs Thompson had come to tell me that her husband had been posted elsewhere, and that they were obliged to leave Fairacre.

'And we don't want to go. Not one of us,' she asserted, 'but it means more money, and if he turns this down he might not get another chance in the future. I'm real sorry about it, Miss Read, and the children don't want to leave any more than we do.'

'Have you got to find a house?' I asked, secretly hoping that this would mean keeping my pupils a little longer.

'No. There's a house with the job, so we can go in at Easter. It all looks fine on paper, but that doesn't change our feelings.'

'Well, at least I shall have them for the rest of the term,' I said. 'But we shall all miss them. They've been model pupils.'

I accompanied her to the outer door. The rain was pelting down again, but a large umbrella stood in the corner of the lobby and Mrs Thompson assured me she would be adequately sheltered on her return to her duties at the shop. I thanked her for letting me know about her plans, and watched her departure across the playground.

I returned to the classroom with a heavy heart.

At playtime, after the dire threats about 'Splashem' to my flock, I broke the sad news to my assistant Mrs Richards, formerly Miss Briggs. She was as upset as I was.

'But this will bring our numbers down to well under thirty,' she cried.

'Nearer twenty,' I told her. 'Mind you, we've been almost as low before, and always managed to evade closure.'

It is one of the shadows which hangs over many villages these days: none wants to lose its village school, and local newspapers, the length and breadth of the country, carry sad stories of battles to keep village schools thriving.

I thought of my recent conversation with Miss Clare, and the large numbers which once thronged Fairacre School. So much had changed over a life time. At eleven years of age, my pupils moved on, instead of staying until fourteen as in Dolly Clare's day. Families were much smaller. With the advent of the car, parents could deliver their children farther afield to a school of their choice. Salaries had increased, and many parents could now afford the fees at local private schools which, for one reason or another, they preferred for their children.

I had faced this problem of dwindling numbers through-out my years at Fairacre. So far we had been spared, but for how long? Many small schools had managed to combine with others for activities such as games, or had shared facilities for common ventures such as film shows, peripatetic lecturers, demonstrators and so forth. This was fine when the schools were fairly close.

Fairacre unfortunately was isolated, except for the neighbouring school at Beech Green. If we had to close, it was most likely that the Fairacre children would be taken by bus the two or three miles to the larger school, where George Annett was head teacher and had an excellent staff. I had no doubt that my little flock would settle there happily, in more modern surroundings and with the added attraction and stimulation of larger numbers which would allow team games such as cricket and football which my youngsters sorely missed.

But what would happen to this venerable old building with its leaky skylight and lobby walls flaking paint everywhere? And what about my beloved school house across the playground, where I lived so contentedly?

Even more alarming, what would happen to me?

All conjectures about the future were brought to a sudden return to the present, by the appearance of a tearful infant dripping water everywhere, who had become the latest victim of 'Splashem'.

I strode out of the classroom into action.

Mr Willet, of course, had heard the news of the Thompsons' departure long before I had, and he seemed to find great satisfaction in telling me so.

'I thought about that old saying,' he said, when I remonstrated with him, 'that one about ignorance being bliss. Seemed to me a pity to shake you out of your fool's paradise.'

I felt somewhat nettled by this remark.

'I'm shaken all right,' I told him crossly. 'This is one step nearer closure, you know, and we shall both be out of a job.'

'Won't worry me,' he said sturdily. 'I can turn my hand to anything. Gardenin', carpenterin', decoratin', grave-diggin', there's allus summat to do. Now with you it's different. What can you do except teach school?'

'I can cook –' I began.

'Not good enough to get a proper job.'

'Well, I could work in a shop.'

'You ain't that quick with money.'

'Or learn to type, and go into an office.'

'The young 'uns would run rings round you. They has *computers* anyway.'

'Perhaps I could do market research. You know, walk about Caxley High Street with a clip-board, and annoy everyone with my questions when they were hurrying home to cook the lunch.'

'You wouldn't be bossy enough.'

I began to feel somewhat mollified by this remark.

'I mean,' he continued, 'you're bossy enough in school with the kids, but you'd never stand up to anyone your own size.'

'Thanks!' I said, back where we had started. 'So what do you suggest, other than the Caxley Workhouse?'

'That closed years ago,' he reminded me. He looked me over speculatively.

'I s'pose you might get married.' He sounded doubtful.

'A desperate measure,' I laughed. 'And not one I'm going to consider.'

'Maybe you're right,' he conceded and began to move towards the door. Then he stopped and turned.

'The first of those new houses is up for sale. Might get some children there, with any luck.'

Mr Roberts, our local farmer, had sold a strip of land a

year or so earlier, and three good-sized houses had been put up by a local builder. They were fairly innocuous in appearance and had decent gardens, but their prices were steep by village standards.

The sale of the land had provided plenty of gossip at the time. Bob Willet told me that his grandfather had always gone to work at Springbourne by a footpath which had once crossed that piece of land.

'Used to save the old boy a good mile,' he told me. 'But after the war that path was never claimed. Roberts's old dad was a cunning one, and it served his purpose to let the path be covered by his crops. There was plenty around here did that, and we lost no end of old footpaths then.'

However, despite local protests, planning permission was granted, and Fairacre now had three new 'executive' houses, whatever that meant.

'It would be marvellous,' I said, 'if we had three families with lots of children coming to live there.'

'Make a nice change,' agreed Bob. 'Mighty few young 'uns in Fairacre coming along as it is.'

'Has anyone heard if the houses have attracted any buyers yet?'

'Two or three of them yuppy types. Real tinkers.'

'Tinkers?' My mind flew to a collection of shabby cara-vans, washing spread on hedges, swarthy men busy with clapped-out cars, and litter everywhere.

'Two-Incomes-No-Kids. T.I.N.K. or tinkers,' explained Mr Willet. 'If that sort comes, it'll be years before you get any of theirs into the school.'

'Well, I shall live in hope,' I told him. 'After all, Fairacre School is still alive and kicking.'

'Just,' agreed Bob Willet, departing.

3   At Amy's

THE following Sunday I prepared myself for Amy's dinner party.

I hoped that it would not be a large one, and was comforted by the thought that Amy had muttered something about six, which would save putting in the leaf of the table. However, knowing Amy, she might well have fallen victim to her own generous instincts and I might find myself among twice the number first envisaged.

In my modest wardrobe I have had, for more years than I can recall, a black velvet skirt and waistcoat to match. What is more, the waistcoat has pockets large enough for handkerchief, purse and spectacle case. They can also accommodate an indigestion tablet, although I knew that this would be quite unnecessary after a meal at Amy's.

The thing was, Amy had seen this ensemble many times over the years, worn with a white silk blouse, a white lace blouse, a black and white spotted blouse, and a fine white woollen blouse for draughty houses.

While I was worrying about the alternatives, a navy-blue foulard which was too tight in the waist, or a pink-flowered silk which I thought made me look like mutton dressed as lamb, I remembered that my only pair of black patent shoes was at the mender's, so that ruled out the black velvet duo.

Now I had only to choose between the navy-blue and the pink. I spent most of the afternoon vacillating between the two, as I marked history test papers in the garden.

The sun was warm, and out of the wind it was possible

to enjoy this early warmth. The rain had done some good, and already the early daffodils were showing their buds. My red pencil slipped to the ground, and I closed my eyes against the sunshine.

Did other women fuss so about their clothes, I wondered? Heaven alone knows, I am the most undressy person alive, as Amy frequently tells me, and my wardrobe is scanty. What did women do who had twenty outfits to choose from? Went quite mad, I supposed, worrying about shoes and jewels and so on to go with the right clothes. Thank heaven I only owned Aunt Clara's seed pearls for my evening adornment, and one or two pieces of costume jewellery.

How did royal ladies cope? Did they choose their own emeralds and rubies or was that decision left to the Mistress of the Wardrobe, or whoever it was? And think of the horror of having to choose something from hundreds of ensembles! I supposed I was lucky with just the choice of my too-tight navy blue or the too-juvenile pink, and fell into a light doze.

When I awoke the sun had vanished behind a cloud, and my arms were covered in goose pimples.

I went into the kitchen and put the kettle on. It should be the pink. My new cream handbag and matching shoes would be quite suitable, and Aunt Clara's seed pearls would tone beautifully.

I proposed to be the belle of the ball. It would make a nice change.

'Well, you *do* look pretty!' cried Amy when I arrived. 'You should wear pink more often. It's so *youthful*. It makes you look like a bridesmaid.'

This was exactly what I had feared, but I did not enlarge on the theme.

Amy herself was in a filmy grey frock patterned with leaves and looked, as always, exactly right.

I was the first to arrive, so we had time to discuss the other guests before they joined us.

'Only Horace and Eve Umbleditch,' said Amy, 'to make a nice comfortable six. And if poor Brian is depressed we can always count on Horace to keep the ball rolling.'

I agreed. Horace, a fellow-teacher, was always an asset in company, as I had known for years.

'And is this Brian likely to be depressed? Where is he, by the way?' I asked.

'Getting dressed, I hope. He was late coming back from Caxley and had a quick shower. He's not a very tidy shower-taker, I'm afraid.'

'I think you are noble to have him at all,' I said truthfully. I imagined a gaunt sad figure drifting about the place, hollow-eyed and monosyllabic, mourning his lost wife and job. My heart bled for him just a little, but even more profusely for my gallant old friend.

'Oh, it won't be for long,' said Amy. 'James is looking out for something suitable for him. Ah! Here are Horace and Eve.'

She made her way to the front door, and I heard welcoming greetings from James and Amy, and Horace's well-known hearty voice.

I have always been fond of Horace, and he had been among the many local bachelors and widowers whom Amy had presented to me, over the years, as suitable husbands. Neither Horace nor I had had the slightest desire to satisfy Amy's ambitions, but we had always enjoyed each other's company. He taught at a local prep school and had recently married the school secretary. I imagine that Horace's loud voice was the result of years spent in making himself heard above hordes of little boys.

We sat with our glasses, exchanging news. I always feel that the inhabitants of the country south of Caxley are much more sophisticated than we are north of the town, and this evening the talk was of opera, a local bridge tournament, and the disgraceful condition of the nearby golf course. Eve and I launched out on a discussion of Caxley shops and their superiority over Oxford, Reading, Winchester and other large conurbations, until we both confessed we had not visited any of the latter for years and so then enjoyed a refreshing fit of the giggles.

Amy appeared somewhat distracted and was obviously listening for the arrival of Brian from upstairs. It would not have surprised me to see her go in quest of him, but she was spared that.

The door opened and Amy's visitor was revealed. Far from being gaunt, hollow-eyed and the picture of melancholy which I had envisaged, Brian turned out to be pink and bouncy, gleaming with soap and good health, and only a few inches over five feet. He apologized for being late.

Amy introduced him to us all as: 'Brian Horner, who was at school with James, and is staying here for a while.' He had a nice smile, a low voice, and a firm handshake. He did not seem to be at all cast down by his circumstances, and I wondered if he were really as unhappy as Amy and James seemed to think.

He was put next to me at the table and although I knew that this time Amy was not thinking of matrimony, I remembered her request 'to cheer up Brain' and set about doing my duty to support my hostess.

As it happened, I had very little work to do. Apart from fixing a bright smile on my face, and laughing politely at Brian's jokes, all that was required was a listening ear.

Brian turned out to be one of those people who can eat and talk at the same time. He did both with great speed, and kept us all regaled with tales of recent holidays – the cottage in Wales which was so damp that fungi grew on the inside wall, the hotel in Greece where the hot tap in the bathroom refused to turn off creating a private sauna *en suite*, and the skiing holiday with no snow.

He told his tales well, and although I had the feeling that he was rather monopolizing the conversation, I put it down to nervousness which so often makes people garrulous. At any rate, it made my duties much lighter, and I was able to enjoy Amy's lovely meal.

Afterwards we sat round the fire with our coffee, and I had time to talk to Horace and his wife who were thinking of moving into a house of their own, a mile or two from the school.

'If we don't do it now,' he said, 'we never shall. It's just too easy to stay on in the school premises until I retire, but then where should we live?'

I told him that those were my feelings about my own school house, and later I was invited to visit them in their present tied home.

The party broke up about eleven. Brian, who had taken only a small part in the conversation about the new home, sighed rather heavily as he said goodbye to Eve and Horace.

'You don't know how lucky you are to be making domestic plans. That's something I miss so dreadfully.'

It was one of those remarks upon which it is impossible to comment, but the pair looked somewhat startled, simply making their adieux and expressing pleasure at making his acquaintance. Perhaps, I thought, watching his sad face, he really is as unhappy as Amy says.

I rang her at playtime next morning to thank her for a splendid evening.

'And did you like Brian?' she said.

'Yes, indeed.'

'Oh, good. He was most complimentary about you.'

I am quite accustomed to this sort of remark from Amy after meeting males at her parties, but could afford to ignore any implications of future romance as Brian was already married, although a grass widower at the moment.

'James thinks the world of him,' went on Amy. 'He is a few years older than James, and was captain of cricket when James was in the fourth form. Quite a hero, according to James, was our Brian. They keep harking back to cricket matches they remember, and going to see Bradman at the Oval when they were boys. The air is thick with Trent Bridge and Lords, and I must say, I find it a trifle over-powering.'

'Any sign of a job for him?'

'There's a possibility of something in Bristol. Another Old Boy, equally cricket-crazy, I gather, has a business there, and James said he would be ringing him today.'

'Good. Must go. I can see a fight developing in the playground. Between *girls* this time!'

I put down the telephone hastily, and went to the rescue.

Hostilities having been quelled, we all returned to the classroom where peace reigned as soon as the children got to work on their pictorial maps of the village of Fairacre.

It grew comparatively quiet, broken only by the stutter of coloured pencils, the drone of a bee, newly-emerged from hibernation, bumbling up and down the Gothic window, and the distant bleating of sheep in a field belonging to Mr Roberts. Soon it would be lambing time and the shepherd would be keeping his vigil. It was good to look forward to may blossom in the hawthorn hedges, tulips in cottage gardens, cowslips on the downs, and lighter evenings to relish such joys.

Meanwhile, I let my thoughts stray to my conversation with Amy. I sincerely hoped that she would soon be free of Brian, and that James's admiration for his school-fellow would result in a steady job, safely in Bristol.

I had noticed before this peculiarly male trait of hero-worship which seems to persist, to a certain extent, throughout a man's life. Usually the object of veneration is a sportsman, as in this case. Many times have I watched a man picking up the newspaper, turning immediately to the sports pages, and brightening or despairing at what was to be read there. The leaders of the nation, the heroes of war, those most eminent in the arts are as nothing compared with the man who scored a century or kicked the winning goal.

Women, I mused, seemed to get over the hero-worshipping stage with commendable speed. The 'schoolgirl's crush' faded by the time the sixth form was reached, and she herself became briefly the object of adoration. Strange that the male should take so long to get over it. Stranger still that it should persist, in so many cases, for the rest of a man's life.

Well, perhaps Brian would benefit from James's feelings.

I remembered that the Bristol business man was also a devotee. Between the two of them, Brian should find a haven.

At that moment, the door opened and Patrick appeared, his gap-toothed grin well in evidence.

'And where have you been?' I demanded.

'Out the back,' he replied. This is the vernacular in Fairacre for the lavatory. 'You never took no notice when I asked. And I *had* to go. So I went.'

I apologized. This did not seem the right moment to explain, yet again, the problems of the double negative. No doubt there would be plenty more occasions.

I put Brian Horner's affairs away, and returned to my own.

Before afternoon school, Mrs Pringle, our dour cleaner, arrived to perform her usual task of washing up the dinner things.

'You'll have to do without me this time next Wednesday,' she told me. 'Just had word from the Cottage that they wants to see my leg.'

The Cottage is our local Caxley Cottage Hospital. Sometimes it is known as 'The Caxley', but this is somewhat confusing as our local bus and our local newspaper are both known as 'The Caxley'.

One catches, or meets people, on 'The Caxley' (bus). To appear in print in *The Caxley* (newspaper) can be a matter of pride or shame according to which page one is given prominence. Naturally, to be mentioned under the heading Court Proceedings can be embarrassing. The Wedding page or Local Charity Events can be a pleasure, and if a personal photograph is included (even if it does look like 'An Explosion in a Pickle Factory', to quote P. G. Wodehouse), it is an added bonus to one's self-esteem.

'So I shan't be able to do the washing-up, or put your place to rights.'

'Well, never mind,' I said. 'I can do it with the children, and it doesn't matter about my house.'

'*Doesn't matter?*' boomed Mrs Pringle, turning puce. 'I was all set to do that brass of yours, and not a minute before time, I may say. I thought of getting Minnie to step in for the day.'

At this my blood ran cold. Minnie Pringle is a niece, with as much sense as a demented hen. I have suffered from her ministrations in the past, and the thought of her at large in the school lobby with the dinner crockery was bad enough. Left to her own devices in my house was not to be borne.

'Definitely not!' I exclaimed. 'We can managed for one day without bothering Minnie.'

Mrs Pringle drew in an outraged breath. Her puce cheeks took on a purplish hue.

'I was only trying to help,' she said at last. 'Small thanks I gets for *that*, I can see. I'll say no more. Just to let you know I'll be catching the one o'clock Caxley to The Caxley next week.'

She limped heavily from the classroom, leaving me to wonder if she would possibly be reading *The Caxley* on The Caxley when she went for her appointment at The Caxley.

As usual it was Mr Willet who came to the rescue later.

'My Alice heard as our Madam Sunshine is off to hospital on Wednesday. You want her to wash up? She says she's willing. And she'll do whatever's needed at the school house.'

'I'd be glad of her help here,' I told him, 'but my house won't hurt. According to Mrs Pringle there's so much wants doing there that another week's neglect won't do much harm.'

'Right. I'll tell her. Mr Lamb mentioned it.'

Mr Lamb is our Fairacre post-master, and much respected, though I had often had the unworthy suspicion that he perused much that passed through his hands.

Bob Willet must have read my thoughts on this occasion.

'There was a postcard from the hospital,' said he. 'I don't say Mr Lamb exactly *reads* things like that, but he sort of *imbibes* them, as he's sorting out the mail.'

It seemed best not to comment.

On the next Saturday morning I had occasion to visit the Post Office myself. Mr Lamb was busy hanging up a multitude of various coloured forms around the glass enclosure which, we all hoped, would protect him in the event of robbers breaking in.

There was a young woman there and, to my delight, she had a boy of about four or five with her. A new pupil, I wondered, with my hard-pressed school in mind?

'Do you know Mrs Winter?' said Mr Lamb. 'She's come to live in one of the new houses.'

I introduced myself and expressed hope that she would enjoy living in Fairacre.

'I'm going back to make coffee,' I added. 'Would you like to join me?'

She smiled and accepted.

'Have you got a dog?' asked the boy.

'No, but I've got a cat.'

He looked pleased. They seemed a cheerful pair, and I looked forward to learning more about them.

We bought our stamps and bade farewell to Mr Lamb.

'What a nice man he is,' enthused Mrs Winter as we

went back to the school house. 'He's introduced me to quite half a dozen people.'

'He did the same for me years ago,' I told her. 'And in those days one still had the older generation calling on the newcomers. It's a pity that nice habit has died out. Really, I suppose, I should have called on you, instead of leaving it to Mr Lamb.'

Over coffee, it transpired that she knew more about me than I had realized.

'You see, I worked with Miriam Quinn for several years and I believe she is a friend of yours.'

'Indeed she is,' I exclaimed, 'although I don't see quite as much of her now that she is married to Gerard Baker and lives in Caxley. How is she?'

She gave me all the news, and it turned out that she herself had succeeded to Miriam's post as personal secretary to the great Sir Barnabas Hatch, the financier.

'It's partly through Miriam that we decided to buy this house in Fairacre. She had always said how happy she had been in the village, and I visited her at Holly Lodge once or twice.'

'And will you continue with your job?'

'I shall indeed. Not only do I enjoy it, but we certainly need two incomes to pay our mortgage.'

'Does Jeremy go to school yet?' I ventured, watching the young boy engrossed in a picture book on the sitting-room floor.

'Play school twice a week,' said his mother, 'but he starts at the prep school in Caxley in September. It has a first-class Kindergarten group, and both my sister's children go there. We can drop him off each morning as we go into the office. My husband works for the same firm, but in another department.'

My hopes for a new pupil were dashed, but I did my best to hide my disappointment.

I showed her round the house and garden, accepted an invitation to tea one Sunday, and we parted company at the gate.

'A very nice addition to the Fairacre community,' I told Tibby on my return to the kitchen.

My encounter with Jane Winter and her little boy gave me much food for thought over that weekend. How things had changed at Fairacre School even in my own time there, let alone in Dolly Clare's! For one thing, there had been almost double the number of children on roll when I took over. The ancient log book showed almost a hundred pupils at the beginning of the century, but of course they could stay at school then until the age of fourteen. Nowadays they left at eleven.

But that was only one reason for the fall in numbers. Smaller families was another. The drift from the land another one. The two or three local farmers who employed a dozen to two dozen men as ploughmen, carters, hedgers-and-ditchers, harvesters, thatchers and piece-workers of all skills, now coped with the two or three employees and barns full of expensive agricultural machinery, supplemented by contractors called in for seasonal work.

There had also been a natural desire by parents to see their offspring better catered for than they had been themselves. A great many in Fairacre remembered the hard times of the thirties, and intended that their children should never be as deprived as they were in their youth. After the war, many of the farm labourers changed jobs and moved into the towns where wages were higher and the hours of work shorter. Consequently, children attending the school were few and far between.

And then there came the pleasures and convenience of owning a family car. Their parents' world had been limited to the miles they could walk, or ride on horseback or in a carriage. For many of that generation and earlier, Caxley was as far as they had ever ventured. Very few had seen the sea, some seventy miles away, and fewer still had been to London, less than seventy miles to travel. Now, it seemed, they could spend their leisure anywhere in the British Isles, or even farther afield.

Even more pertinent, from my point of view, the car could take children out of the village to nearby schools of their parents' choice. The preparatory school at Caxley, to which young Jeremy Winter was bound in September, was a case in point. It had been a thoroughly reliable and thriving school for many years, and was deservedly respected in the community. Many local people had passed through its hands, and in the old days had usually gone from there to the ancient local grammar school. One could see why the Winters would have no difficulty in taking the child in by car, and it was absolutely right that they should have the school of their choice. But it did not help my numbers, alas!

The proliferation of cars in the village certainly contributed, in some measure, to the plight of my own school and many others in the same quandary. But what could be done about it?

When I first came to Fairacre public transport was adequate. There were several buses a day to Caxley and back, and from there one could proceed to larger towns such as Oxford, Reading, Andover, and even Salisbury with a little planning. Now we had several days in the week with no buses at all.

There had been a branch line on the railway to Caxley, much used by school children and other daily passengers. When it closed, in company with hundreds of other lines after the war, there was a definite loss to the community.

To have a car in Fairacre is now a necessity rather than a luxury, and what was once an added pleasure to life is now a vital means of getting to one's living.

Well, there was mighty little I could do to halt the dwindling of my flock. Perhaps the other two new houses would provide some future pupils for Fairacre School.

But somehow I doubted it.

4   Newcomers

MRS Pringle returned to her duties after her visit to hospital. Her mood was more militant than usual. 'That new doctor I saw this time said I was to lose two stone and take *more exercise*. "*More exercise*, young man," I says to him, "if you saw how much exercise I have to take, day in day out, at my work – which is Real Work, I'll have you know, not just looking at legs and writing out bits of paper for the chemist – you would get a real shock." He didn't say nothing after that.'

It was my private opinion that Mrs Pringle had not delivered the tirade quoted but wished she had, and I was being the recipient of her wishful thinking.

'A mere boy he was too,' she went on, puffing about the classroom with her duster. 'Could've been my grandson except I'd have learnt him better manners if he'd been one of mine, I can tell you.'

'Has he prescribed any medicine or ointment?' I enquired, really in order to stem this vituperative flow.

Mrs Pringle sat down heavily on the front desk, chest heaving under her flowered overall. I confronted her glaring eyes as bravely as I could.

'Much too posh for that, this one was. Going to get in touch with our own doctor, I gather, and says he'll see me when I've lost the first two stone. *The first two stone!* He'll have to wait a bit, and that's flat.'

She heaved herself to her feet and made for the floor. It was no surprise to see that her limp was much in evidence.

* * *

March was almost over and before long we should be breaking up for the Easter holidays.

Our vicar, the Reverend Gerald Partridge, paid his usual weekly visit and gave a talk to the children about the coming Holy Week followed by the Festival of Easter.

I always enjoy his visits, and so do the children, but much of his discourse is far above their heads. He had been a brilliant student, I had heard, at his theological college, and this I could well believe. But his beliefs were couched in such obscure and learned language that I found as much difficulty in understanding him as did my class.

However, he has a lovely voice, and kindness oozes from him like honey and this we all appreciate. The children are quite content to listen in peaceful bemusement as the words flow round them, and we all feel rested and happy.

On this particular afternoon, after the children had gone out to play, the vicar broached the subject of our falling numbers.

'I know,' I said. 'It is worrying, but what's to be done?'

'We've faced this before. It was the worrying part for you that my wife and I were concerned about. You can be sure that if the worst happens, which pray to God it won't, we shall all see that you can stay on in the school house.'

'I have no doubt that the education committee would be humane enough to allow that,' I agreed. I wondered if this were the moment to tell him about Miss Clare's wonderful bequest to me. So far, I had kept silent about it, although I had a strong suspicion that the news had been common knowledge for some time in the neighbourhood. I decided to take the plunge.

'As it happens,' I began, 'I don't think I should be entirely homeless –'

'Ah yes! Dear Dolly Clare's house. I had heard of her plans that you should have it.'

How *did* the news get about, I wondered for the hundredth time? I had said nothing, Dolly had said nothing, that I knew. Her solicitors presumably were like the proverbial clams. I suppose things are air-borne in rural parts. There seems to be no other explanation.

'It's true,' I said. 'I am an extremely lucky woman, and Dolly says I can stay at her house whenever I like.'

'Well, that's a great weight off our minds,' sighed the vicar. 'You are going to have a roof over your head one way or another.'

I went with him to the door. A few spots of rain were falling, and I called the children inside, waving goodbye to our chairman of governors at the same time.

Within two minutes the heavens opened and the windows were streaming with rain. At least I had collected my little flock before the chance of playing 'Splashem' had been a temptation.

The rain continued through the night and I lay in bed listening to it gurgling into the water butts. I heard the thump of the cat flap on the kitchen door, and a second thump very soon afterwards. Obviously Tibby had not spent long out in the garden, and had returned to warmth and a dry bed with the minimum of delay. I too enjoyed my bed, and thought how extra snug it seemed with the rain splashing outside.

In the morning it had cleared, and a bright sun was already sparking the raindrops on the edge. A spring morning in this downland country is a joy, and my garden was looking at its most hopeful. The ancient plum tree, brittle with age, was a mass of white blossom, and the grass was 'pranked with daisies', as Robert Bridges put it. I decided then and there that the children should learn his poem *Spring Goeth All in White* that very afternoon, in readiness for all the pleasures of the spring now, and those about to come.

The clematis was showing buds and, in the two tubs by my door, scarlet early tulips made a splash of colour against the faded brickwork of the house. Farther off in the border the daffodils made a brave show behind the mixed colours of velvety polyanthus. I savoured the freshness of it all before going in for my breakfast. Everything was so clean, so new, so hopeful. Before long the weeds would come, and the greenfly. The birds would peck at the polyanthus and primrose, and scatter the earth everywhere as they scratched for insects. The grass would need mowing, the paths would need weeding, the flowers would need deheading.

Never mind! That was in the future. It was bliss enough to relish this early morning vista of young life and fresh beauty, and I proposed to look no further.

On the following Sunday I went to tea at Jane Winter's new house.

I had looked forward to this for some time, for I have the usual curiosity about how others live, and we have had so few really new houses in the village that this was going to be an extra excitement.

Since my arrival in Fairacre, a number of cottages had been sold and renovated. With the decrease in the number of farm workers, many of their homes had gone on the market. Some, but not many in Fairacre, had become weekend cottages for Londoners, but more had been taken by couples working in Caxley, or retired people from the neighbourhood.

This, of course, was traditional. The young couples wanted a garden, and a pleasant place to bring up a family. The retired couples often wanted to leave their town homes which had sometimes been their business premises as well, and were looking for something peaceful and pretty, and easy to run.

The Hales were typical of such people. He had been a history master at Caxley Grammar School for most of his career, and they both enjoyed retirement now in Tyler's Row, a row of small and once shabby cottages which they had converted into one house. The Hales had proved to be a great asset to Fairacre, supporting the church and school, and well to the fore in helping with all our village activities. No doubt the Winters too would join in, although their business commitments would mean that their time was limited.

The front garden of the Winter's house was still rather raw, but the border had been planted with dwarf conifers of varying shapes and hues, and would look pleasant before long. It was obviously planted with an eye to saving labour in the future, which I thought wise. The Mr Willets of this world get scarcer weekly, more's the pity, and what one cannot do has of necessity to be left.

'Come and see the back garden,' said Jane, leading me round the house. There was a newly planted lawn, young grass already sprouting, and the whole area covered with lines of black cotton supported by a forest of sticks.

'The birds are such a pest,' said Jane, 'but I think we're winning. We're planning to have a rockery in the corner, and a long border with perennials at that side. And we're going to get a shrubbery going next autumn.'

'No vegetables?'

'Simply not worth it,' she said. 'We are surrounded with first-class market gardeners, and I can always pop into Tesco's or Sainsbury's from the office. Besides, when would we find the time to tend a vegetable garden? I know my father spends all his days planting peas and training raspberries, but then he's retired.'

It all made good sense, but again brought home to me the change in Fairacre ways. The older people in the village still maintain their vegetable plot in the back garden, and when I came here first a great many grew vegetables in their front gardens as well. The idea of spending money, and energy, in bringing stuff unnecessarily from Caxley on the bus was unthinkable. Only foreign produce such as oranges or bananas needed to be transported, the bulk of fruit and vegetables came from one's own patch and was eaten in season. All the peelings, the outer leaves of cabbages and lettuces and so on, went to the pig, for almost all cottagers had a sty, and even in my own days, most gardens had a family pig in the corner.

Needless to say, there was no pig in this garden. It was very well planned, and given a few years it was going to look lovely, as I told my hostess.

We went indoors to be greeted by Jane's husband Tom, a large and cheerful man who was engaged in bandaging young Jeremy's knee.

'Nothing serious,' he assured me. 'It isn't a hospital job, is is Jeremy?'

The child nodded agreement. There were still signs of tears, but he seemed to be over the shock.

'Our paving stones are still wobbly,' explained Tom, 'and we shall have to get them laid properly, I can see.'

The drawing-room was large and light, and the furniture new and comfortable. Jeremy was prompted into handing round sandwiches and cake, which he did nobly despite the limp, but his father was given the job of delivering teacups.

It was all very jolly, and I enjoyed meeting new people and admiring their splendid possessions. It was stimulating to see the latest bathroom equipment, the modern double-glazing, the fitted cupboards and up-to-date gadgets in the kitchen and the adjoining utility room. The washing machine and tumble drier, as well as some large objects which I could not recognize, were housed here, while the kitchen itself was reserved for the cooking arrangements and also had a large table where meals could be taken. This, I could see, was already the heart of the house, as it is in all real homes.

After tea and the inspection of the house, we returned to the sitting-room and helped Jeremy with a large jigsaw puzzle of Mrs Tiggywinkle.

'He loves Beatrix Potter,' commented Jane.

'What a right-minded child,' I said.

'But I still wish we'd chosen "Benjamin Bunny",' said his father, studying a mottled piece of jigsaw. 'These prickly bits are the devil to sort out.'

I returned home with a pot of home-made jam, a picture drawn by Jeremy, and the comfortable feeling of having made new friends.

Later that evening, as I soaked in my very ordinary white bath, I dwelt on the beauty of the Winter's new home, and particularly on the luxury of their bathroom. The walls were painted a pale green, and the bath, wash-basin, bidet and lavatory echoed the colour. Even the soap was green and the towels too. It was a most beautiful sight.

And yet, not all that long ago, as I well remembered, almost all the water in our village was that which fell from the skies, and ended up in water butts and tanks. It is true that there were several deep wells, and my school house possessed one in which the water was pure and ice-cold. But bathrooms were few and far between, and in my early years at Fairacre I took my bath in front of the kitchen fire enjoying silky rain water in a galvanized iron tub.

Very few houses now were without a bathroom. My own had been adapted from a tiny box room between the two bedrooms, and very well it suited me.

I remember how excited I was when main water was laid through the village, and I turned on my new bath taps. Here indeed was luxury!

There was no doubt about it, I thought as I towelled myself dry, Fairacre folk were a great deal better off these days. Gone were the buckets of hot and cold water to be carried into the house. Better still, gone were the earth privies at the end of the garden which, no matter how well embowered in lilac and elder bushes, were not a pleasure to visit at any time, and at their very worst on a dark wet night.

I would not wish to go back to those days, and yet I wondered if my delight in hearing rain splashing against my windows and gurgling into my water butts did not stem from that long ago time when rain water was welcome and held so dear.

Amy called in one evening, soon after the Sunday tea party, and I told her all about the new house.

'I wish you had somewhere like that to live,' she said somewhat wistfully.

I looked at her in surprise. 'But I've got this – and I love it! You know that.'

'Yes, of course I know it,' said Amy, sounding more like her brisk self, 'but what about the future? What happens if the school closes? *When* it closes, one might say, from all I hear.'

Again, I had to make a decision. Should I keep my secret, as I had done for some years now? Or was it a secret after all? The vicar seemed to know all about Dolly Clare's generosity, and I had no doubt that most of Fairacre knew too.

I resolved to tell Amy that after one or two bequests, I would inherit Dolly's house and its contents. And having told her it was gratifying to see that she really had had no idea of my good fortune, and she was greatly stirred. Amy has a warm and quite emotional nature hidden under the sophisticated veneer, and she rose to give me a hug.

'Gosh, what a relief! I am so *very* pleased for you. Dear old Dolly, she is as far-sighted as she is generous. It is the perfect answer to your problems, isn't it?'

I told her how I felt about it.

'It solves our problems too,' she went on. 'James and I have often thought about what might happen to you when you retired, and he had plans for some kind of trust fund.'

'Good heavens!' I exclaimed. 'It's uncommonly kind of you both, but I shall have a pension, you know, and probably find digs somewhere, or a flat to rent.'

'Well, that doesn't arise now, does it?' said Amy.

'You are a good pair,' I replied. 'Always helping lame dogs over stiles – though I can't ever remember seeing a lame dog being helped over a stile, come to think of it. No doubt it would resent the attention, and bite the helping hand ungratefully. Anyway, how's your latest? Brian, I mean?'

'Still with us, although his daughter took him off our hands for three days last week.'

'So the Bristol job didn't materialize?'

'We don't know yet. The fellow who was at school with James and Brian is in Australia on some high-powered business lark, and then he will want to consult the other directors, so it looks as though we shall have our Brian for some time.'

'Well, I reckon you are both noble. I often think of that somewhat outspoken Spanish saying: "After three days fish, and visitors, stink!"'

Amy laughed. 'Well, at least Brian doesn't do that! He's the most frequently-bathed man I've come across.'

She rose to look out at the garden. 'I can see why you're so fond of this place. It is a little gem.'

'I know.'

'Does it run to a cup of coffee, by the way?'

I burst into apologies.

'Anything will do, my dear, as long as it isn't "This-week's-offer" from the village shop.'

'You shall have the very best,' I assured her, hastening to the kitchen.

5   Easter Holidays

WITH the end of the Spring term in sight, I began to busy myself with innumerable forms and returns which had to go to the local education authority.

More pleasurably, I began to plan some modest entertaining at the school house. During term time my evenings and weekends seem to be filled with such domestic activities as washing and ironing, answering personal letters, attacking anything particularly urgent in the home such as a leaking tap, a spent light bulb, or some feline disorder of Tibby's.

There are also school duties which have to be done in the peace of my sitting-room, such as the ever-present marking, planning of lessons and occasionally the highly necessary job of sorting out a large cardboard carton known euphoniously as 'The Bits Box'.

This useful aid to education contains such objects as cotton reels, buttons, kitchen paper towels, plastic boxes which once held margarine, Gentleman's Relish and other choice comestibles, lengths of elastic, string, raffia, lace, mysterious pieces of metal from old corsets, broken clocks, kitchen gadgets, and heaven knows what beside.

This jumble of rubbish is a constant source of delight to my children whose powers of invention are sparked off by blissful trawling in this rich sea. From the detritus they fabricate windmills, ships, cars, furniture for their dolls' houses or a host of ingenious objects. The Bits Box is much prized, but needs attention now and again. An insufficiently cleaned cereal carton, for instance, soon gets the attention of the school mice who bustle out at night when all is quiet. Sometimes the box itself, redolent of its varied cargo, has to be replaced with a fresh one.

This holiday, however, I intended to invite the Winters and Miriam and Gerard Baker to lunch with me. I should like to have invited Amy and James too, for they are generous in their hospitality to me, but they were going to be away and, in any case, seven people in my small dining-room was rather a squash. They would come on another occasion.

The invitations were accepted to lunch on a Saturday, and I began to ponder on the meal. I enjoy cooking, but it is not much fun providing for one person. It was going to be much more exciting planning an elegant spring luncheon for five.

It seemed a good idea to browse through several glossy magazines for ideas, and these were so absorbing that I found myself studying articles on child behaviour, breast-feeding, bird migration and the pollution of our beaches, before realizing that I had spent an hour in these pursuits and was no farther ahead with my culinary plans.

I turned to the pictures. That rum and chocolate and coconut cake looked really impressive, but the recipe had over a dozen listed ingredients. Also one needed several bowls in use, including one lodged over hot water whilst engaged in melting butter and chocolate together.

I like something simpler. Ten to one the milkman would call at a crucial moment of butter-and-chocolate merging, and all would be lost. Then think of the washing up of all those messy saucepans, bowls and spoons. Besides, a lot of people did not care for rum, or coconut, for that matter.

I turned to another magazine. Did I want a loan in order to buy a house? Was I adequately insured against accidents in the home, hospital treatment, and car crashes? Was my marriage unsatisfactory? (Well, no. I was not bothered about that, priase be.) Had I ever considered becoming a counsellor, or a warden at a residential home?

This was getting me nowhere. I turned firmly to the cookery pages. This was better. 'Spring On The Table'. A rather ambiguous title, surely? However, the pictures were splendid, and the salmon soufflé looked just the thing. But, come to think of it, one really wants the guests absolutely ready and waiting at the table in order to present them with the perfectly-risen dish. Suppose the Winters were late, or the Bakers, for that matter? Too risky, I decided. Far better to be less ambitious and have something I could prepare the day before, such as cold gammon and chicken.

But I am a messy carver, and it might be one of those cold cheerless spring days when one would relish a Lancashire hot-pot or steak-and-kidney pudding, and forget such elegant dishes as cold soup sprinkled with caviare.

I had a look at *Mrs Beeton*. Under April she gives a comprehensive dinner menu for ten people, for eight and for six, and I studied the last eagerly. Would my four guests enjoy six courses starting with tapioca soup, and going on to sweetbreads, oyster patties, haunch of mutton, capon and tongue? Would they have room, after that lot, for rice soufflé, lemon cream, Charlotte à la Parisienne, or even rhubarb tart? I doubted it, and doubted too my ability to provide it.

In the end I settled for a round of gammon, a tongue, both cooked beforehand and carved in the privacy of my kitchen before the guests arrived. In this way, the more shapely and presentable slices could be neatly arranged with some hardboiled eggs on a lordly dish for handing round, whilst the fragments could be hidden in the fridge for home consumption another day. This, with a cheese and tomato quiche, new potatoes and a salad could follow a warming bowl of mushroom soup; and I proposed to make apple meringue and a treacle tart which no doubt the men would like.

All this mental effort had quite tired me, and I went to bed early. I had forgotten to bring up my library book, but *The Diary of a Country Parson* is always by my bed.

I opened it at Wednesday, March 12, 1794, and read with delight the dinner that Parson Woodford provided for five guests that day.

> We had for Dinner some Skaite, Ham and Fowls, a whole Rump of Beef boiled etc., a fine Hen Turkey rosted, Nancy's Pudding and Currant Jelly, Lobsters, Bullace and Apple Tarts, Cheese with Radishes and Cresses.

My own menu looked decidedly parsimonious beside that. But how much more digestible, I thought smugly, as I turned off the light.

The day after we broke up I went to visit Dolly Clare, carrying some magazines and a bunch of daffodils. It was a blustery day with a hint of rain in the air which misted the windscreen and dampened the roads.

I found Dolly sitting by the fire looking as serene as ever but, to my eyes, thinner than usual.

'I don't really want much in the way of food,' she confessed when I enquired after her health. 'I suppose I don't need it these days. I get so little exercise. Mrs John brings me a delicious lunch each day, but it's really too much. Very often half is left, and it seems such a terrible waste.'

'Have you told her?'

'Yes, indeed, but the dear soul continues to bring it. I haven't the heart to say more.'

I told her about Parson Woodforde's dinner party and
my own plans. As always, she showed the liveliest interest.

'Tongue!' she cried. 'Now I always liked tongue, but
haven't had it for years.'

'Come and join us,' I said. 'I could fetch you in the
morning, and bring you back after tea. Will you come?'

She shook her head and laughed. 'My dear, I'm really
not up to visiting anyone these days, but it's lovely to be
invited. I shall just think of you enjoying that tongue.'

'I shall bring you some on the Sunday,' I promised.
'Better still, I'll bring you enough for two and perhaps
you'll let me have it with you.'

She readily agreed, and when I made my way home I felt
glad that I could do something, even if it only rose to
putting aside some helpings of ham and tongue, to tempt
my old friend's appetite.

I had a week before my little party, but before that occurred I was going to be at the mercy of the decorators.

Luckily they would be working upstairs, painting mainly, but also doing some much-needed tiling round the bath and wash basin.

It was one of the reasons for staying at home this Easter holiday. I wanted to keep my eye on the progress of the work, to catch up with such things as taking curtains and bedspreads to the cleaners, having the sweep, getting two decrepit teeth seen to, and shopping for some summer clothes.

Also, I needed to watch my expenditure, and even the most modest guest house would strain my resources at the moment. The painters, the cleaners and the dentist would deplete my bank account seriously enough, without my gadding about in foreign, or even local, parts.

And there was another reason for staying at home. I was worried about Dolly Clare, and did not want to leave her. I called as often as I could, and I knew that Mrs John was in and out several times a day. The doctor too was kind and attentive, dropping in to see her at least once a week, but I wished that I could do more.

I had suggested that she should come to stay with me for as long as she liked, but she was adamant about staying in her own home, which I well understood. I wanted to be at hand if she needed me, though, and this was probably the strongest reason for being glad that I was not going far during this particular holiday.

On Monday morning the two decorators arrived. I had not seen them before, but they had been recommended to me by Mrs Richards's husband Wayne, who was a builder. They seemed a cheerful pair and arrived in a battered van which rattled with pails and paint pots inside, and had an aluminium ladder along the top.

'I'm Perce,' said the fat one.

'I'm Bert,' said the thin one, and I led them upstairs to survey their task.

'Oh dear, oh dear!' sighed Perce.

'Looks a bit rough,' agreed Bert, lugubriously.

I refused to be alarmed. I have come across this sort of approach before. It means another twenty pounds on the bill, if taken seriously, but as I already had their estimate carefully tucked away in my writing desk, I did not worry.

'Bert's going to rub down in the bathroom,' Perce told me, 'while I tackle this 'ere bedroom.'

This was the spare room. Once done, I proposed to sleep in there while they did their worst in my own bedroom.

'D'you mind if we has the tranny on?' asked Bert, patting his portable radio lovingly.

'As long as you keep the volume down,' I said in my most schoolmistressy voice. 'I've some letters to write, and some phoning to do.'

I left them to their work and descended to my room.

Ten minutes later there was a tap on the door. Bert smiled at me. 'You wouldn't have such a thing as an old dustsheet for the floor? The one we've got's a bit skimpy.'

I mounted the stairs and produced a dust sheet from the bottom of the airing cupboard. From the bathroom came the sound of someone screeching and gulping out what I supposed was a song. Fortunately it was somewhat muffled by the closed door, but the heavy drumming made the house throb.

I returned to my letters, only to be disturbed by Perce slamming the front door, and I watched him ambling across to the van. He clambered in and drove off.

He had still not returned when I climbed the stairs again with a mug of coffee for Bert at ten-thirty.

'Where's Perce?'

'He had to go back to pick up some thinners. He won't be long.'

Morning prayers appeared to be emanating from the radio, and I added my own to them. The bathroom was so thick with dust from the rubbing-down operation that it was difficult to breathe, but Bert seemed unperturbed.

I went downstairs to my own coffee. Before I had taken a sip, Bert appeared. 'Could you spare a minute, miss? There's a nasty crack across the top of the door. It may need some time spent on it if it's to be a proper job.'

I climbed the stairs again, and surveyed the crack. It looked pretty superficial to me.

'You must do what is best,' I said. 'If it needs filling, or whatever, then do it. But I should get Perce's opinion when he gets back.'

'Right. I'll do that.'

I went back downstairs to my tepid coffee. Why, I wondered, do men seem to need so much assistance, not to mention praise and commendation, for their tasks? I did not consult anyone about my teaching affairs – just got on with them, and faced the consequences.

At twelve o'clock Perce returned, and joined Bert upstairs. A quarter of an hour later, they both went to the van, and sat inside with their lunch boxes on their knees, and the radio on full blast.

Tibby wandered in, mewing protestingly.

'I know, Tib,' I said. 'I know.'

To give them their due, Perce and Bert were almost finished by Thursday of that week, and I felt that I could begin my preparations for the Saturday lunch without too many requests for pieces of old rag, a dustpan and brush, a kettle of boiling water, old newspapers, a cold chisel, (are there *hot* chisels, I wondered?) and even '*the right time*', now and again. (Who, in any case, is going to give an enquirer the *wrong* time?)

I started on the quiche first, and enjoyed rolling out the pastry to bake it blind. It was going to be filled with cheese, tomatoes and eggs for I had an idea that Miriam Baker, née Quinn, had become a vegetarian. Of course, I thought, rolling busily, if she was one of the really strict ones, vegan or something, the eggs would be turned down, and in that case she would simply have to graze on the salad.

There is something very soothing about cooking if one has the kitchen to oneself and nothing too demanding to cook. With the work almost completed upstairs. I pursued my own plans happily. The tongue and the gammon were waiting to be boiled. I had most of the shopping done. Last minute jobs such as mixing the mustard and taking the egg stains from the forks before general cleaning of the silver, and making sure that there were enough matching napkins – not easy in a household of one – now loomed, but I was beginning to feel that I had the whole campaign well in hand.

I might have known that Fate would pull the rug from under my feet.

Perce and Bert told me at five o'clock that the bathroom tiles would need to be changed over the wash-basin as they were 'too big in a funny sort of way'. (*How* funny? Strange? Comic? Sinister?) They would have to get a smaller size in the morning – that is, Bert said, shaking his head, if they made that particular size in that colour. Should they bring a few samples out to show me? If they couldn't get the same thing, would I like a different one – say, in a *toning* shade? They could get plain white, of course. It was up to me. After all, it was my bathroom, they said fairly, and looked relieved at the thought.

'Does this mean,' I demanded, 'that you won't finish to-morrow?'

They looked aghast at such a direct question.

'Not our fault, miss. Just a bit of a slip-up over the sizing. If we can get the right ones first thing, we ought to get everything done tomorrow. What's the rush anyway?'

'The rush, as you call it, is that I shall have people here on Saturday, and no doubt they will use the bathroom. I want it to be finished.'

Now they both looked hurt.

'Well,' said Bert sadly, 'if that's how you feel, I think we'd better settle for white tiles behind the basin.'

'There's just a chance we might be able to order the same as the others, of course,' added Perce, 'but them tile firms take their time sending down.'

'The same if you can get them, white if not,' I said, in the tone I use to infant malefactors. 'But the job's to be finished by tomorrow. Understand?'

'Very well, miss,' sighed Bert, more in sorrow than anger, in the face of such feminine unreasonableness. 'We'll call in at the stores on our way home.'

I watched them clamber into the van. They were busy talking to each other. It was fortunate, I suspected, that I could not actually hear their comments.

That same evening, while the ham and tongue simmered comfortably on the stove, Mrs Pringle arrived.

'I had to go over the school,' she said, 'so I thought I'd pop in.'

'Do sit down. Coffee?'

'No thanks. It gives me heartburn. But I thought I'd give your brass a rub up with these visitors of yours coming.'

I was torn between gratitude for the kind offer and

irritation at being disturbed in the midst of my preparations.

'Well,' I began, 'I don't think there's any real need, but if you like to come for an hour tomorrow afternoon, I should be grateful.'

'Better make it two,' said she. 'Besides the brass, I expect that bathroom will want doing, and I see them men have made plenty of dust everywhere. You don't want your visitors drawing their fingers along the top of the doors now, do you?'

'My guests,' I retorted, 'would do no such thing, and if they were so ill-mannered they would deserve to get dirty fingers.'

Mrs Pringle snorted derisively, which made me seethe even more.

'Why,' I continued, 'you might just as well suggest that my visitors would scrabble about in the *chimney* while they are at it!'

'And that,' said Mrs Pringle, puffing to her feet, 'can do with the sweep, and that I do know.'

She limped to the door.

'See you tomorrow,' she said.

As always, she had enjoyed the last word.

Bert and Perce appeared the next morning bearing two boxes. One held plain white tiles, the other some beetroot-coloured ones with a green sprig of some unknown shrub in the centre.

'All we could get in that size, miss,' they said. 'That's a very tricky bit of wall there, over that basin. Too close to the door like, and that mirror on the wall takes up a deal of room. I said to Bert at the time we was measuring: "Here's trouble," I said, didn't I, Bert?'

'You did, Perce, you did.'

'You didn't measure it correctly,' I said bluntly, and they looked wounded.

'So which d'you like?' said Perce at last.

'I don't like either,' I told them, 'but it will have to be the white, I can see that, so you'd better get on with it.'

They went aloft bearing the tiles. The box of beetroot ones remained on the table, and I studied the sprig carefully. Could it be yew? Or rosemary? Come to think of it, it looked remarkably like a piece of butcher's broom which examiners like to present to botanical students for identification. There was a catch in it, if I could only recall what it was after some forty years. What looked like a leaf was a stem, or else what looked like a stem was a leaf. Unless it was something called an adventitious root, of course.

I decided not to waste any more time on the matter, and put the box of tiles in the front porch for Perce and Bert to return to the van. Those sprigs, let alone the colour, would have driven me made in a fortnight.

I was now quite reconciled to living with the white ones.

6   A Change of Address

SATURDAY morning was all that an April morning should be. The small birds sang as they went about their nest-building, the daffodils waved their trumpets and the blue sky was dappled with high slow-moving clouds.

My four guests were due at twelve-thirty, and as most of the preparations were done, I even had time to peruse the fashion pages of my daily newspaper.

It appeared that ethnic colours – whatever they might be – were the only possible choice for our summer outfits. Such bourgeois *ensembles* as navy-blue and white, beige and cream were evidently anathema to the fashion writer. Wide belts of leather studded with bronze, or simply thick chains with dangling medallions would encircle the waists of those who had such attributes.

Hats were out too – vivid kerchieves of scarlet or yellow would bind our heads to make us look like Russian peasants or Caribbean mammies. Cardigans, it seemed, were also forbidden. This necessary adjunct to an English summer had been thrown overboard for vivid shawls and ponchos. What you did with your arms whilst attempting to carry a tray and keep your wrap round your shoulders, was anybody's guess, as buttons were taboo. What a blessing I had so little money that last year's despised garments would form the bulk of my summer wear!

'Lucky old Tibby,' I said to the cat, as I threw aside the

paper to go about my duties. 'Only one rigout for winter
and summer! And it always fits.'

The Bakers and the Winters arrived within five minutes of
the half hour, much to my relief.

We all know the friends that are bidden for, say, 'twelve
to half-past', and cotton on to the half-past bit and arrive
at five to one when the potatoes have turned to mush, and
the Yorkshire pudding is black round the edges.

Frankly, I far prefer people to arrive too early, even if I
am struggling into my clean blouse, and the white sauce
has still to be made. At least they are *there*, and you have
them under your thumb, so to speak, and are spared the
anxiety of wondering if they have:

a) forgotten

b) had a crash on the way, in which case who should one
ring first to apprise them of the accident and give the
address of the hospital?

c) been told the wrong day, and may turn up tomorrow
when the food is ruined.

My good friends were welcomed most warmly. The
women knew each other, of course, and there was immediate chatter about their old employer Sir Barnabas
Hatch, but Gerard and Tom had not met. However, within
minutes, over their sherry, they were discussing the merits
of Manchester United and Tottenham Hotspur, and I was
able to slip away to put out the food.

It all seemed to be much appreciated. Appetites were
hearty, and the ham and tongue was consumed by Miriam
with as much enjoyment as the others. Nevertheless, the
carefully prepared vegetarian quiche seemed equally popular
with all. I felt positively smug at the compliments and was glad
that I did not live in earlier, more formal times when young
ladies were adjured never to comment on the food offered,

and to eschew all talk of money, religion and politics; not that the latter two subjects cropped up very frequently, but money, or rather the lack of it, was a more common theme these days.

It was the reason, Jane Winter surmised, for the lack of buyers for the remaining two new houses.

'The price has been reduced by several thousand,' she told us. 'Perhaps we should have waited.'

'Nonsense!' said Tom cheerfully. 'We bought when we wanted to, and got a decent packet for the last place. It's simply that there's not the money about now.'

'There are several "For Sale" boards in our road in Caxley,' said Gerard. 'You can understand people's reluctance to lower the price, but it will have to come.'

'Have you seen any possible buyers at the new houses?' I asked Jane, hoping she would tell me of couples with large families of school age, all bent on living in Fairacre and attending my school.

'One or two elderly couples,' she replied, dashing my hopes. 'Retired people, I think. I spoke to one very pleasant woman. She'd be an ideal neighbour, I'm sure, but they thought the price excessive.'

'He'd had a bakery in Caxley High Street,' said Tom. 'I think it was 'Millers''.'

'Oh, that's a marvellous shop,' I exclaimed. 'It's been there for generations. One of the founders was a brother of an old boy who farmed round here for years. The brother – the baker – used to live over the shop. I had tea there once with one of his daughters. You could see all the life of Caxley from their sitting-room windows.'

'These people moved from there long ago, I gather,' said Jane. 'Now they want to be even further out.'

I found this understandable, but sad. Of course, it had always been thus. The High Street traders, as they grew prosperous, moved to the higher and hillier suburbs of the town, probably only a mile away in Victorian times. Their descendants built their homes a little farther out, on the fields which ringed the town. With the coming of the car, the present generation could live ten or twenty miles away from their business. Many, of course, had sold long ago, which accounted for the national, rather than local, names over the shops in the High Street.

Times change, we know, but I gave a wistful thought to that long-ago tea party overlooking a busy, but not, as now, traffic-clogged Caxley High Street.

My thoughts were interrupted by a question from Miriam about Miss Clare.

'I shall be seeing her tomorrow,' I told her.

'I don't know her as well as you do,' said Miriam, 'but she always struck me as one of the most well-balanced people one could wish to meet.'

I heartily agreed, and gave a brief account of Dolly's early days at Beech Green and Fairacre.

Gerard became vastly interested and wondered if he

could have a television interview with her. Always the professional, I thought!

'Would she come to Lime Grove?' he asked, eyes shining.

'I doubt it. She's very old and very delicate now. It's as much as she can do to get upstairs to bed.'

'We could do it at her house,' continued Gerard. 'Shall I call on her on our way home?'

'Good heavens, Gerard! Have a heart! I should think the very idea would make her collapse.'

The conversation turned to other things, and then the Winters said that they must go and collect Jeremy from his friend's house where he had been invited for lunch, and so the party began to break up.

'I can't tell you how I envy Jane,' said Miriam, as we waved goodbye to the Winters.

I wondered whether she was considering her own childless state, but other matters were on her mind.

'I do so miss the office,' she told me, in a low voice, so that Gerard, who was inspecting the garden, could not hear. 'Barny could be a sore problem at times, but he was always stimulating, and I miss the hurly-burly of all the arrangements to be made, and the comings and goings of interesting people.'

'Can't you apply for another job? I should think anyone with half an eye would snap you up.'

She looked pensive.

'I'm beginning to think about it. Barney has said that when Jane has her holidays he would like to have me as stand-in. But I wonder if that would work. Even if it would be enough.'

'Something will turn up,' I told her, wondering just what.

'When you women have stopped chattering,' said

Gerard, approaching, 'we'll offer our sincere thanks for a lovely time, and let you have a rest.'

They departed, leaving me with much to ponder.

The next day I set off to see Dolly Clare, taking the promised picnic with me. It so happened that I met Mrs John on her way home from calling at Miss Clare's.

'She's looking forward to seeing you,' she told me. 'I've just had to break the news that I shall be away for a week or two. My father is very ill in Cardiff. They seem to think that he is near his end, and I must go to help my mother. Mrs Annett knows, and she has promised to keep an eye on things, but I didn't like telling Miss Clare, I'd be away.'

'It can't be helped, and in any case your family must come first. I'll see what I can do, and give you a ring before you go.'

'Thank you. Actually, I shall set off on Tuesday morning.'

'I'll remember,' I said. 'You've been absolutely marvellous to her, and I know she has always appreciated it.'

I drove on, my mind full of plans.

Dolly was pottering about in her garden. She used a stick for support these days, and moved very slowly, but she was still upright and greeted me with a smile.

We wandered about the garden together. The fruit trees were in small leaf, and the hawthorn hedges beginning to show buds. After a while we went indoors, and I wondered if she would say anything about Mrs John's departure to Wales. It would be typical of Dolly, I thought, to say nothing, independent spirit that she was.

We enjoyed our cold collation, and I was glad to see that she ate a good helping of tongue. The remains I insisted on leaving in her cool tiled larder for another meal, and was about to help her upstairs for her usual rest.

'Rest?' she protested. 'I don't have such a thing when I have visitors. I can have a rest any time. Visitors are rarer and more precious.'

So we sat and talked, but still nothing was said about Mrs John. At length, I broached the subject.

'I met Mrs John on my way here. She tells me that she is obliged to go to Wales. I just wondered if you would like to come and stay with me?'

I had been thinking of this, and other plans, ever since meeting Mrs John. It was true that the workmen were due to tackle my bedroom, but that could be postponed, or I could sleep downstairs for that matter. In any case, the spare bedroom was now in pristine condition should Dolly agree to use it.

But, as I guessed, she would not consider it.

'I shall be perfectly happy on my own. Isobel Annett will pop in, I know, and I have the telephone if I should need help. It's very kind of you, but you have enough to do.'

'Then I have an alternative to offer,' I told her. 'Let me come here to live while Mrs John's away. I can easily drive to school from here, and you would not be alone at night.'

'There's absolutely no need –' began Dolly, but I cut in with a very cunning argument.

'I shall be terribly anxious about you. You shouldn't be alone for hours at a stretch, and I've worried for months now about your sleeping here on your own. Suppose you fell? Or someone broke in?'

She was silent for a moment, and then began to laugh.

'Very well, you artful girl, you win! And thank you very much, my dear.'

So it was settled, and I made up her spare bed then and there ready for my sojourn. My routine could easily be altered. I should leave Dolly about eight-fifteen each morn-

ing, having given her breakfast, and go to Fairacre to let
in the workmen, to pick up the post, feed Tibby, and go
over to the school. At the end of the school day I could
spend half an hour or so in my house, feed Tib again, see
all was well, and return to my temporary home with Dolly.

To say that I had been anxious about her was perfectly
true, and I felt considerable relief at these new arrangements. I only hoped that Dolly would not find my presence
too irksome. As a single woman myself, I knew how
precious one's privacy was, and I was determined to bear
that in mind.

The following day was the last of the Easter holidays.

Bert and Pearce arrive to tackle my bedroom, and set to
work with unwonted briskness. I commented on their progress when I took up their coffee.

'Well, you wants us gone, I expect,' said Bert. 'We likes
to oblige.'

'Besides,' said Pearce, 'we've got another job waiting
over at Bent. They're getting a bit shirty.'

Bert gave Perce what is known as 'an old-fashioned
look', and I guessed that he would be rebuked for his
moment of truth when I had left the scene.

But mention of Bent reminded me to ring Amy and to
tell her of my temporary change of address.

'Good idea,' said Amy. 'I wonder you didn't think of it
before.'

'I certainly did,' I protested, 'but you don't know Dolly
Clare. She "won't impose", as she says, or I should have
been there months ago. Tell me, how are things with you?
Brian still with you?'

'Not for much longer. There's been a general reshuffle
at the Bristol place as they've opened a new office in
Scotland. Brian starts as treasurer in the Bristol office as

soon as things have settled down there. To give the chap
his due, he's willing to push off into digs in the Bristol
area, so maybe he'll do that. James seems to think it
would be unkind to encourage him to go. Still thinking of
those heroic cricket matches of long ago, I surmise.'

'Men are trying,' I replied, and was about to tell her of
my troubles with Bert and Perce in residence, but fearing
that I might be overheard, I forbore to relieve my feelings.

'I was going to invite you to come with me to a charity
concert next week, but I suppose you don't feel able to go
out in the evenings if you are with Dolly.'

'It's nice of you, but I'm going to stay put while I'm at
Beech Green.'

'Fair enough. There'll be other things later on, I'm sure,
but it looks as though I shan't see you for some time. I'm
going with James to see a new factory in Wales. He's a
director of the firm, and I shall be staying on down there
with my aunt. She's ninety-two, and will no doubt walk
me off my feet.'

'Any more jaunts?'

'I may go up to Scotland later. James is also on the
board of this firm Brian's joining, so we may go up to see
how the new office is settling down. But that won't be
until June. I'll see you before then, I hope.'

'As soon as Mrs John gets back,' I promised, 'we'll get
together for a meal somewhere.'

At that moment, Bert appeared. 'Sorry to bother you,
miss, but have you got such a thing as an old kitchen
knife?'

'I heard that,' said the voice on the telephone. It sounded
highly amused.

'See you sometime,' I replied, putting down the receiver.

'Now, Bert,' I said, 'do you really want an old kitchen
knife or "*such a thing* as an old kitchen knife"?'

'We wants an old kitchen knife,' explained Bert, looking puzzled.

'Then say so,' I retorted. 'Though to tell the truth, all my kitchen knives are the same age, so you will have to take care of it. What's it wanted for, anyway?'

'There's a bit of something stuck under the skirting board. An old kitchen knife –' He caught my eye. 'I mean, a kitchen knife'd shift it easily.'

He followed me into the kitchen and I found him the desired object in a drawer.

'And bring it back,' I said.

'Yes, miss,' replied Bert meekly.

For a moment he looked exactly like Joseph Coggs, and my conscience smote me.

But not for long.

That evening I telephoned Mrs John and told her my plans, and hoped that she would have better news of her father when she reached Cardiff.

After that, I walked down to see Bob and Alice Willet to ask for their help at Fairacre while I was away at Beech Green.

As always, they were able and willing.

'We'll look after things, don't you fret,' said Bob sturdily. 'And that cat of yourn will be fed regular. If I can't do it, then Alice will, and Tibby'll get double rations if she's on the job.'

'Well, I think animals miss their owners more than we reckon,' contributed Alice. 'I'll see Tib has any little tit-bits like our chicken liver or meat scraps. Cats like fresh stuff.'

Bob cast his eyes heavenwards. 'That cat's got fatty heart as it is,' he told me. 'Wouldn't hurt it to go on a few days' fasting.'

But I knew it would not with the Willets to look after it,

and handed over the keys, and explained about the where-abouts of the tinned cat food and the milk arrangements.

'We'll all feel better knowing you're with the old lady,' said Bob, accompanying me to the gate. 'I suppose ideally she should have someone living there all the time, but I can't see Dolly Clare standing for that.'

The sun was going down as I passed through the village on my way home. The scent of narcissi and early stocks drifted in the warm air. Soon there would be lilac blossom and mock orange adding their perfume, and then the roses, which do so well in Fairacre, contributing their share too.

Above me, the rooks were winging homeward, black wings fluttering against a golden sky. They were building high this year, I had noticed, a sure sign of a good summer. Dolly Clare had told me that soon after I had come to live in Fairacre. Dolly Clare had told me so many things, just as she had told all those lucky children who had passed through her hands.

There were a great many of us who owed a debt to Dolly Clare. I looked forward to trying to repay her, in a small way, over the next few months.

7 'Love To Fairacre'

THE summer term began with a spell of hot dry weather. Even the wind was warm, and the distant downs shimmered in a haze of heat.

My move from the school house to Miss Clare's had caused the minimum of fuss. Each morning I drove the few miles from Beech Green to Fairacre, having given my old friend her breakfast in bed, and seen to her needs.

Isobel Annett, the wife of the headmaster at Beech Green School and once one of my assistants before her marriage, had arranged to call on Dolly at regular intervals during the day, and other friends also gave a hand while Mrs John was in Wales. I was back around five o'clock having seen to my school and home duties, and we spent the evenings together, before retiring to sleep in adjoining rooms under the thatched roof.

It all worked out very easily, and if Dolly sometimes found so many visitors irksome, she was too well-mannered and sensible to show her feelings. Secretly, I think she was relieved to have support, and was now accepting that she could do less and less on her own. After a life time of independence this must have been a difficult problem to face, but she did so with her habitual grace and good temper.

Sometimes, on these light evenings of early summer we went for a drive, usually threading our way through narrow lanes, fresh with young foliage, up to the cool heights of the downs above Beech Green.

On our way, Dolly would point out various landmarks:

'That cottage,' she would say, 'was where Mrs Cotter lived when I was young. She had ten children, and they all streamed out of that tiny place with polished boots and brushed hair, and the girls in starched white pinafores when those things were in fashion. Heaven knows how she did it on a carter's wage – but she did.'

As we approached a little spinney she would tell me that the very best hazel nuts grew there, and down in a fold of the downs she and Ada, her sister, used to go on September mornings to find mushrooms, in the dewy grass.

And once, as we drove along the lane which eventually led to Caxley, she pointed out an ancient sycamore tree, with limbs as grey and lined as an elephant's, which overshadowed the road.

'I said goodbye to my dear Arnold here,' she said quietly. 'I never saw him again.'

Her hand stole to the locket about her neck, and we drove in silence for a time, our minds troubled by 'old unhappy far-off things, and battles long ago'.

At school, the fine weather was especially welcome. The children relished their playtime outside, I relished their absence from the classroom for a precious quarter of an hour, and Mrs Pringle relished the comparative cleanliness of the school floors. An added bonus for her was the fact that her beloved stoves were not sullied with the inflow of fuel and the outflow of ashes.

She became almost pleasant in her manner, and expressed her approval of my move to Miss Clare's.

'Not that it couldn't have been made months ago,' she added. 'She could have done with help long since.'

I pointed out as mildly as I could that Dolly Clare wanted her independence, and that I had in fact offered my services on several occasions.

'Well, better late than never, I suppose,' she admitted grudgingly. 'And I will say that house of yours is a far sight easier to clean with only Tib in it.'

She bent, corsets creaking, to pick up a drawing pin from the floor.

'That could cause a mort of trouble,' she puffed, putting it on my desk. 'Minnie's Basil had a nasty septic foot after stepping on a tack. Minnie had to take him to The Caxley. Hollered something terrible, she said.'

Knowing Basil as I did, I was not surprised.

'Minnie's going to take all the kids to that new pleasure place they've built the other side of Caxley. Sounds lovely. Switchbacks and a giant dipper, and one of them swimming pools with great tubes you can dive down. The kids'll love it. She wanted me to go too, but I told her my switchback days are over, and I'm not flaunting my figure in a bathing suit even if my leg allowed it.'

It seemed wise to me, but I had to be careful not to agree too enthusiastically in case my old sparring partner took umbrage.

'I'd better bring the children in,' I said, making for the door. Diplomacy or cowardice, I wondered? In any case, the thought of Minnie's children at large on all that machinery made my blood run cold. Which would come off worst, I wondered, the children or the equipment?

'Miss,' shouted Patrick, red in the face with indignation, 'John swored at me. He swored twice. He said –'

'I don't want to hear about it,' I said dismissively. 'Go indoors, all of you.'

'But it was about *you* he swored,' protested Patrick. 'He called you a bad name. He said you was –'

'Never mind,' I said firmly. 'Go back to your desk.'

We had hardly settled down before the vicar arrived bearing a large envelope.

'This really should have come to you,' he said apologetically, after greeting the children. 'I can't think why it was sent to me.'

'Well, you are Chairman of the Governors,' I pointed out.

The envelope contained a sheaf of papers from our local naturalists' society and pictures of a dozen endangered species, as well as innumerable forms for donations, competitions, free tickets for this and that. They all managed to flutter to the floor, much to the delight of the milling crowd who rushed from their desks to rescue them. Such diversions are always welcome to children, and it took some time to restore order.

The vicar smiled benignly upon the scene, and when comparative peace reigned again he asked about Miss Clare.

'I thought I might visit her on my way to Caxley this afternoon,' he said. 'Would it be convenient?'

The Reverend Gerald Partridge, in common with most clergymen these days, was in charge of several parishes, and Beech Green was one of them.

He had been calling regularly on Dolly, but usually in the morning when Mrs John was around. I told him that Dolly would be glad to see him at any time, I knew.

'And you are happy together?'

'Perfectly. At least, I am, and I think Dolly is relieved to have someone in the house.'

'Good.' He surveyed my class. 'And how many on roll now?'

'Twenty-one, including the infants.'

The vicar sighed.

'Of course, there are those two new houses,' he said brightening.

'Have you heard anything?' I asked hopefully. 'The boards are still up.'

'Well, no. But we must live in hope. They are both very

well suited to families. Four bedrooms, I gather. Very hopeful. Very hopeful.'

He gave me his usual sweet smile and departed, oblivious, for once, of the children.

'He never said nothing to us,' said John-the-swearer reproachfully.

'If the vicar never said nothing, he must have said something,' I pointed out, embarking yet again upon the use of the double negative. A fruitless quest, as I should know after all these years, but as the vicar had just remarked, we must live in hope.

Mrs John returned a week or so later, bringing her mother with her for a little break after the sad days following her husband's death.

She was very like her daughter, small and nimble, with the same large dark eyes. She had been a nurse in her young days at one of the foremost Welsh hospitals, and she still had the lilt of the Welsh tongue. It was plain that mother and daughter got on very well together.

Dolly Clare was as pleased as I was to have Mrs John back again. Her presence eased my anxiety, and I suspect that Dolly found her assistance in dressing and other daily activities much more deft than my own efforts.

But I was greatly moved when my old friend asked me to stay on at the cottage.

'It is such a comfort to have you here,' she said, 'particularly when I wake in the night. If it's not an imposition, I should love you to continue here.'

There was nothing I wanted more and Mrs John was pleased too, so that my new routine continued, living in two homes at the same time whilst teaching went on undisturbed.

* * *

On the first Friday of June, I took Dolly's tray upstairs as usual, just before eight o'clock. There was not much to carry for she only had two slices of brown bread and butter, some marmalade, and a cup of weak tea.

She seemed to be asleep, and I put down the tray quietly. She opened her eyes, and smiled at me.

'Thank you, may dear. Just off?'

'Yes. Just off.'

'Goodbye then.'

She sat up slowly, and added as she always did: 'Love to Fairacre,' as I turned to go.

It was my turn to do playground duty at mid-morning, and above the din of exuberant children I heard my telephone ringing.

Hastening into the school house I lifted the receiver. It was Mrs John on the line, and she sounded distraught.

'It's sad news, I fear. She's gone. I found her in her bed when I got here ten minutes ago.'

'I'll come over at once.' I said, and went to arrange matters with my assistant, Mrs Richards.

* * *

I had always imagined that the death of my dear old friend would leave me shattered, probably in tears, and certainly trembling and shocked. But to my amazement, although I felt desolate, my mind was clear and I felt capable of dealing with all the practical problems which I should have to face.

There was a kind of numbness of body and mind which, I had no doubt, would soon desert me, but for which I was grateful when I entered the cottage and found Mrs John. She had obviously been crying, and she was shaky, but she was in control of her feelings.

'She must have gone soon after you left,' she told me. 'I thought she had fallen asleep again, as the breakfast wasn't touched.'

'We'd better go up,' I said.

She led the way up the familiar stairs.

'Mother came with me this morning,' she said, 'And she's done all that was needed. She's better at these things than I am, her being a nurse.'

I could not reply. This was my first encounter with death, and I wondered how I should react.

But there was nothing at all to fear. Dolly lay in her bed as I had seen her so many times. A light breeze lifted the curtain at the open window, and ruffled Dolly's fine white hair. She was in a fresh cotton nightgown, and the gold locket was still around her neck.

'I didn't quite know what to do with that,' said Mrs John, following my gaze.

'Leave it there,' I replied. I could not have removed it. As far as I was concerned, I felt it should accompany Dolly to her grave.

Mrs John carried the tray downstairs, and a little later I followed her.

'I rang the doctor,' she said. 'He's out on his rounds,

but they said they could get him on the car phone, and he'd call as soon as possible.'

'And I'll ring the undertaker,' I said.

I was still in the dream-like state which cushions one from immediate shock, and I found I could do these routine jobs without undue emotion.

'It was good of your mother to cope with things,' I said. 'It's something I've never had to face, but I think I could have done it for Dolly.'

'I was glad too,' said Mrs John. 'As soon as she'd done, she went home to get the children's dinner ready.'

How life jostles death, I thought. But rightly so, for life must go on.

There was a knock on the door and the young doctor, who had succeeded dear old Doctor Martin, came in.

'This doesn't surprise me,' he said, after the first condolences. 'She was very weak when I came two days ago. She was a grand old girl – never complained. I shall miss her.'

I took him upstairs, and waited while he examined Dolly.

'If you'd pick up the death certificate at the surgery,' he said, standing up, 'I'll do it as soon as I get back. It's a simple case of heart failure. Everything has just worn out.'

Gently he drew the sheet over Dolly's face, and I began to have my first tremors.

A few minutes after his departure, a van drew up. Two kindly men from the Caxley undertaker's went aloft with a stretcher, and very soon they descended slowly bearing Dolly, still shrouded in her white sheet.

'She'll go straight to our Chapel of Rest,' said the older man, 'should you want to visit her.'

He dropped something on a side table as he resumed his task, and I watched Dolly go through the cottage door and down the garden path for the last time.

When the van had gone I saw that Dolly's locket lay on the side table. Somehow it seemed cruel to have parted her from it.

I drove back to school, still numbed, told Mrs Richards the news, read one of the Greek legends to the children, heard them recite one of Walter de la Mare's poems and saw them off home. Then I went back to the school house, fed Tibby, made a cup of tea and rang the vicar.

He was greatly concerned, more, it seemed, on my account than Dolly's, but I assured him that I was perfectly calm and that I intended to go to the cottage the next day to write to any relatives I could find, and to tidy up Dolly's things. He suggested that either he or Mrs Partridge would accompany me, but I refused as politely as I could.

I sat down in my quiet sitting-room and drank my tea. It was only then that I remembered that I had had nothing to eat since my breakfast at Dolly's, some eight or nine hours earlier.

It reminded me of that untouched breakfast tray.

I must have been the last person to whom Dolly spoke, and I recalled those last three words:

'*Love to Fairacre.*'

It was now that grief engulfed me. My whole body shook as I returned the cup, clattering, to its saucer, and the tears began.

I seemed to spend all the evening crying, powerless to control my emotions. I did not cry for Dolly, now freed from pain and the indignities of old age. I cried for myself. I should never see or talk to Dolly again, and that, truthfully, was the cause of my tears and my desolation.

For now I knew. I was bereft.

8   Making Plans

NEWS of Dolly Clare's death was common knowledge within twenty-four hours and there were tributes to her from everyone. During her long life she had touched so many other lives as teacher and friend, that it was plain that her influence would linger for many years in Fairacre, Beech Green, and many places farther afield where old pupils had settled.

The funeral had been arranged for a date some ten days distant at Beech Green church, and she was to be buried in the churchyard there, beside her parents Francis and Mary.

In the meantime, I was doing my best to track down any living relatives. I put an obituary notice in *The Caxley Chronicle* and hoped that I might hear of some descendants of her sister Ada.

The son, John Francis, had gone overseas after his mother's death, but somewhere there must be descendants of Mary, the daughter. No one seemed to know what had happened to her.

Dolly Clare had lived so long that almost all her contemporaries had gone, but one elderly lady living in a retirement home in Caxley, wrote to the vicar telling him a little about Dolly and the family, and from this it appeared that Mary had married twice, but no names could be discovered.

I very much doubted if we would hear any more about Dolly's family.

* * *

The funeral took place on a beautiful June morning.

The vicar took the service, a simple one with three of Dolly's favourite hymns. The church was full of roses and sunshine, a fitting setting for the small plain coffin at the chancel steps, whose occupant had always loved flowers and the joys of summer.

There was a large congregation, but most of the people slipped away as just a few of her closest friends accompanied the vicar to the graveside. It was a peaceful spot, shaded by a lime tree already showing flowers. Francis and Mary's gravestone was patterned with moss and lichen, but I saw that there was room below the inscription for Dolly's name and dates, and this I proposed to have done as soon as possible.

Some friends took advantage of the general invitation to come to the cottage for refreshments after the service, and

when they had gone, I locked up the house, and drove back to my duties at Fairacre in time to serve out school dinners.

I thought of Mrs John's remark as I cut toad-in-the-hole into squares: 'Mother went back to get dinner for the children.'

So had it always been. My bedtime reading at the moment was Virginia Woolf's essay about my favourite clergyman, eighteenth century Parson Woodforde. I had come across her remarks on the entry: 'Found the old gentleman at his last gasp. Totally senseless with rattlings in the Throat. Dinner today boiled beef and Rabbit rosted.'

'All is as it should be; life is like that,' she comments.

Everyday life for me was certainly bearing this out.

After my night of weeping, some peace had returned. Although, from now until the end of my own days, I knew that there would always be this poignant sense of loss, yet there was no need for prolonged grief. A long and lovely life had ended, but Dolly would be remembered by many, for years to come. There had been no children of her own as immediate heirs, but all those who had passed through her hands had come under her wise and gentle influence, and this must shape their views and outlook for the rest of their lives.

It was with gratitude, not grief that Dolly would be remembered.

Amy came over to see me one evening soon after the funeral and said that I was looking distinctly peaky.

'Well, if you must know,' I responded, 'it's exactly how I feel.'

She had been in touch by telephone during my stay with Dolly Clare, but this was the first occasion that we had seen each other face to face for some considerable time.

She looked deeply concerned, and I began to feel guilty.

'No, I'm really all right. There was quite a bit to do tidying up Dolly's affairs as executor, and of course I was horribly shocked when it actually happened, but I am over that now.'

'Well, you don't look it. I think you want a tonic, plenty of good food and sleep, and a few days' holiday. Come and stay with us next weekend as a start.'

'I'd love to, but I can't. Perhaps towards the end of the month. We're getting a week off then.'

'Half-term?'

'Sort of. The powers that be are feeling their way towards a four-term year sometime in the future, and this is part of the preliminary trial. Actually, I hope it comes off, though I can't see it happening before I retire.'

'A week at the end of June,' said Amy thoughtfully, and I knew from her expression that she was planning something for me.

To distract her I asked after James and the semi-permanent lodger Brian.

'He's decided to look for digs near Bristol, so we haven't seen so much of him recently. James seemed to think that I was instrumental in pushing him out, but I can assure you I'm quite innocent. I think the idea of ejecting a hero who had once scored a century against Eton or Harrow, or possibly both, was more than James could face. Anyway, I told him that my conscience was as pure as driven snow, and that it was Brian's idea entirely, which it was.'

She began to smile.

'Mind you, when he broached the subject, I didn't cling to his arm with tears in my eyes to dissuade him. And it is lovely to have the bathroom to myself again, I must admit.'

'What about a turn around the garden, like Jane Austen's young ladies?' I suggested.

It was a perfect June evening. Mr Roberts had a field of beans somewhere nearby and there was a wonderful scent of flowers. The wistaria was in bloom, and the Mrs Sinkin pinks, which do so well on our chalky soil, added their scent to the evening air. The ancient Beauty of Bath apple tree had grey-green velvety marble-sized fruit on it and, judging by the plum blossom, we were going to be well off for fruit this year.

After our stroll, which we took with our arms round each other's waists like true Jane Austen characters, we sat on the garden seat to resume our conversation.

'Are you proposing to live at Dolly's now?' asked Amy.

'Not immediately. There's quite a bit to do there, and I don't want to make a long-term decision just yet.'

'Very sensible.'

'Besides, I've everything I need here, and it's so much closer to the school. I certainly do intend to go to Dolly's cottage eventually, as she wanted, but I'm staying here until the end of the summer term, and then I'll see how things go.'

A blackbird came out of the flower border followed by one of its young which was rather larger than its parent. It squawked incessantly as it badgered its harassed father for food, and we watched the two running back and forth across the lawn in their searchings.

Amy slapped her leg and the birds flew off.

'Mosquito!' she exclaimed. 'Just as we were enjoying Paradise.'

'We'd better go in,' I said getting up. 'Every Eden has its serpent.'

'I must go anyway,' said Amy, and I walked with her to the car.

'Tell me the dates of your holidays,' she said.

I told her, and she nodded looking rather mysterious.

'Ah! I have some thinking to do,' she said, and drove off.
Now what is she up to, I wondered?

Soon after Amy's visit Mrs Pringle apprised me of the fact that her niece Minnie had been obliged to go to hospital for a few days.

'So there am I,' she said dourly, 'stuck with those little 'uns of hers. If you could see your way clear to having Basil in school for a day or two, it would a be a real help.'

I felt sorry for my old cleaner and said we could manage Basil in school hours. She seemed relieved, which was more than I was.

Ideally, he should go into Mrs Richards's class. He was not yet five, but lethargic in the extreme. I knew from experience that it took him some time before he could let us know that he needed the lavatory – and then too late.

I decided that I would keep him with my own class. He could have a large ball of modelling clay, paper and crayons. These should keep him 'properly creative' as earnest educationalists say, or 'keep his idle fingers out of Satan's way', as our grandparents would have preferred to put it.

'Is Ern capable of looking after the children while Minnie's away?' I asked. Ern, Minnie's husband, appears to me to be at about the same stage of efficiency as Minnie.

'Not really. Ern don't like children.'

As he had five of his own when he married Minnie, and took on her three as well, it seemed odd that he did not like children. Unless, of course, the eight offspring had been the cause of his dislike.

'How long does she expect to be in hospital?'

'Not long. The doctor said it was her Salopian tubes.'

Confused images of underground trains hurtling through Shropshire vanished when I surmised that Mrs Pringle meant Fallopian tubes, but I did not intend to enquire further. I know virtually nothing about my own, or anyone else's internal organs, and am content to remain ignorant.

Once I had been foolish enough to ask my doctor what he proposed to do to a minor leg injury. He was a painstaking fellow, and after his explicit and conscientious account of the proceedings to be undergone, I vowed never to be enlightened again. On the rare occasions when I have had to go to hospital, I have said: 'Put me out, watch your work, and don't wake me up until all the blood's gone!'

So I did not press Mrs Pringle for details, though I might have guessed that she was more than keen to give them.

'Oh, it only takes a day or two. It's a job that's got to be done if you wants any more babies.'

I was about to ask if Minnie, with eight children already, really hankered for more, when Mrs Pringle continued.

'They just blows them out. They takes one of them instruments —'

'Good heavens,' I cried, 'is that the time? I must get the children in.' I rushed away, and Mrs Pringle, deeply umbraged, limped after me.

Later I went into the infants' class to borrow some simple jigsaws for Basil. The modelling clay had inspired him sufficiently to roll out a worm-like object which he had seemed content to leave at that. My suggestions that he could coil it round and make a flat dish or, even more ambitiously, a small vase, was met with a stubborn shake of the head.

The crayons were not a great success either, and after I had discovered him crunching a particularly virulent-looking green one, I decided that his activities needed to be channelled into another direction.

'Would you like me to have him in here?' inquired my noble assistant, but I could not accept such self-sacrifice.

'Of course,' she went on, 'if we had all Minnie's school-age children, we shouldn't need to worry about the school closing. Besides,' she added hopefully, 'she might have more. She's no age, is she?'

I thought of the Salopian tubes, and agreed that there was every possibility of Minnie's family increasing over the years.

'But strictly speaking,' I told her, 'they are living in the Beech Green area. It's only because Mrs Pringle is taking on the three youngest that we can claim Basil – and then he's not on the roll, of course.'

At that moment, Joseph Coggs appeared in the doorway to announce that our visitor had 'gone to the lavatory'.

As was quite apparent when I returned to deal with the puddle, that was exactly what Basil had not done.

Dolly Clare's cottage, for so I always thought of it, was not neglected. Mrs John went in several times a week to air it, do a little dusting, and generally tidy up, and I went over each weekend, and sometimes during the week after school.

I asked Wayne Richards to come and have a look at it for any signs of immediate repairs which might be needed.

His verdict was favourable on the whole. 'It's pretty sound inside, though there's a nasty damp patch on the kitchen wall. Probably had a tub with brine in it years ago, for salting the pork, and the salt's leaked in. But I could seal that, I think. And there's woodworm up in the loft but there again I could treat it.'

'What about the roof?' I asked.

'You'll have to face having that roof re-thatched in three or four years' time, but it'll do a few winters yet.'

I was glad to hear it. Now that I was a property owner, I knew that I should have to use my meagre savings to put the place in order and I looked forward to doing it. Nevertheless, I could not face such a major job as re-thatching which, I knew from other cottage owners, could run into thousands of pounds.

'I thought of having it redecorated inside,' I said. 'Dolly could not face the upheaval in the last few years, but it really should be done. Could you do it?'

'No problem. Except time. I could give it a good doing with emulsion paint on the walls, and some good hard gloss on the woodwork. That'd do you for years.'

'You'd better give me an estimate for that and the other odd jobs,' I told him, 'and then we'll see what's urgent, and how soon you can start.'

'Right. You thinking of keeping it all white inside?'

'Yes. It looks fresh and cottagey. Besides, all the carpets and curtains go well with it.'

He laughed, and drove off, leaving me to lock up and return to Fairacre. But before I set off I wandered round the garden which Dolly had enjoyed all her years.

It was not as big as my own, and the fruit trees were not as healthy or as prolific. Sometime in the past a knowledgeable headmaster had stocked the school-house garden, and I was well supplied with plum and apple trees, an espalier pear by the garden shed, and gooseberry and black and red-currant bushes.

At times I cursed the bounty of my garden when I returned tired from school duties and was faced by an abundance of red and blackcurrants, all needing to be picked, stripped, washed, bottled, frozen or made into jelly or jam. But my friends were always glad to help me out, and Alice and Bob Willet made good use of my surplus.

With the exception of a sturdy old Bramley apple tree,

Dolly's fruit trees were past their prime, and I resolved to get Bob Willet's advice about replacing them in the autumn. The vegetable plot too, I decided, should be halved. Room for a few lettuces, some new potatoes, spinach and runner beans would suffice. There are several first-class market gardens nearby and in any case I am given no end of fresh vegetables in the autumn and winter, from friends and neighbours who have enjoyed my surplus fruit during the summer.

The flower border too looked in need of attention, and would need a good load of manure later on after I had divided some of the perennials. There were one or two particular favourites of mine in the school-house garden which I proposed to bring over, phlox and penstemon and various pinks.

There was a lot to do; the paths needed weeding, the hawthorn hedges needed a trim, and the laburnum tree by the gate was almost split in two with advanced age and the rigours of many downland winters, but I surveyed my inheritance with love and pride. I hoped to keep Dolly's cottage as well as she had done, and hoped too that I should be lucky enough to have many happy years there, as she had.

Perhaps, too, I should be as fortunate in my end, surrounded by my garden and the distant downs, and sheltered by my own thatched roof.

I was rather touched to receive a visit from Minnie Pringle one evening.

'Come to say thank you,' she said, 'for having our Basil. Auntie don't get on with Basil ever since he spat in the jam she was making. She's funny that way.'

For once, Mrs Pringle had all my sympathy, but it seemed best not to comment on this disclosure.

'Well, it's good to see you up and about again,' I said. 'Would you like some coffee?'

She followed me into the kitchen and I saw her eyeing a bowl of blackcurrants awaiting attention on the table.

'Those are to spare,' I told her, hoping to be let off a tedious job, 'if you would like them.'

She said that she would, and I gave her a bag and let her scrabble away while I filled our mugs.

'Basil wasn't much bother,' I said, nobly squashing the memory of constant sniffing, complete absence of interest in his surroundings, and the regrettable puddle on the floor.

'He liked it,' said Minnie, with her mad grin. 'I wish they could all come here, but they has to go to Beech Green. Ever so strict that Mr Annett is! Give our Billy the cane once.'

'Why?'

'Well, he shut one of the other's fingers in the door. Could've been an accident, I told Mr Annett when I went to complain.'

'And was it?'

'Not really. Billy got some other boy to hold the first one while he slammed the door.'

I changed the subject. Despite my dwindling numbers, I did not feel inclined to welcome any more of the Pringle tribe to Fairacre school.

'And how's Ern?'

'He's a bit cross with me.'

This I knew might well be construed as being violent. Ern is not above attacking Minnie when he disapproves of her behaviour.

'It's Bert, see,' she went on. 'Bert come up the hospital to see me, and Ern didn't like it.'

As Bert has been an admirer of Minnie's for many years and, according to local gossip, the father of two of her young children, it is hardly surprising that Ern views his attentions to Minnie with great disfavour. The two men have come to blows in their time, and Minnie appears to be rather proud of the fact.

'Bert brought me some roses and the nurse put 'em in a vase by my bed, and Ern wanted to know where they'd come from. So I told him. He was that wild!'

Minnie smiled happily at the memory.

'Why did you tell him?'

'He asked didn't 'e? All I done was tell 'im the truth.'

'So what happened?'

'Ern went down 'The Spotted Cow' in Caxley that night, and had a real old turn-up with poor Bert. Blacked his eye, and knocked a tooth out, and made his nose bleed somethin' terrible, Bert said.'

'Bert told you?'

'Yes. He came up to see me the next night with some carnations. I was ever so sorry for Bert.'

I began to feel ever so sorry for poor Ern, but kept quiet.

'Best be getting back,' she said, rising briskly. 'I've left the kids with Auntie, and there's Ern's tea to get. He gets a bit nasty if he has to wait for his tea. Thanks ever so for these currants.'

She bustled off to the door.

'I hope Ern is looking after you properly,' I ventured.

'Nice as pie,' she replied. 'Never laid a finger on me since I come back from hospital. The doctor had a few words with him, see. Mind you, once I'm really better I shouldn't be surprised if he turned nasty about Bert. Funny really, I keep tellin' 'im I knew Bert long before I knew him, so why shouldn't we be friends? But he's real funny that way.'

She skipped off down the path to collect her offspring

from Mrs Pringle's. A stranger, seeing her for the first time, might have guessed her age at twelve or thirteen.

Mentally and morally, I thought, she was a good deal less than that, but it was nice of her to come and thank me, I decided charitably, as I went to get Tibby's evening meal.

Later that week I had another visitor. It was Amy, elegant in a cream trouser suit, and I hastened to brush down the sofa before she sat on it.

'I was stripping redcurrants an hour ago,' I told her, 'and I don't want you to sit on any stray ones.'

'But surely you do that in the kitchen?'

'Not when there's an old film of Fred Astaire's on,' I told her, lifting up a glossy report of some unknown firm which was at one end of the sofa.

Amy settled herself and turned the pages idly. 'I didn't know you had shares in this. James is one of its directors.'

'Aunt Clara left them to me,' I explained, 'with her seed pearls, and a nest of occasional tables which I handed on to one of my god-daughters.'

I saw her studying a page of photographs at the beginning of the booklet.

'I can't think why they put those in,' I said, peering over her shoulder. 'Far better to leave their shareholders in ignorance. It may be the fault of the photographer, of course, but at a quick glance, would you trust any of those with five bob?'

'There's James,' said Amy, pointing to one of the photographs.

I peered more closely. 'So it is. Well, he's certainly the best looking by a long way.'

'Of course,' agreed Amy smugly. 'Now sit down, and I'll tell you why I've come. You haven't a spot of sherry, I suppose? Not that stuff you won at our raffle, I mean.'

'I've got some Croft's.'

'Perfect.'

I poured out two glasses.

'I've been thinking,' said Amy, after an approving sip.

'Oh, Amy,' I wailed. 'Not another prospective husband for me? I've got such a load of trouble already.'

'No, no, no!' tutted Amy. 'How you do harp on *MEN*!'

I was too taken aback by this unjustified aspersion to retaliate, and she continued unchecked.

'It's really about James and his trip to Scotland. He's flying up, a few days before he planned, to meet this fellow.'

She tapped a finger on one of the photographs on the open page beside her.

'They're going house-hunting together before the main meeting.'

'House-hunting? You're not leaving Bent?'

'Nothing like that. They're both on the board of some charity trust for orphans, and they want to start up a home there for the Scottish lot. The point is this. I shall be driving up a little later, and hope you will come with me. James knows a lovely quiet hotel on the Tweed. Lots of salmon on the menu. What about it?'

'Oh, Amy! You are sweet to think of it, but I ought not –'

'My treat,' said Amy swiftly. 'My shares are doing well, and James wants you to keep me company as he'll be so tied up with business affairs. Do say you'll come. We'll take two days to go up, and two back, and have two there. It would do you good after all you've had to do these past weeks.'

She looked at me with such concern, almost tearfully, that I weakened at once.

'It sounds heavenly. Tell me more.'

She proceeded to give me details. A night in the Peak District on our way north. A leisurely drive along the A7 towards Kelso the next day. Visits to Mellerstain House and Floors Castle. It was apparent that Amy had been very busy working out routes, planning little treats such as these visits to lovely houses, and generally becoming acquainted with all that the neighbourhood had to offer.

'Then, yes please,' I said, 'I'd love to come. But I can't let you pay for me, Amy. It's too much.'

'If it makes you feel any better,' said my old friend, 'you can pay for the petrol, and any odd ice-creams.'

'Willingly,' I told her, 'but let —'

'But I warn you,' she said, 'my car is a thirsty one, and I have a great weakness for cornets and wafers.'

'As though I didn't know,' I told her, 'after all these years together.'

9   Holiday with Amy

I T is wonderfully exhilarating to set off on holiday. The days before, of course, and particularly the one immediately preceding departure, are fraught with as much anxiety as anticipation. Have you stopped the milk, the papers, the laundryman? Have you left enough cat food for Tibby? Should you switch off the electricity at the mains? If so, what about the fridge and the light that comes on automatically after dark? There is no end to the household problems.

Personal packing is comparatively easy. I have long given up trying to compete with other hotel visitors in the realms of sartorial chic. To be clean and decent, and not to shame dear Amy, is the limit of my ambitions these days.

Nevertheless, there are decisions to be made. The weather may be hot. It may be cold. Cotton frocks and a thick cardigan may be the basis for one's wardrobe, but it is necessary to have a little more flexibility.

Then there is the problem of underclothes. Should you take enough to ensure a change every day, and possibly an extra outfit in the unlikely event of falling into a Scottish burn or being soaked to the skin in a Scotch mist? Or would it be safe to hope that the hotel bathroom would have one of those clothes lines that pull out from the wall – and sag dangerously when a pair of tights is slung over it?

And what about a mackintosh? Should it be the heavy raincoat just back from the cleaners? The cost of its recent reproofing makes one feel it should be housed in a glass case rather than bundled into a suitcase or the boot of

Amy's car. Perhaps the thin bedraggled one hanging on the peg behind the kitchen door might fit the bill?

But when one is actually in the car, cases stowed behind, keys and telephone number left with the neighbours, and handbag safely on one's lap, then the pleasure begins.

A certain recklessness takes over. What if one *has* forgotten toothbrush, handkerchieves, sun spectacles or talcum powder? Presumably all these can be bought in Scotland.

And what if I have forgotten to leave out the tin opener for Tibby's meal tins, or the bottles for the milkman, or that old piece of bread which I intended to throw out for the birds? Dear Alice and Bob Willet would see to it all.

'Amy,' I said, snuggling back into my luxurious seat, 'I am so happy!'

'That's the whole idea,' she responded, putting her foot down on the accelerator.

We sped northward in great spirits.

By lunchtime we were in the neighbourhood of Warwick, and I was beginning to look out hopefully for a café.

'Don't bother,' said Amy. 'I've brought a picnic. Just keep your eyes skinned for a leafy lane to the left.'

We soon found it, a lovely lane with ferns growing from the banks, and some pink campions among the cow parsley, and we got out thankfully. Even a car as large and magnificent as Amy's cannot quite overcome the stiffening of the human frame.

Amy produced one of those splendid wicker hampers that I always associate with Glyndebourne or glorious Goodwood. There were plates and glasses and cutlery and even two large linen napkins. We sat on the bank amidst the verdure with this splendid object between us. Amy had made smoked-salmon brown sandwiches, and egg and

cress white ones. Lettuce hearts nestled in a plastic box.
Pears and peaches supplied dessert, and two flasks contained coffee and hot milk respectively. There was even a
bottle of sparkling wine to go with the smoked salmon.

I thought of my own slapdash picnics, comprising cut
bread with crusts left on, and the contents usually hanging
out in a ragged manner, followed by a banana or an apple
from the garden. I was lucky if I remembered to put in a
piece of paper torn from the kitchen roll at the last minute.

'This is superb,' I said, trying not to make my napkin
too disgusting with peach juice. 'How do you manage to
do everything so elegantly?'

'My mother taught me,' she answered. 'She was terribly
strict about standards. One of her favourite maxims was:
"Never let yourself *go*!" And she lived up to it too. I don't
think I ever saw her untidy, even in her last illness. She
really was remarkable.'

'You take after her,' I told her. 'She would be proud of
you.'

'Mind you,' said Amy, packing away plates and boxes
briskly, 'she was very bossy with it.'

My private thought was that dear old Amy took after her mother in that too, but it would have been churlish to say so after consuming such a memorable meal.

'Thank you for that marvellous lunch,' I said instead.

We were in the Peak District for our one night stop in time for a refreshing cup of tea, before unpacking.

Then we walked along the path by the River Dove which had remarkably few visitors just then. We stopped to hang over the rail of a wooden bridge, and fell companionably silent as we watched the bright water cascading over the boulders beneath us.

What a benison water is, I thought, watching a wagtail enjoying the spray. Whether we drink it, wash in it, swim in it or simply stand and stare at it, as we were doing now, it has the power to refresh, to soothe, and to exhilarate. It has much the same beneficial properties as sleep, I thought, remembering Macbeth's tributes to that panacea. Certainly, gazing downward with the waters of the Dove below, and listening to the rustle of the Dovedale foliage above me, I could feel the pain of Dolly's absence, and the many petty domestic and school frustrations and worries ebbing away from me. Amy had been absolutely right. I needed to get away from Fairacre now and again.

It was Amy who returned first to the present. 'Let's go on. We haven't worked up an appetite for a four-course dinner yet.'

'Speak for yourself,' I retorted. But we went on all the same, and peace went with us.

The hotel in Scotland was old and grey, and full of years and tranquillity. It stood amid acres of grass dotted here and there with clumps of fir trees. The flowerbeds close to the house were bright with freshly-planted annuals, and some climbing roses, pink and white and red, nodded against the stone walls.

James and Amy had a bedroom on the first floor and from their windows they could see to the nearby valley where the river Tweed ran its course eastward to Berwick-on-Tweed.

I had a room on the ground floor which overlooked a particularly pretty part of the garden, with a bird bath and flowering shrubs, a private small garden of my own, it seemed, adjoining the larger grounds.

James joined us in time for dinner, and was good company. James is one of those fortunate people who really loves his neighbour, and likes to hear all about that neighbour's affairs. I have rarely seen him tired or depressed despite the busy life he leads, and tonight he looked as dashing as ever.

I told him about the photographs of his fellow directors in the only shares brochure which falls through my letter-box, and how he was by far the most handsome. Needless to say, he fairly glowed at the compliment. How vain men are!

'And Ted and I came across two decent little houses at the end of a terrace on the outskirts of Glasgow. I think something could be done with them, and we've asked the architect to see if they could house six children.'

'Who looks after them?' I inquired.

'There will be two foster parents. That's the principle of this charity – family units, not too big, in a smallish house. So far it seems to work. Now, tell me about the journey. Were you very long on the M6? It's quick but tedious, I find.'

Our meal was delicious, and afterwards we strolled in the grounds watching a number of thrushes stabbing the lawns to find their supper. At Fairacre, thrushes are in short supply these days, and it was good to see that they flourished here in the Border country.

I said my goodnights early, for I could hardly keep awake. It was seven o'clock when I woke to a fine sunny morning, and I reckoned that I had slept solidly for nine hours.

That day, James returned to his labours while Amy and I explored the market town of Kelso, some three miles away. We admired its fine square, its friendly shop keepers and, above all, the cleanliness of its streets.

We noticed this throughout our visiting. North of the Border, it seemed, people liked to see things clean and tidy. Caxley streets these days are littered with rubbish thrown down by the people too idle to walk six steps to a nearby litter bin. In the lanes around Fairacre I frequently pick up Coke tins, bottles, crisp packets, cigarette cartons and other detritus which the consumers have simply cast out of their car windows, careless of the damage these things can do to animals and plants, as well as making the countryside hideous.

We went on to visit Floors Castle standing close to the ubiquitous river Tweed which we crossed and recrossed dozens of times during our stay. It was magnificent, and Amy and I coveted the Dresden and Meissen porcelain more than anything else in that delectable array of pictures and furniture.

However, the next day we decided to visit Mellerstain, not far away, and its Adam elegance won us completely.

'"Comparisons,"' quoted Amy, as we gazed upwards at the superbly decorated ceilings, '"are odious," but I think I'd rather live here.'

'Either,' I said, 'would suit me.'

The Border country was gently rolling, with plenty of

cattle enjoying grass far lusher than that which grows on our downs. We drove across to the Northumberland coast, and were refreshed by the salt winds blowing over the North Sea and a good lunch at Bamburgh, where the great castle dominates the little town.

By the end of our break together, my face was glowing as if I had spent days on the beach. I slept solidly both nights, ate the hotel's lovely food as if I were starving, and altogether felt a new woman as we set off for home.

James drove, and our first idea of spending a night in the Peak District on our way back was abandoned.

'Let's get on,' said James. 'I can't wait to get home.'

Sitting in the back of the car, thinking of the places we were now leaving behind, and occasionally snoozing, I realized how much good this holiday had done me. It had put things in perspective. To see those beautiful old houses, their contents, their well-kept gardens, all so enriching to the spirit, had made my own worries seem fleeting. It had also made me deeply conscious of the simple future pleasures I should enjoy at Dolly's cottage, and my good fortune in having friends as dear and generous as Dolly and Amy.

I returned to a host of minor irritations, and a pile of letters. The minor irritations included a leaking tap, a broken saucer of Tibby's, and a colossal branch ripped from the plum tree, its plentiful but unripe fruit scattered on the lawn.

The post included a fair amount of material for the waste paper basket. 'Had I thought of the best way to invest my savings?' (What savings?) 'Would I help a child?' (I already helped twenty-one, and would be glad to have those numbers increased, but under my school roof.) 'Had I considered a fun-filled fortnight on the exotic beaches of Florida?' (Well, no!)

Such missives were easily disposed of, but some heavy-looking correspondence from the office would need my attention, and several more welcome letters from friends. I put the lot aside to greet Bob Willet who hove in sight.

'My word, you look ten years younger,' he greeted me. 'Time you had that break. You was looking real white and spiteful.'

'Thanks,' I said. 'And proper thanks to you and Alice. Did you have much trouble?'

'No. Old Tib bolted the grub, as if starved, as usual. The only thing that went wrong was me droppin' the saucer. And, what's more, the mower's on the blink.'

'Oh dear! And you can't mend it?'

Usually, Mr Willet can cope indoors with anything from light bulbs to domestic plumbing, and outside, of course, he can turn his hand to anything growing, and the maintenance of my simple gardening equipment.

'I reckon it's had its time. We could get someone to see if spares here or there'd be the answer, but it's that old I doubt if anyone's seen 'em.'

'You mean, I shall have to buy a new one?'

'Looks like it to me, but you get someone else's opinion, afore you lash out on a new one.'

This was grim news, but I guessed it was probably the answer.

Bob Willet waved to the battered plum tree.

'That happened the night afore last. Had a sort of mini hurricane. Barmy, it was. Like a whirlwind. Took half the thatch off of Mr Roberts's barn, and flattened a field of barley down Springbourne way. Josh Pringle said three of his bantams was tossed up in the air like shuttle-cocks. But, mind you, you don't want to believe all Josh Pringle tells you. Still, it was pretty nasty while it lasted.'

'Did it do any damage to your garden?'

'Blew a bit of felting off my shed roof, but I got that back next day. And I heard as our Maud Pringle got hit on the head by a bit of guttering as blew off of her house, but no doubt you'll hear plenty about that when she turns up.'

'Coming in for a drink?'

'No thanks. I promised the vicar I'd have a look at his garage roof. He thinks a tile or two's come off, and he's like a new-born babe when it comes to anything like that. Still, he do give a good sermon, and I suppose we all has different talents.'

I watched him stump off down the path, and felt grateful, as I so often do, for Bob Willet's particular and practical talents.

One Saturday morning, soon after my holiday, I bumped into Miriam Baker in Caxley High Street.

I had just emerged from Marks and Spencer's with a bagful of goodies from the food counter, and was on my way back to the car.

'Hello, and what are you up to?'

'Wondering if I have the strength to seek out another cotton frock. Gerard's away with the cameraman for a television programme, looking at a possible site, and I thought it might be a good opportunity.'

'Good hunting then.'

'Oh, I've given up the idea already. My shopping threshold, if that's the term, is pretty low.'

'Then come back to Fairacre with me, and have a Marks and Spencer's lunch.'

'No, really,' she protested, but not very convincingly, and I had no difficulty in steering her towards the car park.

'We haven't seen each other for ages,' I said, stowing parcels in the boot. 'Not since our lunch with the Winters.'

We set off for home, and as we passed through Beech Green I pointed out Dolly's house.

'I heard about that,' said Miriam, 'and we were both so glad it's to be yours.'

'When I'm really settled there you and Gerard must come and see me.'

'Lovely! And when are you moving from the school house?'

'I may go towards the end of the school holidays, if the builders have finished, and it is ready for me.'

'Will you miss it? The school house, I mean?'

I pondered the questions. They had been rattling about in my own mind for some time now.

'Yes,' I told her soberly. 'I shall miss it very much. Some of my happiest years have been spent under that roof, but I should have to face leaving it sometime, and thanks to dear Dolly I have somewhere of my own now to end my days.'

'But what will happen to it?'

'It will be sold, I expect. The church owns the property, and if the school has to close, which seems horribly likely at the moment, I expect my house would be sold too.'

Miriam shuddered. 'I don't like to think of changes at Fairacre.'

'Neither do I,' I replied, swinging into my drive, 'but I'm afraid I've got to face them.'

We both agreed that the grilled plaice stuffed with shrimp sauce, with salad from the garden, was just what we had needed, and coffee cups in hand we sat on the garden seat to enjoy the summer sunshine.

'And now tell me your news,' I said. 'Still regretting leaving Sir Barnabas?'

'Not really, but I've other plans afoot.'

'Tell me.'

'Well, I don't know if I'm an oddity, but I find that

being married is all very nice, but not quite enough for me.'

'You get bored on your own?'

'No. I just miss the job. I suppose I've always been geared to work, and marrying late it's harder to give up the routine. All the youngsters who take the plunge at nineteen or twenty seem delighted to settle down to home-making and babies and such –'

'I thought they had to go on working to pay for the mortgage,' I broke in. 'Bob Willet calls them "tinkers".'

'I didn't find that so when I was at the office. We were always looking out for new girls to replace those who had left. Which brings me to my plan.'

'And what's that?'

'I'm starting an agency, mainly for supplying office staff. As a matter of fact, the only one in Caxley is about to be sold. The proprietor is retiring, and to be truthful it never operated very efficiently, as Barney and I discovered on many occasions when we were desperate for staff. I should thoroughly enjoy it and, though I don't want to boast, I really can sum up people's ability pretty quickly, and also what the employer wants. For instance, nothing would annoy a man like Barney more than one of those motherly types for ever bringing in cups of tea when he was telephoning. On the other hand, you get bosses who just love that sort of attention.'

'You'll be marvellous at it,' I told her. 'What does Gerard think?'

'He's all for it. He has to be away such a lot, and I think he soon realized I was getting fed up with kicking my heels. He's pretty astute.'

'So when do you start?'

'With luck, in the autumn. It means married women with children at school will have more chance to take on part-time jobs. There's been an enormous increase in part-time work as firms have come to see that this is the sensible way of organizing offices. Matching bosses to applicants will be just what I like, and honestly Caxley is in real need of a service like that.'

'Well, the best of luck,' I said. 'I'm sure it will be a wild success, and your name will be blessed by all the Caxley folk.'

'We'll see,' she said, looking at her watch.

'You don't have to hurry back, do you? Is Gerard due back soon?'

'Not till the evening. He's doing a series of documentaries about inland waterways, and is giving the Kennet and Avon canal a thorough scrutiny further west.'

'It sounds pleasant enough.'

'So I imagined, but Gerard says there are an awful lot of snags, like fishermen, and people tramping along the tow path, not to mention mosquitoes and the occasional hostile swan.'

'But surely all those creatures have a right to the canal?'

'Not according to Gerard and his cameraman,' said Miriam.

10   Flower Show and Fête

THE month of July every year in Fairacre is dominated by the village Flower Show. It is held in the village hall, and the funds raised go to two good causes – the Fairacre Horticultural Society and to repairing whichever portion of the church is in most urgent need of attention.

At one time there was also a village fête, held in the vicarage garden, but latterly the two functions have combined and a few stalls outside the village hall, and sports events in the field around it, now take the place of the earlier fête whilst the gardeners hold sway inside the hall itself.

Naturally, this sensible combination took years to accomplish. It had been the vicar's idea, and of course some people thought it was because he did not like to see his lawns spiked with high heels nor his borders damaged by wooden balls bowled erratically in 'Bowling For The Pig'. Those more kindly disposed thought that it was far better to use the village field for the fête side of the occasion.

'Stands to reason,' said Bob Willet, 'folks feel freer on their own patch, and who wants *two* summer dos? There ain't the money about for it, for one thing, with cornets the price they is.'

Personally, I thought it was a much more practical arrangement.

I have spent several fête afternoons sheltering with dozens of others in the vicarage summer-house or barn, with the rain lashing across the stalls, watching the crêpe paper dripping coloured rivulets on to the sodden grass, while tea trays were being rushed into the house for protection.

Under the present scheme we could at least bundle into the hall, even if it did mean enduring the disgruntled comments of the gardening community jealous for the welfare of their produce and lush displays set out on black velvet.

The entrants for the many classes for fruit, flowers and vegetables, had obviously worked for months beforehand to produce their bounty. But the rest of us were busy, too.

As always, there was a cake stall, and a produce stall, and to these I had promised to contribute. Why is it, I wondered, surveying my lop-sided Victoria sponge sandwich, that the cakes one dashes off for home consumption rise splendidly, stay risen, and supply most satisfactory eating? And why, when one hopes to achieve something memorable for public display, does the wretched thing burn, or sink in the middle, or refuse to rise at all?

My first attempt went into my own cake tin, and I turned to a tried and true recipe for almond cake for my contribution to the cake stall. Two pots of gooseberry jelly were to go to the produce stall, with half a dozen Tom Thumb lettuces. More I could not do.

A notice had been put in *The Caxley Chronicle*, and various posters decorated the village and its environs. All that remained to ensure success was a fine afternoon.

It has always been a source of wonder to me that so many English occasions are planned as outdoor events, with not even a tent in sight for shelter from the rain which is liable to appear at any time. It says much for the hope and confidence of organizers. I only know that if I plan some public display at Fairacre school, and the playground is the main venue, I am glad to be able to make a rush for the ancient building with my flock and the visitors when the heavens open. The fact that we shall have to face the wrath of Mrs Pringle is of secondary importance compared with a heavy summer storm.

The combined fête and show was to take place on a Saturday, and the weather forecast was delightfully vague. A band of rain affecting the north west *might* reach our area by midday, followed by brighter fresher weather with increasing winds. The forecaster prudently promised unsettled weather, with a likelihood of showers, but possibly some fine spells. As you were, in fact.

Summer clothes, then, I decided, accompanied by stout shoes for the (possibly) wet grass, and a cardigan and an all-enveloping mackintosh.

In an unguarded moment, I had offered to help Mrs Partridge on the cake stall. This, as everyone connected with fêtes knows, is a veritable magnet for keen shoppers or, if not actual buyers, then astute spectators happy to assess the cooking abilities, or better still, the frailties of those whose products are publicly displayed.

As a vicar's wife, Mrs Partridge takes a firm stand about not opening her stall until after the local celebrity has formally declared the fête open. Of this I entirely approve. When I have assisted at jumble sales, I have often been appalled by the number of articles 'put aside' or 'bought in' in advance by the persons preparing for the event. If not checked, this can result in anything attractive being extracted beforehand, leaving the poor stuff to be sold when the doors open to admit the customers.

I arrived at my station by Mrs Partridge's side some ten minutes before Basil Bradley, our local novelist, was due to open the fête.

'No, no!' Mrs Partridge was saying firmly to a questioning buyer. 'I can't serve anything until we are officially open. But do wait here, and we shall start selling as soon as Mr Bradley has made his speech.'

It was somewhat of a surprise to me when I bent down to tie my shoe lace, to see half a dozen cakes in polythene bags resting on a tea towel in the grass beneath our stall. Clean sheets had been spread over our stall, and hung down to the ground concealing the booty from public gaze, and my faith in Mrs Partridge's integrity was severely shaken.

The vicar rang the school handbell lent by me for the afternoon, and most of the conversation ceased.

He introduced Basil Bradley as 'our old friend, the famous author', and led the clapping as Basil advanced to the microphone. After some alarming cracklings and whistlings, the machine calmed down, and Basil gave his usual charming speech saying how delighted he was to be present, and exhorting us to spend freely in supporting this good cause. I had a strong suspicion that he had no idea where the funds were going. Church roof? Organ fund? New

hassocks? Upkeep of village hall? Never mind, he carried out his duties with great charm and elegance, and did not forget to conclude with the magic words:

'I declare this show and fête OPEN!'

This was the sign for a rush to the stalls, and pudding basins, plastic boxes and ancient Oxo tins began to fill with coins and notes.

Activity on our cake stall was frenzied. It was easy enough to pass over a sturdy fruit cake wrapped in its plastic bag with the price displayed on top. It was quite another matter to manipulate inexpertly a large plastic pair of tongs, in the interest of hygiene, and to insert three, or five, or six, according to demand, small sticky cakes into a paper bag.

Alice Willet's jam sponge sandwiches, and her large batch of fruit scones soon vanished, bought by knowledge-able customers, but an ornate chocolate cake decorated with chocolate icing and beautiful curlicues of chocolate on top of that, remained unbought.

'Too rich, dear,' pronounced the vicar's wife, when I inquired why. 'And it was sent by the owner of that cake place in Caxley. I think people are suspicious of it, and it is really rather expensive.'

At that moment, Basil Bradley arrived on his dutiful tour of the stalls. He was clutching a golliwog, a lettuce, two pots of chutney and a plastic vase which he had just won at the hoop-la stall, and he was followed by Joseph Coggs.

'If that gorgeous cake is not already bespoke, can I buy it?' he asked, after his affectionate greetings to us both.

'You can certainly have it,' said Mrs Partridge, 'and I shall give you a large cardboard box for all your pur-chases.'

Hard behind, the lurking Joseph was given the task of

carrying Basil's box of goodies to the car, which he did with a beaming smile. It was not hard to guess that Basil would reward him handsomely when the time came.

Our stall gradually cleared, leaving only some shortbread fingers and a lumpy-looking bran loaf. I broached the subject of the hidden treasures under our stall.

Our vicar's wife was not discomfited in the least.

'Yes, dear, I know it looks bad, but there are exceptions to every rule. Two of those cakes were put by for Miss Young and Mrs Ellis, both great supporters of the fête, but unable to be here as they are poorly.'

I nodded.

'Miss Young,' continued Mrs Partridge, 'makes those delightful soft toys for the handiwork stall, and Mrs Ellis always makes a most generous donation. The other cakes were set aside for those helpers who couldn't leave their own stalls during the initial crush.'

I said that seemed fair.

'I noticed you looking highly disapproving,' she went on. 'Quite rightly so, of course, but there are times when one must be *flexible*!'

I felt suitably chastened, but not entirely satisfied. However, there was nothing to be said.

'Now we are so slack,' said Mrs Partridge, 'why don't you run along and have a look round? Perhaps have a cup of tea? I'll go when you come back.'

And so I set off to see what the fête and flower show offered, first making my way into the hall to see all the exhibits.

The din was appalling. Somehow one expected a reverent hush among all this beautifully arranged provender, but one might have been standing in Paddington Station, except that it smelt more pleasantly rural. There were wonderful whiffs from the vases of sweet peas and roses, so I went to look at the flower exhibits first. I was not surprised to see that Bob Willet had first prize for six magnificent cream sweet peas. Josh Pringle, the black sheep of the Pringle family, was surprisingly second. I guessed that his wife had done most of the nurturing of his six mauve beauties.

Several of my children had red or blue tickets against their flower arrangements in the Under-Twelves class, including Joseph Coggs. Each would receive a modest monetary reward, and I only hoped that Joe would conceal his from his father, otherwise The Beetle and Wedge would swallow up Joe's prize.

But it was the vegetable tables which really were stunning. Mr Lamb from the Post Office had carried off quite a few of the first tickets. I stood to admire six splendid carrots, almost a foot in length and a good three or four inches round the top, lying straight and true as swords on their black velvet background.

'Grows 'em in one of them oil drums,' I heard one man say glumly to his neighbour. 'Seen 'em there. Plenty of sandy soil and enough slurry from the pigs to feed a field of taters. It ain't natural.'

'Well, he don't do that with his onions,' replied his friend fairly. 'Look at 'em! As big as footballs, nearly!'

'Terrible coarse eating,' sniffed his companion. 'If my missus dished 'em up, I'd throw 'em on the floor, that I would.'

Passions are easily aroused at these exhibitions, as I knew from experience. There would be little rejoicing over Mr Lamb's success, and the tongues would wag tonight in the pub, and not with much goodwill.

I decided to take Mrs Partridge's advice and find a cup of tea. The tea tent was as noisy as the hall, and it was difficult to find a chair which would stand squarely on the tussocky grass floor.

I had just collected my cup of tea and a rock cake when I was hailed by the Winters who were at a table nearby.

'Come and sit with us,' called Jane. 'We're getting our strength up for the men's tug-of-war.'

'Have you had any luck with your flower entries?' I asked, as I knew she was going to put a vase of annuals in the show.

'No luck at all, I'm afraid. And as for my cheese and asparagus quiche which I entered in the cookery section, it was dismissed out of hand as it was baked in a fluted dish.'

'What nonsense!' I said.

'Exactly. But the judge was some terrible old battle-axe from the cookery department of the Caxley Tech so there was no gainsaying her dictum. Anyway, it all helped to swell the number of entries,' she added tolerantly.

'I think this must be the first time we've had a quiche class in the show,' I said. 'How Fairacre is changing! I'm sure we never had anything more dashing than a class for scones and fruit cake in my early days here.'

'It's the same with the vegetables,' agreed Jane. 'All those courgettes and dark red lettuces would have been giant marrows and cos at my mother's horticultural show, if you follow me.'

An ear-splitting crackling shook the tent, and a voice boomed out unintelligible messages.

'The tug-of-war,' cried Jane to her husband, and they struggled to their feet. 'Come along and see what the head of the Winters can do.'

It was half past six by the time Mrs Partridge and I had cleared our stall and packed up all the paraphernalia. We had also done some general tidying, carrying chairs from the tea tent into their usual place in the hall, and retrieving teacups and teaspoons from the grass. These activities, of course, were interspersed with lengthy conversations with other workers, but despite these breaks in our labours, I was dead-beat when at last I arrived home.

It was good to lie on my sofa with only the gentle purring of Tibby in the room. I decided it was the noise rather than the press of people and the physical activity which I found most tiring.

I must have fallen asleep for it was almost eight-thirty when I looked at the clock, and the sun was reddish-gold in the west. It seemed a good idea to make myself a cup of coffee and I went into the kitchen which was still bathed in warm sunlight.

Through the window, beyond my garden, I could see a figure walking round the edge of the field which was already thick with corn. As the man came closer, I saw that it was our vicar, with Honey, his yellow Labrador bitch, following behind him.

I went out to speak to him over the hedge. He often exercised Honey in this field, safe from traffic and other more belligerent dogs, for Honey was somewhat timid as well as being almost soppily affectionate.

'Wonderful day,' he called as he approached, 'and Henry Mawne has already counted five hundred pounds, and more to come!'

I expressed my gratification.

'I'm just making coffee,' I added. 'Come and join me.'

I have a useful gap in the hedge, for which Mr Willet is constantly offering me 'some nice stout thorns' or 'a few real tough old holly bushes'. He cannot understand how I can put up with the gap, but I tell him it saves me walking all round the house to get into the field, and he simply puffs out his moustache with disgust, and says no more.

The vicar entered through the shameful gap, and we

were soon sipping our coffee, with Honey lying at our feet. Tibby had left home in high dudgeon but would doubtless be back in time for a bedtime snack.

'I intended to call on you next week,' said Mr Partridge.

'About end of term?'

'Well, no, not exactly.'

He looked a little uncomfortable and I began to wonder if I had failed in my duties in some way. Perhaps he simply wanted me to play the organ while George Annett was on holiday? Or was I going to be asked to organize some school event for next term?

'Are you happy here?' he asked surprisingly.

'Very, why?'

'In this house, I mean. You haven't thought of moving?'

I felt on firmer ground. 'As you know, I think, I hope to move to Miss Clare's cottage before long.'

'Yes, yes. You had apprised me of that very kindly.'

He leant down and began to fondle Honey's ears. He was rather pink in the face, but whether from his stooping, or my coffee, or simple embarrassment it was difficult to say.

'You see,' he went on, straightening up, 'I met that nice fellow from the education office when I was at a committee meeting in Caxley. Salisbury or Winchester, I can never remember his name. And he rather delicately, I thought, wondered if you would be needing this house much longer. He seemed to have heard about your good fortune with the house at Beech Green.'

'Who hasn't?' I said.

'It's very difficult for me to talk about this,' he said sighing, 'but as the school is now so small, I really think we shall have to accept closure before long, unless something extraordinarily felicitous turns up. What is in the committee's mind, I think, is the sale of your school house, and if it comes to it, the sale of the school building itself if the children are transferred to Beech Green. Of course, both are church property, and it is the church which would benefit from the sale.'

'I had realized that,' I told him, 'but is there any urgency? I had begun to make plans to move before the end of the summer holidays, but nothing's really settled.'

The vicar began to look more agitated than ever, and dropped his custard cream biscuit on the floor. He bent to retrieve it with a shaking hand, but Honey kindly cleared it away for him.

'No, no! Of course there is absolutely no urgency. You can stay here as long as you wish. It was simply that happening to meet dear Rochester he asked if I knew your plans. You know I should give you every support if you decided to stay on here and, say, let your Beech Green property until you wanted it for yourself.'

'I know I should never be homeless,' I told him. 'You've reassured me about that on several occasions, and I'm eternally grateful. But I really do want to live in Dolly's cottage. It was what she wanted too, and I think I can safely say that I hope to move sometime before the winter – possibly before the beginning of term, if the alterations are done by then.'

Mr Partridge rose, looking mightily relieved, and – much to my surprise – gave me a vicarish kiss on the cheek.

'And now Honey and I must be on our way,' he said, making for the door. 'Thank you for that excellent coffee, and for being so understanding. I really have been so worried about broaching the subject.'

'Well, there's no need to worry any more,' I told him, making my way with him to the useful gap in the hedge. 'I'm glad we've spoken about it.'

'I shall sleep more easily tonight,' said he soberly.

'And so shall I,' I assured him.

PART TWO

BEECH GREEN

11   A Family Survivor

THE last day of term, and of the school year, was its usual muddle of clearing up and general euphoria.

Only one child was leaving to go to Beech Green school under George Annett's care. He had a sister there already and was happy about his future. To my delight there would be one new admission to the infants' class in the next term, so our numbers would remain unchanged. Mr Roberts's new farm worker had a son of five years old. He would be warmly welcomed by all those at Fairacre School.

As usual, the vicar called to wish everyone a happy holiday, exhorting them to help their mothers and fathers and to remember the date on which the new term began.

He turned anxiously to me. 'Could you remind me again?'

'September the fifth.'

'Ah yes! Of course!'

He picked up the chalk and wrote the date on the blackboard, looking triumphant as he dusted his hands afterwards.

'Just read it out,' he urged the children.

They chanted it obediently. Was there a touch of indulging-an-old-man, I wondered? But there were no smiles, and they stood politely, without my prompting, as Gerald Partridge departed.

I was particularly glad to start the summer holidays. Wayne Richards, husband of my assistant teacher and owner of a

local building firm, had asked 'if I minded' his men making
an early start in Dolly's house.

So dumbfounded was I by this unusual request that I
simply gazed at him speechless.

'You see,' he explained, 'what with things being so bad
in the trade, I'd be glad to see the two chaps I had in mind
for your little problem, getting some work. I don't want to
stand anyone off, though I reckon it'll come to it before
long.'

'Is it really as bad as that?' I managed to say, when I had
got over the initial shock of a real live builder wanting to
come *earlier* than arranged.

'Things are tight. Even the big firms are feeling the
pinch. People can't afford to move. Can't afford to have
repairs done, for that matter.' He looked at me speculatively.

'You won't have to wait for your money on my little
job,' I promised him. 'I've put aside the amount in your
estimate.'

He hastened to assure me that he had never had any
doubts on that score, but I thought that he looked relieved,
as well he might if more prosperous firms than his were
already suffering.

'The company that built these new places in Fairacre is
going bust, so I heard last night. Nobody's buying, see,
with mortgage rates as they are. They'll have to bring the
price down to get rid of those two that are left.'

'They have already reduced the price,' I said. 'So the
Winters told me.'

'I bet they're cursing they bought when they did,' he
replied. There was a touch of contentment in his expression.
How often other people's misfortune gives gratification, I
thought!

'Well, do start as soon as you like,' I told him. 'I shall be
glad to move in during these holidays.'

Heaven alone knows, I thought after his departure, it will take weeks to sort out my present abode, even the goods and chattels in the rooms themselves. What the cupboards, the loft, the garage and the glory-hole under the stairs would bring forth, I shuddered to think.

Time, and back-breaking work, would tell.

A day or two after this, Amy called in unexpectedly, accompanied, to my surprise, by Brian Horner.

After our greetings, we sat in the garden and I told Amy about my move, possibly in a few weeks' time.

'Splendid!' said Amy. 'Once you've made up your mind it's best to get cracking. No point in drifting along as you so often do.'

'Oh, come!' I protested. 'I'm not quite as bad as that. I'm always telling myself that "procrastination is the thief of time". What a marvellous phrase, incidentally.'

'Not quite as reverberating as that one in our *Handbook for Teachers*,' Amy reminisced. 'Something about teachers in dreary city schools "directing the children's attention to the ever changing panorama of the heavens".'

'I can go one better than that,' I told her, still smarting from her remarks about *drifting*. 'In some scriptural commentary or other, I read once that "Job had often to suffer the opprobrium of anti-patriotism." What about that?'

'I think I can top both those reverberating phrases,' broke in Brian. 'It was said by Dr Thompson, Master of Trinity College, Cambridge from 1866 to 1886, about Richard Jebb: "The time that Mr Jebb can spare from the adornment of his person, he devotes to the neglect of his duties." How's that?'

'Perfect,' we agreed. Brian's final two words emboldened me to ask if he was called 'Basher' because of his cricketing ability.

'Only partly. My full name, I'm sorry to say, is Brian Arthur Seymour Horner, and naturally boys soon called me 'Basher'. What a lot parents have to answer for when they name their children.'

'Excuse me,' I said. 'I must look at my oven. I'm cooking a chicken.'

Amy followed me into the house while Brian meandered about the garden admiring, I hoped, my flower borders.

'I thought he was safely in Bristol,' I said to Amy, in the privacy of the kitchen.

'So did I,' she responded, 'but he has to go to head-quarters with James tomorrow, and so he's spending this weekend with us. I'm quite sorry for him. He misses his wife and home so much. He fairly jumped at the chance of coming to see you.'

'Well, I'm not particularly sorry for him,' I said, slamming the oven door, 'and I've got quite enough to think about without taking on an estranged husband.'

'You're a hard woman,' said Amy, giving me a loving pat, and we returned to the garden.

I was pottering about that evening wondering if Amy would ever be free of Brian Horner. Would James's hero worship survive all the strain that was being put upon it? To my mind, Brian was a mediocre little man, full of self-pity, and I should like to have heard his wife's side of the tale. Still, I told myself more charitably, both James and Amy came very well out of the present situation: generous, and good-hearted. I only hoped that their faith in their friend would remain unclouded.

The telephone bell aroused me from my conjectures, and I was surprised to hear a strange woman's voice announcing herself as 'Dolly Clare's niece, Mary.'

'Well,' I said, 'I *am* delighted to hear from you. Where are you?'

'In Caxley for a few days. My husband – my *second* husband, that is – is over from the States on business, so I came with him to visit some old friends here. They told me about Aunt Dolly.'

'Would you like to come and see the cottage?'

'Indeed I should.'

I went on to tell her about Dolly Clare's legacy to me, but naturally she knew about that from her Caxley friends. I arranged to pick her up two days ahead, and to take her to Beech Green.

'I didn't see as much of Aunt Dolly as I should have liked,' she told me. 'She and mother became somewhat estranged in later life. To be truthful, I think my mother was jealous of Dolly's friend, Emily Davis.'

'What a pity!'

'It certainly was. Anyway, I should like to see the little house again, and perhaps you could spare something of hers as a little keepsake?'

'Of course, I'm sure we can find something,' I told her, and we went on to arrange the time of our meeting.

Later, I began to wonder what could be offered to Dolly's niece. As she had stated in her will, all her trinkets, as she called them, were to go to Isobel Annett who had been such a staunch friend, and this request had been met.

There were several nice pieces of china, and some silver spoons; also a pretty little clock which had graced Dolly's bedroom mantelpiece. Perhaps Mary would prefer some of her aunt's linen, embellished with hand-made crochetwork? In any case, I thought, I was glad to be able to offer a selection of mementoes. She seemed to be the only living tie with Dolly.

I had given several things to people who had been close to my old friend, such as Mrs John, Alice and Bob Willet and various neighbours who had looked after her during her long life. I only hoped that there would be something suitable for Mary to take back.

I suddenly remembered an occasion many years ago when I met an elderly Austrian man and admired a magnificent set of eight mahogany dining-room chairs in his home. His eyes had filled with tears as he said: 'Ah, my dear friend Wilhelm! When he died his good wife asked me to choose a little keepsake. So I chose these chairs.' I had often wondered what that poor widow thought.

I only hoped that Mary would not take a fancy to the cottage staircase or Dolly's kitchen dresser. It was some comfort to remember that she had to transport her choice to the United States eventually, and weight would have to be considered.

Mary Linkenhorn turned out to be a middle-aged, cheerful woman with absolutely nothing in her appearance to connect her with Dolly Clare.

She was beautifully dressed with many fine rings and a three-row string of pearls. Her expensive crocodile shoes had high heels and matched an enormous handbag. I felt that she was perhaps a little too exquisitely turned out for a morning visit to a cottage where possibly Wayne Richards's employees were messing about with plaster and emulsion paint. However, I liked her at once. She was friendly and unaffected, and obviously delighted to be going to see Dolly's house. She chattered about her early memories of the place, and of her affection for her Aunt Dolly.

'My mother, I'm sorry to say, rather looked down on her, you know. She was a bit of a social climber, my mother, I mean, and she felt that she couldn't invite Dolly to meet some of her affluent Caxley friends.'

'Dolly Clare,' I said, 'would have been welcomed in any society.'

'I agree, but mother didn't think so. To tell the truth, my brother and I fell out with her when we were old enough to leave home. We visited her, of course, and always kept in touch by letters when we left England, but there wasn't much love lost. She was a headstrong woman, and we were better apart.'

'What happened to your brother?'

'He went sheep farming in New Zealand, and did very well, but he contracted cancer some three years ago, and died last Christmas.'

We drew in to the side of the lane outside Dolly's cottage, and I switched off the engine.

Mary sat, silently gazing at the little thatched house. I was rather relieved to see that no builders were at work this morning. We should have the house to ourselves.

It was very quiet in the lane, and we were both content to sit there in silence. A lark was singing overhead, high above the great whale-back of the downs behind the village. A young pheasant crossed the road a few yards from the car, stepping haughtily from one grass verge to the other, and ignoring a small animal, shrew or vole, which streaked across the road within yards of the bird. There was a fragrance in the air compounded of cut grass, wild flowers and, above all, the pungent scent of a nearby elder bush heavy with creamy flowers.

Mary broke the silence first.

'It's so small,' she said.

'Actually,' I told her, 'it has been enlarged since your time. Dolly had the sitting-room made wider, and the kitchen too. But I agree, it is a little house. I think that's why I like it so much.'

We climbed out of the car, and I unlocked the front door. The familiar smell greeted me of ancient wood, slight dampness, and the faint smell of dried lavender which

Dolly had never failed to keep in china bowls in each room.

The furniture remained much as Dolly had left it. Some if it would have to go later to the Caxley auctioneers; I had removed anything portable of value to my school house for safety. Beech Green may look idyllic to the passing stranger, but it has its share of villains, as well as a few marauders from elsewhere who take advantage of the nearby motorway to steal anything which will bring them a few pounds, and then make a hasty getaway. It was this hoard which I proposed to display to Mary when we returned to my house for lunch, so that she could choose her keepsake; and this I told her.

Her face was transfixed with pleasure and wonder as she stood inside the sitting-room: 'It still smells the same. Isn't it strange how strongly smells evoke memories? Far more so than sight.'

She crossed to the window and looked across the little garden, now in sore need of attention I noticed guiltily, to the sweep of the downs beyond.

'And the view's exactly the same. What a relief!'

She sat down suddenly, as though everything was too much for her.

'You know,' she said after a while, 'my friends in Caxley dissuaded me from going to visit a place near the town where we used to picnic as children. There seemed to be every wild flower imaginable there – cowslips, scabious, bee orchids and early purple orchids, and lots of that yellow ladies' slipper. They told me it has all gone. A new estate has been built there, and all the trees cut down "Cherish your memories," they said to me, and I'm sure they are right.'

She looked about the room.

'But this has changed so little, and I'm glad you've brought me. Can we see the rest?'

We wandered into the kitchen, and Mary ran her fingers over the old scrubbed kitchen table, ridged with years of service. She peered excitedly into the larder with its slate shelves, and the massive pottery bread crock on the brick floor.

'It's all as I remember it,' she said delightedly. 'Will you keep things as they are?'

'I shall do my best,' I assured her, as we mounted the stairs.

It was plain that work was in progress here, though not at the moment. Dust sheets draped the beds and the rest of the furniture which had been put into the middle of the rooms. Paint pots and brushes stood on newspaper on the window sills, and there was a smell of fresh paint.

Mary gazed out of the window. It did me good to see how much she relished her visit here after so many years, and I was glad that so little had changed for her. It was right, as her friends had said, 'to cherish her memories'. But how much better to find that some of those memories, at least, were still reality.

She was very quiet as we drove back from Beech Green to Fairacre and, I guessed, much moved by all she had seen. I was careful not to break the silence until we had stopped the car outside my home, when Mary seemed to return to this world with a cry of delight.

'But this is a lovely house!' She turned to me, looking perplexed. 'It is so much better than Aunt Dolly's! Can you bear to move away?'

I laughed, and led her into the house.

As we sipped our glasses of sherry, I explained that the school house was virtually a tied cottage, something that went with the job, and when I retired I should have had to have found another abode. That was why Dolly's wonderful legacy to me had been so deeply appreciated. Her house would be my haven in the future.

'But won't you mind what happens to this place when you go?'

'Of course, I shall. I've always loved it, and I think the school authorities would let me buy it if the school were closed down. But that's out of the question. The property will be sold, I've no doubt, and if the school closes, then that will be sold too. It could make a splendid house with care and money spent on it.'

'I hope that never happens,' said my guest.

'So do I,' I assured her, 'but things don't look very promising at the moment. Now, come and have some lunch.'

Afterwards, I broached the subject of a memento and told her about Dolly's valuables which I had stored upstairs.

We went up to inspect them, and I spread out Dolly's

things on the bed for Mary's inspection. She fingered the beautiful old linen, and picked up the pieces of ancient china with great care.

'It's all so lovely, and so difficult to choose. I love this little china cream jug, but I think I'll settle for one of Dolly's tablecloths, if that suits you?'

'Take both,' I said. 'I know Dolly would love to have seen them in family hands.'

She made her selection from the pile of linen. The chosen cloth had a deep edging of hand-made crochet, done years ago, I felt sure, by Dolly's mother Mary, after whom the present Mary had been named.

'I shall use it on very special days, like Christmas,' Mary said.

Later I drove my new friend to Caxley. Only three days remained before she and her husband returned to America, and I was much touched when she invited me to go and stay with them, and have a holiday there.

'Perhaps next summer?' she pressed, as I stopped outside at her friends' home.

'There's nothing I should like more,' I told her, 'but I shall have to think about it.'

We parted with a kiss, and I drove back thinking how good it had been to have contact with this last link with Dolly's family.

Should I ever go to the United States, I wondered? A lot would depend on the future of Fairacre School. Would it still be there? For that matter, would I still be there?

I had plenty to think about in the time ahead, but I was enormously glad to have met Mary and to have been able to give her the mementoes she liked. And at least she had not put me in the position of poor Wilhelm's widow when those Austrian dining-room chairs had been appropriated.

* * *

At the Post office the next day, I was surprised to see Mrs Lamb standing behind the grille in place of her husband.

'He's down at the surgery,' she said, in reply to my enquiry. 'Got a bad back, picking gooseberries yesterday, and anyone would think he was at death's door. You know what men are.'

'Well, I hope it soon gets better. Backs are so painful. Just six air letters, please, and a book of stamps.'

She busied herself in a drawer. 'Have you heard any more about the school closing?' she asked.

Mrs Lamb has been a manager, or *governor*, as I have to remember to call them now, for several years, in company with other good villagers such as Mr Roberts and Mrs Mawne, wife of our local ornithologist, Henry.

'Nothing definite,' I said. 'As you know, we are now down to about twenty on roll, but I have had no word from the office about closure so I'm keeping my fingers crossed.'

'Well, we've trounced the idea before, and we'll do it again,' said Mrs Lamb, slapping down my purchases in a militant manner. 'There's not a soul in Fairacre who wants the school to close. That must count for something.'

I said that I hoped so.

'You don't think,' she went on, a note of doubt now in her voice, 'that you leaving for Dolly Clare's place might make them think of shutting the school?'

The thought had never occurred to me, and although I did not think that my removal a few miles distant would affect the authority's decision, I was somewhat taken aback.

'I don't imagine it will make the slightest difference,' I said, trying to sound reassuring. 'After all, I spent several weeks commuting from Dolly's house to school during her last illness.'

'That's what I said to Maud Pringle when she came in yesterday. There's a fair amount of gossip about the school at the moment.'

This I could well believe, and I made my way homeward with all the old familiar worries buzzing in my head like a swarm of bees.

It really looked as though the school might close. It would not be just yet, as we should have had fair warning if such a step were imminent. I remembered the vicar's blackboard message about the dates of the coming term, and felt a faint comfort.

But I really ought to give some serious thought to my own future. My departure from the school house would probably mean that it would be put on the market. That I had already faced. But what should I do if the school closed? I felt sure that I would be offered another post in the area, possibly at Beech Green School if there were a suitable vacancy. There were a dozen or so schools in Caxley and nearby which might employ me. But did I want to go elsewhere? I certainly did not.

I could, I supposed, take early retirement, but could I afford to? And wasn't I still an active person, wanting to work and, though I said it myself, able, healthy and experienced? I should soon be bored, kicking around at home, and I remembered Miriam Baker's remark about 'being geared to work'. Like most people when working, I professed to loathing it, but deprived of it I should probably be far less content.

As I came towards the church, I saw that Bob Willet was busy digging a grave, and I went across to speak to him. He looked hot with his labours, and pushed his cap to the back of his head.

'Fair bit of clay over the chalk in this 'ere graveyard,' he said, clambering out and taking a seat on a conveniently placed horizontal grave stone over the tomb of Josiah Drummond Gent. He nodded towards his work. 'Poor old Bert Tanner. Went last week.'

I made to sit beside him, and he dusted a place with his rough old hand.

'Bit damp, you know. Don't want to get piles. Nasty things, piles.'

'I shan't hurt,' I said. 'I'm pretty tough.'

'You needs to be these days,' he observed, and a companionable silence fell between us as we let the peace of the place envelop us. A country churchyard is a very soothing spot among all our 'rude forefathers', including Josiah Drummond Gent, whose last resting place was providing us with a comfortable, if chilly, seat.

'Heard any more about our school shutting?' he said at last, breaking the silence.

'Not a thing. I don't think there's any cause to worry just yet.'

'Looks as though it's bound to come, though. I hates all this 'ere change. New houses, new people, that dratted motorway, you moving out before long. It's *unsettling*, that's what it is.'

'I shan't be going far,' I pointed out. 'In a way I shall only be carrying on where dear old Dolly left off. So there's a nice comforting piece of continuity for you.'

Mr Willet sighed.

'I s'pose you could look at it like that. There's still plenty that stays the same. Digging graves, for instance, and them downs up there. They won't change, thank God.'

The stone was beginning to strike some chill through my summer skirt, and I rose to go. Mr Willet heaved himself to his feet, and grasped his spade again.

'Ah well! My old ma used to say: "Do what's to hand

and the Lord will look after the rest." I'd best get on digging.'

He jumped neatly into the mottled clay and chalk hole of his making, and I went to embark on what my own hand should be doing.

12   Relief by Telephone

I WENT to Beech Green on most days during the summer holidays, to see how the refurbishing was getting on, and to take over a few pieces of furniture, china and so on from the school house.

Wayne Richards was doing me proud, I felt, and the basic decorating was done within two weeks, and rejuvenated the whole place. I felt immensely pleased with my new home.

I had got our local electrician to inspect all the wiring, and the plumber to check his work in the cottage. To my relief all was in good repair. It looked as though I should be able to move in before term started, unless any unforeseen problems cropped up.

The biggest headache was the state of the garden, and I took Bob Willet with me one hot day, to get his advice on it. He mooched about it in a thoughtful mood, taking particular note of the ancient fruit trees.

'Almost all have had their day,' he told me. He stood by an ancient plum tree. Brown beads of resin decorated the trunk, and some of the topmost branches were already dead.

Bob's brown hand slapped the wrinkled bark.

'You thinkin' of replacing any of 'em?'

'Is it so bad?'

'In my opinion, yes. The only tree here as is worth its salt is that old Bramley and the yew tree. They'll be good for another fifty years, but these 'ere fruit trees should be out before they falls down.'

I nodded my agreement.

'I think I'd like a new plum tree – one of the gage type, if possible – and perhaps a couple of new apple trees. But I agree there's no need for more.'

'Come early autumn I'll bring a lad up with me and we'll get this lot down.'

He moved on to a James Grieve apple tree which was already leaning over at an alarming angle.

'Tell you what, Miss Read, these 'ere trees'll give you a nice lot of firewood for the winter.'

He turned his attention to the neglected border, and shook his head.

'Hopeless?' I hazarded.

'Best to dig up the lot and start afresh,' was his verdict. 'It's that full of twitch and ground elder nothing won't grow well there.'

And so it went on as we did our tour of inspection. Only the soft fruit bushes, black and redcurrant and gooseberry bushes passed his ruthless inspection. Even they, it

seemed, could do with 'a good old spray against the bugs'.

We went into the house to arrange matters. As always, Bob had some practical advice.

'I've got a young lad in mind, nephew of Alice's over Springbourne way. He's a good worker, when he gets the chance. Just been stood off from one of those Caxley firms as has gone bust. Tip top gardener he is. Shall I get him over?'

'Yes, please. I suppose we could make a start on that border?'

'The sooner the better,' said my old friend forthrightly, as he rose to go home.

August seemed to hurry by at an alarming pace with so many things to do in both my abodes. Luckily there were no urgent maintenance jobs to be done at the school house, as the upstairs rooms were now in pristine condition and, apart from getting new mats for the kitchen floor sometime, I felt that I could sit back.

In any case, I did not propose to do any more to my present home. The outside maintenance was the responsibility of the school authorities, and I was only responsible for things inside; I felt that I had done my duty honourably throughout the years. With the possible closure of the school hanging over me, it seemed prudent to postpone any long-term decisions for my domestic arrangements at the school house.

My social life during the holidays was limited to a few outings to friends, a short trip to Dorset to see an aged aunt, and entertaining my cousin Ruth for three nights at the school house – 'probably,' I told her, 'for the last time.'

'It's sad. I shall miss it,' she said. 'Will you?'

'Naturally, but I should be far more upset if the school were to close. As it is, I have Dolly's house to enjoy, and all the fun of new neighbours at Beech Green with the continuing of life as the village school teacher here.'

I took her to see my new property. The work was well on the way to completion, and privately I reckoned to be in by the end of August.

Ruth was enchanted with it, and it was good to have her whole-hearted approval. She is a wise woman, and I have always respected her judgement.

'Well, the next time you come,' I told her, 'you will be sleeping under that thatched roof.'

We were blessed with warm sunshine while she was with me, and we had several picnics, and two visits to nearby National Trust properties. August is not my favourite month: there is an end-of-summer look about the countryside, shabby and worn, before the glory of autumn transforms it.

But the verges of our lanes were still bright with cranesbill, and the tall grass was dusted with minute purple flowers. The lime trees had shed their yellow bracts, but the remains of the flowers still fluttered moth-like among the foliage.

I was sorry when Ruth had to go. There are times when I realize how much I miss family ties. This was one of them as I drove her to Caxley station.

'Come again soon,' I urged her. 'Come for Christmas in the new house.'

'Nothing I'd like more, but I'll have to let you know,' she replied, and with that I had to be content.

That evening I was surprised to get a call on the telephone from Mr Salisbury. He is the representative from the local education office who attends our school governors' meetings, and acts as the line of communication between the local schools and the education authority. He performs his rôle admirably, being kind and tactful. I wondered why he should be ringing me personally, presumably on a school matter.

After polite inquiries about my state of health, he began to approach the purpose of his call.

'I happened to meet Gerald Partridge recently,' he said smoothly, 'and he mentioned the fact that there was a little disquiet in the village about Fairacre School.'

This is it, I thought, feeling slightly sick. He is going to warn me about closing the place before the next governors' meeting.

'I do want to put your mind at rest, Miss Read. There is no suggestion of closing the school in the near future.'

I sat down abruptly on the chair by the telephone. My legs did not seem capable of supporting me.

'That's good news,' I croaked. 'Naturally, I've been anxious as the numbers are so low.'

'They are indeed,' he agreed, 'but they may pick up before the next school year. In any case, that side of the matter will be kept under review, and you would be apprised of any official decision in good time.'

'I was sure of that,' I told him.

'No. The other matter was rather more personal.'

He cleared his throat while I thought, now what? Had I forgotten to return some vital forms? Had an angry parent complained about me? Was I about to get the sack for some unknown misdemeanour?

'It's really about your tenancy of the school house,' he went on. 'I gathered from Gerald Partridge's remarks that you were proposing to live at Beech Green sometime in the future. Is that correct?'

'Yes, indeed,' I replied, and went on to explain my plans as far as I knew them myself. 'I was going to bring this up at the next governors' meeting,' I added. 'I realize I have to give a month's notice.'

'There is absolutely no hurry on our side for you to leave the school house, you know. You have been a model tenant, and we should all be very sorry to see you go. I only rang so that I could get matters straight before anything official was put into writing.'

I said that I appreciated the courtesy, and felt that perhaps I should have mentioned my plans earlier.

'Indeed no! There's nothing to blame yourself for, but I am delighted to have had this little talk.'

He went on to more general subjects such as the traffic congestion that morning in Caxley, the early harvest this year, and ended up with his hopes for more children at Fairacre before long.

I agreed fervently, and with mutual compliments the conversation closed.

As the end of August approached, the school house began to look pathetically bare. My future abode, on the other hand, was in danger of getting seriously overcrowded, although I was happy and excited at the prospect of moving in.

Amy came over one morning to help me pack books, a formidable task, and a particularly dirty one as it happened. We swathed ourselves in overalls against the dust of years which was being blown off, or slapped off, the contents of my book shelves.

'I should have thought you could have got Mrs Pringle to dust these now and again,' observed Amy.

'Mrs Pringle,' I told her, 'doesn't hold with books. If I'd let her have her way, she would have had a bonfire of the lot in the garden. She maintains that *reading* keeps decent folk from *proper work* like polishing and scrubbing and dusting book shelves. By the way, Mrs Pringle insists on "doing me" at my new home on a Wednesday afternoon.'

'Well, I'm glad to hear it,' said Amy. 'Do you really want to keep this *Historic Houses and Gardens Guide for 1978*?'

She held it up by one corner, looking fastidious. Her usually well-kept hands were filthy, I noticed guiltily.

'Throw it in the junk box,' I said, 'and let's have some coffee.'

We washed our filthy hands at the kitchen sink, and sat down exhausted with our coffee cups.

I had switched on the television to catch the news on the hour, but we'd found ourselves confronted with an old black and white film. The heroine, wearing a black satin suit with aggressive shoulder pads, and a minute pill-box hat with sequins and an ostrich plume was sobbing noisily on a settee. At the other end sat Cary Grant, ebony-haired and looking greatly concerned.

'Aw, kid,' he said, 'don't take on so,' and produced a beautifully laundered handkerchief which he pressed upon his weeping companion.

She proceeded to mop her cheeks, being careful not to touch her mascara.

'Gee, you're so kind,' she gulped. 'I bin silly.'

I switched them off.

'I wonder,' said Amy meditatively, 'why weeping women in films never have a handkerchief? I don't know about you, my dear, but I can truthfully say that I *always* have a hanky on me, thanks to my mother's training. Although I did know two sisters who *shared* one when they went out to parties. I remember one saying to the other: "Have you got *the handkerchief*?" I was appalled.'

'And quite rightly so,' I said. 'D'you want more coffee or shall we get on?'

We returned to our labours, and later that day took the books, a box of china and some garden chairs over to

Beech Green. Our load needed both cars, and Amy arrived before I did. I found her sunning herself on an old bench under the thatch at the back of Dolly's cottage.

'If ever you want to part with this,' she said dreamily, eyes still closed, 'let me know.'

'Not a hope,' I told her. 'I intend to stay here, like dear Dolly, until I'm summoned hence.'

I unlocked the door, and we manhandled our heavy loads into the house.

The books went into the new shelves without much bother, but it was quite apparent that cupboard space was beginning to run short. I could see that Wayne Richards would have to be prevailed upon again, but not until the Christmas holidays, I hoped.

When we had done all that we could, we sat down to recover. The sun was shining into the sitting-room, and I thought of the many times I had sat here with Dolly, enjoying her company and the peace of her home.

I looked at Amy with renewed affection. It was good to have an old friend under my new roof. I began to tell her about the telephone call from Mr Salisbury, and the relief I felt at knowing the closure of Fairacre School was not imminent.

'That's marvellous,' agreed Amy, 'but what hopes are there of new pupils?'

'Not too bright immediately,' I told her, 'but we are waiting to see if two large families come to live in the new houses.'

'Or in your school house,' observed Amy. 'I take it that it will be on the market sometime?'

'I suppose so,' I said, and was surprised to find the idea distinctly upsetting. Somehow, *other people* in *my* house, was an unpleasant prospect.

Amy was studying me with some concern. 'You must worry,' she remarked.

I have no secrets from Amy. We have known each other too long for dissembling.

'I do,' I said truthfully. 'I worry about the school itself, that dear shabby old building which has seen generations of Fairacre folk under its roof. I worry about the children, and the parents, and grandparents.'

'But what about *you*?' pressed Amy.

'Funnily enough, not so desperately. I should probably be worrying far more if Dolly had not been so generous to me. But I'm pretty sure I would be offered another post locally, or I could contemplate early retirement, I suppose.'

'Would you like that?'

'Half of me fairly leaps at the idea, but the other half wonders if I should get restive after the first few months of euphoria. Like Miriam Baker,' I added, and began to tell her about Miriam's plans.

After this we parted, Amy driving off southwards to Bent, while I locked up the house and then drove in the opposite direction to Fairacre.

The village seemed deserted, and nothing stirred near St Patrick's and its churchyard. It was a golden evening of great calm, the kind of post-harvest lull when the stubble is still in the fields reflecting a warm September effulgence.

I remembered that I needed some of the children's readers to check an order list I was sending to the office, and went to the school before going home across the playground.

The brickwork threw out considerable warmth, and I could smell the drying paint round the window panes. Mrs Pringle had 'bottomed' the place at the end of the summer term, and would be up again in a day or two to see that all was ready for our opening again soon.

Meanwhile, the school had remained locked. A few dead leaves whispered on the porch floor, as I inserted the massive key into the Victorian lock. The woodwork was warm against my hand, and I suddenly noticed that the crack of the door was sealed with a criss-cross of gossamer threads, spun by a host of small creatures who had been undisturbed for weeks.

I stood numb with shock, the key motionless in my hand. This, I suddenly realized, would be the state of this well-loved school for ever, should its doors finally close. Dust, cobwebs, flaking paint, a few dead leaves, an overall acceptance of time's ravages and the onslaught of the seasons.

It must have been several minutes before I could find the strength to twist that key and return to the present. But as the gossamer threads broke, and the familiar scent of the old schoolroom assailed me, I found my eyes were wet.

13   Two Homes

I MADE the move into Dolly's cottage before the end of the summer holidays, as I had planned. But only by the skin of my teeth.

As everyone who has moved house knows, there are always *snags*. The day before the move, I returned to the school house from the Post Office to find a roll of stair carpet in the porch. This was supposed to have been delivered to Dolly's house where Mrs John was awaiting it. I rang the firm who expressed surprise and said: 'I'd better hang on to it, didn't I?' as the men could pick it up with my other 'bits and bobs' the next morning. And yes, yes, they'd certainly be at my place (School House wasn't it now, at Beech Green?) by nine o'clock prompt.

I straightened out that one, rang Mrs John to apologize for keeping her waiting all the afternoon, hauled the unwieldy package further into the porch in case it rained, and hoped for the best.

At ten o'clock the next morning, I rang the removal firm again. The same man answered. I recognized his adenoidal symptoms.

'That's funny! The chaps as left that stair carpet had a note for you.'

'It's not here.'

'Well, we're working you in with a party at Cirencester.'

'How do you mean? "Being worked in"?'

'Well, there's a full load going to Cirencester, see, and a half-load being picked up there, and the chaps will call at yours for your bits to fill up the space, see, and drop it off at Beech Green on the way home, see. Save you all a lot of trouble.'

'There's quite enough here to be getting on with,' I said tartly. 'So when can I expect this half-empty van from Cirencester?'

'About midday.'

'So I should hope.'

'With luck, that is,' said Adenoids. 'This way you save quite a bit of money, you know.'

'It doesn't save my time and temper,' I snapped back, crashing down the receiver.

It was perhaps fortunate that I had been unable to catch Tibby earlier. That astute animal had seen the cat basket which I had attempted to hide in the cupboard, recognized it at once as the carriage which conveyed animals to the vet, and had made for open country. Luckily, just before twelve, Tibby appeared, accepted the last of the milk, and was corralled in mid-sip, poor thing. Together we sat, awaiting the van's return from the party in Cirencester.

In the quiet, denuded room, I had plenty of time to look back over the years I had spent beneath this roof. They had been happy ones, busy with worthwhile work and enriched by Fairacre friends. Should I feel as secure at Beech Green, I wondered? Time would tell.

By one o'clock Tibby and I were still waiting, and both hungry. Tibby had some rather unpopular cat biscuits in the cat basket, and I dined on two somewhat fluffy wine gums from the bottom of my handbag.

At two o'clock the van appeared, loaded up the last of my removables and took off for Beech Green.

Tibby was put on the front seat of my car, protesting loudly at this indignity, and I drove away to our new home.

* * *

Later that night, I climbed the stairs at Beech Green, weary with all the day's activities. Tibby was settled in the kitchen below, the doors were locked and the empty milk bottles stood on the doorstep.

Everything was quiet. I leant out of the bedroom window and smelt the cool fragrance of a summer's night. Far away, across Hundred Acre field, an owl hooted. Below me, in the flowerbed, a small nocturnal animal rustled leaves in its search for food.

A great feeling of peace crept over me. The tranquillity of Dolly's old abode and my new one enveloped me. I knew then that I had come home at last.

My link with the school house was not entirely broken.

At the governors' meeting the matter was discussed with all the sympathy I knew would be shown. Mr Salisbury, from the office, was among those who sat in some discomfort in the schoolroom after the children had gone home.

I explained my position, knowing full well, of course, that my move to Dolly's cottage was known to all present, but these formalities must be observed. I ended by saying that I proposed to vacate the school house at Michaelmas, the end of the present month, so that it could be put on the market if that was, in fact, to be its fate.

Here Mr Salisbury intervened. He was empowered, he told us, to make quite clear that there was absolutely no hurry in this matter. It would be perfectly in order for me to stay at the school house until the end of the year, giving me more time to see to my affairs. Any decision about the house's future would be taken then.

I was truly grateful for this gesture. It meant that I now had ample time to clear up my domestic matters.

The rest of the business went much as usual. The school

log book was produced and handed round. The punishment book, its pages unsullied, was also scrutinized. The chairman, the vicar, thanked us all for coming, and the meeting dispersed into the September sunshine.

Although almost everything of mine was now installed at Beech Green, I had left one bed and a chair beside it, in my old bedroom. This I had done for two reasons. Firstly, I might need to stay overnight if school affairs kept me late during this interim period, or if some unexpected weather hazard made it difficult to get home. Secondly, I had always used the school house in any emergency with the children. A sick child would be taken over there to lie down whilst help was fetched and parents informed. Somehow I felt safer in keeping a place of refuge close to the school in case of sudden need. Naturally, when the end of the year came I should have to face making other contingency plans, but it was good to know that these temporary arrangements had the blessing of the school authorities.

I went home to Beech Green that day, very much happier in mind.

The golden weather continued, and people were looking for blackberries along the hedges. It was plain that we were going to have a bumper crop of apples, and even the farmers could find little to deplore after an unusually good harvest.

'Want a marrow or two?' asked Mr Willet. 'A *proper* marrow, I mean, not these 'ere soppy little runts what gets cooked whole. Courgiettes, or some such name. I reckon it's pandering to women as is too idle to cut the skin off a decent marrow. I fair hates to see a dish of them little 'uns, like a lot of chopped-up eels, and my Alice knows better than to serve 'em up.'

I refused the marrow – or marrows – as kindly as I could. A lone woman simply cannot cope with a full-sized marrow, and Mr Willet's were mammoth.

'I thought you might like to make a bit of jam,' he said, looking hurt.

'I don't eat much jam.' I said apologetically.

'There's always bazaars as could do with it,' pointed out Bob. 'Good causes. Charity. All that.'

'Well,' I began weakly.

'I'll bring you up a couple,' he said swiftly. 'Put a nice bit of ginger and lemon with it, and it'll sell like hot cakes. Mrs Partridge has made twenty-five pounds of it with the marrows I took up to the vicarage last week.'

This looked to me as if the local market for marrow jam would be overloaded already, but Mr Willet's undoubted dismay at my reluctance to accept his bounty had to be assuaged.

'I'm sure I could cope with one of your lovely marrows,' I said bravely. 'It's just that, living alone, you know – '

'Well, that could be righted,' observed Bob sturdily, 'if you wasn't so picky about chaps.'

He turned to go, leaving me speechless.

'I'll look you out a couple of beauties,' he promised, stumping away.

Those 'couple of beauties', I told myself ruefully, would probably make another twenty-five pounds of marrow jam to add to Fairacre's surplus.

One Saturday morning, soon after receiving four massive marrows from Bob Willet, I went into Caxley to buy a pair of shoes. I tried on about sixteen pairs which were either too tight or too loose, the wrong colour or design, and finally settled for the pair which hurt least, looked un-obtrusive, and hoped for the best.

Still in a state of shock at the price asked for the shoes I took myself to the store's restaurant and ordered coffee. At that moment I was hailed by Horace and Eve Umbleditch at a nearby table, and I was invited to join my old friends.

'Just the girl we wanted to see,' cried Horace. 'We've been hearing about your move, and wondered if your school house was going to be put on the market.'

I told them my story up to date, and that a decision about the house would be taken in the New Year, but it looked highly likely that it would be for sale then.

'But not if the school stays open, surely?' asked Eve. 'Won't the house be kept in case the next head teacher wants it?'

I explained that the school had been reprieved for the time being, but in any case the chances were that anyone appointed after I had retired, sometime in the future, would probably want to live elsewhere.

'When I came years ago,' I told them, 'cars were not so abundant. I was jolly glad to have the school house on top of my job, so to speak. But nowadays the head of Fairacre School could live anywhere within striking distance by car. In any case, the school house is really only suitable for a single person.'

'Any hope of building on?' said Horace, stirring his coffee thoughtfully. 'Eve and I were wondering if it would suit us. We're in the same position as you were – living in a tied house virtually – and it's high time we found a place of our own.'

'It might suit you very well,' I answered. 'You have seen it, I know, but if you really are considering buying, do come over at anytime and have a good look at it. I love the place dearly, and it would be lovely to think of you there. But don't forget, you are cheek by jowl with the school, and all the noise that causes.'

'We've thought about that. But after all, we should be away at our own school when your children are there, and we have long holidays when Fairacre School would be empty too. It might work out very comfortably.'

The conversation then turned to the past school holidays which they had spent in France, and to my own spell in Scotland with Amy.

We parted with renewed promises about their visiting the house, and I drove back to my new home at Beech Green wondering if my old house would one day see the Umbleditchs happily settled there.

I must say, I liked the idea.

The garden at Dolly's was beginning to look tidier, thanks largely to Bob Willet's efforts. He cycled over from Fairacre when he could spare the time, and did a stout job on the neglected borders, sometimes assisted by Alice Willet's nephew.

Under his direction I too did my stint, and on some days I was assisted by Joseph Coggs who was always willing to come back with me in the car, eat a substantial tea, pitch into digging and weeding, hedge-trimming or tending a bonfire, and earning a modest sum in payment.

I enjoyed his company. He was never going to be an academic person. His parents' distrust of 'book-learning' was partly shared by all the Coggs' family. But he loved natural things, flowers, birds, curiously-shaped stones, the evolution of tadpoles into frogs – in fact, anything which involved the living world and its past in the countryside around him. He had an enquiring mind retentive of all that really appealed to him. Moreover, the sense of wonder, which so often fades as a child grows older, remained as keen as ever, and we spent many happy hours together restoring the old garden.

'The next real job,' said Bob Willet when the three of us were sitting on the bench under the thatch surveying the result of our back-breaking labours, 'is them old trees.'

He was looking with great disapproval at the ancient fruit trees which were looking decidedly sick.

'That old Bramley will do a few years yet,' said Bob, 'but I'd have them two plums and that pear and greengage out as soon as they've dropped their leaves. Riddled with canker, I'll lay. Best put in some new stuff – bush type, I'd say so as you can pick 'em easy.'

I agreed to all his wise advice. When the time came, I knew that Mr John and George Annett would give a hand in getting the trees down. Meanwhile, Joe and I were content to obey our mentor, and went on with our humble weeding and other unskilled labour under his watchful eye.

The spare bed in the near-empty school house was used only twice during the next few weeks. One of Mrs

Richards's little boys looked flushed and was tearful. On investigation, we discovered an ominous rash on his chest, and whipped him across to the school house before the rest of the infants showed the same symptoms. As it turned out, our fears of measles or chickenpox were groundless. A new jersey, desperately tickly, had irritated the poor child's chest, and he was back in school within two days.

On the second occasion, I occupied the bed myself after a long evening of gardening. I was splitting up the roots of my favourite perennials to take over to the Beech Green garden, and found that my back was in such a parlous condition that driving was next to impossible.

An early night under the old familiar roof eased the pain, and I was able to nip over to Beech Green to feed Tibby before breakfast. The poor animal had missed supper, and I was greeted coldly.

After friends had been given any particular object of their choice, surplus furniture from my old house, and from Dolly's had been sent to the auctioneers and had brought in a tidy sum. Dolly, I felt, would have approved.

The thatched roof insulated the cottage well, keeping it snug in winter and cool in summer. The ceilings were low, so that the rooms soon warmed up when the electric fire was on, and I found the staircase easier to negotiate than the rather steep one at the school house.

I relished my new home, and looked forward to returning to it after each day at school. I began to realize that a few miles between one's place of work and place of home made all the difference to one's relaxation. Hitherto I had gone between house and school many times between dawn and dusk. In truth, I was always on duty, and fair game for any parent or governor who wished to drop in and discuss school matters. Now I was less vulnerable, and I appreciated this change in my life.

Tibby too seemed to enjoy an environment without children, and explored the new hedges, trees and ditches with fresh energy.

We settled into this different routine with great satisfaction, now that the worries of the move and the clearing-up of Dolly's affairs were over, though nothing could take away the sharp sense of loss which overcame me now and again. The pungent scent of southernwood by the back door, the photograph of Dolly which hung over her desk, and the sight of the bright rug she had made for the landing, all sent a pang of loneliness through me. How potent such inanimate things are!

Horace and Eve Umbleditch came to see me one Saturday soon after our encounter in Caxley, and we drove over to Fairacre to see the school house.

'It doesn't look at it's best unfurnished,' I warned them, 'but at least it is all newly decorated upstairs, and you'll get some idea of size and outlook.'

It was a balmy afternoon, and the school-house garden was looking tidy. I still had the key, of course, by courtesy of the school governors, and water and electricity were still available. Our footsteps echoed hollowly on the bare boards and the uncarpeted stairs.

'This looks very monastic,' observed Horace in my old bedroom. He was looking at my lone bed, chair and electric heater. There were no curtains at the windows and no covering on the floor. Somehow it looked even more bleak than the completely bare rooms elsewhere, I realized.

I explained about the emergency arrangements.

'But I really think it's time to get the removal men to take these few things to the sale room. With luck, I'm not likely to need them again before the end of term, and anyway I must make other plans after that.'

After they had looked at the house, we sat on the grass in the sunny garden. A bold pair of chaffinches came close, hoping for peanuts. A lark sang high above us, and in the distance we could hear the bleating of Mr Roberts's sheep.

'It's a blissful spot,' said Eve.

'It is indeed,' agreed Horace, chewing a piece of grass lazily. 'It would be worth waiting for if you think it will really find its way on to the market.'

'Not for me to say,' I responded. 'But all the signs point that way. Sometime in the New Year, I imagine.'

We returned to Beech Green for tea. They were both very quiet on the journey there, obviously mulling over all that they had seen.

'And what's the village like?' enquired Horace when I had poured the tea. 'I suppose we should be looked upon as newcomers, and not really accepted.'

'That would depend on you,' I said. 'If you really want to join in, I've no doubt you would soon find yourselves president of this, and secretary to that, sidesman at the church, umpire at cricket matches, and a dozen other offices.'

'Well, we *would* like to join in,' said Eve roundly. 'I was brought up in a village, and it's one of the reasons we should like to make our home in one.'

'The only snag is,' added Horace, 'we should obviously have to be away most of the day, just like the rest of the village commuters. I suppose you have such bodies in Fairacre?'

'We do indeed. It's one of the more obvious changes in the village, and I really don't see what can be done about it. When I look back to my early days at the school, I can remember how close-knit the families were. I suppose Mr Roberts and his neighbouring farmer were the two main employers in the village, and I know there were the old familiar names on my school register which were in the log book almost a century ago.'

'And aren't there now?'

'A few. Nothing to speak of. So many have moved away, and when the cottages have become empty they have been sold for far more than the original village people could afford. It's happening everywhere. On the other hand, you can understand people wanting to bring up their children in the country, and if they have the money to pay for a suitable piece of property, and are game to have miles of travelling each day to work, who can blame them for buying village houses?'

'Like us,' commented Horace.

'The only objection I have,' I added, 'is that the children don't come to my school!'

'Take heart,' said Eve. 'They may come yet. After all, it's not going to close, is it? You told us that the other day.'

'It will be a miracle if it survives for another few years,' I replied soberly. 'I sometimes wonder if the authorities are waiting to see how low the numbers will fall, and if perhaps the whole property – school, school house and the ground – will then be put on the market. It would be a valuable property if that happened.'

'I noticed a shop in the village,' said Eve. 'Do you use it?'

'Indeed I do. It's the Post Office as well, and I suppose I do almost all my weekly shopping at Mr Lamb's, and get stamps and post things at the same time. Now and again I have to trundle into Caxley, mainly for clothes and the like, but I go as little as possible, parking gets worse and worse.'

'And is that the only shop?'

'Afraid so. Years ago things were different. Bob Willet

was telling me the other day that when he was a boy there
was a thriving blacksmith at the forge, a baker, a carpenter,
a cobbler, a man called Quick – who was extremely slow –
who was the carrier between local villages and Caxley.
Fairacre must have been a busy place, and quite noisy too
with plenty of horses about and the forge clanging away.'

'Sad, really.'

'The saddest part for Bob Willet was the demise of the
old lady who used to keep the Post Office when he was
young. She sold a few sweets, and home-made toffee was
twopence a quarter. Guaranteed to pull out any loose teeth,
too, in a far more enjoyable way than a trip to the dentist.'

'My favourites were gob-stoppers,' said Horace remi-
niscently. 'The sort that changed colour as you sucked
them.'

'And mine were licorice strips,' continued Eve. 'My
mother wouldn't let us have gob-stoppers. She said they
were *common*!'

'Not common enough for my liking,' said Horace, 'on
threepence a week pocket-money, I never got enough of
them.'

And with such sweet-talk, the question of house-buying
was shelved for the rest of the afternoon.

14   A Mighty Rushing Wind

AS we entered October the weather became very unsettled. There were squally showers, the wind shifted its direction day by day, and Mrs Pringle began to complain about the leaves which were making her lobby floor untidy.

Her complaints became even more strident when I proposed that the two tortoise stoves would have to be lighted.

'What? In this 'ere mild spell? I'd say the Office'll have a thing or two to say, if we starts using coke this early. It's tax-payer's money – yours and mine, Miss Read – as pays for the coke.'

'Children can't work in chilly conditions,' I retorted.

'Chilly?' shrieked Mrs Pringle. 'They'll be passing out with heat stroke, more like.'

Nevertheless, the stoves were roaring away the next day, and we were all the better for it. Except, of course, Mrs Pringle, whose bad leg definitely took a turn for the worse.

Bob Willet, who much enjoys our little fights at a safe distance, approved of the stoves being lit.

'We're in for a funny old spell,' he forecast. 'You noticed how early the swallows went this year? They knows a thing or two. And them dratted starlings is ganging-up already. Flocks of 'em in them woods down Springbourne way, messing all over they are, doin' a bit of no good to the trees.'

'Well, what does that mean?'

'Something nasty in the weather to come. That's what

all that means. Birds know what to expect before we do. I'll lay fifty to one – that is if I was a betting man, which I'm not, as you well knows – as we'll have a rough day or two before long.'

I always take note of Bob Willet's prognostications. He is often right. But apart from the veering weathercock on St Patrick's church, all seemed reasonably normal on the weather front.

Or it seemed to be until midday on a fateful Wednesday. The dinner lady appeared, bearing a stack of steaming tins, and looking wind-blown.

'Coming over the downs was pretty rough,' she said. 'The wind's getting up. I heard a gale warning on the van radio.'

'I shouldn't take a lot of notice of that,' I said. 'Ever since that really dreadful gale two or three years ago, the weathermen have been only too anxious to give us gale warnings, and half the time they never materialize.'

'Well, we'll have to see. I know I'm going to be glad to get home today,' she replied, bustling away to her next port of call.

As the children tucked into macaroni cheese and sliced tomatoes, followed by apple tart and custard, the wind began to drum against the windows. Half an hour later, the gusts increased in intensity, and when I went across to the school house to see if all the doors were secure, I was blown bodily against my gate, and could barely get my breath.

It was at this stage that I saw the door of the boys' lavatory wrenched from its hinges and hurled towards the vicarage garden wall. I had a brief inspection of the school house exterior, decided that it was as safe as it could be in the circumstances, and struggled back to the school. Somehow the children must be evacuated to their homes before flying tiles and torn branches endangered us all.

Mrs Richards and I held a council of war as the windows rattled, and leaves and twigs spattered the panes.

Those who had a parent at home were dispatched at once, with strict instructions to run to safety and then to stay indoors. One or two others had telephones in their homes, and these we could forewarn about their children's early return. Several of them offered to pass on the message and mind neighbours' children with their own, until they returned from work.

It was lucky that the telephone lines were still intact, and I rang Mr Lamb at the Post Office to tell him that I was closing the school, and would he pass on the news.

'You're doing the right thing,' he assured me. 'I've just seen Roberts's tarpaulin blow off a straw stack across the road. Might have been a handkerchief the way it floated up!'

I also rang the vicar who said he would come at once

with his car, and house any odd children (I had plenty of those, I thought) until their parents could collect them. Looking at the school clock, I said that I hoped I had not brought him from his lunch.

'Only from banana blancmange,' he said, 'and I don't like that anyway.'

Poor Mr Partridge, I thought replacing the receiver. I should have liked to have offered him a slice of our own excellent apple tart, but as usual it had all been polished off.

By a quarter to two, almost all our little flock had departed, and I said that I would run Joseph Coggs and his two younger sisters to their house before I made my way home to Beech Green. It had not been possible to get in touch with the Coggs' parents, but Joe assured me that Dad was off work (no surprise, this) and Mum got back from helping out at Mrs Mawne's at two o'clock.

Before I locked up, I put things to rights at the school, windows and doors secured, and tortoise stoves battened down, and saw Mrs Richards off towards her home.

The car was quite difficult to handle when the gusts hit it on my way through the village, but I deposited my passengers as Arthur Coggs opened the door himself.

He thanked me civilly, and although there was a strong smell of beer, past and present, he seemed comparatively sober, and I left my charges with a clear conscience. I then battled my way to Mrs Pringle's and told that lady not to attempt to go up to the school.

'It can all wait,' I shouted to her outraged face at the kitchen window.

'But what about them stoves? We should never have lit 'em.'

'I've damped them down.'

'And the washing-up?'

'Stacked on the draining board. That'll keep. Just *don't go out!*'

At this stage the window was all but wrenched from her grip. She gave a gasp, slammed it to, and I returned to the car to make my way home.

It was a frightening journey. The road was strewn with leaves and quite large branches from the trees, which were bowing and bending in an alarming way. There was an ominous drumming in the air which I had never heard before, and it was as much as I could do to drive a steady course along a road lashed with this hurricane-force wind.

About halfway home, I rounded a bend to encounter a damaged car, two others and an ambulance whose lights were flashing in warning. Two men were just sliding a stretcher into the shelter of the ambulance, and when it moved off towards Caxley, I saw how badly damaged the small car was.

The branch of a beech tree, thicker than a man's leg, had obviously been torn from the trunk and landed on the unfortunate driver's Fiesta. The two men had manhandled the branch to the side of the road, but although cars could just about pass, it was going to cause a hazard, especially when darkness came.

I wound down my window to shout any offer of help, but the two men assured me that the garage men were on their way.

I had hardly driven another quarter of a mile when I found a fully grown tree straddling the road, blocking it completely. Panic began to seize me. What now?

It was beginning to get eerily dark which added to my uneasiness. Could I get down the little road to Spring-bourne, I wondered, and make a detour to my cottage?

It was a narrow lane, little used except by walkers, but I knew it well from my ambles with Miss Clare in earlier days. I turned the car, and made for the lane. It came out near the village of Springbourne, and from here I could take a similar narrow lane up the side of the downs beside a spinney which I hoped would shelter me from the worst of the wind.

I was in luck, but the screaming of the wind in the little wood was unnerving, and I was horrified to see that already quite large trees had been uprooted and were lying at all angles among the others. How the damage could ever be sorted out was going to be a sore problem, and how many small animals had already lost their homes, one could only guess.

I emerged into Beech Green half a mile from my home, and was thankful to see it again. After putting the car away, I stood in the shelter of the house to see what damage had occurred in the garden.

A lilac bush was already upended, and roofing felt on the garden shed was flapping dangerously. No doubt it would be ripped off completely before long, but I was too exhausted to bother much about it.

Miss Clare's ancient fruit trees, which Bob Willet proposed to take down, were swaying so violently that I doubted if they would survive another hour of this onslaught.

I struggled indoors, and looked for Tibby. There was no sign of him, and I was beginning to fear that he was outside somewhere in the maelstrom, when he emerged from under an armchair, attempting to look at ease. It was plain to see that Tibby was just as scared as I was, and it was good to have a fellow coward to keep me company.

I rang Mrs John, one of my nearest neighbours, to see if she and the children were safe, and although she sounded as frightened as I was she assured me that all was well.

'Mr Annett's closed his school as well,' she told me.

'The school buses came early, and let's hope everyone's got home.'

It was amazing to me that the telephone was still in order, but how long, I wondered, before the power cables came down and we should be without electricity?

I switched on the kettle while the going was good, and prudently looked out my old Primus stove, a torch and some candles. I checked that I had stocks of kindling wood, coal and logs in my house, and felt that I could do no more.

It seemed worse when darkness fell, and during the night I feared that the thatch might be ripped from its rafters, and the rattling windows might be torn out.

It was the incessant noise that was hardest to bear. The wind screamed and howled. It drummed and throbbed. Every now and again there would be a strange thump as something heavy, such as the wooden bird table hit the side of the house. Or there would be a metallic clanging as some unknown object, such as a dustbin or part of a corrugated iron roof collided with another.

I cowered beneath the bed clothes, glad to have Tibby at the end of the bed. What on earth would daylight show?

It showed chaos on a scale I could never have envisaged. Five of the condemned fruit trees were completely uprooted displaying great circles of chalky roots. The sixth leant at a dangerous angle. Only the old Bramley apple tree remained, and a sycamore and two lime trees. The border which Bob and Joseph had so carefully prepared was strewn with twigs and leaves, not to mention an upturned bucket and part of the shed roof.

It was hardly surprising to find that the electricity had gone, so I soon had my Primus going.

'Cornflakes for me,' I told Tibby, 'and Pussi-luv for you.'

Thus fortified, I rang the highways department to see if there was any chance of getting to school. A harassed individual told me that all roads within six or seven miles of Caxley were impassable, and 'to stay where you are, my duck'.

I rang Mr Partridge who sounded distraught and begged me not to venture out, and then Mr Lamb.

Although the wind had somewhat abated, it was still difficult to hear clearly as the line crackled. But Mr Lamb gave me more news of Fairacre damage.

'Tiles everywhere. Dozens off the church roof and the school, and your house, Miss Read, has had the chimney through the roof. You be thankful you weren't there. One of the big trees fell clean on it. Bob Willet's been up to have a look, and he's fair shaken, I can tell you. He's rigged up a tarpaulin to keep the worst of the weather out.'

He promised to let as many people as possible know that school would be closed until further notice, and Bob Willet had offered to put a notice on the school door if anyone should have managed to fight their way there. We could do no more, but I was desperately worried.

I spent the rest of the day trying to get some order out of the chaos outside, as the wind gradually died down.

Luckily the thatch had weathered the storm, and the house had stood up sturdily to the battering. The garden was such a shambles that I could do little there but rescue buckets, flower pots and even a water-butt which had all been shifted from their rightful homes.

It was not cold, but I lit a fire for comfort. Tibby and I both needed it.

As soon as possible, I intended to get over to Fairacre to see my school and the school house. I was very much worried by Mr Lamb's message. But at least the children should be safe. I dreaded to think what could have befallen them if the hurricane had arrived earlier.

Meanwhile, I rang friends and neighbours who all had hair-raising tales to tell, and then finally, Amy, at Bent.

To my surprise it was James who answered, and he sounded breathless.

'I thought it was the hospital,' he said.

'The hospital?'

'Amy's there. I thought there might be news of her.'

My heart sank. The sight of that battered car and the stretcher being put into the ambulance came back to me with devastating clarity.

'Tell me what's happened?' I quavered. I sat down. Somehow my legs had suddenly ceased to support me.

'She went into Caxley just before things really got too fierce, to take a load of clothes to the Red Cross shop. She packed the car in that side road, and struggled round with her parcel, but by that time things were getting pretty hairy.'

'So she wasn't in the car when whatever it is happened?'

The memory of yesterday's smashed car began to fade slightly, but what horrors would take its place?

'Tiles were sliding off roofs, and poor dear Amy caught one on the side of the head. Laid her out, of course, but the Red Cross ladies saw it happen and carried her into the shop, and did some much needed first-aid. They managed to get her to hospital, still unconscious, and bleeding like a stuck pig.'

'And how serious is it?'

'Not sure yet. They've stitched her ear on again.'

My inside, never really up to this sort of thing as a squeamish woman, gave a disconcerting somersault.

'But you haven't seen her yet?'

'I'm just off now, as a matter of fact. She came round last night, but our lane's blocked and we've a couple of trees down in front of the garage. I'm going to walk across the fields to the main road, and a friend there says he'll take me into Caxley. They've managed to clear the main road evidently, which is a stout effort, but I can't see how we're going to get Amy home until things are easier for travelling.'

'Well, I won't hold you up,' I said. 'My love as always to poor Amy, and I'll see her as soon as possible.'

'I'll keep you posted,' promised James. 'Now I must get into my wellingtons.'

This news, of course, haunted me for the rest of the day. Would pretty Amy be scarred? That she would face any affliction with enormous courage, I was well aware, but I hoped that nothing permanent would remain. A head wound, I gathered, could have some nasty consequences.

The wind had now died down, and across the south of England the gigantic task of clearing up was beginning. The highways' staff had worked heroically, and a great many of the main roads were clear enough to allow at least one-line traffic to proceed. There was still no electricity in our immediate area, but mercifully the telephones still seemed to be in order. I did my best to pull the worst of the debris in my garden to one side, and also walked among the rubble to see how the village of Beech Green had fared.

It was a sorry sight. Mr Annett's school roof had a dozen or so tiles gone, and someone's chicken house had been blown into the playground. The churchyard, where dear Dolly was buried, was almost covered with two fallen trees and scattered leaves and branches. The church itself, apart from a smashed window, appeared unscathed.

People were in a state of shock, scarcely able to believe what had happened in the space of twenty-four hours. But luckily there seemed to have been no casualties. George Annett had sent his pupils home early, as I had done, and the damage to his school had occurred during the night.

Tibby and I relied on the Primus stove for our cooking, and the open fire for warmth and comfort. But reading was impossible, I found, and I wondered yet again how people managed to read and write by candlelight years ago. Even my ancient Aladdin lamp scarcely threw enough light for reading, and I found myself listening to my battery-run radio for hours on end, before going early to bed. It was clear that our part of the country had suffered severely.

I rang the hospital the next morning to be told that Amy was 'as well as could be expected and quite comfortable'. (With an ear newly sewn on?) She was due to go home during the day, so obviously their lane at Bent was now passable.

To my relief, I found out too that it was now possible to get along our own road from Beech Green to Fairacre, but beyond that it was still blocked.

I got out the car and set off. The devastation on each side of the road was shocking. Fully-grown trees, mainly the beeches, had been plucked from the ground and lay with their roots, in great circles of chalk, pointing upward and outward. Where they had fallen they had brought other trees crashing down, and the work of restoring these woods to normality could not be imagined. Most of the fallen timber would have to remain where it was.

The thatch had been badly ripped away on a pair of cottages, and a corn stack had collapsed and the bales scattered for yards around. Garden fences seemed to have suffered most, for almost all lay flat on the ground. The insurance firms would be busy, I reflected. Thank goodness my new home was covered.

I drove into my old driveway, stopped the car and sat for a moment surveying the wreckage. One of the tall fir trees behind the house had fallen right across the roof and there was no sign of the substantial chimney. A gaping hole midway across the ridge of the roof, however, gave evidence that the missing chimney was somewhere inside the house.

The school building appeared to be only slightly damaged. Again, as in Beech Green school's case, a few tiles lay shattered in the playground, and I could see that the glass of the skylight was broken. But the lavatories across the playground were in a bad way. The doors had been ripped off and one or two of the china lavatory bowls were smashed.

I got out of the car to examine things more closely, and was surprised to see Bob Willet and two other young men emerge from the back door of the school house.

'Ah, I reckoned you'd be along soon,' said Bob. 'Fair old bluster, weren't it? You want to see inside? I've got the key here, but you'll have to watch your step. One of the stairs is busted.'

I followed him inside, and up the old familiar staircase. There was a large puddle on the landing, and my bedroom door leant at a drunken angle.

I stopped in the doorway and surveyed the chaos. The chimney, which indoors looked enormous, had crashed on to my bed, splintering it and the chair by it into match-wood. Soot had tumbled and blown everywhere, and the new paintwork was ruined. Rain had added to the damage, and my heart sank at the sight.

It was only when Bob Willet spoke again, that I realized how lucky I was to be alive.

'Good thing you moved to Beech Green,' he said. He nodded towards the crushed bed and its rags of filthy bedclothes. 'You wouldn't have stood much chance under that lot.'

I agreed, much shaken.

Bob studied me closely.

'We was just going back home for a cup of coffee. Alice has kept the Rayburn in all this time. Come and join us.'

I accompanied him thankfully.

15   Harvest and Havoc

I WENT to see how Mrs Pringle had fared, and found that lady had taken the onslaught of the elements as a personal affront.

'Washing blown clean off the line,' she told me. 'Mrs-Next-Door picked up some of it, but I'm still missing two pillow slips.'

She paused, and dropped her voice to a confidential whisper. 'But the worst of it is I've lost a pair of bloomers. Good winter ones, too, and I don't care to think of 'em being picked up by *some man*.'

'I don't suppose it would worry him,' I said cheerfully.

Mrs Pringle bridled. 'It's not his feelings I'm bothered about, it's mine. What do I say to him if a *man* brings them back?'

'Just thank him and leave it at that,' I said, rising to go.

Something looked different about her garden, I thought, looking through the kitchen window.

'Fred's workshop's gorn,' she said, following my gaze. 'Proper fussed he is. We found some bits of it round the back of Mr Roberts's barn. It was insured, but all his craft-work's gorn.'

I felt very sorry for Fred Pringle. The little shed at the end of the garden was really his haven from his wife. In it he found pleasure in constructing models made with matchsticks. The smell of glue, cardboard and thick paper always clung about Fred Pringle. His thick fingers had made hundreds of objects over the years, ranging from a model of St Patrick's church to innumerable calendars which always

hung fire at the local bazaars, as not everyone wants a
Swiss chalet, rather askew, or a rustic bridge, slightly uphill,
adorning their walls for a whole year. Nevertheless, Fred
continued to turn out dozens of articles, which might
appear useless to others, but which provided hen-pecked
Fred with pleasure and privacy. Now all that had gone,
blown away by that mighty rushing wind which had shattered so many homes as well as hopes.

'I hear as you might have been killed in your bed,' said
Mrs Pringle conversationally, as we went to the door. 'Bob
Willet said as it was all struck to kindling wood.' She
spoke with relish.

'That's so,' I replied. 'The chimney fell through the roof.'

'I never did hold with that bed being where it was,'
continued the lady primly. 'For one thing, anyone could
see you if they'd a mind, being in full view of the window.'

'Well, it only overlooked the playground,' I pointed out.
'By the time the children arrived I was downstairs anyway.'

'There's such a thing as Peeping Toms,' said she darkly.

Her manner changed as she opened the door. 'Ah well!
That's the end of that worry, isn't it?'

For once she sounded almost cheerful, and I made my
way to the gate.

News of the devastation became more general as roads
were cleared slowly, and people started to put things to
rights.

We seemed to have caught the severest onslaught, unlike
the earlier hurricane which had done most damage in the
counties south of us. Now we were all in need of builders,
electricians and plumbers, as well as haulage contractors,
timber merchants and any company, in fact, which owned
heavy shifting machinery.

The great landed estate which surrounded and included

the village of Springbourne, and was renowned for its splendid collection of trees, had lost eight hundred of them in the two days of violent weather. The ancient cedar tree in Fairacre's vicarage garden, under which so many tea parties, bazaar functions and the like had taken place, was now stretched across the lawns and flowerbeds. Nearby the vicar's greenhouse lay in ruins, and his newly-potted geranium and fuchsia cuttings lay among the shattered glass.

There were horrific tales of people trapped in their homes, cattle and sheep mutilated by flying debris, or stampeding panic-stricken into distant parts.

But, it seemed, the travellers had the worst of it. Cars had been crushed by falling timber, roads blocked, and electricity cables and telephone wires brought down. It was impossible, as I knew from my own short but nerve-racking journey home from school, to get to one's destination directly, and a good many traffic accidents had occurred through frightened drivers trying to get through impossibly narrow lanes, or even cart tracks, in order to get home.

Abandoned cars were everywhere, adding to the chaos, and it was amazing that there were so few outright fatalities. As it was, the casualty departments of the local hospitals had worked overtime, patching up the stream of people with cuts, bruises, broken limbs and head wounds.

That afternoon I took out my car, and drove through the wrecked countryside to see Amy who was now on her way to recovery in her own home.

I found her sitting on the sofa wearing a very fetching white turban of bandages. It was at a rather rakish angle and, as usual, she looked quite stunning, although rather paler than usual.

We greeted each other affectionately, and she assured me that she was practically back to normal.

'And there won't be much of a scar,' she added. 'I've been experimenting with my hair style, and I can cover the one by my hair-line, and the ear bit will be invisible any way.'

I asked, somewhat tentatively, if it had healed properly.

She began to laugh. 'I don't intend to harrow you by displaying my wounds like some Indian beggar. I expect James gave you some horrific description which upset you for hours. I know you so well.'

'I was a bit shattered to hear you had had your ear sewn on again,' I admitted.

'Too bad of James to put it like that,' she said severely. 'He knows what a coward you are. Actually, it was really not much more than a nick at the top, and only needed four or five stitches. A very neat little job someone did, and I'm eternally grateful.'

We spent a pleasant hour or so comparing notes on our respective horror stories, and she was suitably impressed by my tale of the roof damage at Fairacre school house.

'Does this mean that it will be a total loss? Will it be worth repairing?'

'Oh, I should think so. I know Wayne Richards has been asked to come and look at the job, though when that will be, heaven alone knows. He's up to his eyes in emergency jobs, but he's promised to make good the lavatories so that school can open again. I imagine he'll inspect the school house then.'

'Heavens, you were lucky!'

'I know it. I have a lot to thank dear Dolly for, and now she has virtually saved my life. The thing that really irks me is the thought of all that wasted time and energy in decorating upstairs earlier this year.'

I told her about Eve and Horace's interest in the little house, and she looked thoughtful.

'Why don't they try for one of those new ones if they really want to live in Fairacre?'

'Too expensive for them. And too large too, I expect. After all, they have no family.'

'Well, they could soon put that right if they got a move on,' said Amy. 'Mind you, they must be fortyish, so there isn't a lot of time to spare. These professional women do run it a bit fine these days when it comes to babies.'

'Two incomes no kids,' I said quoting Bob Willet.

Amy sighed. 'I wish I'd had the sort of inside that coped with a nice string of babies, but there you are. So *unfair*, isn't it?'

'We live in an unfair world,' I told her. 'Shall I make us a cup of tea to cheer us up?'

'A splendid idea,' said Amy.

It was ten days before Fairacre School could open again, and I spent the time trying to tidy my own house and garden at Beech Green, and visiting the school to see how the repairs were getting on.

Wayne Richards had done a mammoth job on the school

itself, coping with roof tiles, the smashed skylight and damage to the porch. But the biggest job was putting the lavatories to rights, and work was held up by trying to get new lavatory pans which appeared to be in short supply.

'Lord knows why,' said Wayne, sounding exasperated. 'I can't believe the gale smashed many lavatory pans. It's my belief the plumbers at Caxley are finding it a fine excuse for shilly-shallying.'

'We can't start school until they are there,' I pointed out.

'Don't you worry. You'll get the first I can lay my hands on, and that's a promise.'

His assessment of the damage to the school house roof was less bad than we had imagined, much to the vicar's and the other governors' relief. Horrific though the damage looked, the rafters could be replaced, and a rather less massive chimney erected above the repaired roof. The decorating would have to be done all over again, but I was told that it would not involve me in any more expense, for which I was relieved.

The repairs would take some time, but as there was no one living there now, it was not considered such an emergency job as so many others. A stout tarpaulin was fixed over my poor little home for so many years, and it had to wait its turn in the repair queue.

'It will definitely be put on the market then,' the vicar told me. 'And as for the school —' His voice died away.

'That's going on, full steam ahead,' I told him, with a conviction I did not wholly feel.

'Of course,' he agreed, rallying slightly. 'Why, of course!'

We had hardly got back into school routine, it seemed to me, when half-term was upon us.

Of course, I had to hear the children's accounts of the great tempest, some so hair-raising that I was forced to conclude that many of my flock had more imagination than I had realized.

However, as a resourceful teacher, I made good use of all this stimulating material; and essays, illustrations and even a long poem had 'The Storm' as subject matter. The fact that one of Mr Roberts's cows had been lifted from its field and deposited in John Todd's bedroom, and that one of the young Coggs twins had seen God sitting on a cloud directing the whirlwind had to be put in perspective, but Ernest's account of finding washing from someone's line entangled on the hedge near his garden sounded plausible. The fact that a pair of lady's bloomers was among these items made me uneasily aware that they could have been Mrs Pringle's.

Ernest's house certainly lay in the path of any wind blowing from the Pringle domain, but I thought it prudent to keep my suspicions to myself.

Luckily, no one had been hurt, although the cat from 'The Beetle and Wedge' had vanished, and Patrick reckoned it was 'stone-dead under that barn door as blew off what Mr Roberts should have lifted, but never done it'.

I was about to unravel this sentence when arguments arose around the class giving various heated conjectures about the fate of the unfortunate cat, and I let the grammar lesson go. There is a limit to a teacher's endurance.

The day before we broke up for half-term, we went over to the church to take part in dressing it ready for Harvest Festival. This is an annual pleasure, and we share the work with experienced ladies from the floral society, and such stalwarts as Mrs Partridge and Mrs Mawne who do their best to keep everyone in order.

The more ambitious floral ladies are given to making

arrangements with little tickets on them saying such things as: 'The Earth's Bounty' or 'From a Thankful Heart'. These are usually set out in rustic baskets with a lot of cornstalks and highly-polished apples and, although to the layman's eye they look much of a muchness, there is a great deal of unladylike jostling for major positions in the church.

Fortunately, the school children know their place, and traditionally keep to such modest decorating as a row of carrots and turnips along one window sill, a tasteful display of upended marrows round the base of the lectern, and a giant pumpkin which is allowed pride of place in the church porch when the ladies have lined the stone bench there with moss and finished adorning it with such sophisticated articles as wreaths of bryony, sprays of blackberries, and corn dollies.

The vicar was doing his duty by commending all the work. I caught him looking doubtfully at one of the floral ladies' efforts which consisted of a basin of flour, some wheat ears and some sprays of oats, and which bore the label 'Our Daily Bread'.

'My grandpa,' said one of the children, grandson of a local baker, 'could have given you a *real loaf* to put there.'

The vicar looked as though he heartily agreed with this sensible suggestion, but as the floral lady was within earshot he contented himself with a smile, and a kindly pat on the boy's head.

The church had got off lightly in the storm, although one of the stained-glass windows had been damaged. It had been put up about 1860 in honour of some local worthy, and I had never liked it. The colours reminded me of those in the paint-box of my childhood, Crimson Lake, Prussian Blue and Gamboge. Furthermore, it made that side of the church very dark, and I had often thought how much more suitable a clear window would have been.

'I suppose we shall have to repair it,' said the vicar sadly, 'but they are having difficulty in matching the glass.'

'Perhaps it could be replaced by a plain glass window,' I said daringly.

'That would be a *very* nice idea,' said the vicar beaming, 'but it might offend the family.'

'Are there any about?'

'A step-grandson, I believe, in Papua, New Guinea.'

'Is he likely to worry?'

The vicar sighed. 'I'm afraid we can't risk it. We must restore this one as best we can.'

He gave me a conspiratorial smile, and I went to inspect the children's artistic endeavours.

On Sunday the church looked magnificent. All the harvest decorations glowed against the ancient stone of the walls. The brass lectern shone with extra-zealous rubbing, and the silver on the altar shone in a ray of sunlight from the south windows.

Even more heartening was the size of the congregation. We country folk enjoy Harvest Festivals. For us it is the culmination of the year, when we can see, smell, touch and taste the fruits of the twelve months' labour. It is significant that St Patrick's church is even fuller for this festival than at Easter or Christmas. The hymns too are well known and loved, and we sing them lustily, our eyes on the marrows and apples from cottage gardens, and the grapes and peaches from the greenhouses of local wealthy families.

We all joined robustly in singing our favourite harvest hymn:

> We plough the fields and scatter
> The good seed on the land,
> But it is fed and wor-hor-tered
> By God's almighty hand.

Looking around the congregation it occurred to me that there were probably only half a dozen or so among us who had really ploughed a field. There might be rather more who had scattered seeds, if only a few sprinklings of hardy annuals in the flower border, or even some mustard and cress on a wet piece of flannel in a saucer.

No matter, we enjoyed our singing, although when I heard Mr Roberts behind me booming out the line, 'The winds and waves obey Him', I wondered if he questioned the obedience of the elements after all we had suffered so recently.

The vicar gave his usual homely address about being thankful for the fruits of the earth, and the satisfaction of seeing the results of our labours, which would be going to the local hospital in the next few days, and we all streamed out into the autumn sunshine after the closing hymn and blessing, mightily content.

It was one of those autumn days, crisp and clear, when the sky has a pellucid quality which is rarely seen in other seasons. The hedge maple had turned a brilliant yellow and the beech trees above the hedges were a deeper gold. A few hardy summer wild flowers such as knapweed, yarrow, and cranesbill still starred the verges and banks, brave survivors of summer heat and the ferocity of the recent storm.

Reminders of it still littered the countryside, and no doubt would continue to do so for many months to come. Some of the copses were criss-crossed with fallen trees and would be impossible to clear. Fine avenues of beeches and lime trees showed sad gaps where full-grown trees had toppled like nine-pins, and loved landmarks, like the vicar's ancient cedar tree, were now no more.

But despite the wreckage, the autumn scene on this vivid Sunday was beautiful. It gave one comfort and hope to see the modest flowers, the blazing autumn woods, and to hear the lark singing above the immemorial downs.

There may be many changes in Fairacre, I thought, but the seasons come round in their appointed time, steadfast and heartening to us all.

It so happened that it was one of the few bright days we had that autumn.

November wound along in its gloomy way, and the tortoise stoves at the school were certainly needed to keep out the chilly dampness.

In no time at all, it seemed, Christmas loomed. Mrs Richards insisted on coaching her class in the mid-European dances which she so enjoyed. The sound of hand-clapping and foot-stamping, never entirely co-ordinated, nearly drove me mad, but I managed to refrain from outright complaint.

'Makes a lot of *dust*,' said Mrs Pringle gloomily, 'all that banging about on them floorboards. They're not up to it after a hundred years. Besides, there's some as says there's a well under that room.'

'A *well*? There can't be!'

Mrs Pringle drew in two of her chins, folded her arms and looked portentious.

'Bob Willet's uncle, dead now of the quinsy, always maintained the school had a well. This 'ere room of yours was the only schoolroom then, and the children used to get their water from the well just next door. When they built on the infants', they covered it up.'

'But that's nonsense,' I protested. 'Both rooms were built at the same time, and in any case, why cover up the well if it was in use? There was plenty of space to build an adjoining room elsewhere.'

'I'm simply telling you what Bob Willet's old uncle said,

and a more truthful God-fearing man you couldn't wish to meet in a day's march. Went to chapel twice on Sundays regular, and played in the Salvation Army band in Caxley if they was a cornet player short.'

'I'm not doubting his morals,' I replied, 'but I think he was mistaken, that's all. I just can't believe it.'

'Of course, if you're calling me a *liar* —' began Mrs Pringle, getting very red in the face.

'Don't be silly —' I broke in. 'It's not you I'm criticizing, it's just so obvious that this present building was all done at the same time. You can see that by the foundations and footings, and if there had been a well, then it would have been filled in, that is if they had been so stupid as to want to build over it.'

Mrs Pringle began to limp heavily about the room giving sharp little slaps at the partition with her duster. I let her get on with it. Sometimes she sees fit to change the subject when she is getting the worst of it.

Today was a case in point.

'Our Minnie,' she said, in a slightly less belligerent tone, 'left Ern last week.'

'Good heavens! For good? How will she manage with all those children?'

'That's her headache, not mine,' said my old adversary, sinking heavily on to a front desk. 'She had a bit of a turn-up with him last week over some papers the kids had crayoned on. Seems it was something about the poll tax he had to answer. He took his belt to Basil, and Minnie flew at him.'

'Oh dear! What happened then?'

'Well, you know she's never really broke with that Bert of hers, and she caught the next bus to Caxley to say she'd settle in with him, as he's always been so loving and that.'

'What about Basil and the younger ones?'

'She took 'em too, and a bit of money Ern always puts by regular for the electric and that, in a tobacco tin. Bert was out when she got there, and when he got back about nine he wasn't best pleased to see that lot on his doorstep.'

I could understand it.

'He took 'em in overnight, but told Minnie she couldn't stop with him. They had a blazing row, I gather, and our Minnie said she dursn't go back to Ern because of nicking the money, as well as not really liking the fellow much.'

'But she *married* him!' I interrupted.

'Well, yes, I suppose she did, but girls do funny things and then live to regret it. Our Minnie's never been what you'd call *steady*.'

That I could thoroughly endorse, but held my tongue.

'So there she was,' continued Mrs Pringle, 'on the streets of Caxley with them three kids next morning when Bert went off to work. At her wits' end she was.'

And that would not take long was my private comment, but I let Mrs Pringle, now in her stride, continue with the saga.

'Give Bert his due, he did let them have breakfast there, egg and bacon too, before he locked the door on 'em all, and left them to fend for themselves.'

'So she's back home again?' I said, one eye on the school clock, and one ear on a lot of shouting in the playground. I should have to stop this enthralling tale very soon.

'She went to the police,' said Mrs Pringle, seeing through my endeavours to hurry up the narrative. 'They was uncommon nice for policemen, and took her back to Springbourne, and had a word with Ern before he set off for work. He's got a few odd jobs to do these days. Not much, mind you, but it all helps.'

'What did the police say?'

'That,' said Mrs Pringle primly, 'is not for me to say.

But I *gather*, only *gather*, mark you, that they pointed out that Minnie was his wife, and that they didn't want to have to come out again to sort out any domestic disputes, and the courts had quite enough trouble as it was, so he'd better let bygones be bygones. And with that they left.'

'So all's well?'

'Not really. As I say, she's liable to fly off the handle any time as far as I can make out, which is why I told you.'

'Oh?'

'It's quite on the cards that our Minnie will be coming to ask you for a job at your house, and I think you should be warned.'

'Thank you,' I said, my heart sinking. 'It was good of you to warn me.'

'Of course, whether you believe what I've told you, or not, is your affair, Miss Read. I've been called a liar once this morning, so I'll say no more.'

Before I could get my breath she made for the lobby – and there was no hint of a limp on this occasion.

16   Gloomy Days

THE end of the Christmas term is always hectic. As well as our Christmas concert, it is traditional to invite parents and friends to tea in the schoolroom, and the children enjoy acting as hosts and hostesses on this occasion.

Alice Willet made her usual enormous Christmas cake, presents were distributed from the Christmas tree, carols sung, and we all streamed home after the vicar's customary blessing.

To say that I was tired, as I went back to the haven of my new home, is an understatement. Advancing age, I told myself, as I went up to bed before nine o'clock.

But, on comparing notes with others during the welcome holiday, I found that this exhaustion was general, and we started to blame the aftermath of the recent hurricane as well as the short dark days, for our lassitude. 'Delayed shock', we told each other, and felt all the better for finding a solution, even if it were a wrong one, for our inertia.

I spent a few days with my cousin Ruth, who could not travel to Beech Green as her car was laid up, leaving Tibby in the care of Mrs John. I looked out some redundant clothing for a future jumble sale, made marmalade, re-read some of Trollope's Barchester novels, and had one or two modest tea parties.

During this gently recuperative period Amy came over from Bent. She had quickly recovered from her injuries, and had no scars which were visible, but she too looked tired.

'I'm a bit worried about James,' she said, when I inquired after her health. 'Mind you, he's often rather low after Christmas. I think he suddenly realizes he's spent too much money.'

'Well, that goes for all of us, doesn't it?'

'He's so idiotically generous. He always buys me a piece of jewellery, for one thing, and I dread to think what this year's wrist watch cost. And the office people always get fantastic presents as well as their usual bonus.'

'And what news of Brian?'

'That's funny. We invited him for Christmas Day, but he rang to say he couldn't manage it. No reason given. James seemed very upset, and was quite sharp with me. Had I written a *really welcoming* letter? Could I have offended him in some way? And then a lot of guff about how sensitive Brian was, and how humiliated he felt about his broken marriage, and so on. Really, at times I could *slap* James, he's so childish.'

'We're not allowed to slap children these days,' I observed, 'although John Todd had a fourpenny one from me on the last day of term, when I found him picking at the icing on the Christmas cake.'

'I should have given him an eightpenny one,' said Amy approvingly.

We turned to other topics.

'I saw Horace and Eve over Christmas, and they were devastated to hear about the school house. Any news?'

'Not yet. It is still sheltering beneath its tarpaulin, and a dreadful noise that makes too when the wind gets round the south-west. It flaps and rumbles. Quite alarming, I think, but Wayne Richards assures me it is as safe as houses – which seems an unfortunate comparison in the circumstances.'

'Any more Fairacre excitements?'

'Jane Winter is expecting, and not too pleased about it. Sir Barnabas has begged Miriam to return to the office while Jane's away, but Miriam's already in the throes of getting her new agency going, so she has had to refuse.'

'And my friend Mrs Pringle?'

'Flourishing like a green bay tree,' I told her, and added the news of Minnie Pringle's domestic troubles for good measure.

'Has Minnie asked for a job here yet?'

'Fingers crossed,' I replied, '*no!*' And if she does my heart will be as flint.'

'What a tough old woman you are!' laughed Amy. 'When you are dead and gone you will be remembered as the Stony-hearted Spinster of Fairacre.'

'I may not be remembered at all,' I pointed out.

Amy looked serious. 'Do you ever think about such things? About dying, and so on?'

'Frequently. Particularly since Dolly went. She's one of those that will be remembered, that's for sure.'

'I suppose so. It's one of the things that being childless upsets me. After all, you live on in your children, really. And the work you leave behind, I suppose. It must be a great comfort to artists and furniture-makers and so on to know that people will enjoy their work and remember them for years. I shall leave no children, and mighty little worth remembering in the way of work.'

'Cheer up, Amy,' I rallied her. 'You'll leave lots of happy memories among your friends. Me, for one!'

'Thanks,' said Amy. 'I presume that you imagine I shall pop off before you. I tell you here and now that my relatives, on both sides, totter on to their nineties, and my Uncle Benjamin stuck it out to a hundred and one and got his telegram from the Queen.'

'Good for him. And for you, of course.'

'Tell you what, though,' continued Amy, 'we all seem to go deaf after ninety.'

'Never mind. That's a long way ahead, and they do the most marvellous things with hearing aids these days. Do you think a cup of coffee would keep you going?'

'Definitely,' said Amy.

Term began with grey skies and a wicked wind from the east. Even Mrs Pringle agreed that the tortoise stoves were needed, and a great comfort they were as the draughts from the skylight and under the ancient doors whistled around the schoolroom.

Mrs Richards had a very heavy cold, and was accompanied everywhere with a box of tissues. I had earache, no doubt from the malevolent skylight above my head, and most of the children seemed to have coughs or colds or both.

'January,' I told Mrs Richards at playtime, 'should be done away with. Christmas well behind us, and only gloomy months ahead.'

'I agree,' she said, 'but Bob Willet says it will get warmer once the snow comes.'

'Is that his forecast?'

'That's right. He told me we'll get a fall before the week's out.'

'Well, I hope he's wrong this time,' I replied.

But of course he was not.

By Friday afternoon the first flakes began to fall, much to the delight of the children who were up and down like jacks-in-boxes to catch a glimpse of the weather through the high windows.

By playtime the flakes were whirling fast, and it was impossible to see the school house across the playground, so thickly were the snowflakes descending. The coke pile was covered in a mantle of white. The branches of the trees were beginning to sag with their burden, and the fence tops and hedges looked as though they had been decorated with sugar icing.

I closed school early and went into the lobby to see that each child was well wrapped up before going out into the elements. Most of them were well protected in anoraks and woolly scarves, but as always the Coggs children were poorly shod and had no gloves to protect their hands.

'I'll run you home,' I said, surveying their shabby shoes which would soak up snow within three minutes. They exchanged happy smiles as I saw off the others, and then locked up.

As I packed them into the car, I looked up at my old home. The tarpaulin was invisible below its covering of snow. The downstairs windows were plastered with the enshrouding whiteness, and the scene was enough to wring the heart. Never had I seen the little house looking so forlorn and neglected. Could it ever be repaired and made into a home again, I wondered?

My journey home, after dropping the Coggs children was uneventful, although the snow was still falling heavily. One thing, I told myself, tomorrow was blessed Saturday, and there would be no need to face an early journey to school.

I set about my usual preparations for bad weather while the light remained, bringing in extra coal and logs, looking out candles and my trusty Primus stove, in case we had a power cut. I left a spade in the porch in case I had to dig my way out the next morning, and I went early to bed.

It was good to get between the sheets, nicely warmed with a hot bottle, and the fact that the wind had started to howl round the cottage only emphasized the snugness of my bedroom beneath the thatched roof.

Let the elements rage, I thought drowsily, as I nestled deeper beneath the bedclothes!

I ought not to have been so complacent. When morning light came, I was appalled at the amount of snow which surrounded my home, and stretched in billowing waves and whorls of whiteness, as far as the eye could see.

The wind had whipped the snow into enormous drifts. Hedges had disappeared. Garden walls and gates were engulfed, and against some of the nearby houses the snow was so deep that it was within a few feet of the upstairs windows in places. There must have been a fearsome blizzard during the night, and I hastened downstairs to see how my house had fared.

I was fortunate in that the wind had piled the snow at the side of my home, and with the help of the spade I could clear a way out of both front and back doors, although I doubted if I should ever be able to dig a path to my gate.

An eerie light flooded the house, partly reflected from the snow, and partly from those windows which were plastered with it and filtered the morning light.

I soon had my kettle on, and was thankful that the electricity had not failed. But I was perplexed that Tibby had not appeared. Surely that comfort-loving animal had not ventured out during the night?

The weather men gave gloomy forecasts of more snow to come although the northern half of the kingdom would come off worst, evidently. As it was, I found my own attempts at snow-clearing later that morning were quite exhausting enough.

I remembered Dolly telling me about a very old man she had known as a child at Beech Green. He was the grandfather of her close friend Emily Davis, and had been caught in the great blizzard of 1881. By the time he was discovered, many hours later, he was suffering from severe frost-bite and lost some fingers. Ever afterwards, Dolly told me, he wore a black leather glove on the maimed hand, and it was this that fascinated her. I only hoped that we were not in for the same length of horrific conditions as that memorable winter.

It was good to see the snow plough chugging along during the morning. There was something to be said for mechanized transport, I thought, waving to the men as they passed by slowly. In 1881, even the stout shire horses had to remain in their stables while the weather was at its worst. Today, a poor benighted traveller trapped in the snow, as Emily's grandfather had been so long ago, would be rescued by a helicopter, and whisked into hospital. Change, I thought, was often deplored. In these conditions it was welcome.

By mid-morning, there was still no sign of Tibby and I began to get alarmed. There were no tell-tale footprints around the house, but then they would soon have been obliterated in last night's conditions.

I rang the Annetts and also Mrs John in the hope that they had seen him, but there was no help there. I called until I was hoarse, hoping to hear an answering mew from some over-looked shelter, but nothing happened. I had gloomy visions of the poor animal entombed beneath the blanket of snow like John Ridd's sheep in *Lorna Doone*. How long could a cat survive without food in such a situation? One thing, Tibby had plenty of surplus fat to live on, as Bob Willet was fond of pointing out, but would the cold kill him?

I began to get more and more agitated as the hours passed, and remembered all the captivating ways of my truant, and how much his companionship meant to me. By the time early evening began to cast its shadows, I was near despair. At that moment, the lights began to flicker ominously, and I decided that it would be as well to delve into the recesses of the cupboard under the stairs to find the ancient Aladdin lamp stored there.

I undid the door, and bent double to locate the lamp in the gloom. A lazy chirruping sound met me, and Tibby emerged sleepily and greeted me with much affection. Relief overcame my initial irritation with the maddening animal. Why had there been no response to my anguished cries? Why, last night of all nights, had he decided to sleep in that cupboard? I suppose I must have left the door ajar on my first visit there for candles, and then automatically shut it in passing later on. In any case, it was good to see my old friend, and a double portion of Pussi-luv vanished in a twinkling.

Snow fell again that night, and the paths so exhaustingly cleared were white again. The roads from most of the villages into Caxley were partially open, but around Fairacre itself, I gathered, the drifts were still deep. It looked as though, yet again, my school would have to remain closed.

I rang the office first thing on Monday morning to get an overall picture. It was not very encouraging.

'All schools closed for the next three days,' I was told. 'The school buses and the dinner vans are going to have great difficulty in getting around. Some can't even get out of the depot yet. We'll be in touch on Wednesday, and simply hope that the thaw will have come by then.'

I talked to Mr Lamb and the vicar on the telephone, and they assured me that everyone possible would be told the position.

Gerald Partridge sounded unusually despondent. Snow had seeped into his beloved church and ruined a pile of new hymn books. Even worse, the organ was found to be thoroughly damp from some hitherto unsuspected leak from the roof, and repairs to it could cost a fortune.

'And what about the school and the school house?' I asked him, hoping to deflect him from his own worries.

'I'm afraid I haven't been into the school. Bob Willet has been unable to get up to it yet, there is such a great snow drift in the lane, but I struggled out with Honey to just behind your old home and it looks none the worse for the snow. The tarpaulin has stood up wonderfully against the weather.'

I said I was relieved to hear it.

'Incidentally,' he continued, 'the diocese has definitely decided to put it on the market as soon as it is habitable again. It should be ready by about Easter, if all goes well.'

'Well, it's a dear little house as I know. It should sell, I think.'

'One wonders. Or will it be the *third* empty house in Fairacre? I hear that the price of those two new ones has dropped again. It is definitely not the time to try and sell one's property.'

'A buyer's market. Isn't that the expression?'

'I believe so. But there seem to be no buyers about. I suppose they can't *buy*, until they have *sold* their own.'

'There are such people as first-time buyers,' I told him, thinking of Horace and Eve. 'Perhaps they'll turn up in time.'

'One can only hope,' agreed the vicar. But he sounded very unhopeful as I rang off.

We were closed for a week. It was a frustrating time for everyone. Two days of the seven we were without electricity, and I found that half a day coping with oil stoves, candles and matches, was quite enough for the small amount of pioneering spirit I possessed, especially as the only source of hot water was a kettle lodged on the Primus stove which took forever, it seemed, to come to the boil.

After that, I was heartily fed up with automatically and vainly switching on in every room I entered, only to be frustrated yet again.

The snow plough had made me thankful for mechanized transport, and now I realized all too clearly how much we took for granted in our all-electric houses. It was probably salutory to be reminded of our dependence on this source of power, but it did nothing to improve our tempers.

I found myself using methods of cooking, lighting and heating which Dolly's mother had used daily in this self-same cottage years before. The open fire had to be kept going with coal and logs, and I left the sitting-room door open at night so that some heat would penetrate into the chilly bedrooms.

The lamps had to be trimmed and filled, and the candles replaced. I even rolled up an old rug to stuff against the bottom of the outside door to keep out the wicked draughts, and wished I had the straw-filled sausage of Victorian times to do the job, as Dolly had described.

When at last the power returned, we were all mightily grateful to those men who had restored it, and we counted our blessings with thankful hearts.

It was quite a relief to return to school.

Bob Willet had done a magnificent job in clearing the playground, and Mrs Pringle gave me a graphic account of the state of her beloved tortoise stoves after a week's neglect.

'They was that damp and mildewy you could've written your name on 'em. And all down one side there was the beginning of rust where the water had run along a beam from that dratted skylight, and dropped down on to my poor stove. We'll have to get another load of blacklead

from the Office, and if they gives you any hanky-panky, Miss Read, just let me speak to them.'

I promised to do that, rather looking forward to such an encounter. Mrs Pringle, in defence of her stoves, is a formidable figure, and I trembled for any of the staff at the Caxley Education Office who questioned her demands. What can they know of blacklead, who only red tape know?

The children were full of tall stories about the snow and the havoc it had caused. Patrick told us that his little brother fell in a drift near Mr Mawne's and they only found him because he was wearing a red bobble hat and the bobble stuck up from the snow.

Ernest then capped this with a long rigmarole about his father's bike which was hidden for days by the front gate. But when John Todd tried to make us believe that he had rescued Mr Roberts's house cow single-handed from a snow drift in a neighbouring field, I thought it was time to put a stop to matters. Imagination is one thing; downright lying is another.

'To your desks,' I ordered briskly. 'We'll have a really stiff mental arithmetic test.'

I was not popular.

17   Minnie Pringle Lends a Hand

WE were all very thankful to tear off JANUARY from our calendars and to look hopefully at FEBRUARY.

The days were now perceptibly longer, and I took my first walk-after-tea of the year, in the light. The catkins were a cheerful sight, fluttering from the bare hedgerows, and the bulbs in the garden were poking through. A clump of early yellow irises were already in flower. I had given the tiny bulbs to Dolly some years earlier, and she had planted them under the shelter of the thatch where they thrived.

The birds were busy, bustling about, full of self-importance as they scurried about their courting.

Life was beginning to look more hopeful after all we had endured from gales, snow and flooding.

The children's coughs and colds faded. At playtime they could get into the playground for exercise and fresh air, and altogether I began to enjoy a period of relaxation and to make plans for a variety of outdoor pursuits in the months ahead.

Alas for my euphoria!

As one might expect, I was about to have my comfortable rug snatched from under my feet, and of course it was inevitable that Mrs Pringle would do the snatching.

She caught me in the lobby as soon as I arrived. I might have guessed from her unusually cheerful face that something was up.

'My doctor,' she began importantly, 'though a poor tool

in many ways, as well you know, Miss Read, says I'm to
have a thorough check-up on my leg, and I've got to go to
The Caxley for an X-ray.'

'Oh dear! When?'

'Friday. Not till the afternoon, so I can do the washing-
up. But he says I may have to lay up for a bit.'

'Well, there it is. I'm glad you told me. Are you in pain?'

The reply was as expected.

'I'm *always* in pain, as well you know. Not that it stops
me doing my duty. Never has! My mother used to say to
me: "Maud, you are your own worst enemy with that
conscience of yours. Can't you ever *spare* yourself?" And I
used to say: "No, mother. I'm just made that way. What
needs to be done, I must do, cost what it may in time and
trouble." And it's the same today.'

'It does you credit,' I said, paying a tribute to this
eulogy of self-satisfaction. 'Let's hope the X-ray shows
nothing seriously wrong.'

Mrs Pringle limped about rather more heavily than usual
while the hospital mills ground their slow way through her
data. The results were that she should rest the leg for a
fortnight and then have another examination.

'Don't worry,' I said, on hearing the news, 'we can
easily manage for two weeks. I believe Alice Willet might
sweep up, and Bob has always been helpful about the
stoves in an emergency.'

'If you let Bob Willet lay so much as a finger on my
stoves,' said Mrs Pringle, puffing up like an outraged
turkey, 'I shall give in my notice.'

I have heard this threat so often that I take it in my
stride, but I felt sorry for my old adversary in her present
afflictions, and simply said that I'd see Bob only *filled* and
did not attempt to *polish* her two idols.

Unfortunately, Alice Willet had promised to go and stay

with a sister who herself was just out of hospital, so it looked as though we should have to muddle along on our own.

'Of course, our Minnie could come,' said Mrs Pringle. She sounded doubtful, and with good reason. We both know Minnie's limitations. 'She's not a bad little cleaner – if watched.'

'Oh, I don't think it's as desperate as that,' I replied, wondering if that could not have been expressed more tactfully. 'I'll look around,' I added hastily.

But in the end, when Mrs Pringle had taken to her bed and sofa for the allotted time, it had to be Minnie who came to provide help and havoc in unequal portions to Fairacre School.

During Mrs Pringle's absence, I took to staying on after school to supervise Minnie's activities, and to protect the more vulnerable of the school's properties from her on-slaught.

I discovered that she was comparatively safe with such things as desk tops, window sills and the floors. Anything horizontal presented little difficulty, and I felt she was really getting quite proficient with broom and duster. But vertical surfaces seemed to defeat her. She took to sweeping a broom down the partition between the two rooms, bring-ing down anything pinned thereon such as the children's artwork, pictures cut from magazines and the like.

'Well, look at that!' she cried in amazement, gazing at the fluttering papers on the floor. I helped to pick them up, and stopped her attacking another wall with her broom.

On one occasion, in my temporary absence, she tried her hand at window-cleaning. She had begun an energetic attack with a rather dirty wet rag, well coated with Vim,

and was fast producing a frosted-glass effect when I arrived back.

She was anxious 'to have a good go', as she put it, 'at Auntie's stoves', but knowing what I should have to face on Auntie's return, I was adamant that she should not touch the stoves. In fact, I did my poor best to clean them myself, knowing the withering scorn which I should receive in due course from Mrs Pringle, but at least that was better than risking Minnie's ministrations with, possibly, more Vim, or even metal polish, which would be impossible to get off.

The fact that Minnie was unable to read complicated matters, as the directions for use on the cleaning packets meant nothing to her. Neither could she tell the time, so she relied on me to see her off the premises before I locked up.

Nevertheless, the hour after school which we spent together at our labours, had its compensations, and I grew daily more fascinated by Minnie's account of her love life which was considerably more interesting than my own.

I had not liked to ask about her marital affairs after Mrs Pringle had given me the account of Minnie's flight to Bert in Caxley, and his refusal to let her stay. But Minnie blithely rattled away as she dashed haphazardly about the schoolroom with her duster.

'Ern was a bit nasty with me for a time,' she admitted. 'I s'pose he's jealous of Bert.' This was said with some satisfaction.

'Naturally,' I responded. 'You married him. He expects you to live with him.'

'Oh, I don't see why!' said Minnie, standing stock still in her surprise. A troubled look replaced her usual mad grin. 'I knew Bert long afore I met Ern. He bought me some lovely flowers when I was up The Caxley having my Salopians done.'

I decided against correcting Salopian to Fallopian, and to ignore the past use of the verb 'to buy' when it should have been the past tense of the verb 'to bring'. I get quite enough of that sort of thing in school hours, and I did not propose to do overtime.

'But Minnie,' I pointed out, concentrating on the moral issue, 'if you made a solemn contract at your marriage you should keep it. You are Ern's wife, after all. You married him because you wanted to, I take it.'

'Oh, no!' said Minnie, smiling at such a naive suggestion. 'I married Ern because he had a council house, and my Mum was that fed up with us under her feet, so that's *really* why.'

I must say, I found this honesty rather refreshing. Plenty of people with greater advantages, both mental and material, than Minnie, marry for the desire for property rather than passion, and who was I to criticize?

'Mind you,' went on Minnie, taking a swipe at the black-board and nearly knocking it from the easel, 'that council house doesn't half take a bit of cleaning. I really like my Mum's better. Life don't always work out right, do it, Miss Read?'

And I agreed.

Now that the weather had returned to normal, the repairs to the school house went on apace.

Wayne Richards enjoyed visiting his two workmen, and also gave a hand himself. The fact that his wife was close at hand, and that he shared our school tea-breaks seemed to please the young man, and we found him good company.

'Take about three weeks,' he told us, standing with his back to us and looking out at the repair work through the schoolroom window. The mug steamed in his hand, and he did not appear to be in any great hurry to leave us. I began to find that, on the mornings he shared our refreshment, it was I who had to shoo him out so that I could get on with my work.

Every now and again the vicar called to note progress, and the children had to be discouraged from purloining pieces of putty, odd bits of wood and roof tile, and curly wood-shavings which the wags among them used as ringlets fixed over their ears. At least it made a change from the coke pile which was their usual illicit means of finding ex-ercise.

There was a good deal of noise, not only from the workmen themselves, but from vans and lorries which drove up to deliver materials or to remove the vast amount of rubble that this comparatively small job seemed to en-gender.

I was glad that I could leave the scene of battle each day to seek the peace of my new home at Beech Green.

I grew fonder of the cottage as the time passed. It was full of memories for me, not only of dear Dolly herself, but of the people she had told me about, who had lived there before. Her parents, Mary and Francis Clare, her sister Ada whose daughter I had met, her friend Emily Davis who had visited this little house all her life, and had ended it under this roof, as Dolly had done later, all seemed to me to have left something intangible behind them: a sense of happiness, simplicity, courage and order. I am the least psychic of women, and am inclined to suspect those who lay claim to extra-sensory experiences, but there is no doubt about the general reaction most people have to the 'feel' of a house.

Some houses are forbidding, cheerless and indefinably hostile. Others seem to welcome the stranger who steps inside. Dolly Clare's was one such house. I felt that I was heir to a great deal of happiness, and I blessed the shades of those who had lived in and loved this little home, and who had now gone on before me.

One morning, Bob Willet accosted me as I arrived at school.

'Time I come up to do a bit of pruning up yours,' he told me.

'Sunday?' I suggested.

'Best not. My old woman's got these funny ideas about working on Sundays. Anyway, we've got some tricky anthem Mr Annett's trying out at morning church. What about Saturday afternoon? Alice is off to Caxley wasting her money on a new rig-out.'

I said that Saturday afternoon would suit me well.

'Gettin' on with the job all right,' he said, nodding towards the school house. 'Wonder when it'll be up for sale? Vicar tells me the diocese copes with all that business.

Should make a bomb, nice little place like that. That is if it sells at all, the way things are.'

'Well, the new houses are still hanging fire, I gather. I don't see as much of Fairacre these days, but I haven't heard of anyone being interested.'

'There were two blokes looking at them the other day. Shouldn't think they were buyers though. No women folk with 'em. More likely council or summat. Got nice suits on, and clean shoes.'

'That sounds hopeful.'

'No telling. Maybe just looking to see there's no squatters got in. They was definitely *officials*.'

'How can you tell *officials*?'

Bob Willet ran a gnarled thumb round his chin. 'Don't know entirely. But there's a *look* about 'em. Sort of *bossy*, if you takes my meaning. The sort as carries a brief case and talks posh.'

'Well, I hope they don't come to live here,' I said. 'They don't sound very Fairacre-ish to me.'

As luck would have it, that Saturday afternoon was fine and mild. Over near Beech Green church the rooks were busy with their untidy nest-building. They cawed and clattered about, twigs in beaks, energetically thrusting each other away from disputed sites. The sun gleamed on their black satin feathers. Every now and again, one would swoop down into the garden to rescue one or two of Bob Willet's pieces of pruning.

'Dratted birds,' he exclaimed. 'Only fit for a pie.'

He looked at me suspiciously. 'D'you feed 'em?'

'Well,' I began guiltily, 'I put out a few things for the little birds. You know, the chaffinches and robins and so on, and sometimes the rooks come down.'

'You'll get rats,' said Bob flatly. '*Rats* not rooks, and I bet you don't know how to cope with *them*.'

'I should ask your advice,' I said, at an attempt to mollify him. 'In any case, I've probably got rats already. You can't live in the country and imagine you are free from all unpleasantness. I've learnt to take the rough with the smooth.'

'Well, if you wants my advice now, it's stop feeding the birds. Not that you'll take it, I'll lay. You women is all the same, stubborn as mules.'

I have heard this before from Bob, so could afford to laugh.

'That young Mrs Winter's another bird-feeder,' he went on. 'You should see her garden! Peanuts hanging up everywhere. Coconut halves, corn all over the grass. 'Tis no wonder their lawn's taking forever to get growing. The birds eat all the seed.'

'How are the Winters? Really settled in now?'

'She's not too pleased about this new baby on the way, but still sticking to her job until she durn well has to stop. My Alice worries a bit about her, but I tell her it's not her affair.'

He straightened up and looked over the rest of the garden.

'I'll make a start on them straggly roses after tea,' he said. 'That is,' he added, 'if there is any tea?'

'There's always tea,' I assured him, hurrying indoors to get it.

That evening I had a telephone call from Horace Umbleditch. He began by apologizing for disturbing me. 'You must be busy,' he added.

'I'm only looking through the telly programmes,' I told him, 'and wondering if I want a discussion on euthanasia, a film about the victims of famine in Africa, the increase of parasites in the human body, or one of those mindless games where you answer a lot of idiotic questions, and the audience goes berserk with delight when you win a dish-washer you don't want.'

'There's a nice Mozart piano concerto on the Third,' said Horace.

'Thanks for telling me. I'll listen to that and get on with my knitting. What can I do for you?'

'The grapevine has it that your house will soon be ready for the market. We're still interested. Do you know any more about it?'

'Not really. I've no doubt the diocese will be putting it into a local agent's hands before long. Why don't you ring Gerald Partridge and tell him that you are interested? No reason why you shouldn't get first chance at bidding for it.'

'D'you think we've a chance?'

'Definitely. Nothing seems to be moving much in the property market, and you're in the happy position of first-time buyers, not waiting about to sell your own before buying another.'

'That's true. There's another reason really. We're expect-ing our first. A bit late in the day, but better late than never.'

I expressed my great pleasure.

'So you see, it would be nice to have a home of our own before the baby arrives. How do you like the idea of an infant in your old home?'

'It gives me no end of delight,' I assured him. 'Now, do ring the vicar and tell him all. I know he will help you.'

We rang off, and I savoured this delicious piece of news as I pursued my knitting to the accompaniment of Mozart.

I hoped that my friends would one day live in my old house, and dwelt on the many teachers who had lived there before; Mr and Mrs Hope, Mr Wardle who had trained

Dolly Clare for her teaching career, and his wife, Mrs
Wardle, who had been such a stern martinet during needle-
work lessons.

It was, like Dolly's, a welcoming house, and I sincerely
hoped that Horace and Eve would be able to live there,
and be as happy as I had been for so many years.

The mild early spring weather continued and raised our
spirits.

During this halcyon spell I invited the Bakers to tea one
Sunday. Miriam's agency was doing well, and her chief
problem at the moment, she told me, was to find a first-
class secretary for her old boss, Sir Barnabas Hatch, when
Jane Winter took time off for motherhood.

'He rings me at least once a day,' she said, 'imploring me
to come back. Sometimes I feel sure that Jane is present
and it must be most embarrassing for her. I've told him it
is quite impossible, time and time again, but dear old
Barney can't believe that he won't get his own way if he
keeps at it.'

'Is such a job well paid?' I asked. I thought the amount
she told me was astronomical, and wondered why I had
taken up teaching.

Gerard, busy toasting crumpets by my fire, added his
contribution. He was engaged, it seemed, on a script for a
television company, about the changes in agriculture since
the 1914–18 war, and at present was studying the wages
earned by farm labourers at that time.

'I came across a quotation from A. G. Street,' he said,
surveying his crumpet and returning it to the heat. 'He
reckoned that a man working a fifty-hour week in the
1920s earned about thirty shillings. That's *real* shillings, of
course, now worth our fivepence.'

'But surely they lived rent free?'

'Not always. His argument was that a man who could plough, pitch hay, layer hedges and shear sheep was a skilled worker. Many farm labourers, he maintained, were under-rated and under-paid.'

'Things have improved though?'

'Well, the wages have gone up certainly, but now a man is expected to be a mechanic as well, with all this sophisticated farm machinery. There's more risk of accidents too these days. Mind you, I wouldn't mind ploughing a field sitting in a nicely-warmed cabin with my earphones on, but shouldn't offer to plough behind two or three horses, with only a sack over my head and shoulders to keep out the weather.'

'So, on the whole, you think things have improved?'

'Definitely. But I still think A. G. Street was right. Farm workers are skilled men, even more skilled now than in his time, and I should like to see that recognized.'

'Well, they are a rare breed now in Fairacre. The vicar showed me some parish records the other day, and the number of farm workers came to almost eighty, what with carters, hedgers-and-ditchers, ploughmen, wheelwrights, shepherds or simply "Ag. Labourers". Now Mr Roberts only has two men to help him. What a change!'

'Isn't that progress?' demanded Gerard.

'It doesn't help my school numbers,' I said sadly. 'There used to be nearly a hundred children at Fairacre at one time. Now we've only twenty-one.'

'Cheer up,' said Gerard, blowing the flames from his cookery. 'Have a nice crumpet. Well done, too.'

18   Country Matters

IT was quite a pleasure to welcome Mrs Pringle's return to her duties. I am not really quite as slatternly as she is fond of telling me, but even I could see that the school was looking increasingly shabby under Minnie's haphazard care.

She gasped at the sight of the stoves, but I defended my efforts on their behalf.

'Now, come on,' I told her, 'you know they're not too bad. Why, I used nearly half a tin of that blacklead stuff.'

'That's the trouble,' retorted Mrs Pringle. 'You only needs a *touch* of that, and *plenty* of elbow grease, which these 'ere stoves haven't had in my absence, as is plain to see.'

However, she seemed pleased to get back after her enforced idleness, and even agreed that her leg was 'a trifle – only a trifle, mind', better than it had been. Her doctor's treatment, she admitted, grudgingly, 'could have been worse'. High praise indeed from Mrs Pringle!

It was good to get back to our normal routine, and I was glad to leave school at the usual time and not have to supervise Minnie's ministrations.

She had departed with her wages, a box of shortbread as a parting present from me, incoherent thanks on her side, and secret relief on mine. A little of Minnie Pringle goes a long way, and although I am sorry for the girl, I find that taking responsibility for such a hare-brained person is distinctly exhausting.

Amy called one afternoon just after I had arrived home.

Looking very elegant in a grey suit, she deposited a paper bag on the kitchen table.

'I bought some penny buns on the way here,' she said. 'I guessed I'd be in time for tea.'

'I bet they were more than a penny,' I observed.

She ruminated for a moment. 'Come to think of it, I believe they were about half-a-crown each. Can that be right?'

'I shouldn't be surprised. Very welcome, anyway.'

We munched happily, and Amy told me that she had been to lunch with the widow of one of James's directors.

'He died some months ago. Great pity. He was dear, and very generous with his pots of money. He's left a pile of it to that trust for orphans. He was one of the founders actually. James was very cut up when he went, and still misses him.'

I enquired after James.

'Still worrying about that wretched Brian. He doesn't tell me much, but I don't think that man is settling down very well in Bristol, and of course James won't hear a word against him from the people there. Anyone who plays cricket as well as our Brian must be above reproach, James thinks. All rather trying, I find. However, he is taking me to the opera next week for a treat.'

'What are you seeing?'

'That Mozart one about those two silly girls who are so thick they can't recognize their own fiancés.'

'*Cosi Fan Tutte*,' I told her.

'Ah! thanks for reminding me. At least the music should be lovely, and the sets and the costumes pretty. Unless, of course, the producer sees fit to set it in some back alley of an industrial town, with all the characters in dirty jeans and sweat shirts.'

'Keep your fingers crossed,' I advised. 'Have another

penny bun. I seem to recall that there were even *halfpenny* buns when we were young.'

'There were indeed. And how sad that phrase: "When we were young" sounds! Nearly as sad as: "*If only*" which people are always saying. You know: "*If only* I had known he was about to die. *If only* I had been nicer to my mother. *If only* I hadn't married that man." Terribly sad words.'

'For me,' I said, 'the saddest words I know were put into the mouth of Sir Andrew Aguecheek in *Twelfth Night*.'

'But surely he was just a buffoon?'

'Maybe. But when I hear him say: "I was adored once", it breaks me up.'

Amy surveyed me thoughtfully.

'For such a tough old party,' she said at last, 'you are remarkably vulnerable. Now tell me all the Fairacre news.'

My prime piece of news about the sale of my old home, she had already heard from Horace and Eve, and she speculated about this.

'I told them that I thought they should try for one of those new houses while they are about it. After all, with this baby on the way, and possibly another while Eve is young enough, a larger house than your two-bedroom abode would be much more sensible.'

'What did they say?'

'They saw the point, but it's much too expensive for them to contemplate. So I suppose they will go ahead with an offer as soon as they can.'

I told her about Horace's telephone call, and my advice to have a word with the vicar.

We went on to gossip about Jane Winter's approaching confinement and Miriam Baker's new agency.

'And Gerard is writing a novel,' Amy told me.

'He was working on a script about farm labourers' conditions earlier this century. Has he given that up?'

'I'm sure he hasn't. He's just pottering along with the novel at the same time, but he says it's much harder than he imagined. I think he really started it because he's bought a word-processor and he likes to play with it.'

'But he'll have to think what to put in the word-processor, won't he?'

'That's evidently the trouble. He says that he is very conscious of keeping his readers interested, and he quoted Wilkie Collins's advice to Charles Dickens: "Make 'em laugh, make 'em cry, make 'em wait". He thinks he can make 'em laugh and cry, but making 'em wait is the tricky bit. He's dying to take his readers into the secret right from the start, but then would they want to go on reading?'

'Well, I'm glad to hear he is at least considering his readers. Far too many writers these days seem to write purely to relieve their feelings, and pretty dreary the result is. Good luck to Gerard!'

'If that's the time,' said Amy, looking at her watch, 'I must be off, or it will be baked beans on toast for James tonight.'

The vicar called at the school the next morning, accompanied by his yellow Labrador, Honey.

The vicar is always welcomed by the children with appropriate respect and affection. His dog is welcomed with rapture. Honey reciprocates with much bounding about, slavering, panting and licking any part of a child's anatomy that is available to him.

I am fond of dogs, and Honey is particularly adorable, but one cannot deny the fact that she is a destructive element in the classroom. Work ceases. Pockets are turned out, revealing a surprising amount of contraband delicacies such as bubble gum, toffee, biscuits and chocolate. All these secret hoards are readily raided by their owners for

tit-bits for Honey, who never fails to gulp them down ravenously.

Meanwhile, the noise is enormous, and the vicar and I stand
helplessly until, after a few minutes, Honey is put on her
lead and my own charges are hounded back to their desks.

'That nice fellow Umbleditch rang me,' says the vicar, when
partial order has been restored. 'It would be a great pleasure to
have him in the parish. I've told him the position. Somehow I
think the builders have been a little sanguine in thinking that
the house will be ready by Easter. What do you think?'

'Builders are always sanguine. I've yet to meet anyone
who has been able to get into their homes at the time the
builders have forecast. Anyway, Easter's only a few weeks
away. I can't see the job being finished by then.'

'My view entirely, and I think Mr Rochester at the office
feels the same. He is in close touch with the powers-that-be
in the diocese, of course.'

'Well, we can't do much about it, can we? I mean, the
builders have the last word.'

The vicar began to look rather worried, and patted
Honey's head distractedly. 'Mr Rochester, I mean, Mr Winchester – '

'Salisbury,' I broke in.

'Yes, yes, of course, *Salisbury*! He was mentioning the
future of the school again.'

'But that was settled, surely?' I said, feeling alarmed. 'We
were to stay open.'

'Of course. We were told that quite unequivocally. He
was simply wondering if you have any news of fresh pupils
arriving in the coming year.'

I thought of Jane Winter's baby and Eve Umbleditch's,
but they would certainly not be ready for school by September next.

'Not a word,' I said, 'but I live in hope.'

'We must all do that,' said Gerald Partridge resignedly, and departed with Honey who, hopeful to the last, gave backward glances at her generous hosts.

In the week before the school broke up for the Easter holidays, we had a visit from Henry Mawne.

Henry and his wife own the most beautiful house in Fairacre, a Queen Anne building much the same age as the vicarage, but even more splendid.

An ornithologist of some note, we are very proud of Mr Mawne, and look out for his nature notes, and sometimes rather erudite letters, in *The Caxley Chronicle*. He is very good at visiting Fairacre School, and we can usually welcome him about once a term to give us a lecture on birds.

In a school such as ours it is particularly useful to have people dropping in. The children need to see other faces, hear other voices, and generally find stimulation in other people's points of view. Henry Mawne always appears to enjoy his visits, and so do we.

On this occasion he came bearing an armful of rolled illustrations about birds of prey. A band of willing helpers rushed to undo the tapes and to hang the pictures over the blackboard. Henry Mawne bore their enthusiasm with complete patience, but it was some minutes before we could get all the pupils into a receptive frame of mind.

'Anyone fidgeting or interrupting,' I said firmly, 'will spend the next half hour in the lobby.'

Silence reigned.

'How do you do it?' whispered Henry admiringly, his back to the class.

'Years of practice,' I told him. 'And self-preservation, of course.'

He began his talk, and the children listened attentively. Some of the birds of prey were familiar to them. They are quite used to seeing sparrowhawks winging their way along our hedgerows, disturbing the small birds who soon become their victims. The kestrel is another common bird in these parts, hanging motionless in the sky ready to drop like a stone upon any luckless small animal or bird below.

'My dad,' interrupted Ernest, 'don't call it a kestrel. He says it's a wind-hover.'

Henry Mawne embroidered the theme that this alternative name engendered, and then went on to birds which are rarely seen in Fairacre, the smallest hawk, the merlin, and the hobby which has been seen locally during some summers.

But it was the picture of the golden eagle which impressed them most, probably because of its size and its fierce looks.

'It sometimes strikes at a new-born lamb,' said Henry, 'or any other small helpless creature, but it's not nearly as fierce as it looks.'

'Do Mr Roberts know?' quavered Joseph Coggs. 'There's a lot of young lambs on his farm.'

'They're quite safe,' Henry assured him. 'You'll only find golden eagles in Scotland, and then only in the wilder parts.'

The class appeared relieved.

Henry turned to me. 'Would it be possible to take them to that falconry north of Oxford? Perhaps we could get a mini-bus, or arrange a few cars one afternoon?'

These remarks were made very quietly, and expressively to me, but there was a murmur of approval from the front row.

'Would you like to see real birds of prey one day?' I asked the children.

The roar of ecstasy was unanimous, and Henry beamed affectionately at his audience.

'We'll try and fix up the outing next term,' he assured them. 'Miss Read will come too, of course.' He turned to me and added in a conspiratorial whisper: '*To keep order.*'

Henry Mawne was not only generous with his time in encouraging an interest in birds, he also presented the school with a fine wooden bird-table to replace the old one which had been shattered in the autumn storms. The children welcomed this addition to the playground, but Mrs Pringle considered it 'a nasty great object, encouraging all sorts of vermin'.

'We've got enough mice in the handiwork cupboard,' she said darkly, 'without a lot of corn and nuts and that hanging up. There was definitely a mouse in that paper cupboard what you're leaning against.'

I moved hastily away.

'Unless it was a *rat*,' she added, sounding pleased.

'Anyway the bird table is going to stay there. It was exceptionally kind of Mr Mawne to present it to us, and I don't intend to hurt his feelings.'

Mrs Pringle snorted. '*His* feelings indeed! I'll have you know that everyone remembers *your* feelings when he took advantage of you soon after he come here.'

I was taken aback. I know that villagers have long memories, but that little misunderstanding happened years ago and, in any case, it was not I who was expecting a proposal of marriage from the newly-arrived stranger, then, it had seemed, a bachelor, but the village folk themselves who had cast me in the rôle of ageing bride.

And I did not care for Mrs Pringle's use of the phrase: '*took advantage of you*'. It made me sound like some backward fourteen-year-old raped by a sex maniac. I was certainly not the former, and nor was poor Henry Mawne the latter but, as usual Mrs Pringle managed to give a comprehensive clout with her remarks.

I decided to rise above it, and changed the subject. 'Has Fred found his shed yet? He must miss it.'

For two pins I would have added; 'To get away from you,' but I forbore with Christian charity, and hoped my guardian angel was taking note.

'Part of it fetched up by Mr Roberts's cattle shed, and he brought the bits back on his trailer. The vicar said he'd let Fred have what was left of his tool shed after the storm, and Josh Pringle gave him a hand putting it all together.'

'That was good of the vicar,' I observed. 'A case of true practical Christianity.'

'He knew Fred missed somewhere to do his art-work,' said Mrs Pringle.

'And to have a peaceful place of his own,' I felt compelled to add.

I could almost hear my guardian angel scratching out the earlier entry.

'It keeps him from getting under my feet,' replied Mrs Pringle. '*That's* what the vicar really had in mind!'

I might just as well have saved my breath, and have had a rare entry in my angel's credit column, after all.

Easter was early this year, and I was glad to have some time in my little house.

I was beginning to realize with increasing intensity, the expense involved in being a property-owner. When I lived in the school house, all outside work was paid for by the school authorities, and I was responsible only for indoor maintenance.

Now, despite Wayne Richards's earlier repair work, I found that a mysterious damp patch had appeared in the corner of my bedroom ceiling. On investigation, Wayne traced it to the lead flashing at the base of the chimney stack just above the thatch.

'Must've been the gale,' he said, shouting down from the top of his ladder. 'All bent up, it is. That's your trouble, Miss Read. Won't take more than a day to put it right.'

He descended carefully, and brushed a few wisps of straw from his trousers.

'But I thought lead was terribly heavy stuff,' I protested. 'Isn't that what they use for roofs?'

'True, but it's soft too. Once it gets bent, it sort of rolls up under pressure. Why, the parish church in Caxley lost yards of it in the storms. Took six men to get it into the lorry.'

He gave me an estimated price for the job, and I fixed a day for his men to come and see to it. I have no doubt at all that his price was a fair one, but it gave me a shock. My old winter coat would have to wrap me up for another season, I could see that.

Visits from the plumber, the electrician and the telephone people, all took a good slice from my pay packet, and I began to do some careful budgeting for future repairs. At least it was my own property I was maintaining, and this gave me enormous satisfaction. I did not have to notify anyone of things which needed to be done, for it was now my decision, and I could employ whom I wanted, and have the work done when it pleased me.

I knew from experience how frustrated some of the nearby cottagers had been when they had gone to their employers with a list of things needing to be done. Cracked windows, leaking roofs, damp walls and dozens more defects were often met with either downright refusal or grudging agreement to do the minimum.

'He told me what did I expect for ten bob a week,' one man told me, 'and us with a bucket catching the raindrops in the kids' bedroom.'

I had sympathized. There were many many with conscientious landlords, but there were certainly others who seemed callous.

But now that I was a house-owner and realized just how much was needed to keep my own modest home in good repair, I was beginning to feel sympathy with the owners of so many rural homes. Many of these properties in Beech Green and Fairacre were well over a hundred years old, some almost three hundred, and there was something needing to be done to them practically every month. It was hardly surprising that so many were put on the market for others to repair and to spend their money on.

Nor was it surprising that council houses were proliferating, but even these were often too much for country people to afford, and there was a drift to the towns where there was often cheaper property to rent, and also more work available.

I thought of Gerard Baker and his present work on the change in agricultural matters during the present century. He was dealing with general change involving mechanized farming, intensive rearing of animals, the drastic reduction of men needed on a farm these days, and the rise in wages and conditions.

I too, in my small way, could vouch for change. From being a dweller in a tied-house, I was now a property-owner.

Surveying Wayne Richards's written estimate, I thought to myself: 'It's heavy going being a home-owner. But worth every penny.'

Luckily, the weather stayed fine for the holidays, and Wayne was able to get on with the flashing round the chimney. Better still, it was done in one day, as he had promised.

I had made no plans to go away, but took several day

trips to places I enjoy visiting. One was to Great Tew, the renowned Cotswold village which went through a sad period of neglect some time ago, but has now been restored to its former beauty.

Amy came with me on one or two occasions, and we lunched one day at Kingham Mill, and visited some of the lovely Cotswold villages which we knew from experience would be clogged with traffic in the summer but were relatively empty early in the year.

'Isn't it strange,' remarked Amy, 'that so many of these villages appear to have no people around? And all these cultivated fields never seem to have anyone working in them.'

'You'd better listen to Gerard's programme when it's on the telly,' I told her. 'You'll hear all about changes in country life.'

'But there doesn't appear *to be* any country life,' protested Amy. 'That's my point.'

'There's plenty in Fairacre,' I told her, 'particularly in my school. Far too much going on most of the time, especially when Mrs Pringle appears on the scene.'

'But in my youth,' continued Amy, surveying the empty rolling fields around us, 'you would see men ploughing the fields, or layering a hedge, or scything the verges –'

'But it's all done with machinery now.'

'Of course, I know that! But you used to see washing blowing on the line, and women sitting in the sun shelling peas. Where are they now? There must be washing to do, and peas to shell, even now.'

'They're inside with their washing machines and tumble driers. And the peas are in nice clean packets in the freezer. You're harking back to those dear days beyond recall. But think, Amy, would you really want to go back to boiling clothes in a copper, and stirring them about with a copper stick? And then rubbing them on a wash-board?'

Amy laughed. 'Of course not. Not that I ever boiled clothes in a copper, though my dear old granny did, and I used to help her hang them out, using lovely hazelwood pegs the gypsies used to sell. And come to think of it, what's happened to real gypsies who used to sell pegs and paper flowers at the back door?'

'They're all in their fabulous mobile homes,' I told her, 'watching the telly with one eye and the tumble drier with the other.'

'And shelling peas?'

'Not likely.'

'It seems so extraordinary that things have changed so drastically in the country in such a comparatively short time.'

'Gerard will tell you all about that,' I assured her.

19   Problems for Friends

I T was quite a pleasure to return to school after the
Easter holidays. I suppose that it is partly that I am
'geared to work', as Miriam Baker once put it. I
always welcome a break from it, but after a time I begin to
feel uneasy and somewhat guilty.

Then, too, I was now really settled in to the routine of
living at Beech Green, driving the few miles to Fairacre,
and not bobbing back and forth across the playground to
see how things were faring in the school house. In many
ways it was a more ordered existence, and I found it much
to my liking.

After a short spell of cloudy weather, the sun had
returned with all the pleasures of spring. Daffodils were
out in cottage gardens, and primroses starred the banks on
the road from Beech Green to school.

Mr Roberts's lambs were frisking about, untroubled by
golden eagles safely in Scotland, and the dawn chorus of
thrushes, blackbirds, and finches of all kinds, greeted me
when I awoke. The snowdrops had withered, the catkins
which had fluttered so bravely through the winter months
were now tattered, and as frayed as the dying flowers of
the yellow winter jasmine. They had played their part in
keeping hope alive during the darkest days of the year, but
now bowed out to let the larger and more showy flowers
take the stage.

But although I welcomed the spring as rapturously as the
children did, and despite my more settled way of life now

that I had become used to the changed rhythm of my day,
I felt a secret unease.

The vicar's remarks last term about the fact that my
school might close despite assurances to the contrary had
brought back the fear that had always lurked at the back of
my mind. I tried to remind myself that this had been faced
for years, and that still the school remained open. I told
myself that I had been assured that although the school
house would be put on the market, the school would
continue. But I still worried, and all the old bogeys about
my future came back to haunt me.

Should I take early retirement? Could I afford to? The
expense of keeping my own small property in good heart
had been brought home to me pretty sharply recently, and
the thought that old age and general infirmity must be
faced one day, with all the added expense that that would
bring. In any case, it came back to the fact that I was
'geared to work' and would miss it.

But what about working in someone else's school, the
other alternative? I knew myself well enough to know that
I should hate it. For too long I had been monarch of all I
surveyed, and had my own way in most things. I thought
of having to fall in with the wishes of a strange head
teacher, undertaking methods of which I probably disap-
proved, sharing a staffroom with dozens of others, and my
spirits quailed. After all this time, I recognized that I should
not be an admirable member of a team. Mrs Richards
and I worked happily together, but of course it was I who
really prevailed as head mistress when it came to the
crunch.

No, the thought of teaching in another school, no matter
how splendid the building or how angelic the staff, could
not be contemplated. I should just have to soldier on as
things were at Fairacre, comforting myself with Mr Salis-

bury's promise, and the slight hope that particularly large families would decide to make their homes in the village before too long.

Horace and Eve came to see the school house one afternoon. By now the roof repairs were done, but the garden still showed signs of the builders' recent activities. There were indentations on the lawn where the ladders had stood, the shrubs and flowerbeds were dusty with the débris from the roof, and there was a battered air about the whole place. Nevertheless, the job itself had been well done, and the new roof tiles matched the old ones admirably.

The estate agent had let them have the key, and they had spent an hour looking over the interior, until I finished the afternoon session.

They followed me to Beech Green for tea, and were full of plans if their offer were accepted.

'One of the things I mentioned to the agent,' said Horace, 'was that we should prefer to do the decoration ourselves. It might mean a lower price, for one thing, and in any case it always seems to me a mistake to re-decorate a house just to sell it. Usually the new owner can't bear the colour scheme, and sets to and repaints as he wants it. Also, it might mean a quicker sale, and everyone would be happy.'

'When do you expect to hear?'

'Heaven alone knows! You know how these matters drag on. The thing is, we've made our offer, and I doubt if many other people will with the market as it is. We'll keep our fingers crossed.'

It was good to see them so hopeful as they drove away, and I only wished that they would see those hopes fulfilled.

* * *

One morning towards the end of April, before the school bell was rung, Mrs Pringle informed me that someone was looking over one of the empty houses.

'Good!' I cried. 'Did they look as though they might have children?'

'Not as far as I could see,' replied Mrs Pringle. 'More like *grandparents*, I'd say.'

'That's right,' agreed Mr Willet who had joined us. 'More like folk from the council again, I reckon. I recognized that old trout from Caxley as is on the District Council. Wonder what's up?'

'Checking on the drains and that perhaps,' surmised Mrs Pringle. 'Don't do to leave a place uninhibited too long.'

'*Uninhabited,*' I corrected automatically.

'Like I said,' agreed Mrs Pringle. 'You don't want no one in it for too long.'

Here was the double negative rearing its ugly head again, but I did not join battle.

'Looked more like buyers wanting a bit added,' said Mr Willet. 'They was looking at the kitchen side. Maybe they want one of these glass-house places stuck on. All the go, them conservatories these days.'

'Perhaps one of those people was a buyer,' I speculated.

'That young woman as is expecting,' continued Mr Willet, 'said she thought they looked at both houses.'

'Definitely drains!' pronounced Mrs Pringle. 'They shares a septic tank no doubt.'

'I never saw them looking at but just the one,' said Bob. 'Mr Annett had us in early for choir practice. Trying out a new anthem, he was, and a right pig's breakfast we made of it, I can tell you. Some modern thing, it is. What's wrong with a nice bit of Stainer, I want to know? So anyway, I never saw as much as Mrs Winter did from her kitchen window.'

He sounded disappointed.

'All I hope,' I told him, nodding to Patrick to ring the bell, 'is that they are building on to accommodate their large families.'

'That's what's called *"wishful thinking"*,' he shouted, above the din, and departed.

I came across Jane Winter myself one dinner hour when I was calling at the Post Office for the school savings' stamps. She looked remarkably well, with that radiance that pregnant women so often show, once the first uncomfortable months are over.

'Yes,' she said, 'I certainly saw those people, and a couple of men have visited the houses once or twice. What's going on?'

'I've no idea. Perhaps two couples – old friends or something – have decided to retire together. It sometimes happens.'

'But the houses are too big for retired folk,' she said.

'Sometimes they have lots of grandchildren who come to stay,' I surmised. 'But honestly, your guess is as good as mine.'

I enquired about the coming baby.

'Not long now, thank heaven. To tell you the truth, we were both a bit miffed about it when we first knew, but now I'm quite looking forward to having a baby in the house again.'

'The old wives' tale is that those that aren't ordered always turn out the best,' I told her.

'That's a consoling thought,' she laughed. 'Perhaps this one will be able to keep us in our old age.'

We walked back towards my school and her home in good spirits.

* * *

Amy rang me one evening soon after my meeting with Jane. She sounded worried, and wanted to know if I could spend the next Friday night, and perhaps Saturday too, with her at Bent.

'James has to be away, and he's heard such a lot about people breaking in that he doesn't like the idea of me being alone. Besides, he still looks upon me as an invalid after that bang on the head.'

'I'd love to come. What time, Amy?'

'Come to tea if you can manage it. If not, soon after. And many thanks. James will be grateful.'

'So shall I. Have you had more than usual robberies in Bent?'

'As a matter of fact, we have. Mrs Drew, our daily, seems to have fresh instances ever time she comes, but at the moment the poor soul is laid up with her back, so I don't get the gossip, good or bad.'

'Anything serious?'

'Just a displaced vertebra somewhere from the sound of it, but you know how painful backs can be. Sometimes –' she broke off. 'Sorry, I forgot how squeamish you are.'

'I don't mind *bones*. It's *insides* I can't take. All those tubes, and squashy bits.'

Amy laughed. 'Well, anyway, I won't curdle your blood with any more horrors. See you on Friday, as soon as you like.'

I must admit that I wondered once or twice why James was so suddenly anxious about leaving Amy alone. He often had to be away from home on business, and surely the fact that there were burglars about could not be the whole story. I looked forward to hearing more.

April was on its way out, and I looked forward to May, to my mind the loveliest of all the months. The hedges were breaking into leaf, and the trees' stark branches were beginning to be clothed in a veil of swelling buds, soon to become a mantle of fresh green.

I drove to Amy's about six o'clock, and found her picking narcissi in her garden.

'Smell those,' she said, thrusting the bunch under my nose, and I sniffed rapturously.

'Bliss!' I told her. 'Now tell me all about James's concern for you. I'm intrigued.'

'Come and have a drink, and I'll tell you as much as I know.'

She dropped the flowers into a jug of water as we passed through the kitchen, and we were soon comfortably settled in the sitting-room, glasses in hand.

'It's a sad story, and to be frank, I'm much more worried about James than he is about me.'

'Is it something to do with Brian?' I ventured.

'It has *everything* to do with Brian,' said Amy, putting her glass down on a side table with a bang. 'The little rat!' she added violently.

I gazed at her speechless. It is not often that I see Amy in a fine temper.

'He's hopped it. Scarpered. Gone to ground. Vamoosed. In short, he's nowhere to be found. And what's upset James so much is the fact that he had arranged an interview for Brian with one of his high-powered city pals – no easy task – and of course that wretched Brian didn't turn up. He'd vanished, and so had the money.'

'Good lord! From the Bristol firm?'

'That's only part of it, and a small part at that evidently. Our Brian has been pinching funds from his various places of employment for years now. They think he plays a fairly minor rôle in a group of wide-boys with nice little bank accounts in various places abroad.'

'I can't believe it. I must admit I always thought that he was a rather mediocre little man, but I should never have credited him with enough savvy to be an international crook. Where is he, I wonder?'

'He could be anywhere. Bolivia or Brazil or one of those islands where people stash their ill-gotten gains. He obviously took a plane from Bristol. Last Thursday I think.'

'But can you fly to Bolivia from Bristol? I thought you could only hop across to nearby places like Paris and Madrid.'

'Presumably you can change planes at Paris and Madrid,' snapped Amy crossly. 'Don't be so pettifogging!'

I apologized meekly. It was quite obvious that Amy was deeply upset. In the silence that followed I turned over the word 'pettifogging' in my mind. I had looked it up recently for a crossword I was doing, and I felt sure it had said something about 'a cavilling lawyer', which could not possibly apply to me. Perhaps Amy meant to use the word 'pernickety'? In any case, this was not the time to discuss such niceties of the English language with my suffering friend, and I put forward a less controversial question.

'Won't Interpol catch him?' I ventured.

'Of course they're doing their stuff, and so too is the fraud squad, I gather, but people like Brian and his dubious friends are always one jump ahead, and poor old James seems to think we'll never see him again.'

'Jolly good thing too! And after all you and James did for him! Makes my blood boil!'

'I think James is dreading the possibility of Brian being brought back to face trial. Although he's furious about being let down over that interview, he still can't bear the idea of having to be a witness against Brian. Frankly, I should enjoy it.'

'Me too. But then women are much tougher than men.'

'You'd think that this business would have turned James

completely against that little horror, but it hasn't. He's had the most terrible shock, his idol with feet of clay, and all that, but he's still besotted. He makes idiotic remarks, such as: "Can't hit a man when he's down." "Brian always played a straight bat." "He must be covering for someone." Really, sport has a lot to answer for when it comes to men's thinking.'

'Don't you argue with him?'

'Of course I do, until I'm blue in the face, but then James starts to blame the women in Brian's life. He would have been perfect if his wife hadn't left him. She should have stuck by him. Loyalty should come first, and all that guff. I must say I wonder if she didn't suspect things years ago, and removed herself while there was time.'

'So James is in Bristol now?'

'Yes. He's meeting this old school friend who employed Brian. I expect there'll be a lot of wailing and gnashing of teeth over the fall of their cricket hero. More about that, I'll bet, than the plight of the shareholders.'

'Maybe the employer will be made of sterner stuff.'

'I hope so. The point is that I'm truly worried about James. He looks so wretched and ill. Brian has properly let him down. For a really tough business man, he is extraordinarily soft-hearted, and this really has hit him badly. I wanted to go with him, as I don't think he should be driving when he's so upset, but he and the friend and the firm's accountant are going through the books and will be hours on the job, evidently. Then they've got the other firms to contact, and the police. He'll probably be down there for the whole of the weekend. Can you stay?'

'Of course I can. Poor old James! What a wretched underhand sort of affair it is!'

'Hardly cricket, is it?' agreed Amy, with a wry smile.

* * *

Naturally, it was an anxious weekend. Every time the telephone rang, Amy rushed to answer it, hoping for news from James.

He rang just as we were off to bed on the Saturday night, telling Amy that he would be home on Sunday evening, and to see if all was well.

'How was he?' I asked.

'He sounded very weary, and says there's more to do than any of them realized. No news of Brain, as you might expect, but there's another complication.'

'What's that?'

'One of his erstwhile colleagues, at a previous job he had, has also vanished into thin air. Looks remarkably suspicious according to the police. This other chap's a real hard nut with a record. The police want him for other matters. James reckons he's had a strangle-hold on poor Brian.'

'And nobody's seen Brian or this other fellow getting on a plane?'

'No. They're now beginning to wonder if they are still in this country, lying low.'

'Perhaps it will be easier to pick them up,' I offered, consolingly. I was worried on Amy's behalf. She looked pale and drawn, and I felt that I should really be doing more for her than I was.

'Let's go to bed,' I said. 'You look all in, and James will never let me be a wife-sitter again if he finds you under the weather.'

We made our way upstairs, and I hoped that Amy's exhaustion would let her sleep. As for me, sleep was impossible, and I found myself thinking of idiotic ways of tracking down Brian. It must have been about three o'clock when I hit upon the ruse of attending the coming summer Test matches at Lords and the Oval (school matters allow-ing, of course), when I fell into an uneasy sleep, where I was busy making marrow jam which refused to set, with Bob Willet and Mrs Pringle in the school lobby.

It was quite a relief to wake up.

I left Amy in the early evening, knowing James would be back very soon, and feeling that I must do some school marking, as well as a few household chores before Monday morning.

A white froth of cow parsley lined the verges below the sprouting hedges, and I thought how lucky I was to live in Beech Green.

My own garden looked exceptionally tidy after Bob Willet's pruning and general clearing up, and in the growing dusk I pottered around outside noting the tulips now breaking into flower, and the little knots of tightly-furled buds on the old Bramley apple tree. The wicked storm, the snow, the horrors of winter and all it had brought seemed far away and long ago, and I rejoiced in the summer so soon to come, before going indoors to face my duties.

It is always annoying to me when people think that a single woman's work is over when she comes back from her daily grind. After all, her home needs as much cleaning, her clothes as much laundering, her food as much cooking, her correspondence as much answering, as any other woman who spends her day at home. Added to these domestic chores are the necessary tasks which she brings back from the school or office. In my case, I have a considerable amount of marking and preparing of lessons to face after school hours, and when people point out that I have lovely long holidays, I reply firmly that I need them.

Mrs Pringle comes to Beech Green on Wednesday afternoons on the convenient Caxley bus, and I must admit that she thoroughly 'bottoms' the cottage before I get back to share a pot of tea with her, and run her home to Fairacre. On the few occasions when she has had to miss her stint, the place certainly lacks that extra gloss.

On the Wednesday following my weekend with Amy, we sat in the garden with our mugs. To tell the truth, it was hardly warm enough, but we could just about stand the coolness in the air, and it was good to realize that summer had arrived.

'You been to see them new houses lately?' asked Mrs Pringle. 'Getting on a treat they are with them kitchens.'

'I don't get down that way very often now,' I confessed. 'I miss strolling around Fairacre in the evenings. Somehow I just get in the car and head for here these days.'

'Well, the boards are down, of course, and from what I hear they've both been bought.'

'Must be two retired friends,' I said, repeating my earlier prognostication. 'Or maybe an old couple and a married son or daughter.'

'At that price?' queried Mrs Pringle. 'With that sort of money they could buy Buckingham Palace. No, it's my belief they've been brought by some rich firm for retirement homes, to put their pensioners in.'

'But they couldn't house more than four or six pensioners,' I protested. 'I still plump for two families. Want to make a bet?'

Mrs Pringle bridled, as I knew she would.

'I am not a betting woman, as well you know, and it's a good thing the children aren't here to listen to such a scandalous idea. I should have thought that Arthur Coggs with his betting and swilling would be enough trouble for Fairacre, without the headmistress of the school uttering such wickedness.'

By this time she was red in the face with wrath, and I hastened to apologize. Her feelings were not assuaged by my trying to make amends, and we drove to Fairacre in heavy silence.

She struggled from the car at her gate, and turned to give me a parting message.

'What you said,' she told me, 'is an abomination in the sight of the Lord. Betting indeed!'

With a final snort she turned towards her gate, as always the victor in any of our battles.

20   Good News

MRS Pringle's guesses about the future residents in the new houses were echoed by one or two other people in Fairacre. Mr Lamb favoured my own view that probably two fairly well-off friends had decided to be neighbours.

'If you were retired,' he said, 'you'd like to have someone handy to help you out when you had an accident, wouldn't you? Someone told me that they reckoned they might have been bought by Caxley folk who came from these parts originally. You know, made their pile and now returning to their roots. It happens sometimes.'

Mrs Pringle stuck to her pensioners idea. Bob Willet favoured two families, unknown to each other, who had just happened to buy at the same time.

The children's interest was desultory. Only old people had been seen looking at the premises. Who cared about new folk? It was their own families in Fairacre that really mattered.

The vicar seemed rather guarded in his conjectures, I thought, simply expressing the hope that they would be church-goers.

In any case, there were other and more pressing things to think about. The summer term is always busy. We have the school sports day, weekly trips to Caxley's swimming bath for the older children, the annual outing to the seaside, and the village fête in July.

This particular summer we also had the trip to the falconry arranged by Henry Mawne, and we were lucky to awake to a glorious June morning. Only my class of ten children were making the trip, while Mrs Richards held the fort at school.

We decided to go in three cars. Henry drove his with three excited children as passengers, Mrs Mawne accompanied us in her beautiful Rover, with four more, three in the back, and Ernest in the front passenger seat, full of importance because his aunt lived somewhere near the birds of prey centre, and he assured everyone that he knew the way.

I had Joseph Coggs beside me, with Patrick and John Todd, the two most unreliable boys in my school, in the back. My eagle eye gleamed at them from the mirror, and I had threatened to deposit them on the road *anywhere* if I saw the slightest sign of bad behaviour.

It was a wonderful drive and my three were remarkably appreciative. One would have thought that, country-dwellers as they were, the rolling Cotswold scene would not have affected them. But they noticed the difference in architecture, the honey-coloured stone of the village houses compared with their own native brick and flint with thatch or tile atop.

We had taken picnic lunches with us, and stopped at a quiet spot by the river Windrush, known to Henry from his fishing days. In addition, I had brought enough apples for everyone, and Mrs Mawne had been even more generous with some chocolate apiece, so that it was a very happy and well-fed company that watched the bright water and the willow branches trailing in it.

By half past two we were waiting in the grassy centre for the display to begin. We saw owls, hawks and merlins in all their glory of flight and intermittent obedience to the falconer, and the children were awe-struck.

One at a time they were encouraged to don the leather

gauntlet, and to feed the bird which landed there. Some were rather timid about it, but I was touched by Joseph Coggs's reaction to this new experience. He was entirely without fear, his face rapt, as the great owl swept silently to his outstretched arm to take the bait. Of all my country-bred flock it was Joe who had the strongest link with wildlife. When the other boys were drawing vehicles, it was Joe who was drawing birds and trees, and now this affinity was more than ever apparent. Joe's dark eyes gazed in wonder at the yellow eyes of his new friend. They seemed in complete accord, and I knew that today's experience would mean far more to Joe than to any of the other children.

They were still excited on the way home. Patrick and John in the back boasted about their bravery at the centre. But Joe sat silent, his eyes shining at the memory of all that he had seen.

It was sometime after this that Horace Umbleditch rang to tell me the good news that their offer had been accepted, and the school house would be theirs.

'And when do you expect to be in?' I asked.

'Sometime next term, I think. We'll spend the summer holidays here, decorating and doing the garden –'

He broke off suddenly.

'You won't mind us altering your garden?' he continued.

'Good heavens, no! It's not my garden now, you know, and in any case it's been altered every time a new head teacher took over. I think I inherited Mr Hope's spotted laurels when I came, but they were soon uprooted.'

'Eve will see this term out and has given in her notice. She's remarkably fit, but we both think it's a good idea for what she calls "a geriatric mum" to take things gently.'

'Very wise,' I agreed, and we went on to discuss the

problems to be overcome to make my old home into their new one, until a strange smell began to emanate from the kitchen and I found that a pan of milk had spread itself over not only the stove, but a few square yards of kitchen floor as well.

The vicar enthused about the news when he called in soon afterwards.

'Mr and Mrs Umbleditch called on me, you know, when they were negotiating for the buying of the house. A charming pair. A great asset to the village, and I gather that Mr Umbleditch has a fine tenor voice. He will be much welcomed by Mr Annett. They are both regular church-goers too. All *very* satisfactory.'

I said that I thought they would settle very happily in Fairacre. 'After all,' I went on, 'they have wanted to live here for a very long time.'

'Fairacre is the perfect place to live,' asserted the vicar. 'I have been fortunate to be appointed to this living. I do so hope that all our newcomers will enjoy the village as keenly as we have.'

This was said with some emphasis, and I wondered if he had prior knowledge of other people coming to share our environment.

The children were out at play, and we were alone in my classroom.

'Have you had any news about the two empty houses?' I asked.

He began to look slightly embarrassed. 'Well yes, my dear Miss Read, I have, and I don't know whether it is quite in order to tell you.'

'Then please don't,' I replied. 'There's nothing worse than being told a secret, and having to keep mum when people inquire. Forget about it.'

'No, no. I really can't do that, and I don't suppose for a minute that there is really anything *secret* in the news. It's just that I haven't brought the letter with me.'

This began to get curiouser and curiouser, and I started to feel all the well-known prickles of fear, envisaging a letter to Mr Partridge, as chairman of the school governors, from our old friend Mr Salisbury about the dwindling numbers at Fairacre School.

'Have you heard of the Malory-Hope Foundation?' asked the vicar.

'Never.'

'You have heard of Sir Derek Malory-Hope, I'm sure. He was a well-known –'

But well known for what remained a mystery, for at that moment Mrs Richards appeared with a howling child who was dripping blood from a grazed knee.

I hurried to get the first-aid box.

'Heavens!' exclaimed the vicar, gazing at the great wall-clock. 'Is it really so late? I am due at a meeting in Oxford at four o'clock. I will call tomorrow with the letter.'

We bandaged the knee, provided a boiled sweet as medicine, and comparative peace reigned again.

I forgot about the vicar's visit until after school when I asked Mrs Richards if she had ever heard of someone called Malory-Hope.

'Isn't he that rich man who gave a lot of money to the Soldiers, Sailors and Air Force Association? Wayne's dad had something to do with it when they were raising money for that hall in Caxley.'

'Oh, I've never heard of him, I'm afraid.'

'It was in *The Caxley*,' said my colleague, looking rather shocked, 'with photos. He opened the hall, cut ribbons, and pulled curtains back over plaques – all that stuff. You must have seen it.'

'Sorry, I missed it.'

'He lived somewhere around here. Died some months ago, and there was a big memorial service. That was in *The Caxley* too.'

I had no recollection of that item of news either, but I did not admit it to Mrs Richards. Obviously she read her *Caxley Chronicle* with far more attention than I did. I should just have to wait for the vicar's letter to explain these mysteries.

Bob Willet was scraping up the coke which had dribbled away from the pile in the playground. I put my question to him while it was still fresh in my mind.

'Bob, have you ever heard of someone called Sir Derek Malory-Hope?'

'The chap what died last year? All over the *Caxley*, it was. He was a good bloke, rolling in money. Give a lot of it away though.'

'I must confess I'd never heard of him.'

'What put him in your mind?'

I said that the vicar had mentioned him when I had asked about the empty houses.

'Did he now' said Bob, leaning on his spade. He looked thoughtful. 'Did he now?' he repeated, before returning to his labours.

When I arrived home, *The Caxley Chronicle* was lying on the mat with one or two uninteresting-looking envelopes. I made myself a mug of tea, and took it and the paper into the sitting-room, and made myself comfortable on the sofa. Tibby, unusually affectionate, leapt on to my lap, and we settled down together happily.

There was a rather nice photograph on the front page of an old mill, situated on the River Cax, some miles downstream from our market town. According to the caption, it had been mentioned in the Domesday Book and funds were now being raised for its restoration.

Among the donors I saw that 'The Malory-Hope Foundation' had contributed a substantial sum.

I have noticed before that when a new name, or simply a new word, crops up, it appears again quite soon. Here it was again: a body, unknown to me yesterday, now cropping up in my life twice in one day.

I turned to this week's deaths. Not that I am particularly morbid, but it is as well to check who has fallen off the bough recently, to save one from asking brightly about a husband who has gone before. There was no one I knew personally, but one of the entries was embellished with a verse:

> To Heaven you've gone
> Dear Dad who we love
> To Mother who is waiting
> All glorious above

I set about correcting it.

The first line could stand.

The second line should have 'whom' instead of 'who'.

The third line was frankly disgraceful. Why not have: 'Where Mother is waiting', or if one wanted 'Dear Mum' to match the earlier 'Dear Dad' thus: 'Where dear Mum awaits you'?

As for the last line it was simply lifted wholesale from *Hymns Ancient and Modern* Number 167, and was the second part of the opening line of: 'O worship the King'.

I have often thought of offering my services, 'free, gratis and for nothing', to *The Caxley Chronicle* in order to overhaul their list of these funeral rhymes, which they presumably keep in their offices and from which bereaved families may make their selection. I have never got down to actually approaching the editor; it would need a good deal of tact.

While I was still wondering how one could achieve one's aim, the telephone rang, and I leapt to answer it, catapulting poor Tibby to the floor.

It was Amy.

'Am I interrupting anything?'

'Only the reading of *The Caxley*.'

'Good! I was just wondering –'

'Before I forget,' I broke in. 'Do you know anything about the Malory-Hope Foundation?'

'Of course I do. Derek Malory-Hope started it. He died last year, and James and I went to his memorial service. You must have seen his obituary in *The Caxley*, surely?'

'I seem to have missed it.'

'I had lunch with his widow some time ago. Come to think of it, I called on you on the way back. Remember? Anyway what's the connection?'

'I just saw that the Foundation has given a hefty sum towards repairing an ancient mill near Caxley.'

'That's right. James mentioned it. Not that he has much to do with that side of their work. He's mixed up with the other part, the Hope Trust. You know, the orphan bit.'

'What orphan bit?'

'You must remember,' said Amy impatiently. 'Those houses in Scotland.'

I cast my mind back to our holiday together, and saw again Floors Castle, Mellerstain and Sir Walter Scott's pile. Not an orphan in sight as far as I could recall.

I said as much to Amy.

'*Not us*,' she shouted in a most unladylike manner. 'We didn't visit the houses I'm talking about! James did. In Glasgow. For the orphans up there.'

I said I still did not really understand.

'Let's forget it,' said Amy. 'Anyway, besides the mill

involvement, why are you worrying about the Malory-Hope Foundation?'

'The vicar mentioned it.'

'*The vicar*?' Amy sounded thunderstruck.

After a pause, she resumed in a more normal voice. 'This conversation becomes more surrealistic every second. Let's start again. I really rang to see if you would be in on Saturday afternoon, as James has to go to Fairacre on business and he could drop me off as we come through Beech Green.'

'Perfect. Come to tea, and I'll make some of that sticky gingerbread James likes.'

'You spoil him. Sometimes I think James married the wrong woman.'

'I'm certain he did!' I said, and put the telephone down smartly, before she could reply.

I spent an uneasy night wondering about the vicar's letter, and the information Amy had provided about the Malory-Hope activities. More specifically, I worried about James's part as a busy member of the Hope Trust, or as Amy put it, 'the orphan bit'.

If James, on the Trust's behalf, had bought Fairacre's two empty houses, did Amy have anything to do with it? If so, was I involved? Had I been whining more than usual about lack of pupils? Was it possible that my dwindling numbers had made James look into the possibility of the houses being bought by the Hope Trust, just as the Glasgow ones had been?

If it were so, how would it affect me, and my friends in Fairacre? I began imagining crocodiles of orphans, all clad in a dreary uniform, roaming the village street under the stern eye of their jailers. The mind boggled at this Dickensian scene, though there would hardly be enough orphans to form a crocodile if they only had those two houses as their home.

This brought me to even more conjecture. Surely it would be reasonable to have a much larger establishment to house orphans? It seemed very extravagant to use an ordinary family-sized house for such a project. On the other hand, had not James said something once about 'family units' in connection with his Glasgow excursion?

I tossed and turned until my bedroom clock showed a quarter to four, when I must have fallen into a far from dreamless sleep, for Gerald Partridge and I, accompanied by Mrs Pringle, were busy herding about fifty real crocodiles into Mr Roberts's sheep dip at the foot of the downs, to immunize them against crocodile-tetanus to which, as we all know, reptiles are particularly vulnerable because of their webbed toes –

I was fit for nothing when the alarm went at seven.

Naturally, I was anxious for the vicar's visit the next morning to see if the promised letter would give any further information.

Assembly came and went. Playtime came and went. School dinner came and went, and the vicar was still absent.

Mrs Richards departed with my class for the swimming bath at Caxley, while I took myself into the infants' room for the usual Friday afternoon lessons.

After a short session of modelling tea trays complete with saucers and cups, and such intricate pieces of workmanship as teaspoons and crumpets, I embarked on two short poems by Robert Louis Stevenson. I am a great believer in stuffing young children's heads with worthwhile verse which they will have safely stored away for the rest of their lives.

And so we learnt 'The Cow' and 'Happy Thought' from *A Child's Garden of Verses*, and I felt the afternoon had been profitably spent. I had quite forgotten my worries about the Hope Trust, empty houses and Amy and James, when the vicar arrived, envelope in hand.

It was time for the children to go home, and the vicar obligingly helped me with shoe laces, coat buttons and all the sartorial problems of young children.

Then, when the school was empty, he handed me the large envelope and roamed the classroom while I read.

It was headed The Malory-Hope Foundation, and had an impressive list of directors, among whom, I noticed were James and, to my surprise Sir Barnabas Hatch, erstwhile employer of Miriam Baker.

The letter was extremely polite and pointed out that negotiations had been satisfactorily completed, and that the Hope Trust, part of the above Foundation, was now the owner of the two Fairacre houses. Their local director, Mr James Garfield, would give himself the pleasure of calling upon the vicar, and the chairman of the Parish Council, Mr Lamb, to explain matters in greater detail and to hear local people's views and suggestions.

It was envisaged that each home would house four, or possibly five children, with a house-father and mother to care for them. The children would be of school age, viz: from four and a half years to eleven. A leaflet explaining the aims and work of the Foundation was enclosed, and the same information had been sent to Mr Lamb.

So that was why James was making a visit to Fairacre next Saturday was my first thought. The second was had I got some black treacle for the gingerbread?

I looked across at the beaming face of the vicar, and only then did the true impact of this momentous news hit me. I felt stunned. The room gyrated in the oddest way, and I became conscious of the vicar's face close to mine. The smile had changed to an expression of concern.

'My dear Miss Read, are you all right? It is a shock, I must admit, but a *nice* one, isn't it?'

I pulled myself together. 'It's incredible,' I croaked. 'An answer to a maiden's prayer, definitely.'

'And to a vicar's,' said Gerard Partridge soberly.

Mrs Richards always saw off the children when she returned on Friday afternoons from swimming, and although I was longing to tell her the great news, I was glad to have some time to myself to think it over. I drove home still in a state of shock, but remembered to stop at Beech Green's village shop for the black treacle.

After tea I set about making the gingerbread, and the cottage soon became redolent with the fragrance of cooking. As I went about greasing tins and mixing ingredients, my mind tried to come to terms with this amazing news.

Eight new children! Was I right in thinking that the letter had said from four and a half to eleven years of age? I should have almost thirty in my school, and that would mean that it would remain safe from closure.

I still wondered why our village should have been selected by the Hope Trust for its two new homes. Had James and Amy somehow connived in this happy arrangement, for my especial benefit? If so, it was embarrassing for me, although typical of their generous spirit.

I could only possess my soul in patience until I saw them the next afternoon.

Their car drew up at twenty past two, and Amy, elegant as ever, came in whilst James waved, and went on his way to Fairacre. I should like to have babbled away about all my hopes and fears but managed to appear fairly composed. In fact, it was Amy who made the first reference to our telephone conversation.

'So have you found out any more about the vicar and the two new houses?'

She sounded genuinely interested, and not at all like a conspirator.

'Amy,' I said, 'you'll never believe this.'

She listened attentively, her eyes growing rounder every minute.

'And I must admit,' I confessed, 'that I thought you might have had a hand in it.'

'Cross my heart and hope to die,' quoted Amy, making the appropriate gestures. 'Although, of course,' she added, looking rather pink, 'I may have mentioned your worries to James. Or, come to think of it, you often told us about them yourself when James was present.'

This was true enough. We awaited James's return with as much patience as we could muster, and prepared the tea tray ready for his arrival. The gingerbread had turned out satisfactorily dark and sticky.

James was his usual cheerful self, and greeted me affectionately. We were halfway through our tea when I broached the subject which meant so much to me and my school. James listened smiling, and then began to explain.

'First of all, I must make it plain that Amy knew nothing about it. I didn't tell her a thing, knowing she can't keep a secret for two minutes anyway.'

'Well!' gasped Amy outraged.

'But, *unknowingly*, she did set things in motion, because she told me about your two empty houses and how steeply they had dropped in price. Of course, my tough old business instincts were aroused, and I thought of the Trust.'

'But why at this precise time? Haven't you got other possible plans in this area?'

'Since Derek's death we've had a large amount left to the Hope Trust, as you know, and we wanted more premises in these parts. He was a great believer in the family idea, and the next big project is to found a whole village, rather like the Pestalozzi one in Sussex. But that's not going to be ready for many a year, and so we are carrying on with the policy we have already. We've found that a few children get settled very quickly in a community, and the local school can absorb them easily. That's why we keep the units to school ages approximately, some like the Fairacre one's from roughly five to eleven, then some from eleven to about sixteen, and of course there are a number of babies' homes. We learnt a lot from visiting well-established places like Barnardo's.'

'It's wonderful news for me,' I said. 'It makes the future really hopeful. When will they come?'

He laughed, and took a third piece of gingerbread. 'I can't see them sitting in your desks until next year at the earliest. We've got to interview the couples who will be in charge of each house. Luckily we've got a splendid list of applicants, but we take a lot of trouble in matching them to the neighbours as well as the children.'

It all sounded perfect, but I still had an uneasy twinge of guilt. 'James,' I said tentatively, 'you didn't do this for some quixotic reason, such as pleasing Amy and me?'

'You flatter yourself,' he said sturdily. 'I can assure you I started the negotiations for two reasons only. The first was to put into operation Derek's wishes. The second reason was that I could not resist a bargain, and we shall never see house property as cheap again. Satisfied?'

And with that I had to be content.

Just before they went, James said: 'I'm taking Amy away for a break. She's never really recovered from that bang on the head, and I didn't help by inflicting that little rat Brian on her. You can be sure *that* won't happen again!'

On Monday morning I broke the good news to Mrs Richards who was as thrilled as I was.

'So Fairacre School is safe?'

'It looks like it.'

'Isn't that marvellous?'

'Marvellous, indeed; and I'll let you choose this morning's hymn to celebrate it.'

She went to the piano stool and began to leaf through our shabby copy of *Hymns Ancient and Modern*.

'What about "Let all the world in every corner sing"?' she enquired, swivelling round.

'Perfect,' I said.

At that moment I noticed Joseph Coggs, framed in the doorway. He was looking hopeful.

'Yes, Joe,' I said. 'It's time for the school bell. You can ring out the glad tidings to everyone in Fairacre.'

FAREWELL TO FAIRACRE

with illustrations by John S. Goodall

To Eileen and Mike with love

Contents

PART ONE

CHRISTMAS TERM

CHAPTER 1

Term Begins

The first day of term has a flavour that is all its own.

For one thing, it invariably dawns fair and bright, no matter how appalling the weather has been in the days preceding it.

In fact, the last two weeks of the school summer holidays had been cold and rainy, washing out any plans for picnics or gardening which I had made. As headmistress of the neighbouring village school of Fairacre, I had hoped to spend the last weeks of my summer break in tidying the garden before the autumn leaves swamped the place. Now such plans had been thwarted, for I must return to my school duties.

On this particular September morning, the view from my kitchen window was bathed in sunlight. Dew sparkled on the lawn where a thrush hastened hither and thither with an ear alert for worms below. Spiders' webs decorated the hawthorn hedge with medallions of silver lace, and the branches of the old Bramley apple tree were bowed down with fruit.

Beyond this spread Hundred Acre field dotted with sheep, and farther still the misty bulk of the downs against the sky.

I was lucky to live in this pretty downland village of Beech Green. Luckier still to live in the cottage which was now my home, for it had been left to me on the death of a dear friend and colleague, Dolly Clare.

She had lived there for most of her long life, arriving at the age of six with her sister Ada, and her parents Francis and Mary Clare. It was Francis who had rethatched the cottage, and some of his tools had been used, years later, by a young thatcher who inherited them.

When Dolly told me, in the last years of her life, that she had left the cottage to me, I was overwhelmed at such generosity.

All my working life I had lived either in lodgings or in the tied school house at Fairacre. More prudent teachers had invested in property, as I should have done, but somehow I had never got round to taking out a mortgage, and the years slipped by as I enjoyed my rent-free time as headmistress of Fairacre school.

But a few years earlier, my former assistant and dear friend had left me this lovely home, and I have never ceased to be grateful.

The village of Beech Green is some two or three miles from Fairacre, and Dolly Clare had cycled there and back each school day for many years. I was luckier and had a car to shelter me on my daily journey. We get plenty of blustery winds in this open area, and Dolly must have had many rough journeys in her time, but I never knew her to be late for school, and she always looked immaculate in the classroom, no matter how severely the elements had battered her on the way there.

The kitchen clock said eight o'clock. It was time I tore myself away from all the delights before me, and set off for a new term.

Tibby, my fastidious cat, oozed through the cat-flap and surveyed my offering of the most expensive cat food on the market with considerable distaste, before walking away, and I made my way to the garage.

The morning air smelt as seductive as the flowers which scented it.

It was sad to have to leave the garden, but there was no help for it.

Term had begun, and I must be on my way.

At first sight, Fairacre school looked much as it did a hundred years ago. A low one-storey building with Gothic windows and porch, it did its Victorian best to imitate St Patrick's venerable pile near by.

The playground was dappled with sunshine and the shadows of lofty trees in the vicarage garden next door. In one corner stood the pile of coke which would soon be needed for the two tortoise stoves inside.

A few children were already rushing about in the playground, and one or two of the most effusive galloped up to throw their arms round my waist in exuberant greeting. Such affection would be somewhat muted, I knew, as the term progressed and we all settled down to our usual workaday relationship, but it was very cheering to be greeted as if risen from the dead, and I was glad to see them in such good spirits.

My curmudgeonly school cleaner, Mrs Pringle, was not quite so welcoming.

'That skylight,' she told me dourly, 'has been up to its old tricks again.'

I thought that Mrs Pringle was also up to her old tricks, damping any enthusiasm she encountered on this bright new morning. The skylight was an enemy, of many years standing, to us both.

'Anything special?'

'All this 'ere rain has done its worst,' she informed me with satisfaction. 'Dripped all over your ink stand, run under the map cupboard, and nearly got to *my stoves.*'

Here her voice rose in a crescendo and her jowls grew red and wobbled like a turkey-cock's. The two tortoise stoves at our school are the idols of Mrs Pringle's life, and she ministers to them with love and blacklead and all the considerable power of her elbow.

'I'll get Bob Willet to have a look,' I promised her.

Bob Willet is our school caretaker, sexton and grave-digger at St Patrick's church, and general handyman to whoever is in need of his services in Fairacre.

He is an expert gardener, a steady church-goer and a good friend to all. Our village, without Bob, would lose its heart.

But Mrs Pringle was not to be placated so easily.

'I can't be everywhere at once. I come up here twice a

week regular all through the holidays, and there's not many school cleaners as can say the same. I've worked my fingers to the bone for all these years, as well you know, and for what thanks?'

I looked at Mrs Pringle's fingers which were nowhere near the bone, but rather resembled prime pork sausages.

'Well, I thank you. Often.'

'But do those dratted kids?'

At this point a posse of the dratted kids appeared in the doorway, beaming broadly.

'It's bell time, miss. John Todd says it's his turn, but he done it last morning of term.'

'*Did it*,' I corrected automatically. Not that it would make the slightest difference, but once a teacher always a teacher.

'Anyway,' I added, 'it's a new start today, so Eileen may ring the bell.'

Term had undoubtedly begun.

Ever since I arrived at Fairacre some years ago, we have had the threat of closure hanging over our heads.

It is a two-teacher school and seems to have been so for most of its long life. When I came, the numbers were between thirty and forty on roll, but early log books show that occasionally the school numbered around a hundred pupils.

In those days families were large. It was nothing to have four or five children from the same family under the school roof at the same time. Also, of course, children stayed until the age of fourteen, but in these rural areas it was not uncommon for them to leave at twelve if they had been offered a post. Most of the boys went into farming, and most of the girls into service.

During my time, my schoolchildren ranged in age from five to eleven years, and after that they proceeded to George Annett's care in the school at Beech Green where they stayed until fifteen.

The plight of our falling numbers over the years was a constant headache, and only a year or two earlier they had fallen to about twenty. My assistant teacher, Mrs Richards, who taught the infants, and I thought that the outlook was gloomy.

But amazingly help was at hand. Two new houses in the village were bought by a charitable housing trust, part of the Malory-Hope foundation, the brain-child of a much-loved local philanthropist. One house was already occupied. Here a married couple in their forties were in charge of four children, the youngest five years of age and the eldest ten. All four had been at Fairacre school now for one term, and were welcomed by Mrs Richards and me, as well as all those who had the welfare of our school at heart.

The other house was awaiting five children, but one would be a baby. Nevertheless, the thought of four more children, of school age, to swell our numbers in the near future was decidedly heartening.

There had been some plumbing problems with the second house which had held up the arrival of the second family, but we all hoped that we should see our new pupils by half term, at the end of October, or certainly by Christmas.

The Trust had been set up, some years earlier, by a wealthy and philanthropic business man. It began as a housing scheme for the orphans of men who had served in the armed forces, and today it still gave such orphans priority. But as the Trust's work expanded, other children were accepted, and the founder's basic desire for family units was respected. Not more than five, and usually four, children were looked after by a married couple in a small home. They attended the local schools, and took part in general activities, and the regime seemed to work admirably.

I must admit that when the news broke in Fairacre that two families would be housed in the Trust's latest acquisitions, there were a few misgivings from the older inhabitants. Mrs Pringle, of course, was one of the gloomier forecasters.

'I've heard tell as some of these kids come from towns.'

'What's wrong with that?'

'Remember them evacuees? All town lots they were. And brought no end of trouble. Head lice, fleas, scabious —'

'Scabies,' I corrected automatically.

'As I said,' continued Mrs Pringle, undaunted. 'Not to mention bed-wetting and *worse*.'

'Well, these aren't evacuees, and are being properly brought up. Frankly, I'm looking forward to them, and so are the children.'

'You'll regret it,' said my old sparring partner. 'Mark my words.'

But her dark forebodings had not come to pass. The four new pupils had settled into Fairacre school very well, were accepted by the children with the easy camaraderie of the young and, to my mind, were a very welcome addition to the establishment.

The golden September weather continued. The children still wore their summer clothes and complained of being 'sweatin' 'ot, miss', but continued to rush around the playground, and occasionally up and over the coke pile when they thought they were unobserved, so they did not get a great deal of sympathy from me when they pleaded exhaustion from the weather conditions.

But I relished this balmy spell of weather. We had some lessons out of doors, particularly those which involved reading, either by me, or on their own.

Sometimes I suspected that the combined siren voices of a distant tractor driven by someone's dad, the cawing of the rooks above us in the vicarage trees and the humming of innumerable insects around us took more of the children's attention than the printed pages before them. But this did not perturb me greatly. They would remember those golden moments long after the stories had faded from their memory.

Sometimes I took my class for a nature walk. This was always exhilarating, particularly when we traversed the village street on our way to the chalky paths of the downs. A mother, on her way to see Mr Lamb at the Post Office, would greet us warmly. A distant tractor would be pointed out enthusiastically.

'My dad's over there. They're havin' swedes in that field this year.'

Someone would wave from an upstairs window.

'My gran,' said Ernest, waving back. 'She has a nap on her bed after dinner.'

Such encounters were very cheering, but I could not help noticing that there were far fewer people about in the village than when I first came to Fairacre years ago.

Now it was the norm for both parents to go to work, and nowadays at a distance, travelling by car. Certainly, both parents had worked in earlier times, but usually within walking distance of their houses.

Mr Roberts, our local farmer, probably employed eight or ten men when I knew him first, and their wives helped at the farm house or at nearby large homes with domestic work. Usually it was part-time work for the wives, for they arranged matters so that they could be at home at midday to dish up a meal for their husbands and any of the family who were at hand. A number of my schoolchildren went home to a midday meal when I first started teaching at Fairacre. Nowadays all stayed to school dinner. It was a sign of the times.

A few hundred yards beyond the edge of the village, a path led upwards to the downs. The first few yards were shaded by shrubby trees. The wayfaring trees grew here, their oval grey-green leaves encircling the masses of white flowers so soon to turn brown and change into autumn berries. Brambles clutched at legs, their fruits already forming into hard green knobs, and here and there a second flowering of honeysuckle scented the air.

But as we ascended we left the scrub behind, and found ourselves in the high windy world of true chalk downland.

We sat puffing on the fine grass and enjoyed the splendid view. There were pellets of rabbit droppings around us among the tiny vetches and thymes of the grassland, and the small blue butterflies which inhabit chalky places fluttered about their business, ignoring intruders.

We pointed out to each other various points of interest.

'There's the weathercock,' said Patrick. 'It says the wind's in the east.'

'Soppy!' commented John Todd. 'You be lookin' at his tail.' An ensuing scrap was quelled by me.

They noticed washing blowing on a distant line, a train making its way to Caxley station some ten miles away, and a herd of black and white Friesian cows behind Mr Roberts' farm house.

Was this, I wondered guiltily, really 'A Nature Walk'? Was it, more truthfully, 'An Afternoon's Outing'? Whatever it was, I decided, watching the children at their various activities or non-activities, it was, as Shakespeare said of sleep,

> *Balm of hurt minds . . .*
> *Chief nourisher in life's feast.*

We picked a few sprigs of downland vegetation and some twigs from the shrubs at the foot of the downs as we returned, as a sop to the Cerberus of education.

John Todd had collected a pocketful of rabbit droppings which he maintained were going to be used as fertiliser for his mum's pot-plants. My only proviso was that his collection should be put into a paper bag until home time. I heard him later telling another boy that he thought he might sell some to his granny.

Sometimes I think that John Todd will end up either in jail, or as a millionaire. He will certainly make his mark somewhere.

I relished returning to my Beech Green home on those golden afternoons of early term time. The gardening jobs which had waited during the rainy holidays were soon done, and Bob Willet came to lend a hand on Saturday mornings when he could spare the time.

'You heard about Mrs Mawne?' he asked, as we sat with our mugs of coffee in the sunshine.

'No. What's happened?'

'Been took to hospital. Lungs, they say.'

This was bad news. I liked Mrs Mawne, a strong-minded busy soul who took an active part in Fairacre affairs, and looked after her husband Henry very well. Henry was a well-known ornithologist and naturalist and wrote, not only for our *Caxley Chronicle*, but also for more erudite publications. At one time, when it was thought he was a bachelor, and before his wife returned to him, Fairacre had been busy arranging what it considered a suitable match between Henry and me. Naturally, neither of us knew anything about these romantic plans, and very cross we were when light dawned.

'Is it serious?'

'Must be if she's in hospital,' said Bob, who appeared to regard these institutions as the seemly place to die in. 'She do smoke, of course. Don't do your tubes any good.'

'And what about Mr Mawne? Can he look after himself?'

'Shouldn't think so,' said Bob cheerfully. 'Probably frizzle a hegg and bacon.'

'That's something, anyway.'

'Not as good as my Alice's steak and kidney pudden, or her rabbit pie with a nice bit of onion in it.'

'Well, you're spoilt,' I told him.

'That's right,' he agreed with much satisfaction.

He drained his mug and went back to his weeding.

During the next week, Henry Mawne appeared at school.

This was no surprise, as he is a frequent visitor bringing pamphlets and posters about birds and other natural matters which he thinks will interest the children. They always enjoy his visits, and sometimes he stays for half an hour and gives an impromptu nature lesson.

On this occasion I thought he looked older and shabbier. I enquired after his wife, and he shook his head sadly.

'Not too good. The medics tell me she had a slight stroke yesterday. Nothing to worry about, they tell me.' His face grew pink. 'I ask you! Nothing to worry about indeed! They told me not to visit her last night, but I'm damn well going up this afternoon.'

'I'm sure you'll find her getting on well,' I assured him,

hoping that was the truth. 'Lots of people have strokes, and are as right as rain soon after.'

He was not to be comforted, however, and took himself off after a few minutes. It was sad to see him suddenly so old.

'What's up?' I heard Patrick whisper to Ernest.

'Mrs Mawne. She's been struck.'

'Struck? By lightning or something?'

'No, chump! With a stroke, like that chap down the pub.'

'But he's all —' began Patrick looking horrified.

'That'll do,' I said firmly. 'You can stop talking and get on with your work.'

Resignedly, and with heavy sighs, they returned to their labours, while I sorted out a pile of forms to take home to study in peace before returning them to our local education office. Somehow, there seemed to be more than ever these days, and I did not relish an evening poring over them.

Henry's sad face haunted me. If his wife were laid up in hospital for any length of time it might be a good idea to have him to a meal one evening.

What Fairacre and Beech Green would make of the matter I did not know, nor care. If two middle-aged old dears could not enjoy a meal together without scandal it was a pity.

Nevertheless, I resolved to ask our vicar Gerald Partridge and his wife, or failing that, my old friends George and Isobel Annett to join the party. Decorum apart, four would fit nicely round my table, and make more cheerful company for a sad man.

Mrs Pringle, when she appeared at midday to wash up the dinner things, knew all about Mrs Mawne's troubles. With lugubrious relish she told me about several stroke sufferers of her acquaintance. None, it seemed, had survived, or if they had, she told me, it was a great pity considering the plight in which they were left.

'I don't want to hear anymore,' I told her roundly, and left her quivering with anger and frustration amidst the washing-up steam.

Later that evening I tried to settle down to those wretched forms, but found my attention wandering. Mrs Pringle's ghoulish enjoyment of disaster, which I can usually dismiss with some amusement, irritated me unduly on this particular evening. I had lived long enough with her, in all conscience, to be able to ignore her habitual gloom, but I had to admit that latterly she had riled me more than usual.

Was she getting even more trying, or was I getting crabbier? Of course, we were both getting older and our tempers became less equable. Even so, I thought, stuffing the forms into a file and abandoning the task for the moment, should I be feeling quite so depressed?

Perhaps I was sickening for something? Perhaps I needed more stimulus? Perhaps I needed company? Even Tibby seemed to have deserted me on this particular evening, going about some private feline business.

I walked out into the garden, still troubled. Heavy clouds had rolled up from the west, and no doubt rain would fall during the night. This was the first overcast evening we had seen for many days, and it fitted my mood. The air was still, somehow menacing, and I shivered despite the humid warmth.

I would go early to bed, I told myself, and read the latest Dick Francis book, and perhaps plan my proposed dinner party.

> *We get the Hump,*
> *Camelions Hump,*

as Rudyard Kipling said. Doing something was the cure for that, and tomorrow I should be myself again.

I was in bed by nine o'clock.

CHAPTER 2

Old and New Friends

The roads were wet when I set off for school the next morning, feeling rather more cheerful after my early night.

Mrs Pringle was limping heavily about her duties, and was decidedly off-hand with me. Mrs Pringle's bad leg is a sure pointer to prevailing conditions. If she is in one of her rare moods of comparatively good temper, she walks at her normal waddle.

If, however, the limp is noticeable, it means that she is resentful of all the work she is called upon to do, or she is in a flaming temper about one of her pet interests. Anything connected with the misuse of her precious tortoise stoves, for instance, puts her in a rage and the limp is most pronounced. When Mrs Pringle's leg has 'flared up', as she says, we are on guard.

Obviously, the present malaise was the outcome of my short shrift with her over Mrs Mawne's condition, and I did not propose to do any mollifying. She must just get on with it.

In my first months at Fairacre I had worried about Mrs Pringle's feelings, and had done my best to apologise for any hurt which I might have done her unknowingly. Now I knew better, and it was Bob Willet who had opened my eyes not long after my arrival.

'Don't you take no heed of that ol' besom's tantrums,' he told me sturdily. 'Maud Pringle's been a bad-tempered old bag ever since she was born. Turn a deaf ear and a blind eye.'

It was sound advice, and nowadays Mrs Pringle's temper and her bad leg's combustibility held no terrors for me.

Mrs Richards, my assistant, was on playground duty after we had finished school dinner, so I walked down to the Post Office to buy boiled sweets to replenish the school sweet tin, and to pay in some of the children's savings. This thrifty habit had started, years before my arrival, as a wartime effort, and somehow continued.

Mr Lamb greeted me with his usual *bonhomie* and his habitual crack about how many sweets I got through.

I asked after Mrs Mawne. Mr Lamb has his finger on the pulse of Fairacre life and knows more even than Mrs Pringle.

'Much the same, Mr Mawne told me. He's just been in for some eggs. Must be living on 'em, I reckon. They're keeping her in hospital for at least another week. He visits daily, afternoons mostly.'

Armed with this knowledge I decided to go ahead with my invitations that evening, and returned to my duties.

One of Fairacre's major interests at this time was the completion of the second new home which was to house five more children under the Trust's guardianship.

The first home was now flourishing, and the couple who ran it had settled happily among their neighbours. Their charges who had swelled my school's numbers were good-tempered easy children, and gave me no trouble.

The couple for the second home had been appointed, and were frequently seen watching last-minute alterations to their new house. The plumbing problem which had held up proceedings seemed to have been overcome, and it was generally expected that the family would arrive some time in October.

After school one day I walked over to make myself known to the man and woman who were working in the garden.

'We were going to call on you,' the man said. 'You'll be having our children I believe.'

'And very welcome they will be,' I told him.

We introduced ourselves. They were Molly and Alfred Cotton, and they already knew their neighbours and co-hosts the Bennetts from next door. They also knew Mr Lamb, Bob Willet and Jane and Tom Winter who lived close by.

The Winters' home was one of the three new houses to be built recently in the village, and Jane and Tom had moved in some time earlier. They were a friendly pair, and their young son Jeremy had made friends with the four newcomers as soon as they had settled in. The Cottons were delighted with their appointment as joint wardens to their five children, and it seemed pretty obvious to me that they would be a great asset to the village.

'You won't be having all our children,' Molly told me. 'The youngest is not walking yet, and the next up is only four. The two brothers, seven and nine, will come to you, and the girl who is ten.'

I said that I should welcome them, and asked a little more about their family.

'The two brothers and the baby are all from one family,' said Alfred. 'They were saved by neighbours from a fire at their home. The parents perished.'

'That's a terrible thing!'

'They're young enough to have half-forgotten it,' said Molly, 'but I think the older boy, Bobby, still gets nightmares about fire. It's one reason why they have been moved right away, to give them a fresh start.'

'Well, you are doing a fine job,' I told them.

'Not very well paid though,' added Alfred, in a semi-jocular way.

Much later I was to recall that rather odd remark..

My old home at Fairacre, the school house which stood only a stone's throw across the playground from Fairacre school, had been badly damaged by a storm a few years earlier.

Luckily, no one was hurt, and I had already removed to Dolly Clare's cottage at Beech Green.

The repairs took some time, but eventually it was restored and put on the market. To my delight two friends of mine had bought it, and now lived there with their baby.

Horace and Eve Umbleditch had met at the preparatory school where he taught and she had been the school secretary. They had adopted village life with enthusiasm, and were generally liked. Horace had been roped in by the vicar as a general help to Henry Mawne, who made himself responsible for the finances and general welfare of St Patrick's. Now that Henry was so much engaged with his wife's illness, Horace was being called upon to do more, which he undertook very cheerfully.

I called to see Eve and the baby one afternoon after school. Young Andrew was sitting in his pram, bouncing about with enormous energy and making a bleating noise which his fond mother told me was singing.

Eve was ironing, but seemed happy enough to stop and put on the kettle.

'Horace won't be in for some time. Rugger practice,' she told me.

'Do they start as young as that?'

'Well, they all rush about wherever the ball happens to be. You don't see much *passing* of any elegance and skill, but they have a rattling good puff about, and get fearfully dirty and hungry, and everyone's happy, so I suppose it does them good.'

She looked through the window at the pram. The bleating had stopped.

'He's dropped asleep,' she said. 'I always suspect sudden silence. It usually means he's found something to eat. He made quite a meal of his pram strap last week.'

We sipped our tea, and I looked about my old sitting-room with affection.

'Tell me,' said Eve, sounding worried. 'Do you *mind*?'

'Mind?'

'About us living here. In your house.'

'Good heavens, no! Why should I? It looks lovely to me. And it isn't my house now. It was only *lent* to me, so to speak, while I taught at Fairacre school, just as it was lent to my predecessors.'

She looked relieved.

'I still can't believe it is our house. Well, *will* be when the mortgage is paid,' she added with a smile. 'I still feel that it belongs to you.'

'I promise not to haunt you,' I said, 'but I know how you feel. The ghosts of the Hopes, who taught here years ago, always seemed to be about, largely I think through Mrs Pringle's constant reminders of how *clean* Mrs Hope had kept the place, in contrast to my own sketchy house-keeping. I gather from Mrs P. that Mrs Hope dusted the tops of her doors daily, and any visitors had to brush their clothes and take off their shoes before entering.'

'I don't believe it.'

'Frankly, neither do I, but you know Mrs Pringle! She

has a way of telling you the most outrageous things, with such concentrated venom that one begins to think they are true.'

'Well, we're happy as sand-boys here, and I hope that all these other newcomers will settle in as contentedly as we have.'

She went on to tell me that she had made friends with Jane and Tom Winter and the Bennetts who were the foster-parents near by, but had not yet met the Cottons.

She asked after Mrs Mawne whom she knew, and with all this exchange of news about old and new friends it was six o'clock before I realised it.

'Tibby will be pretty off-hand with me,' I told Eve, as I hurried to my car.

'And Horace will with me,' she replied, 'if I don't get our dinner in the oven.'

We departed to cope with our respective tyrants.

Plans for my modest dinner party went ahead.

The Reverend Gerald Partridge and his wife would be away for a week visiting friends in Norfolk, but Isobel and George Annett, who lived near me at the school house in Beech Green, said that they would love to come.

They and Henry Mawne were invited for the next Wednesday evening when the house would be at its cleanest after Mrs Pringle's ministrations in the afternoon.

Now what should I give them? was the next problem. Cold salmon and salad would be elegant, and easily prepared, but already the evenings were getting an autumnal feel about them, and hot food is somehow more welcoming.

I put my load of school forms, records, files and general correspondence to one side – yet again – and let my thoughts dwell much more pleasurably on my entertaining.

Something that would look after itself in a casserole, I decided. Who wants their hostess in the kitchen at the last minute stirring sauce?

I thought of lamb cutlets, pork chops, steak and kidney. Perhaps rather heavy as an evening meal for four middle-aged people, I decided.

A brace of pheasants, a present from the farmer Mr Roberts after his final shoot of the season, still lay in the freezer. But pheasant can be surprisingly tough, and not everyone likes it. What about fish? A halibut steak apiece, in a good white sauce, would suit me well, but did my guests like fish?

In the end, I took the safe and rather mundane way out by settling for chicken, jointed neatly by the butcher for my proposed casserole, and served with seasonal vegetables supplied by Mr Willet from his garden.

I would make an apple and blackberry pie, and a raspberry mousse for dessert, and nice easy accommodating melon for starters. I had some fresh coffee beans, and if I could remember to buy some chocolate mints I should be well set up.

Having settled this in my own mind, I picked up the armful of school papers, thought better of it, put them all back, and watched a television programme until it was time for bed.

I found that I was ready for bed much earlier these days, and when I had time to think about it I felt vaguely worried by my increasing tiredness.

It was still a pleasure to see friends, to write to those at a distance, or to talk to them by telephone. I had real joy in planning such simple entertaining as my little dinner party. Even a jaunt to Caxley at the weekends held a certain excitement.

But, I had to admit that school these days was increasingly demanding. The actual teaching, and the company of the children, I still enjoyed. The fact that the fear of closure, because of dwindling numbers, had now receded, thanks to the advent of the two new homes provided by the Trust, was an enormous relief, and by rights I should be feeling on top of the world.

But I was not. There was nothing physically wrong with me, no sinister pains or lumps in evidence. It was just that somehow the sparkle seemed to have gone out of life.

From school life anyway, I told myself. I remembered Eve Umbleditch's anxiety about my relinquishment of the school house which had been my home for so many years. Could I, subconsciously, be missing it? I did not think so. I was blissfully content with Dolly Clare's cottage at Beech Green.

Certainly, my routine had been slightly altered. I needed to get up earlier and to make sure that the car was ready for its daily short drive.

But I had always woken early, and was at my liveliest in the morning hours, so that nothing could account for my present malaise. Of course, I was getting older, and expected to be slower, but I was beginning to feel worried by the mound of paperwork which seemed to accompany me everywhere.

Like most people, I had never taken kindly to form-filling, but when I looked back to my early years at Fairacre, it seemed to me that I used to dash them off, send them back to the education office, and forget the whole affair. Now each morning brought a pile of work, usually marked 'Urgent', and I was beginning to feel submerged and desperate.

I told myself sternly that most people had the same problems and one must just soldier on. With any luck, I should adjust to my load, just like a tired old cart-horse.

It was on one of these evenings when I was being firm with myself, and trying to whip up enough energy to tackle at least some of my papers, that my old friend Amy rang.

We first met at college many years ago. She was, and still is, pretty, vivacious and intelligent. She gave up work when she married James after only two years' teaching, but occasionally took on a short spell as a supply teacher in local schools, 'to keep my hand in', as she puts it. Occasionally, she has helped me at Fairacre school, and she has certainly not lost her touch.

Our friendship has stood the test of time remarkably well, despite our different circumstances. Amy is much more sophisticated than I am, is a wonderful wife to James, and a wonderful hostess to the important business friends they entertain. She dresses exquisitely, keeps up-to-date with the world of music, theatre, films and painting, and generally puts me in the shade, where I am very content to stay.

The one really trying trait in Amy's character is her desire to see me married, and I have lost count of the various men she has paraded before me in her quest to find me a suitable partner. I am loud and vehement in my protestations to dear Amy, but it does no good. She cannot believe that any woman can be happy without a man in the house.

I constantly point out that I should find a husband a nuisance. I do not want to wash socks, thread new pyjama cords through hems with a safety-pin, listen to news of rugby teams, the stock market, golf averages and, in the case of older men, their war-time reminiscences. Besides, even the nicest men snore, and I like a peaceful bedroom.

Luckily, on this occasion, husbands were not on Amy's mind.

'It's about the opera,' said Amy, after our usual enquiries after health. 'There's a good company coming to Oxford. Care to join me one evening? James will be in China on some trade lark.'

'What's on offer?' I am no opera fan. The idiocy of the plots I find infuriating, and I don't know enough about music to appreciate the finer points. In any case, I have exceptionally acute hearing, and find the noise excessive. Before now I have sat through an entire opera with cotton wool in my ears, to the disgust of the opera-lovers around me. Even so, I have returned home with a splitting head-ache.

'They're only doing two,' replied Amy. '*Madame Butter-fly and Die Fledermaus.*'

'Which do you favour?'

'Well, I like Puccini's music, but I like *Fledermaus* because it's such a romp. I want you to choose.'

'I do draw the line at *Madame Butterfly* because the plot's even more silly than most, and I can't stick Lieutenant Pinkerton, nor that ghastly inevitable toddler who turns up, and Butterfly is such a *wimp* —'

'Say no more,' said Amy, 'I gather you don't like it. So *Fledermaus* it is.'

I felt suddenly guilty.

'But Amy, if you prefer —'

'I'd rather see the Strauss one, actually. I love Frosch, the jailer, and all his bits of business.'

'You're sure?'

'Positive. I'll send off for the tickets today. It's not until early December. Make a note of the day now, my dear, as I expect you'll be up to your ears in end-of-term jollities by then.'

I told her about my dinner-party plans, and about poor disconsolate Henry Mawne.

'Well,' said Amy briskly, 'your company should cheer him up. He was always so fond of you.'

She hung up before I could protest.

There was a nip in the air as I drove to school the next morning. Already the swallows were gathering on the telephone lines ready for departure to sunnier places. The rose hips glowed like scarlet beads in the hedges, and the first few puffs of wild clematis seed-heads were a foretaste of the grey clouds which would soon obscure the bushes over which they clambered.

Autumn in this part of the world is always lovely, for we are blest with magnificent clumps of beech trees which thrive in this chalk country, and their blazing bronze lights the landscape when the sun shines upon them. I relish, too, the fruits of the earth, the blackberries, the crab apples, the sloes, and most of all the miraculous mushrooms, overnight pearls, which are a source of constant pleasure to those who come across them.

I am ready, too, for the domestic pleasures of colder days.

There is great satisfaction from the open fire in the cool evenings, particularly if it is fed with wood gathered by oneself. With the curtains drawn against the dark outside world, what could be more snug?

And yet I am sad too at the onset of winter. I miss the flowers, the smell of cut grass, the singing birds, the humming bees, and all the scents and sounds of summer. The smell of autumn bonfires, the departure of the swallows, the bare brown fields and the basket full of blackberries are small consolation for that golden summer sun.

When I arrived at school that morning, a little knot of children had gathered round a ladder on which Bob Willet was perched.

He was replacing a tile which had slipped a foot or two
from its rightful place, and had lodged in the gutter.

'Been meaning to do this since the summer holidays,' he
called down. 'You got enough rain through that dratted
skylight without another leak here.'

I agreed. Our school is over a hundred years old and
needs constant vigilance to keep it weatherproof. Under
Bob Willet's care we are kept warm and dry. The skylight,
though, has defied generations of builders, and leaks whenever the wind and rain come from the south-west, its usual
quarter.

He gave a final tap to the tile and began to descend the
ladder. The performance over, the children began to look
about for different excitements.

'Miss, miss,' called one of the new children who lived in
the Bennetts' house. 'May I ring the bell?'

So far, the child had been very quiet, a pretty pale girl
but shy. To offer to ring the bell was a great advance.

'I ain't rung it for *ages*!' growled Joseph Coggs. I have a
soft spot for Joe, whose home and family are poor and
pathetic, mainly because Arthur Coggs, the father, is incapable of keeping a job and lives mostly in the local public
houses.

'You often ring it,' I pointed out. 'But Alice has never
done it. You can go inside with her, and get the bell rope
down for her.'

'But can I ring it?'

'No. Perhaps just *once* to show her, and then it's Alice's job.'

Beaming, the two departed, and the rest drifted away to
savour their last few minutes of freedom.

'I hear you're having Mr Mawne to supper this week,'
said Bob. He was lowering the ladder carefully.

The way that news flies around a village never ceases to
dumbfound me.

'Yes,' I said shortly.

'That's nice of you,' commented Bob. 'Poor old boy looks pretty glum these days.'

I did not answer, but began making my way to the school porch.

Bob Willet straightened up, red in the face from his exertions.

'There's a lot in Fairacre says you're a tough old biddy, but I allus maintain your 'eart's in the right place.'

He trudged off, leaving me speechless at Fairacre's assessment of my character.

Tough old biddy indeed!

CHAPTER 3

A Broken Evening

Mrs Pringle, of course, knew about my proposed evening party almost as soon as I did.

I do not think she approved of my invitation to Henry Mawne. She probably thought me *fast*, and possibly *loose*.

But she was graciously pleased to approve of my inclusion of the Annetts in the invitation. She knows both well. Isobel, in her single days, was my valued assistant after Dolly Clare's retirement, and her neat ways were much approved by Mrs Pringle.

'Leaves the classroom a fair treat,' was her summing up, and praise could go no higher.

George Annett has been organist and choir master at St Patrick's for many years, and has put up with Maud Pringle's contralto bellowings, not unlike a cow deprived of its calf, for all that time. By nature a quick and impatient man, he certainly finds Mrs Pringle a sore trial in the choir.

Her singing is powerful but not accurate. She tends to be slightly behind the rest of the choir in time, and decidedly flat when it comes to high notes.

Nevertheless, she is a faithful member of the choir, and takes a proprietorial interest in the chancel woodwork, particularly the choir stalls, as a forebear of hers was one of the carpenters and joiners who refurbished that area during Victoria's reign.

She approved of my having the party on a Wednesday evening.

'Give me a chance to do you properly on Wednesday afternoon,' she said. 'Leave out that cutlery of yours and I'll give it a good go, and get the egg out of the forks.'

I said that I should be grateful for such help.

'Of course, the windows really wants cleaning, and that carpet's never been the same since you tripped over with the cheese sauce in your hand. And to my mind, that fireplace always looks *tawdry*. Never comes up like my stoves here.'

'Well, you can't expect it. The stoves get attention every day.'

'That's true,' agreed Mrs Pringle with smug satisfaction. 'I takes a pride in 'em. I suppose if your head's full of book-learning it hasn't got enough go left in it to notice the filth around the place.'

Whether this was a compliment to my intelligence, or a real back-hander to my domestic standards, I could not be sure. A bit of both, I thought, and decided to let it pass without comment.

In any case, Mrs Pringle likes to have the last word.

On the evening of the party everything looked splendid.

The table was spread with my best tablecloth, which had been left to me by Aunt Clara, together with her seed pearls and a very welcome hundred pounds, some thirty years ago. The glass and silver sparkled, and a vase of late roses stood in the centre of the table.

I felt that my ancient place mats rather let the side down, but they were pretty on top, if shabby, and no one was likely to turn them over to examine the deplorable state of the baize backing during a polite dinner party.

The evening was chilly, and I thought of my chicken

casserole simmering away in the oven with some satisfaction. Perhaps I should have had soup for starters instead of melon? Too late now, I told myself, and went upstairs to change.

Through the bedroom window I could just see, as the dusk deepened, that the Bramley apples were almost ready to pick, and a few autumn leaves were strewn on the lawn. Mrs Pringle had set a fire for us, and it was now crackling away, throwing cheerful flickers of rosy light on the walls of my sitting-room, and glinting on the newly polished copper and brass.

The Annetts were the first to arrive. Isobel was in a pretty dove-grey knitted suit and a handsome silk blouse, and George very spruce in his Sunday suit and a dashing Liberty tie.

'My!' he exclaimed, warming his hands at the fire. 'You have made it all look so splendid! Dolly would be so pleased to see it.'

'I wish she could,' I replied. 'I only hope I can care for it as well as she did.'

Henry drove up a few minutes later. He looked a little less strained, I thought, as we asked for the latest bulletin on his wife's condition.

'A little better, they said, when I rang just now. But no hope of her returning home, evidently, until all the tests are favourable.'

We all agreed that it was far better to stay a little longer in the nurses' care, and to get really strong before facing the rigours of home affairs.

'Have you met our newcomer yet?' asked George. 'You'd be interested in him, Henry. He has written a book about birds of prey.'

'Not old Jenkins?' said Henry.

'That's right.'

'We were up at Cambridge together. Never kept in

touch though. Where is he? He married some frightful woman in Kenya.'

'Well, she died out there, and he's returned home. He's taken that little house just off the road between here and Fairacre. Up Pig Lane.'

'It's called Downland Lane now,' I pointed out. 'Some of the new people thought Pig Lane was vulgar.'

'I still call it Pig Lane,' said Henry.

'So do I,' said George roundly.

'I'll look him up,' promised Henry. 'I read his book. Not bad at all, considering Jenkins wrote it.'

I left them to it while I went to dish up.

I must say that my guests were most appreciative, and I basked in the warmth of their compliments. I am told that in some circles it is not considered polite to comment on the food served, but in these parts we take an active interest in the food put before us, and have no inhibitions about expressing our pleasure. I was grateful for my visitors' enthusiasm and pleased to see their hearty appetites.

The conversation flowed easily. The newcomer was described by Henry, as he remembered him at university, as 'a decent sort of fellow, but a bit of a dreamer'.

George Annett wanted to know if he could sing. Both the Fairacre and Beech Green church choirs were in need of male voices.

This led to next spring's Caxley Festival, then a concert the Annetts had been to in London, and on to more homely affairs such as the imminent glut of apples, the failure of our local runner beans, and the good fortune of Fairacre school in having found eight or nine new pupils to stave off the possibility of closure.

We adjourned to the fireside again, and I served coffee and passed round the box of mints which I had managed to remember.

It was while we were thus happily engaged that the telephone rang and I went to answer it.

A woman, sounding rather weary, spoke to me.

'This is the County Hospital. We are trying to get in touch with Mr Mawne – Mr Henry Mawne – and have been told that he is staying with you.'

I was somewhat taken aback by this suggestion that Henry was a resident in my home, but replied that Henry Mawne was here at the moment and that I would fetch him.

I returned to my friends feeling extremely worried. It must be serious news if the hospital were urgently seeking Henry.

They stopped their conversation as I entered, and looked up, coffee cups suspended.

'It's the hospital, Henry,' I said gently.

Henry struggled to his feet, the colour draining from his face.

I led him through to the telephone, and made him sit down before handing him the receiver, and then returned to the Annetts. They looked as shaken as I felt.

'It must be his wife,' whispered Isobel. 'But she was getting on so well. He said that he rang before coming here.'

The happiness of the evening was suddenly shattered by this interruption. I refilled coffee cups, and went about my duties as a hostess with a very sick feeling.

Henry reappeared after a few minutes. His face was ashen.

'I must go at once,' he muttered. 'She's conscious, asking for me. The sister said something about a rapid deterioration.'

He looked so shaky that I hastened towards him to propel him to a chair, but he motioned me away distractedly.

'I'm so sorry, but I must go at once. Thank goodness I've got the car outside.'

'Let me give you some more coffee before you go,' I urged, but he would have none of it.

'I must hurry. I intended to give the hospital this number before I left home, but forgot. Luckily, Bob Willet was potting up in my conservatory and got their message. But, of course, he had to look up this number, and there was some delay. It's urgent that I set off.'

George stood up. 'I shall drive you,' he said firmly.

Poor Henry's face crumpled, and for a moment I thought that he would break down. But he took a deep breath, thanked me very touchingly for the evening, and went with George to the car.

'But how will you get back,' whispered Isobel, 'if Henry stays?'

'There are always taxis,' said George, following his passenger, who was now opening the car door. 'Stay here until I ring from the hospital.'

We went to see them off, sending all sorts of hopeful messages to the invalid, but with heavy hearts.

'Heaven help all three of them,' I said to Isobel, when we were back by the fire. I held up the coffee pot.

'I couldn't, thanks. Let's wash up.'

'No, no!' I protested, but was overborne.

'Please. We won't do any good moping here. Let's mope while we do the dishes and wait for George to ring.'

And so we did.

It is some twenty miles to our County Hospital, and it was over an hour before George rang to say that he was returning by taxi. Henry was staying overnight and his car had been left in the hospital car park.

'And his wife?'

'Touch and go, I gather, but she spoke to Henry, which comforted him greatly.'

'I'm glad you drove him,' I said. 'He was in no state to be in charge of a car.'

'I'll be with you in half an hour,' he promised, as I handed the receiver to Isobel.

He kept his word, and we all had the final drink of the evening before the two set out to walk home.

The stars were out, and the night was still and chilly. I returned from my gate breathing in the unmistakable scent of autumn.

On the whole, I thought, as I put down on the kitchen floor some delectable remains of the chicken for Tibby, it had been a happy evening. But what a sad ending!

And what would the morrow hold for poor Henry?

The next morning Bob Willet met me in the school playground in a most unusual state of agitation.

'I've been that worried ever since the hospital called,' he told me. 'I didn't want to give 'em your number and upset the party, but they was so pushy – kept on and on – and in the end I thought I'd do as they said. I do hope that was right.'

'Absolutely,' I told him, and went on to explain the urgency of the matter and that Mr Mawne was staying with his wife.

He seemed much relieved. 'That's a comfort to me. If there's one thing I hates it's a Meddlesome Mattie, and I couldn't sleep last night for wondering if I'd done the right thing.'

'You did. And your vegetables were much appreciated.'

'And my brights?' boomed Mrs Pringle, who had appeared in time to hear the end of our conversation.

'They made the place look like Buckingham Palace,' I assured her.

With comparative peace restored we all three returned to our daily round.

Amy came to see me that evening, bearing a large suitcase filled with cast-off clothes and household linen, for an imminent school jumble sale.

'Good heavens, Amy!' I exclaimed, turning over some elegant jumpers and skirts. 'I think I shall take first pick.'

'Not your colours, dear,' replied Amy, settling herself on the sofa. 'Besides, it's quite wrong to snaffle all the best things before the sale starts. It's done far too often at Bent and elsewhere, but I hoped that Fairacre had more moral integrity.'

'My, my, Amy! You make me feel like an opium-runner or white-slaver! In any case, we have an admirable practice in Fairacre when it comes to jumble sales and bazaars.'

'And what's that?'

'The helpers are allowed to pick one object – and one only – before the doors open. After all, they've done the donkey work, and it does seem to work well.'

'I shall introduce the practice at Bent,' promised Amy. 'Now tell me how the party went.'

I told her all. She shook her head sadly.

'Poor woman! One wonders if it would be kinder to see her go if things are as bad as that. Poor Henry, too: he will be lonely.'

She looked at me with the speculative gaze I have learnt to dread.

'Like a cup of coffee?' I asked hastily.

'Love one. And by the way, James sent a message to say that your second house will definitely be ready at half term.'

Amy's husband was one of the directors of the Malory-Hope Trust, and his particular part in its work was the seeking of suitable family-sized houses for the orphans in the care of the Trust. He had recently been instrumental in buying some terraced houses in Glasgow for this work, and since then the two new Fairacre houses which had remained empty for so long.

I had wondered if James had thought of the possible closure of my school when the Trust had purchased this new property, and I had certainly felt somewhat guilty about the school's dwindling pupils.

When I taxed James with my guilty fears, he was hot in denying it. The fact was, he told me, that the property was never going to be as cheap again, so that he knew he would be getting a bargain on the Trust's behalf. Secondly, Sir Derek Malory-Hope, the original founder, had been keen to have several local homes and had expressed this wish a short time before his death. James, as his friend and colleague, was simply carrying out his desires.

I accepted this explanation absolutely, but I was aware that the decision to buy the two houses had been a life-saver for the school I had cared for so long. We were all much indebted to the Malory-Hope Trust.

Amy and I sipped our coffee, and I was conscious that she was watching me closely.

'You look rather tired,' she said. 'That dinner party must have worn you out.'

'Not the party,' I told her, 'but I must admit that the news from the hospital shook us all.'

'It must have done. But James and I have thought you've seemed under the weather for some time. Are you overworking?'

'Me? Overworking?' I cried. 'Amy, you've known me long enough to know that I have an in-built laziness that makes sure that I don't strain myself.'

'Well, I know you *procrastinate*, and you *dither*. Look at the dozens of jobs you've thought about over the years and never applied for. And here you are, wasted and washed up, still at Fairacre.'

'Thank you for those few kind words. You make me feel like a dish cloth.'

Amy laughed, and patted my arm. 'No offence meant, and none taken I hope, but seriously, you do look a little *wan*. What about having a check-up with the doctor?'

'I'm not bothering him. He's quite enough to do with people who are really ill.'

'Then take a tonic. An iron tonic might be just the thing.'

'The sort you take through a straw so that your teeth don't go black? I haven't done that since I was about six.'

Amy snorted impatiently. 'No, no! They have *pills* these days. Sometimes I wonder where you have been all these years.'

'Here,' I said cheerfully. 'And here, Amy dear, I propose to remain.'

'Hopeless!' sighed Amy.

I studied my face in the looking-glass when I went to bed. As far as I could see, I looked much the same. Older, of course, hair greying, jaw-line definitely heavier, plenty of lines here and there, but I was still recognisable, I thought.

It was nice of Amy to worry over me, but unnecessary. I certainly felt tired, and once or twice had been slightly dizzy, as when the vicar had told me about the new pupils who would be attending Fairacre school. And, of course, I was reluctant to get up in the mornings, but with autumn beginning to cast its chill across the country this was understandable. As for consulting our hard-pressed doctor, the idea was simply ludicrous, I told my reflection sternly.

Two days passed with no real news about Henry Mawne's wife, who remained critically ill in hospital.

Henry was at home, staying within earshot of the telephone, and with his car ready to set off if a call came.

We all worried about him, and even Mrs Pringle seemed genuinely sympathetic, curbing her usually ghoulish comments and simply shaking her head when Bob Willet mentioned the invalid.

But one evening Gerald Partridge rang me. Our vicar's voice was shaking.

'I heard about midday,' he told me. 'She died without regaining consciousness, and I've been with Henry. He's taken it very quietly and bravely. I think he knew all along that it was hopeless. I grieve for the poor fellow.'

I asked about funeral arrangements.

'Family only at the county crematorium. No flowers or letters, as she directed. And the remains will go to the family plot in Ireland. A melancholy journey for Henry. I have offered to go with him.'

It was a short conversation and I put the receiver down feeling very sad.

Another link with Fairacre life was broken.

Half term came at the end of October, and I spent most of it in the company of my cousin Ruth who lives in Dorset.

Her parting words were, 'You look better than when you arrived,' which I found faintly disquieting. How dilapidated had I looked on arrival, I wondered?

I returned to find four Christmas catalogues, as well as the usual letters.

Could Christmas really be so imminent? Visions of carols to be learnt, a nativity play, the usual Fairacre school party given to friends in the village, paper chains, Christmas cards and calendars to be constructed, all passed before my inward eye, and I thought, like Wordsworth, of the bliss of solitude.

Ah well! I had done it before, I comforted myself, and no doubt I could cope with it again.

Mrs Pringle greeted me with the news that the Cottons' house was now in order, and that the children would be coming to school, probably that very morning.

I viewed the prospect with pleasure, and hoped that they would settle with us as happily as their next-door neighbours, the Bennett children, had done.

Sure enough, as Joseph Coggs pulled the school bell rope, a blissful smile lighting up his gipsy-dark face, Mrs Cotton arrived with three of the five children.

There was a fair-haired girl of about ten, and two brothers of seven and nine. These two, I knew, were the children who had lost their parents in a fire. A younger child, not related to the brothers, would be eligible for admission next term when she would have her fifth birthday. An even younger girl, sister to the two brothers, was still only a toddler, and it would be some time before I had the pleasure of entering her name in the school register.

All the three newcomers came into my class. There was a certain amount of staring and whispering among my old hands, but within half an hour the three had settled in, and there was a general atmosphere of acceptance from new and old pupils.

The brothers seemed to be exceptionally well advanced in their school work. They had been attending a school in a neighbouring county, and I began to wonder if my teaching methods were behind the times. Were these two unusually forward, or were my children less intelligent? Was I falling down in my duties? Perhaps I should go to those refresher courses always being urged upon me by the school authorities. Too often such missives ended up on the wastepaper pile, together with all those harrowing appeals to save deprived people, starving children, diminishing rain forests, endangered species and sufferers from a multitude of agonising diseases.

I am far from callous, and frequently have a few sleepless hours at night worrying about these horrors which come tumbling through the letter-box. But there is a limit to my ability to help, and I simply support four or five pet charities, and have done so faithfully over the years.

Perhaps those pamphlets about evening classes and weekend refresher courses should be rescued from the pile, and studied earnestly?

Certainly my three newcomers seemed to be well in advance of Fairacre's standards in reading, writing and arithmetic.

I was filled with misgivings.

*

Our vicar usually takes prayers at the school one day a week, but a message came to say that he was accompanying Henry Mawne to Ireland for the interment of his wife's ashes, and would not be able to come to the school as usual.

Mrs Pringle seemed to take this news as a personal affront.

'Poor Mr Partridge, having to go all that way for a burial! If Mrs Mawne had been laid to rest decently in Fairacre churchyard, he could have come to school like he always does, and I could have got my stoves polished just as usual.'

I enquired why the vicar's visits should upset the stoves' routine.

'They always gets a special blackleading before vicar's day,' she told me. 'Surely you've noticed?'

I had to admit that I had not. Her breathing became heavier than usual, and her face turned red with outrage.

'Sometimes I wonders,' she puffed, 'why I spend my time working my fingers to the bone in this place, day after day, week after week —'

She paused for breath.

'Year after year,' I prompted helpfully.

'Pah!' said Mrs Pringle, and limped away.

That combustible leg of hers would register disgust, I knew, for the rest of the day.

CHAPTER 4

Personal Shock

Henry Mawne was in Ireland for three weeks, staying with his wife's relations.

During that time he sent me a sad little note thanking me for the evening he had shared at my house with the Annetts. He described it as 'a warm and comforting spot in a bleak world', but felt that he was slowly getting back to normal after the distress of the past weeks.

The vicar was only away for two nights, returning immediately after the service in which he had taken part.

He told me something about it when he called just after school closed one wet afternoon.

I was unlocking my car when he arrived, the children and Mrs Richards having departed.

I went to greet him, and made tracks for the school door, but he waved me back to the car, and we sat side by side watching the splashing of raindrops into the playground puddles.

'I found the occasion very moving,' he said. 'Such a green and lovely spot. I think Henry might be persuaded to stay permanently. He met his wife there, you know, and her family are being very pressing.'

'Would it be a good thing? Is there anything to bring him back here?'

Gerald Partridge looked troubled. 'I hope he does decide

to stay here. He is such a tower of strength to me over church affairs, and he is very well-liked in the locality. Also he said that this drier climate suits him better,' he said, surveying the puddles.

'In any case,' I said, 'he will have to return to do something about the house, I imagine.'

We sat in silence for a few minutes, the rain drumming on the car roof, and the windscreen running with water.

'Henry said how much he had enjoyed his evening with you,' said the vicar. 'But he thought you looked rather tired.'

My heart sank. Did I really look such an old hag these days?

'You are well, I hope,' went on the vicar, turning in his seat to study me anxiously.

'I'm fine,' I said firmly. 'Right as a trivet, whatever that may mean.'

'Good, good! Can't have you under the weather, you know. It's a miserable time of year.'

'I'll run you back,' I said. 'The rain's getting heavier.'

We trundled through the gathering gloom of a November afternoon, and I dropped him at his front door, refusing his kind invitation to tea.

Driving under the dripping trees to Beech Green, I pondered on this recent display of concern for my health.

Maybe I should get an iron tonic, as Amy had suggested.

The thought was disquieting, but I put aside my health problems after tea, and bravely settled down to some of my growing pile of paper work.

I found it heavy going, and by seven o'clock I was beginning to wonder, yet again, if all these questionnaires and forms were really necessary.

While I was looking back to the relatively free-from-form days of yesteryear, in a nostalgic mood, Amy rang to enquire after my health.

'What about that iron tonic? Have you seen the doctor? Are you sleeping and eating properly?'

'Oh, Amy!' I cried. 'It's sweet of you to be so concerned about me, but I am perfectly healthy. Simply lazy, that's all.'

'Well, I don't believe that, and all I wanted to say was that I hope you will come for a weekend soon, and we can see that you get a proper rest and some food.'

I began to feel like a victim of some national catastrophe being rescued by the Red Cross from starvation, homelessness and disease.

'What are you doing now?' queried Amy.

'Filling in quite unnecessary forms which should have been at the office last week.'

'That's no good to you,' said Amy firmly. 'Put them away, have a tot of whisky and go to bed.'

'I don't like whisky.'

Amy tutted impatiently. 'Well, hot milk then. With perhaps a raw egg in it.'

'It would go down like frogs' spawn! I couldn't face it.'

'What a tiresome girl you are! Anyway, take things quietly, and do let us know if we can do anything. Think about a weekend here. Any weekend suits us, except the next one. I've Lucy Colgate coming for the night, and I don't suppose you want to meet her?'

'Definitely not,' I agreed. Lucy Colgate had been at college with Amy and me. Amy, being of a more kindly disposition, had kept in touch, but I had always found Lucy pretentious, self-centred and irritatingly affected. I found that a little of Lucy's company went a long way.

'But thank you, my dear, for thinking of me, and I'll look forward to a weekend at Bent with enormous pleasure.'

After promising to eat, sleep, take iron tablets, consult my doctor in the near future, put my feet up whenever possible, and to Keep in Touch, I put down the receiver and went to feed Tibby.

The next morning my alarm clock failed to go off, and I awoke twenty minutes later than usual to a dark wet day.

Hurrying to the bathroom I noticed a heaviness in one foot, and supposed that I had been sleeping with it trapped under me.

Stumbling about, getting dressed, I felt annoyed that my foot and leg were taking so long to return to normal. However, there was absolutely no pain, and by the time I had snatched a hasty breakfast of cornflakes and a cup of coffee, I had forgotten the discomfort. It would wear off, I told myself, when I found that I had a slight limp on my way to the garage.

I drove to school determined to ignore a certain numbness in my left foot when using the clutch. Time to worry when something hurt, I told myself, and before long was so immersed in my school duties that I really did forget the trouble with my foot.

Preparations for Christmas were already starting, and Mrs Richards and I had decided that it was a year or two since we had embarked upon a nativity play, and that this Christmas we would produce a real masterpiece.

We had a number of Eastern costumes and various other props in a large box. We also had three shepherds' crooks which were stored in the overcrowded map cupboard along with rolled-up aids to education with such outdated labels as 'The British Empire 1925' and 'Aids to Resuscitation 1940'.

The vicar was enthusiastic about this project and invited the school to perform in St Patrick's chancel one afternoon towards the end of term.

'I think we might even have a collection. I'm sure that lots of parents and friends of the school would like to contribute to the Roof Fund.'

On this particular afternoon Mrs Richards and I took the children across to the church for a preliminary assessment of this natural stage offered to us.

The church was unheated, and uncomfortably dark and dank. I sat with the older children in the cold hard pews whilst Mrs Richards was busy positioning her children around the imaginary crib in the chancel.

As well as the physical discomfort I felt remarkably tired, and could have nodded off if I had been alone. It seemed a long time before Mrs Richards had arranged her groupings to her satisfaction, and I was glad to stir myself to take her place with my own class.

In the gloom I stumbled on the chancel steps but saved myself from falling by grabbing a choir stall.

We went through this first tentative rehearsal of positioning and then decided that it was too cold to linger. On our way back, Bob Willet hailed me from the churchyard.

'All right to bring you up some keeping apples?' he called. 'Alice's sister's given us enough for an army, and I've got to come your way after tea.'

I said that would be fine, and we made our way back to school.

'You're limping,' said my assistant. 'What's wrong?'

I told her about my numbed foot.

'Surely it shouldn't be *numb* for hours!'

'Well, sometimes it *tingles*,' I assured her. 'It's nothing. It doesn't hurt.'

'I should see the doctor,' said Mrs Richards.

'I should see the doctor,' said Bob Willet, when we were sitting at the kitchen table later that day.

He had watched me pouring tea into two mugs, and commented on my shaking hand.

'It's nothing,' I said shortly. I was beginning to get rather cross with all this advice. First Amy, then Mrs Richards, and now Bob. 'The pot's heavy, that's all.'

'Well, I've seen you pouring tea for years, and never seen you wobblin' about like a half-set jelly afore.'

'Those apples,' I said, nodding towards the box he had brought, and keen to change the subject, 'are more than welcome. Will they keep all right in the garden shed?'

'Wrapped up in a half-sheet of newspaper,' said Bob, 'they'll be sound as a bell till after Christmas.'

He finished his tea, and I bade him farewell at the door. The rain still pattered down, the trees dripped and the ground was soggy.

I returned to the kitchen. Should I wrap the apples now, or get on with the children's personal records as requested by the office?

Frankly, I felt too tired to face either. I leafed through the *Radio Times*, and was offered 'Sex Slavery in Latin America', a modern play described as 'explicitly sensual', or a quiz game which I knew from experience plumbed the depths of banality, to the accompaniment of deafening applause from the captive audience.

I cast the magazine from me, and eyed Tibby, blissfully asleep in the armchair.

An excellent idea, I thought, and went upstairs to my own bed.

The rain had stopped when I awoke next morning, and I told myself that now all would be well after such a long and deep sleep.

My foot still hampered me, and I had to admit that I was wobbling 'like a half-set jelly' as Bob Willet so elegantly put it. Perhaps I really ought to visit the doctor? The prospect was depressing.

Not that I had anything against the young man who was one of several who had come after our well-beloved Dr Martin who had died, but I did not relish spending part of my evening in his company. At least, I thought hopefully, as I drove to school, it would mean postponing those wretched personal records that were beginning to haunt me.

The vicar came to take morning prayers, and said when he left that I looked rather tired and that he hoped that I was not over-doing it.

Mrs Richards insisted on pouring the hot water into our coffee mugs at playtime as she could see that I was 'not quite right yet'.

Mrs Pringle, arriving to wash up after school dinner, said that her aunt, although a strict teetotaller, had 'staggered about' just as I was doing, 'looking as drunk as a lord'.

Joseph Coggs, who kindly accompanied me to my car at home time, carrying yet another heavy file of papers, said that his gran 'walked just like that, all doddery-like'.

I decided that it was high time to visit the doctor.

There were only four of us in the waiting-room, the other three unknown to me. One had an appalling cold which needed noisy attention into dozens of tissues which she stuffed after use up the sleeve of her cardigan. I did not feel that this was very hygienic, especially as a wastepaper basket stood nearby. However, I thought charitably, the germs were being kept closer to her own vicinity by her present method of disposal.

The other two were obviously a married couple, passing magazines to each other, and occasionally speaking in a hushed tone as if in the presence of the dead.

I helped myself to a magazine which soon posed some problems for a respectable single woman.

Question: Was I worried about my present sex life?

My answer: Not in the least. But nice of you to ask.

Question: Was my doctor sympathetic to my sex problems?

My answer: No idea. In any case I should not be troubling him with such matters this evening.

I got up to change this magazine for an ancient *Homes and Gardens*, which surely should provide more acceptable reading matter, when the door opened and I was summoned into the presence.

I knew **Dr Ferguson** slightly, and he was pleasantly welcoming. I explained my symptoms in unmedical terms, and he listened attentively.

After some questioning about my family history, he took my blood pressure and pulse, listened to my chest with an ice-cold stethoscope, and then said, 'There's nothing to worry about. I think you have simply had a very mild stroke.'

'Nothing to worry about?' I squeaked in horror. 'A stroke?'

'Not if you are sensible. Lots of people have slight strokes. There is no pain usually, and after a day or two one is over it.'

'But suppose I get a *bad* stroke? What can I do to stop any sort of stroke?'

I must admit that I was feeling thoroughly shocked by his diagnosis. Me, a stroke? It was unthinkable!

'The first thing to do is to face this calmly. It is not serious. It is simply a warning. Your body is telling you to avoid any sort of strain, mental and emotional as well as physical.'

I thought of my daily encounters with Mrs Pringle, and reckoned that my emotional strain, in just that one quarter, must be excessive.

'You are in sound health, except for slightly high blood pressure. I'll give you some tablets for that. The only advice you need is something you know already. Rest as much as possible, keep to a sensible diet, and *don't worry*! Come and see me in a week's time.'

He scribbled a prescription, handed it over and I rose to go.

At the door I turned.

'You know I am a teacher. Am I likely to have the sort of stroke that would knock me out in front of the children?'

He looked at me soberly, considering my question seriously, and I liked him for that.

'It is not likely, but it cannot be ruled out entirely.'

'Thank you,' I said, and tottered out to my car.

I could not get to sleep that night.

I have been exceptionally fortunate in having good health, and rarely had to take time off from school. One takes such a happy condition for granted until some blow, like this one, makes one realise that the body gives way occasionally.

My last question to Dr Ferguson had been the outcome of my main worry. I remembered, with painful clarity, the scene in the infants' room so long ago when Dolly Clare had collapsed.

She had been smitten with a heart attack, and had fallen forward across her desk. Her white hair lay in a puddle of water from an overturned flower vase. Her lips were a frightening blue colour and her eyes were closed. Gathered round her were a dozen or so terrified children, some in tears, and it had taken me some time to collect my wits and hurry them to my own room while I attended to the patient.

The incident had shocked me deeply, and had never been forgotten. Now I was facing a similar problem.

Here I lay, in Dolly Clare's bedroom, wondering what to do. Had she felt as I did now, shaky and full of doubts?

Dr Martin had told me on that dreadful afternoon that she had suffered one or two earlier attacks but had refused to give in. Would the same thing happen to me? Should I collapse as she did in front of a class of horror-struck children?

And what sort of state should I be left in? I thought of several people who still suffered from the effects of a stroke. Some were speechless, some were immobile, some were mentally affected. Was that to be my future too?

I tossed and turned, trying to find some comfort. I reminded myself of the doctor's words. It was only a warning. My general health was sound. I simply had to take things gently.

But how on earth could I? Visions of all that paperwork, of the extra effort needed for our Christmas celebrations, of Mrs Pringle and her infuriating ways, floated before my sleepless eyes. It was interesting, I noted, that the children did not readily spring to mind as an irritant, only as a vulnerable element to be protected.

At four o'clock I descended to the kitchen and made a pot of tea. Sitting there drinking, with a bleary-eyed Tibby hoping for an early morning snack, I began to think seriously about taking early retirement. I had just over two years to do. Should I be able to hang on? Was I truly fit enough to teach properly?

I remembered my surprise at the high level of ability shown by some of the new pupils. Were they naturally more intelligent or had they been better taught? It was a dispiriting thought.

Much troubled, I limped back to bed and fell into a few hours of exhausted slumber.

Of course, by the time I drove over to Fairacre, everything seemed brighter. The fears of the night, like a flock of malevolent vultures, had flown away, and I was sure that the doctor's words were true.

I had been given a warning, and that was all. If I did as he advised and took things sensibly, there was no reason why I should not continue at Fairacre school until my allotted time was up.

My foot seemed much better, and I entered the lobby in a buoyant mood.

Mrs Pringle was cleaning the wash basins, but turned to confront me, Vim tin in hand.

'I can see you've had a poor night of it,' she announced with ghoulish satisfaction. 'I was told you'd been to see the doctor. Bad news?'

'He said that I was in good health,' I snapped. I suddenly wished that he could be present to see just what I had to face every morning.

Mrs Pringle's expression was expectant. I knew that she was hoping for an account of everything that had passed between the doctor and me. I was determined not to fuel the fire, and strode with great dignity towards my classroom.

It was unfortunate that I tripped over the mat. Mrs Pringle gave a gasp which could have meant 'I told you so', as unharmed, but very cross, I went to my desk.

School affairs went on as usual for the next week or two, and gradually I began to get over my shock.

I remembered to take the prescribed tablets now and again, and went to bed earlier than usual, and duly visited the doctor as requested.

He seemed quite pleased with me, and spent a few of his precious minutes talking generally about my way of life.

Did I ever feel lonely, he asked me? Could I get domestic help easily? Did I have bouts of depression? He had found that some women of about my age were unhappy at times, probably because they were past child-bearing.

I must admit that this appeared an extremely odd remark to make to me. He was obviously a kindly and sympathetic man, and I recalled the somewhat impertinent personal questions posed in that women's magazine out in the waiting-room. But surely most married women of my age would have had what family they wanted – or did not want – and were quite looking forward to an easier time now that their children were off their hands.

'Of course,' he went on hurriedly, before I had time to comment, 'you don't have quite the same anxieties, as a single woman.'

'I rather think,' I told him, 'that most women, whether single or married, look forward to a sprightly middle age.'

'Well, I'm certain you will have one,' he assured me, as he ushered me out. 'There's no need for you to come again unless anything worries you.'

I sang all the way home.

CHAPTER 5

End of Term

The relief at my return to normal health gave a great lift to my spirits.

Suddenly I was inspired to tackle all kinds of jobs I had been postponing for weeks.

The dreaded paperwork began to diminish after several evenings of concentration, and I took part in the Christmas preparations with renewed vigour.

Thoroughly frightened at the thought that I might be smitten again, I took care to go to bed earlier than usual and to take my tablets regularly. I admit that I had been terribly scared.

I told no one about my stroke, but did tell kind enquirers that I had slightly high blood pressure which was responding to the prescribed tablets.

Over the years I have discovered that it is as well to provide something for curious minds to pore over. A flat denial of everything only whets the appetite of gossip-seekers. A judicious amount of truthful fact, willingly handed out, is enough to protect the main issue from being revealed.

Sounding disappointed, Mrs Pringle grudgingly admitted that I was 'looking quite bonny again'. Bob Willet said he was glad to see me 'picking up', and Mrs Richards said how good it was to see me as I 'used to be'.

It was early in December when the Annetts invited me

to supper to meet the Beech Green newcomer John Jenkins, the friend of Henry Mawne.

Henry too had been invited and picked me up on his way from Fairacre. He seemed to have settled back into his usual routine, and had acquired a housekeeper after whom I enquired as we drove the short distance to the school house where the Annetts lived.

'A bit bossy,' said Henry. 'I have to leave my shoes in the porch, and she will keep giving me onion sauce with everything. Still, she keeps the house very clean, and her cooking's passable. Nothing like as good as yours though.'

I felt gratified, although I doubted secretly if my efforts were any better than the housekeeper's.

Henry and John had already renewed their friendship, but this was the first time I had met John. He was a handsome man, tall and thin, with a mane of silvery hair and very bright blue eyes.

He looked ten years younger than the plump and bald Henry, but of course, I thought charitably, he has probably not had poor Henry's recent unhappiness.

It was a cheerful party, and as Isobel is an excellent cook we tucked into delicious food and drink. George Annett was in great form and was doing his best to persuade both men to join the choirs of their respective parish churches. He did not have much luck.

And then he turned to me and said something quite surprising.

'I hear you are thinking of retiring.'

I was considerably taken aback. My secret fears had been communicated to absolutely no one. What is there about country air which seems to dispense one's best-kept secrets to all and sundry?

'I have over two years to go until I'm of retiring age,' I managed to say.

'Oh! I somehow thought you had early retirement in mind. I'm soldiering on until sixty-five if my health allows. I must admit I'd like to go at sixty, but we can do with my salary for a little longer.'

'Retirement's really hard work,' observed John Jenkins. 'Everyone wants me to join something.'

'Like the choir?' said George.

John laughed, and Henry added, 'Well, I've been far busier as a so-called retired man than ever I was in business. Still, I do manage to enjoy my bird work, and that reminds me.'

He began to fumble in the breast pocket of his jacket, and brought out a leaflet.

'I'm giving a little talk with slides in Caxley early in the New Year. Would you like to support me?'

Of course we all agreed. John Jenkins said that he was sure he saw a sparrow-hawk near his bird table recently. George Annett mentioned the sighting of a green woodpecker, and my own decidedly inferior contribution was a pair of robins in my garden.

It was pelting with rain when we were about to depart.

Henry offered John and me a lift to our respective doors, and we splashed away after sincere thanks for a splendid evening.

After we had dropped John we drove the quarter of a mile to my home. On the way Henry asked me what I thought of John.

'Very good-looking,' I replied. 'Good company too.'

'I think he's improved with age. Mellowed a bit. He was pretty insufferable at college.'

'Probably shy,' I replied, 'and throwing his weight about to prove that he wasn't. Lots of young people are like that.'

'Well, that's a charitable way of looking at it, I suppose.'

He was silent for a time, and then gave a gusty sigh as we drew up at my gate.

'Will you be seeing much of Jenkins?' he asked.

'I doubt it,' I replied, a little surprised. 'Until we all go to your meeting, I don't suppose our ways will cross.'

'Good,' said Henry, sounding much relieved, and drove off, leaving me to splash to my front door feeling mystified.

The next weekend was spent at Amy's and there, for the first time, I unburdened my recent troubles upon my old friend.

Amy took the whole affair rather more seriously than I did, and enquired about the tablets. Was I taking an iron tonic as she had suggested?

'Well, no,' I confessed, 'but the tablets may have iron in them.'

Amy looked sceptical, but did not pursue the issue.

'And you are taking care?'

'Yes, honestly. I was too frightened by the first business to do otherwise. I'm fine now.'

I proceeded to tell her, with some pride, of all my post-stroke activities, but she was not congratulatory, rather the reverse.

'You'll have another if you rush at things like a bull at a gate. You never learn, you know.'

She sighed, and looked sadly at me. 'I don't know what I'd do if anything happened to you. You mean a great deal in my life, and I don't like to see you in this sort of situation. Can't you retire?'

'Not while I'm fit. In any case, I gather from retired people that they work harder than ever when they have attained that happy state.'

'Rubbish!' retorted Amy. 'That's their own fault for

taking on far too many activities for comfort. I know how persuasive people can be, telling you it's only a once-a-month short meeting of this or that charity, and then you find there are half a dozen sub-committees and you are the chump of a chairman. James is always getting caught that way – and he hasn't even properly retired yet.'

'I promise not to fall into that trap,' I said meekly.

'My mother had a very slight stroke, I remember,' said Amy meditatively. 'She woke one morning and couldn't speak clearly. Luckily, she took it all as a great joke and in two days' time she was normal again. But we were all rather scared, I remember.'

'What age was she?'

'About our age, I suppose. My father took enormous care of her always, and we had about four doctors in the house within twenty-four hours. They had to stand up to a barrage of questions from my father. I should think they were glad to get out alive from our house.'

'Wonderful for your mother, though, to have such a champion.'

'Of course. That's one of the reasons I worry about you so much. If only you would marry some nice man. Henry, for instance. He's devoted to you, and he's so well-mannered.'

'So was Dr Crippen, I believe.'

'How provoking you are! Have you seen poor Henry since he returned?'

'Briefly. He is still very upset over his wife's death.'

I told her about the Annetts' party, and her eyes brightened at the thought of yet another man, John Jenkins, who might fall victim to my middle-aged charms. I decided to change the subject, and asked her to keep two dates free, one for our nativity play, and the other for our annual Christmas party.

'Does that include James too? I know he'd like to see the new children. As well as the old, of course,' she added.

I assured her that James would be more than welcome, and the question of a possible husband for me was shelved.

But only, I suspected, for the time being.

Rehearsals for the nativity play seemed to take up an enormous amount of time. The vicar had presented me with a list of services to be held in the church until the end of term, but pressed us to use the chancel at any other time for our rehearsals.

Consequently we trudged, twice, and sometimes thrice, a week through the churchyard to continue our preparations.

Somehow it always seemed to be raining, but nevertheless I found the churchyard a pleasant place, despite the dripping yew trees and the few rain-spangled upright cypress trees, so reminiscent of sunnier climes.

The grey tombstones glistened in the rain, and the magnificent square gravestone above the long-dead Sir Charles Dagbury, which listed to the north-east, dripped steadily from one side upon the wet clay runnel cut around it.

I thought of the seventeenth-century poet's line:

The grave's a fine and private place,

and although I knew that Andrew Marvell was addressing 'His Coy Mistress', and that the next line was

But none I think do there embrace,

nevertheless I relished the fineness and the privacy which I trusted that earlier Fairacre folk were now enjoying around me.

The church too had its usual calming effect on us all. It seemed pointless to worry about my health, fresh forms from the office, that ominous drip in the kitchen discovered that morning, Tibby's coughing attack and the present shortcomings of our rehearsals, when one considered that these ancient walls had witnessed the hopes and troubles of generations of Fairacre people. I think we all returned to school much refreshed in body and spirit after our efforts.

As always, the parents rallied splendidly to help us with costumes and props for the play.

The new Cotton girl was chosen to play Mary, and very good she was too, having natural grace, a sweet face and a clear voice. Mrs Cotton, her foster mother, sent over a blue frock which she hoped, in the little note attached, would be suitable for Mary's robes.

Unfortunately, it was heavily besprinkled with a flower pattern, and I was obliged to take it back after school.

To my surprise, she seemed unusually agitated about this.

'It's all I have,' she told me. 'Do you want me to buy some plain blue material?'

I assured her that it would not be necessary, as I thought that I might have a plain blue curtain at home which had once hung in Dolly Clare's bedroom, and would be ideal for draping round Mary.

She seemed mightily relieved, answered my inquiries about the children in a rather distracted way, and we parted amicably. As I returned, I told myself that she was probably anxious about a saucepan on the stove, or the toddler left sitting on an unseen chamber pot, and dismissed the matter from my mind.

The property box furnished us with a considerable amount of the costumes required. Mr Roberts, the local farmer and a school governor, provided hay for the box which represented the manger. The ox and the ass had been cut out of heavy cardboard years before, and had weathered their sojourn stuffed behind the map cupboard with remarkable endurance. Once dusted, and an eye redrawn, they were as good as new, we told each other.

The shepherds were clothed in dressing gowns, but here again it was quite a job to find suitably subfusc attire. Gaily patterned bath robes were paraded before us, sporting dragons, Disney characters and a panda or two. Where, I wondered, were the old-fashioned boys' camel-coloured numbers which I remembered from my youth?

After much searching we found one or two, and reckoned that the wardrobe and properties were at last complete.

We gave our first performance one afternoon in the last week of term. I was very grateful to the vicar for letting us have the beautiful chancel for our stage. Usually, any end of term function takes place in Fairacre school, and we are obliged to force back the wooden and glass partition between the two classrooms to make one large hall. Then there is the usual scurrying about for chairs from the school house and public-spirited nearby neighbours, not to mention some rickety benches from the village hall and the cricket pavilion which arrive on a trailer of Mr Roberts', and have to be manhandled into place for the great event, and manhandled back again to their usual home.

On this occasion our audience sat in the ancient pews and had a clear view of the chancel. Mr Bennett, the foster-father at the first Trust's home, had emerged as an electrical wizard, and had volunteered to arrange temporary lighting. This threw the stage into sharp contrast with the dimness of the surrounding building, and gave the performance a wonderfully dramatic setting.

The play went without many hitches. At one point, the

cardboard ox fell down in a sudden draught from the vestry door, and Joseph's crêpe beard came adrift from one ear. This, however, was replaced swiftly by one of the shepherds, hissing 'stand still, stand still!' whilst adjusting the wire over his classmate's left ear, and we all waited for the performance to continue.

It would not have been right to have a school affair like

this without some minor mishap, and we all thoroughly enjoyed ourselves.

The vicar closed the proceedings with a suitable prayer, and we filed out into the misty afternoon feeling all the better for celebrating, in our homespun way, the birth of Jesus.

The last afternoon of term was given over to our own school tea party. It has been the tradition at Fairacre for the pupils to entertain parents and friends. Amy and James were present.

Mrs Willet, who has the largest square baking tin in the locality, always makes the Christmas cake, and it is a job to get her to take the money for the ingredients. But this we insist on doing from the school fund, although I have never been allowed to pay her for the many eggs which go into it.

'I wouldn't *dream* of it,' she always says. 'They are our own hens' eggs, and it's our contribution to the party.' And so I am obliged to submit.

The cake usually has two robins, a church about the same size as the robins, and four Christmas trees, one at each corner, all standing in the snowy icing. Birds, church and Christmas trees are old friends and warmly welcomed each year, but on this occasion we had six attractive choirboys, about three inches high, all holding hymn books and obviously making the rafters ring from their open mouths.

'My neighbour brought them back from Austria,' said Mrs Willet proudly. 'I thought they'd make a nice change.'

Everyone agreed, although I think some of us rather agreed with Joseph Coggs who was heard to remark, 'Them robins was nicer!'

*

On Christmas Eve I drove to Bent to spend the Christmas holiday with Amy and James.

They were as welcoming as ever. The house was looking very festive with holly and ivy, and plenty of scarlet satin ribbon everywhere.

The three of us spent the first evening on our own, all of us glad of a few quiet hours after our Christmas preparations and before the busy day ahead.

Amy enquired anxiously about my welfare and I told her that I was now as fit as a fiddle, as right as a trivet, at the top of my form, and all the other descriptions of perfect health. She did not appear to be satisfied.

'Honestly, Amy,' I said, 'there's no need to worry about me.'

'Well, I do. I don't like the idea of your living alone. Anything might happen. By the way, I met your nice John Jenkins last week.'

'He's not *mine*,' I pointed out tartly, 'and I don't know him well enough to say that he is *nice*, but how did you come across him?'

'At a Caxley Society meeting. He gave a talk about an Elizabethan house he knew well, somewhere in Somerset. I was most impressed, and if it hadn't been such short notice I would have invited him to supper on Boxing Day.'

I knew that Amy had arranged this festivity for a few old friends, but was relieved to hear that John Jenkins was not to be present. Amy's match-making efforts are well meant, but decidedly obvious.

'What did you think of our nativity play?' I enquired.

Amy was enthusiastic, and I congratulated myself on steering her mind to another subject.

'And now tell me how you think the new families are settling,' said James, and I was able to give him an encouraging report on school progress.

We went early to bed, and I was asleep before half-past ten.

Christmas Day passed in the usual familiar pattern of present-opening, church service, turkey, plum pudding, siesta and a therapeutic walk after it.

We listened to the Queen, we agreed that a cup of tea was all that could be faced at four thirty, and Amy and I did a little desultory preparation ready for the next day's buffet supper.

I must say that twenty-four hours later, it looked remarkably elegant, spread out on a long table with a poinsettia in the middle of the starched white cloth.

Horace and Eve Umbleditch were there from Fairacre and two couples from near by in the village of Bent. We all moved about, plates in hand, catching up with the local news.

'Mrs Pringle called the other evening,' Eve told me. 'She was collecting prizes for the Fur and Feather Christmas whist drive, and practically asked me to show her over the school house.'

'And did you?'

'I didn't have much option. She approved of most of our alterations, and said that it was a lot *cleaner* than when you lived there. Horace said that I was not to tell you, but I knew you would relish a typically Pringle remark like that.'

I said she was right.

'What an old faggot she is,' went on Eve. 'She wanted to know how much the alterations had cost, and various other more personal matters such as had I been able to breastfeed my baby at my advanced age. Really, she takes one's breath away! On parting, she said she could always "help me out" if I wanted a cleaner.'

'I hope you put a stop to that offer.'

'I did!'

At that juncture Amy came round with some crackers for us to pull. The contents were unusually splendid, including pretty little brooches and key-rings and other baubles, but the reading of the enclosed riddles made the most fun.

They were all of the 'When is a door not a door? When it's a jar,' sort of standard, taking one back to one's comic-reading days.

Horace read his out to the assembled company, sounding mystified. 'Why is milk so quick?'

'"Why is milk so quick?"' echoed James. 'That doesn't make sense.'

'Neither does the answer,' said Horace, still bemused.

No one could offer any answer to the question and we all begged to be put out of our misery.

Horace read slowly, '"Because it's pasteurised before you see it."'

There were some groans and some laughter. Horace still looked perplexed.

'Pasteurised,' explained James. 'Past your eyes before you see it.'

'Good grief!' said Horace. 'Who thinks up these things?'

'Have another drink,' advised James. 'It'll take the taste away.'

I returned home after the break feeling relaxed and happy.

Tibby deigned to acknowledge me, which was unusual. Normally I have to make overtures with sardines or other acceptable peace offerings after an absence from home.

The weather was mild, and I wandered about the garden on that Wednesday morning admiring the beauty of bare winter branches silhouetted against a pale blue sky. A blackbird was busy scrabbling for grubs in the border, and somewhere in the distance, high above the downs, a lark was scattering its sweet notes. It was good to be back.

I went into the kitchen and put on the kettle to make coffee. Before I could put in the plug, a sharp pain shot through my head, and another through my chest.

The kitchen shelves, the table, the sink, all began to follow each other round and round in growing darkness.

It was almost a relief to hit the floor and give up.

PART TWO

SPRING TERM

CHAPTER 6

Should I Go?

It would be Mrs Pringle, of course, who found me.

She had gone to the school with a freshly washed pile of tea-towels ready for the start of term, and had found that the skylight was leaking, yet again, in my classroom.

She was hastening to catch the Caxley bus, before returning to Beech Green for her usual Wednesday 'bottoming' of my home. But she decided to drop off on the way to give me the news, and then to beg a lift from one of her Beech Green cronies who, she knew, always drove to Caxley about twelve on a Wednesday.

I must have lain there for about half an hour. She managed to support me to the couch in the sitting-room, and then rang the doctor.

It really was most providential that she had called in, at this unusual time, and although I dreaded the dramatic account which would soon be circulating around Fairacre and Beech Green, I was truly grateful for my old adversary's timely help.

I had tried to thank her but was frightened to find that my speech was most peculiar, and my tongue felt twice as large as usual. Also, the dreaded shaking had returned, and I was glad of the cup of tea Mrs Pringle held to my lips, and the rug she spread over me.

'I shall stop with you for the rest of the day,' she told me, 'and see the doctor in.'

She rose from the end of the sofa, and surveyed me sternly.

'May as well get on with the brights while we're waiting,' she said. 'I've never seen them candlesticks look so rough.'

She departed to the kitchen bearing them, and I heard drawers and cupboards being ransacked.

I lay there, bemused and shaken, to the accompaniment of Mrs Pringle's lugubrious contralto singing:

'Oft in danger, oft in woe.'

Very appropriate, I thought, wondering what the future held for me.

I must have dropped off for when I awoke I heard Mrs Pringle talking to someone in the kitchen.

'I thought to myself, "Well, Maud, if you nip into Caxley on the eleven, you can get the slippers at Freeman, Hardy & Willis and the brawn at Potter's for Fred's tea and catch the two o'clock back to Miss Read's for the brights.

'But that skylight was a blessing in disguise this time. "Best report that, I thought, and no time like the present," so I got off here and lucky I did.'

'It was indeed.'

I recognised Isobel Annett's voice.

'And there she was laying,' went on Mrs Pringle, (eggs or bricks, I wondered?) 'and my heart turned over. I thought she'd passed over, I really did.'

'I must see her,' said Isobel. 'Is she upstairs?'

'On the couch,' replied Mrs Pringle, sounding somewhat offended at being interrupted in her dramatic monologue.

Isobel came in, followed by Mrs Pringle. I had closed my eyes hastily. I could hear Mrs Pringle's breathing.

'I think we should get her to bed,' said Isobel.

I opened my eyes, and nodded, not daring to speak.

'Can you manage it?' asked Isobel, putting an arm round me. I nodded again, and we tottered entwined to the stairs, followed by Mrs Pringle.

'Could you make a little bowl of bread and milk?' asked Isobel. 'I think she might manage that.'

Mrs Pringle, debarred from the pleasure of undressing me, retired to do her allotted task.

She was limping heavily, I noticed, but was too concerned with my own troubles to worry much about it.

Dr Ferguson arrived and was reassuring.

'Luckily you haven't broken anything in the fall. And this is just another warning, like the first. It's simply hit other senses this time. I think your speech will be much better by the morning. The worst thing is this bang on the head, but it's coming up nicely.'

He fingered a lump on the right-hand side, making me wince.

'Stay there,' he told me, 'and I'll pop in tomorrow morning after surgery.'

I heard his car drive away. Some time, I thought dazedly, I should have to make all sorts of decisions. But not now. I was too tired to bother.

I turned my aching head upon the pillow, and fell asleep.

Amy came to look after me for a day or two, and then bore me back to her house at Bent with Dr Ferguson's blessing.

Normal speech returned within three or four days, and apart from the lump on my skull which diminished daily, and the overpowering feeling of exhaustion, I felt much as usual.

I wrote to thank Mrs Pringle, and also spoke to the vicar, telling him that I hoped to be fit to return to school as soon as term began. According to the doctor I had suffered from mild concussion, after my headlong collision with the cooker, as well as the second stroke which had triggered off the chain of events.

It was fortunate that all this had occurred in the holidays, but I had plenty of time, as I pottered about at Amy's, to consider the future. I had been given two 'warnings', as the doctor called them, in as many months. I had been lucky to get away with only a bump on the head as a secondary injury. As Dr Ferguson had said, I could have broken a leg or hip as I fell.

Memories of Dolly Clare's classroom collapse so long ago, and visions of other victims of strokes, all came to haunt me. My old dread of such an attack happening at school, in front of the children, was my chief anxiety, and I admitted this to Amy one quiet evening as we sat knitting by her fire.

I had marvelled at the way she had refrained from scolding me throughout her invaluable nursing, but now, confronting my fears, she spoke in her usual decisive manner.

'It's time you packed it in,' she said. 'I know you've only about two years to do, but whatever's the point in knocking yourself up, and starting retirement as an invalid?'

I said that the doctor had assured me that I should recover.

'He said that the first time,' retorted Amy, 'and you say yourself that you felt quite well, and did all the things he had told you, but even so you've had this second attack. To my mind, it's a more severe one. And with your speech affected what good would you be as a teacher?'

The same dismal thought had occurred to me, of course.

'Would you be terribly unhappy if you gave up your job?'

'I'd miss the children. But no, on the whole I think I'd enjoy being a free woman.'

'Have you got enough to live on? Would you have to wait to get your pension?'

'I've got quite a bit stashed here and there, and I'd have to find out more about the pension. I think I might get it immediately, but in any case, I can get by.'

'Well, James said that I was to tell you that we can tide you over, and you are not to worry.'

'James,' I said, 'is an angel in disguise.'

'Pretty heavy disguise too,' said Amy drily, 'when his breakfast's late.'

We shelved the problem of my future, and had a glass of Tio Pepé apiece.

A few days before term began I returned home. I felt

strong enough to face the rigours of school and my own simple house-keeping. Tibby was somewhat stand-offish, as might be expected, but came round after an extra large peace offering of Pussi-luv.

My first visit was to Mrs Pringle to present her with a china cake dish she had admired in Caxley, and had described to me some weeks before.

A rare smile lit up that dour face when she undid it, and I renewed my thanks for her timely help.

'I truly thought you'd gone,' she told me. 'Like a corpse you lay there, and I was going to straighten your limbs before they stiffened, when you gave a groan.'

'That was lucky,' I commented.

'It certainly was! That's when I heaved you on to the couch.'

'You were more than kind. And now I must be off.'

It was plain to me, as I met one or two old Fairacre friends in the village, that my stroke had been well documented.

Mr Lamb at the Post Office shook my hand, and said it was good to see me back. He did not actually add 'from the dead', but I sensed it.

Jane Winter, one of the newcomers, said, 'My goodness, I didn't expect to see you looking so well!'

Joseph Coggs, playing marbles outside the chapel, said he thought I was still in hospital because I'd been struck dumb. Mrs Pringle had said so to his auntie.

I replied in clear and rather sharp tones.

Mr Willet emerged from his gate, and entreated me to come in, to sit down, to give him my coat, and to have a cup of coffee which Alice was just making.

I accepted gratefully.

'Well,' said Bob, as we sat at the kitchen table with our

steaming mugs, 'I didn't believe half what Maud Pringle said, but we was all real scared to hear the news.'

'Not as scared as I was,' I told him. 'I'm not used to being ill.'

'You take care of yourself,' said Mrs Willet. 'We don't want anyone else in your place at the school. Everyone was saying so, weren't they, Bob?'

'So what's the news?' I asked hastily, changing the subject.

'Not much. Except for Arthur Coggs.'

'I thought he was safely in prison.'

'He come out about a fortnight ago. You know how it is these days. These villains get sent down for six months, and they're out again before you can draw breath. Remission, or some such. Anyway, he's out, and got one of his religious turns again.'

'Oh dear!' I exclaimed. We all know what havoc Arthur Coggs' religious turns can cause. On one occasion he had knocked up the Willets when they were asleep, and filled with burning zeal and too much strong beer had attempted to save their souls.

On another occasion he had entered the church during Evensong and started a loud tirade, punctuated with inebriated hiccups, on the after-life of those present in the congregation. Two sidesmen had removed him to the churchyard, but not before he had overturned a pot of gladioli in the church porch, and ripped a warning about swine fever from the noticeboard hard by.

On the present occasion evidently he had trespassed into the Women's Institute meeting at the village hall, whilst the members were engrossed in a cookery demonstration.

The demonstrator was a young woman with little experience. She was nervous before the twenty or so elderly women, who sat clutching their handbags on their laps and watching the proceedings with critical eyes. Her employers, a firm of flour manufacturers, had given her a course in pastry-making of all types, and this knowledge she was now imparting to her audience.

She had spent some time showing them different sorts of flour in half a dozen small bowls, and then continued with the making of choux pastry, puff pastry, and hot-water pastry for raised pork pies and the like. Whether she imagined that the women before her still ground their own flour from their harvest gleanings, no one could guess, but the rather condescending nature of her patter definitely irked them.

Had she but known, nine out of ten of those present had long ago given up making their own pastry, and rummaged in the local shops' refrigerator cabinets for nice ready-made packets marked 'shortcrust' or 'puff', and with no sticky fingers or mixing bowls to worry about.

It was while the earnest young woman was attempting to raise hot-water pastry round a jam jar that the interruption occurred.

It was not entirely unwelcome. The tea ladies were already beginning to whisper to each other about switching on the urn, when the door from the kitchen burst open, and Arthur Coggs, clearly the worse for drink, stumbled into the hall.

He approached the table unsteadily. The demonstrator, with a squeak of panic, retreated behind it, floury hands to her face in alarm.

'Get out, Arthur Coggs!' shouted one brave woman, but was ignored.

'Ish thish,' demanded Arthur, 'the 'all of shalvation?'

'No, it isn't,' said Mrs Partridge, the vicar's wife, coming forward to take charge as president. 'This is the village hall, and well you know it. Go home now!'

Arthur turned a bleary eye upon her. He put one hand on the table to steady himself, and smacked it down upon a wet mound of pastry.

'I've seen the light,' he began, amidst outraged murmurs. 'I bin a shinner, but now I'm shaved. And I'm going to shave you lot too.'

'Oh, no you're not, Arthur,' said Mrs Partridge firmly. 'You are going home, or we shall send for the police.'

She attempted to edge him towards the door. A large dollop of pastry fell to the floor, and was flattened under Arthur's boot.

'My pastry!' wailed the demonstrator, bending down to rescue it. The table gave a lurch from the activities around it, and the jam jar with its skirt of raised pastry rolled to join the mess on the floor.

'The police?' echoed Arthur. 'They needs to shee the light too.'

At this point, three more women came to Mrs Partridge's aid and manhandled the protesting saviour-of-souls into the kitchen.

'I'll just switch on while we're here,' said one, eminently practical, despite holding one of Arthur's ears.

Protesting vociferously, Arthur was bundled through the back door.

'I gotta meshage for you,' he shouted, 'a meshage from the Lord!'

'Well, you'd better go and tell the vicar,' replied Mrs Partridge, giving him a final push.

They slammed the door and bolted it.

'The idea!' puffed one.

'He ought to be put away!' said another.

'Won't the vicar mind?' queried the third timidly, as they went back to the hall.

'He can cope with Arthur,' replied Mrs Partridge. 'I have the WI on my hands.'

She swept in like a triumphant general at the head of his troops, and was greeted with cheers.

The New Year opened with a bitter wind blowing from the east.

The ground was iron-hard and white with frost until mid-morning. The ice on puddles scarcely had time to unfreeze during the day, before darkness fell at tea time and the temperature plummeted again.

Tibby and I went out as little as possible. Indoors we

were snug enough, for the fire burned brightly in this weather, and my new curtains kept out any draughts after nightfall.

I had plenty to do indoors. There were always school matters to deal with, as well as domestic jobs over and above the usual daily round. I turned out a store cupboard, marvelling at the low prices I had paid only a few years earlier, and even came across a tin of arrowroot which bore a label for one and ninepence. After such a length of time, the contents were given to the hungry birds. They appeared to be delighted with this vintage bounty.

As the first day of the spring term grew closer, I gave more and more thought to the future. Amy's advice about retirement was sensible, I realized, but it seemed so terribly *final*, the end of my useful life, so to speak, and with what would I fill my days?

On the other hand, was it fair to the school to struggle on with this constant dread at the back of my mind? I should not be the woman I was before these attacks, and I was reminded again, most uncomfortably, of the abilities of the new children in comparison with the indigenous Fairacre pupils whose accomplishments were not so high. Was it my fault? Were my teaching skills waning as I grew older? Was I pulling my weight?

There was no one that I could turn to to answer these questions. It was up to me to make a decision.

> '*There is a tide in the affairs of men,*
> *Which, taken at the flood, leads on to fortune,*'

I said to Tibby.

Tibby yawned again.

'Or, of course, *misfortune*,' I added. 'I might be a perfect fool to give up, and live till ninety in dire penury.'

Tibby yawned again.

'Which means,' I said severely, 'that you would have to live on *scraps*, and not Pussi-luv. And you would not be having the top of the milk, because we should both be on the cheapest sort, and in any case I should be *watering it down*!'

Oblivious to my warnings, Tibby rolled over to get the maximum benefit of the roaring fire, leaving me to wrestle with my doubts and fears.

The first day of term seemed even more bitterly cold than usual. I told myself that I had risen earlier and so the world was still in its night-time icy state.

The road to Fairacre was glassy, and the car did a few minor skids which could have been a problem if there had been traffic about. I drove slowly and was glad to enter the school playground and park the car.

Mr Willet had sanded the surface of the playground, for which I was grateful. I guessed that my pupils would not share my feelings, for there is nothing the boys enjoy more than a good long slide across the frozen asphalt, with a long line of them hurtling, one after the other, 'keeping the pot boiling'.

The school was warm. Mrs Pringle, resigned to the fact that winter was really here, had stoked up the two tortoise stoves and it was a joy to get indoors out of the bitter cold.

Mrs Pringle was flicking along the windowsill with a yellow duster, as I entered. She surveyed me morosely.

'You seem to have picked up,' she said. I thought she sounded a little disappointed.

'Thanks to you and other good friends,' I told her as cheerfully as I could.

'You want to keep in the warm,' she advised. 'The stoves is fair red hot.'

This was an over-statement, but I took it as a kindly gesture to a convalescent, as Mrs Pringle departed to the lobby.

It was good to be back. I looked round the empty classroom, with the bare shelves and nature table awaiting the fruits of the children's labours. The trappings of Christmas had gone. The paper chains, the Christmas tree, the nativity play, the school party, and all the other excitements of the end of term, were now behind us.

Here, in this empty and quiet room, I awaited the new term. Outside I could hear children's voices, and soon the room would be loud with the noise of children clamouring to tell me their news, scuttling from desk to desk, laughing, teasing and all sniffing from the cold world they had just left outside.

I went to let them in.

I had come to a compromise agreement with myself.

I would see how I coped with the first few weeks of term, and then decide whether I was fit to carry on or whether the sensible thing would be to retire.

A newly retired friend had mentioned that she had given in her notice before mid-February when she proposed to retire at the end of the school year in July. It seemed a long time to me, but when one considered that the post had to be advertised, applicants interviewed and *their* notices to be given in, it was absolutely essential to have this time in hand.

In a way, it helped me. I should have to make up my mind and stand by my decision. During that first week or two of term, I took stock. I felt well enough, but tired easily. I certainly did not have the burst of energy which followed my recovery from the first 'warning', but I was capable of teaching, doing my paperwork in the evenings, and coping with everyday living. What I had to admit was that I had really no resources of strength for any extra crisis that might crop up.

I recalled several emergencies which had occurred at school over the years. A child broke its leg, and I had to track down the mother, take them both to hospital, and leave the school for a good half a day to my assistant to run in my absence.

I myself had been smitten one day with a violent bilious attack which involved many a hasty trip to the lavatory, and eventually complete absence from school when I spent the rest of the day in the school-house bathroom.

Then there were always minor crises in a building as old as Fairacre school. The skylight alone was a source of sudden upheavals involving instant attention. And beside these structural defects there was the constant problem of *Mrs Pringle*.

Matters came to a head one day towards the end of January. The weather was still wickedly cold, but no snow had fallen. Mrs Pringle moaned daily about the work it made for her, the extra fuel needed for the stoves, the journey along slippery roads to take up her duties, her bad leg, the doctor's warnings, and so on.

Just before school dinner time one of the infants fell and hit his head on the corner of a desk, and Mrs Richards and I were hard put to it to stop the bleeding. We put as much pressure as we safely could on the wound, while the poor child screamed blue murder.

'You'd better take him into Caxley casualty,' I said, 'and I'll track down his mother. I think she works at Boots. She'll meet you at the hospital I expect.'

The two set off in Mrs Richards' car, the screams slightly muffled by a boiled sweet from the school sweet tin. I coped with my extended family of pupils, until my assistant returned at two o'clock.

'They stitched him up, and he and his mother came home with me. He's much calmer, and has been put to bed. Look, it's begun!'

She pointed to the window, and there were whirling snowflakes, so thick that it was impossible to see the school house, my old home, across the playground.

We closed school early, and I had a nightmare journey over the few miles to Beech Green, for the roads seemed even slipperier than before, and the windscreen wipers could not cope adequately with the raging blizzard.

It was a relief to get indoors and to put the kettle on. As I drank my tea, I found that the old familiar shakes were back. Worse still, I was horrified to find that tears were coursing down my cheeks.

I replaced my cup with a clatter into the saucer, and leant back, defeated, in the chair.

This was it. It was time to go.

CHAPTER 7

The Die is Cast

Once I had made my decision I felt better immediately. It was a Friday when school matters had come to a head and reduced me to such a demoralized condition. I spent the weekend contemplating the results of my overnight plans, and on the whole I felt mightily relieved.

Now and again, as I went about my weekend chores, I had twinges of doubt. Was it pride that made me loath to join my retired friends? Did I think that I was still as energetic and as capable as when I was appointed to be head teacher at Fairacre school? Did I imagine, when I surveyed myself in the looking-glass, that I looked younger and livelier than my contemporaries? Was I really able to cope with another two, or possibly more, years before I retired?

The honest answer to these questions was 'No'. Since my first stroke – mild or otherwise – I was not the robust and carefree woman that I had been. The second attack had robbed me of the small amount of self-confidence I had nurtured since the first. It was time to face reality.

And so I pottered about that weekend, and faced the future. February would begin in a day or two's time, and I should let the vicar know first, as head of the school governors and a dear friend of many years, just what I had decided to do.

Then I should confide in Mrs Richards, asking her to keep the matter to herself for a day or two while I composed a letter of resignation to the local authority.

I spent some time reviewing my financial arrangements. My newly retired colleague in Caxley had told me that my small teacher's pension would be paid as soon as I retired in July. I should also receive a substantial amount as my 'lump sum'.

This was comforting news. Moreover as I had told Amy, I had some savings in Caxley Building Society, and a wad of Savings Certificates somewhere upstairs, not to mention my useful Post Office book which was frequently raided in emergencies, but I had the inestimable good fortune of owning my own home, thanks to dear Dolly Clare's generosity. Few people, facing retirement, could be so happily placed.

I had no family problems, no husband or children to consider. I was my own mistress, and apart from the recent minor health setbacks, I was hale and hearty.

By the end of that weekend which had started so disastrously, I was beginning to look forward to my more leisured existence. Forewarned by my contemporaries, I should not make the mistake of being bounced into various village activities except those of my own choosing. But I should be able to be useful to my friends in various ways, babysitting for Eve and Horace Umbleditch, for instance, or running non-driving neighbours to Caxley when needed.

My ties with Fairacre would not be severed, for Bob Willet and Joseph Coggs would come to help in the garden, and Mrs Pringle would be with me every Wednesday until death did us part, I felt sure.

I went to bed on Sunday night facing a rosy future.

*

I had rung the vicar and asked if I might call after school on Monday.

'Come to tea,' had been the reply, and here I was pulling up outside the vicarage door which stood open hospitably.

'Tea first, and business later,' decreed Mrs Partridge, proffering buttered toast.

The fire crackled. Outside the birds were squabbling at the bird-table, an easterly wind ruffling their feathers and rattling the leaves of the laurels near by. It was good to be in the warm with old friends.

'Now tell us the news,' said Gerald Partridge when he had removed the tray to a side table.

I told them.

Dismay contorted their faces as I explained my plans, and I began to feel horribly guilty. But I soldiered on until the end of my monologue, and then waited for comment.

To my surprise, the vicar rose from his chair, enveloped me in an embrace and kissed me on both cheeks.

'What shall we do without you?' he cried.

'We shall have to manage,' said his wife resolutely, watching her husband return to his chair. She turned to me. 'It's a terrible blow, you know, but I'm sure you are doing the sensible thing. We've been so lucky to have you at the school for so long. And you've given us plenty of notice, thoughtful as always.'

'Won't you change your mind?' pleaded the vicar.

I shook my head. 'I've thought about it for ages,' I told him. 'I'm going to miss the school, but I feel I must go.'

'How we shall miss her,' he said, so mournfully that I felt he could not have been more cast down if I were emigrating to Australia.

'I shall only be at Beech Green,' I pointed out. 'And I hope you'll come and see me frequently with all my other Fairacre friends.'

They looked a little more cheerful, and we began to discuss the practical side of the matter.

'We have a governors' meeting this month,' said Gerald Partridge, 'so we can tell them then.'

I told him about sending in my resignation, and informing those involved. I think we were all feeling more settled when the time came for me to depart.

The wind was still whipping the bare trees, and sending flurries of dead leaves across the road, as I drove home. It was already dark, and it was plain that the night would be rough and cold. It was the weather to be expected in February, when the children had perforce to spend their playtime indoors and the lack of fresh air and exercise dampened the spirits of us all.

I looked ahead through the rain which now spattered the windscreen, at the windy road which led to home.

Before next winter, I told myself, I should be enjoying the comfort of my own fireside in the afternoons, while my successor coped with Fairacre school. And the skylight, of course. Not to mention Mrs Pringle!

I turned into my gateway in roaring high spirits.

It was during this bleak spell of weather that Henry Mawne gave his lecture on 'Birds of Prey' at Caxley.

Two days before the event John Jenkins rang up to say that he would give me a lift.

'Saves a lot of us wandering round trying to find a parking place,' he said. 'It begins at seven. Shall I pick you up at six thirty?'

'That's fine,' I said. 'Unless you'd like to come and have tea here first?'

'I should like that very much,' he said, and it was left that he would arrive at about five. I decided that it would be as well to provide something fairly substantial, such as crumpets, or sandwiches perhaps, so that we were fortified for Henry's evening.

The next day Henry rang.

'I'll pick you up at six,' he announced. 'Must get in a bit early to see about the plugs. Every hall I go to seems to have different electrical arrangements. Such a nuisance, but I have a first-class adaptor.'

I explained about John and invited him to join us.

'Well, that's cool, I must say,' spluttered Henry. 'He knows we made the arrangements last time we met. I said I'd pick you up.'

He sounded genuinely put out, and I tried to make amends.

'Honestly, Henry, I don't remember us making a set date. I'm sorry if it throws out your plans. Can't we all go in together?'

'No, we can't,' he snapped. 'Leave it as it is, now you've made this muddle with John. I'll see you after the meeting.'

He rang off, leaving me thoroughly cross. I was positive that we had made no arrangements to meet, and in any case, that was weeks before when we had met at the Annetts' party. How like a man to put the blame on me! And if he resented my inviting John Jenkins to an innocent cup of tea, he must just get on with it. I had plenty to occupy me without worrying about foolish old men who behaved like infants.

What a blessing it was to be a spinster!

In no time, of course, it was the talk of Fairacre that I was going to retire.

Mrs Richards' eyes filled with tears when I told her, and I was obliged to find the box of tissues kept for infant eyes and noses to put her to rights again.

'I think I'll give up myself,' she wailed. 'I honestly can't face working with anyone else.'

I did my best to brace her, and before long she was herself again, much to my relief. What would the children think if *all* the staff – both of us – resigned at the same time, I said?

Bob Willet said everyone would grizzle about me going but he and Alice had said for a long time I was looking peaky and I worked too hard. I rather enjoyed the last part of his remarks. I so rarely get the chance to feel a martyr.

Mrs Pringle responded typically. It was her opinion, she told me, that I should have gone months ago. (My enjoyment of Bob Willet's assessment of my worth vanished immediately.)

'You've been off-colour ever since that first funny turn,'

she continued. 'Shaking like a jelly. Tripping over things. Forgetting to shut the skylight. Sharp with the kiddies. Pecking at your good school dinner. I said to Fred, long before Christmas, "You mark my words, Fred, she'll either crack up and end in the county asylum, or the doctor'll make her see sense and retire." Those was my very words.'

'Well, luckily,' I said, as mildly as I could in the face of this tirade, 'I'm taking the second course. So far, at least.'

Mr Lamb at the Post Office said that I would be sorely missed, and maybe they would appoint a man next time which might make some of the children mind their Ps and Qs. This left me wondering how far my disciplinary powers had deteriorated in the past months and if, perhaps, I should have given in my notice years before.

But on the whole, I received nothing but kindness from my Fairacre friends and parents, and far more compliments than I deserved. Perhaps one had to go before one was really appreciated? I was reminded of the glowing obituary notices in *The Caxley Chronicle* dwelling on the sterling merits of local characters 'beloved by all'.

The children, of course, were much more realistic, wondering if my retirement would mean a half-holiday for them, who would take my place, and was I going because I was too old? Or was I *really* ill?

'You're not going to die?' queried Joseph Coggs interestedly.

'Not just yet,' I assured him.

John Jenkins proved to be good company. He had travelled in many countries, and had a cottage in the south of France which he visited for several months of the year.

His Beech Green house was providing him with plenty of household repairs, and these he seemed to be enjoying.

The Annetts had told him about my proposed retirement, and he asked me about my plans.

'I shall enjoy feeling free,' I told him. 'I look forward to visiting friends, and parts of the country I haven't yet seen.'

'Won't you miss the work? The routine? Setting off at the same time each day, and so on?'

'Good lord, no! Why, do you?'

'I did at first,' he admitted, 'but then I think men find it harder to adjust to retirement than women.'

I pondered this as I poured out our second cups of tea. There was truth in the statement. I could think of half a dozen men of my acquaintance, usually successful business men, who had been unsettled and irritable in the first months of retirement, nearly driving their wives mad.

'Women have wider interests, I suppose,' I answered. 'Everyday jobs like cooking and housework, and all the things that have to be looked after in a house. So often a man devotes himself to just one aim, like building up a business, or running an efficient office. When that's taken away he feels lost.'

'I certainly went through that stage. Felt useless, finished, chucked aside. That's why I took on so many voluntary jobs in the village. Too many, I realise now. Don't you make that mistake.'

I promised that I would not, and soon afterwards we set out to the school hall in Caxley where Henry was to give his lecture.

He came bustling up to meet us as we entered, and I was relieved to see that he appeared in excellent spirits.

'Everything in splendid form here,' he cried. 'The head-master was absolutely spot-on about the electrical equip-ment. And two sixth form boys to do the heaving about. By the way, I've booked a table for supper after the show. At the White Hart, if that suits you?'

We thanked him warmly and found our seats.

The hall filled up very satisfactorily, considering how bleak and unpleasant a night it was. Left alone I should have stayed by my fire. Obviously a great many people were more public-spirited.

The lecture on 'Birds of Prey' was vaguely familiar, and I recalled that Henry had given a simple version of it to our school some time before. We had followed it up by paying a visit to a Cotswold falconry, and a good time had been enjoyed by all.

Henry spoke well, and the slides were magnificent. There is something primitively splendid about the fierce eyes and cruel beaks of eagles, kestrels and the like which compel fear as well as admiration. We all sat enthralled, and although Henry's lecture lasted well over an hour no one fidgeted.

Half an hour later we were sitting at a table in Caxley's premier hotel, a comfortable old building, once a coaching stop, with ample stabling at the rear.

As well as Henry and John, the headmaster and his wife were present, and the master who had been instrumental in getting Henry to give the lecture.

'I hear you are retiring soon,' he said to me.

'At the end of the school year probably,' I replied, marvelling yet again about the dispersal of news.

'Well, if you want something to do,' he went on, 'I can find you a little job publicising the work of our local nature society. Very worthwhile, and you would meet lots of people.'

'I've often seen you at concerts,' broke in the headmaster, 'and I know you are fond of music. Do come and hear our school orchestra one day.'

'And you must join our Ladies' Club,' added his wife. 'We meet every third Wednesday of the month, and have really first-class speakers. Some of them charge over a hundred pounds, so you can see we get only the best.'

I began to see how tough I should have to be to resist all the pressure about to engulf me.

John Jenkins came to my rescue. 'I've already warned her about taking on too much when she retires,' he remarked.

'And so have I,' added Henry. 'There will be quite enough scope for her in Beech Green and Fairacre, I'm sure.'

'We'll return to the attack later,' said the headmaster, with a smile, and I was thankful that the conversation turned to rugby prospects for the rest of the season, and I could enjoy my excellent meal without harassment.

I was pleased to see Henry so jovial again, for although he had annoyed me by assuming such a possessive air when he had rung me about driving in, I was sorry to have upset him unwittingly. He was still in a sad state after losing his wife, and I did not want to hurt him further.

But my complacency was short-lived. At the end of the evening, after we had said goodbye to the Caxley contingent, Henry turned to me and said, 'Shall we set off then?'

'I can run her back,' said John quickly.

'No need. I pass the door,' responded Henry.

'Don't you worry,' replied John. 'You've got to unpack all your gear when you get back to Fairacre.'

I began to feel like a bone between two dogs. Both men were getting pink in the face.

'I'm afraid I left my gloves in John's car,' I faltered.

'In that case,' said John swiftly, 'you had better come back with me, as arranged.'

Henry took a deep breath, turning from pink to crimson in the process. 'Very well,' he managed to say, 'if it's *arranged* then there's nothing to say, is there?'

'Thank you for a really lovely evening,' I said weakly, but found that I was addressing his back.

John took my arm in an irritatingly proprietorial manner, and we made our way to the hotel car park. I was sorry that the evening had ended so unhappily, and said so to John as we emerged into the road.

'He'll get over it,' he said dismissively. 'The trouble with Henry is that he's such an old woman. Always was.'

I felt that this was as unkind as it was churlish. After all, Henry had arranged the evening, given us a first-class dinner, and been a genial host until the last few wretched minutes.

We continued our journey in silence. The headlamps lit up the hedges and grass verges glistening with a hard frost. An owl flew across our path intent on finding prey in this harsh world.

As we approached Beech Green, I roused myself enough to give John polite thanks for the lift, and he responded, equally politely, about tea.

'I will see you in,' he said as we drew up at my gate.

'Please don't bother,' I said. 'You have been most kind, and as you see, I have left the light on.'

We wished each other good night, and off he went, much to my relief.

For the time being anyway, I had had quite enough of John Jenkins' company.

In the week following our Caxley evening, more snow fell. Luckily, it was not too heavy, but the ground was so iron-cold and hard that it lay for several days without thawing much.

The children's Wellingtons stood in a row in the porch, but I was surprised to see that the oldest Cotton girl, who had played Mary so beautifully in our nativity play, was the only child in shoes. Naturally, they were soaking wet, and I put them near the stove to dry.

'What's happened to your Wellingtons?' I asked. The two younger boys had come to school in theirs.

'Too small, miss,' she replied. 'Mum's getting me some in Caxley on Saturday.'

'Her shoes are too small as well,' piped up one of her brothers, and the girl flushed with annoyance.

'Well, you all grow fast at this stage,' I said cheerfully, 'and run your poor parents into a lot of expense.'

An odd look passed between the two children. A warning? Fear? Embarrassment? There was no telling, but we continued with our work and I soon forgot about this transitory and uneasy feeling.

February began as cheerless as the last few days of January had been. Consequently my bird table was thronged with finches of all colours, as well as robins and sparrows. Beneath it the blackbirds and hedge sparrows bustled about, and on one occasion a spotted woodpecker joined the gathering, scaring the small birds away from the peanuts which he attacked energetically with his powerful bill.

But by mid-month a welcome change occurred. The wind veered to the south-west, the air became balmy, and the last vestiges of snow, which had lain beneath the hedges, gradually melted away.

Our spirits rose steadily with the temperature. For one thing, the children could go outside to play, which was a relief to us all. The evenings were drawing out. It was possible to have a walk, or for the children to play outside, after tea, and the curtains were drawn at around six o'clock rather than four.

My resignation had gone to the office, and I had received an extremely kind and flattering letter from the Director of Education, no less. I was beginning to wonder if I had done the right thing by resigning.

Just as one feels much better when one has rung the dentist for an appointment and the pain stops immediately, so I felt now. The relief at having made a decision – even if it were the wrong one – was overwhelming.

I did not have many of these twinges of doubt. I knew only too well that the course I was pursuing was the right one.

Amy was particularly helpful at this time. She called one afternoon when I had just returned from school, and we had tea together. The window was open, and the curtains stirred in the warm breeze. A bowl of paper-white narcissi scented the room. Spring had come at last.

'I get restless at this time of year,' said Amy, lighting a cigarette.

'It's time you gave up smoking,' I told her. 'Don't you read about all the horrors it does to your lungs, not to mention unborn babies?'

'I'm not too bothered about my lungs after all these years, and there never have been any babies to worry about, worse luck.'

I felt a pang of remorse. Amy and James would have made ideal parents, but Fate had deemed otherwise. It was one of the reasons, I guessed, that James was so exceptionally good in dealing with the children and their parents in the Trust housing scheme.

'Easter's early this year,' went on Amy, blowing a perfect smoke ring. 'What are you doing?'

'Getting the outside painting done. Wayne Richards says he'll come as soon as we break up.'

'Is that your assistant's husband? The one with the handsome beard?'

'The very same,' I told her.

'And how long will he need to paint the outside?'

'Lord knows. A week, I suppose. Why?'

'James is off on another Trust venture around Easter. I think he hopes to find a house or two in the Shropshire area – lovely part of the country. I wondered if you would like to keep me company.'

'It sounds lovely.'

'No need to make plans yet. I'll have to fit in with James's arrangements, but bear it in mind.'

I promised enthusiastically, and we went out to look at the garden.

It was a cheering sight after the past gloomy weeks. The green noses of innumerable bulbs had pushed through the wet earth. The lilac buds were as fat as green peas, and the honeysuckle was already in tiny leaf.

In one corner I had planted dwarf irises, *reticulatum* and *danfordiae*, and already the purple flowers of the former and the cheerful yellow ones of the latter were making a brave show now that the weather had changed.

Only the ancient trees remained bare, but even so I felt that there was a haziness in their all-over aspect, as if the buds were beginning to swell and ready to burst very soon into the glory of Spring.

Amy sniffed rapturously.

'Bliss, isn't it?' she said.

'It is indeed,' I replied.

CHAPTER 8

Medical Matters

The spring term is not my favourite of the school year. The weather is at its most malevolent, and children's complaints such as whooping cough and measles seem to crop up in the early months with depressing regularity.

This year was no exception, despite the natural robustness of the Fairacre young. The two Cotton boys succumbed to measles and two of the Bennett children next door were also casualties. Joseph Coggs was absent too with influenza, which would no doubt spread to the rest of the family.

Mrs Pringle, relishing the news of each new sufferer, added her own contribution to the list.

'Minnie's Basil has got the croup. Cough, cough, cough, and what he brings up you'd never believe.'

I attempted to escape from these horrors into the lobby, but was confronted by her bulk.

'And she's expecting again,' she added.

'What? Minnie?'

'Who else?'

'But the baby can't be more than a few months,' I protested.

'Twelve. No, I tell a lie. Must be fourteen months now.'

Frankly, I was appalled at the news. Minnie Pringle, Maud's scatterbrained niece, has the mentality of a twelve-year-old and is already the mother of several children, and stepmother to four or five of her husband's by his former marriage. How they all manage to eat and sleep, and even breathe comfortably in their Springbourne council house, has always been a mystery to me.

'Ern's turned nasty about it,' continued Mrs Pringle.

'He might have thought of that before,' I replied tartly.

'He don't reckon it's his,' said Mrs Pringle.

This took the wind out of my sails, of course. Come to think of it, reason told me, Ern might well be right. Minnie's relationships with the opposite sex were always remarkably haphazard.

'But he must know, surely,' I said. 'And Minnie must know.'

'She don't rightly remember,' said Mrs Pringle, taking a swipe with her duster at my desk and thereby removing the hymn list for the month.

I stooped to pick it up, trying to come to terms with Minnie and Ern's attitude to parenthood. The trouble with me is that I constantly try to rationalize matters. When one is dealing with the Minnies and Erns of this world reason does not come into it, but I never learn.

'So what's happening?'

'Well, Ern give her a good hiding for a start, but he's letting her stay, and says the baby'd better look like him, and not that Bert, or there'll be real trouble.'

At the mention of Bert, one of Minnie's more persistent admirers, my heart sank. I had once had to face him in my own schoolroom, and very unnerving the encounter was.

'But surely,' I protested, 'she isn't still seeing Bert? I thought he'd moved to Caxley and broken with her.'

'There's always the bus,' said Mrs Pringle. She began to move towards the door.

'Mind you,' she said, 'I don't hold with all our Minnie

does, but when it comes to *love* there's nothing to be done. Minnie's always had a loving nature, and Bert always came first. Ern don't seem to understand that.'

She disappeared, leaving me exhausted with other people's problems.

My own particular problem that day was a visit to the doctor's surgery for a routine check-up.

The waiting-room was full, as always, and I had my usual difficulty in choosing reading matter from the pile provided. Should it be a ten-year-old copy of *Autocar*, *The Woodworker*, or last Easter's copy of *Woman and Home*?

I settled down with this last offering and soon became absorbed in the cooking pages. Why didn't my steak and kidney pies turn out like the one in the picture? Mine always collapsed round the pie funnel, leaving a white china steeple arising from the ruined pastry roof around it.

Two women were busy discussing the reasons for their presence. One had a straightforward boil on her neck which was covered with a large sticking plaster.

I felt truly sorry for her, particularly as she was getting scant sympathy from her friend who had far more interesting symptoms to describe.

There are times when I curse the fact that my hearing is so good. Give the woman her due, she spoke in low tones as befitted the intimate nature of her disclosures, but I could hear every word.

'It's a blockage, you see, dear, in the *tubes*. They lead to the womb and all that part. In the privates. I never remember the name of the tubes.'

Mrs Pringle, I recalled, named them 'Salopian tubes', which had a nice healthy, if erroneous, air of Shropshire about them.

'So what will they do?' enquired the friend, now resigned

to the fact that her boil was of very little consequence in the face of such competition.

Her companion's voice dropped even lower. 'Dilation, I expect. And then blowing out.'

'I don't like being messed about with down there,' said her friend primly.

'Well, I can't say I *relish* it,' agreed the other, 'but needs must when the devil drives, as my old mamma used to say.'

She began to rummage in an enormous handbag.

'I cut out a bit from the woman's page of the *Mirror*. It was all about this business. I brought it along for the doctor to see. It might give him a lead, I thought. He's only young.'

I wished I could be an invisible witness at this confrontation, but at that moment my name was called, and I had to leave this gynaecological saga behind me.

Dr Ferguson was as welcoming as ever, but looked decidedly careworn. He was going to look a jolly sight more so, I thought, when the tubes-lady took my place.

'And how do you feel?'

'Splendid. No problems.'

'Good. I'll just take your blood pressure.'

He got out the paraphernalia from a drawer and began to wind the soft stuff round my arm. Why such a simple action should be so unpleasant I have no idea, but as the band tightens I am always convinced that I am about to be asphyxiated.

Reason tells me that I am being absurd. The contraption is nowhere near my throat and lungs. Nevertheless, panic rises in me, and I feel that I should tell the doctor to knock off the top five or six degrees of whatever the thing is registering, on account of my acute cowardice.

'Fine,' he said, releasing me from my bonds. 'Down quite a bit. Tablets are working well.'

There were a few routine questions. Tongue, eyes, neck glands were examined, and I was about to escape when he said, 'I hear you're retiring. Will you have plenty to do?'

'More than enough,' I assured him.

He sighed. 'You see, I always think that you single women *need* a job. To make up for the lack of motherhood, you understand. Women *need* motherhood.'

I thought of Minnie. She ought to be the picture of health and serenity at this rate.

'They need children to *fulfil* themselves biologically. It's not just "the patter of tiny feet", I don't mean that.'

'I get plenty of the patter of not-so-tiny feet,' I said. 'Thirty-odd children, from five to eleven years of age, make a pretty deafening patter on bare boards.'

'I'm sure of that.' He began to look less worried, to my relief. I did not want to add to his professional cares on my behalf.

'Honestly, I'm looking forward to retirement now. And if I find that I miss the children, I can always pop into school for a visit. Not that I shall do that very often. I'm planning to be too busy to look back.'

He smiled, and looked his usual cheerful self. I felt virtuously that I had done him good, as I made for the door.

The tubes-lady was rising from her chair, the *Mirror* cutting in hand.

Poor chap, I thought, as I departed. That will give him a relapse, after all my rallying efforts on his behalf.

As I lay in bed that night waiting for sleep, I pondered on my doctor's attitude to single women.

It was obvious that he felt that we were to be pitied. We

had missed one of the most wonderful experiences in life. We were, in that ghastly phrase, 'unfulfilled'.

What made him think in this way? Was it a dislike of *waste*? Here I was, for example, a perfectly healthy – well, nearly – specimen of normal womanhood, with all the right interior equipment, I imagined, for reproduction, the tubes, orifices and appropriate spaces, but they had not been called upon to function.

This did not worry me, so why should it worry him? When I thought about it, I felt I had got off lightly in the reproduction stakes. So many of my married friends told me, in nauseating detail, of their experiences of childbirth, that I was glad I was spared the experience.

I could truthfully say that I had never missed having children. When I watched my friends coping with the problems of babyhood, sleepless nights, changing nappies, enduring the screams of teething, and then the later traumas of childhood illnesses, and the still later, and still more anxious, perils of their children's teens, I felt that I was lucky indeed.

Of course, I realised that I had a full-time job with children which might unconsciously have compensated for my spinsterhood. I was glad that I had reminded my kind-hearted doctor of this.

But why, if it were not the waste of my organs which upset him, was he still unhappy?

Could it be that he was *romantic*? So many men are. We are brought up to believe that it is the female of the species that has the hearts-and-flowers attitude to love, who craves attention and decks herself to catch a mate. In fact, it is the other way round. It is the male who brings flowers and chocolates, and dresses himself in fine array.

Take pigeons, for instance, or any other bird. The female is happily pottering about pecking up her breakfast, and the male bird is in a state of wild excitement, his ruff bristling, head down as he circles, making amorous rumblings from the throat. The female takes no notice. She has quite enough to do at the moment, and her wooer's attentions are rather a nuisance. She is definitely not the romantic one.

My thoughts drifted to Minnie Pringle. What would happen to her and that large family? Ern had been warned some time earlier by the police when he had attacked one of his wife's admirers. Poor Minnie was a fool, but more sinned against than sinning, and I was sorry for the children of that stormy household.

Well, I thought, snuggling down into my comfortable bed, maybe it would all blow over and I should hear no more of Minnie's troubles.

But there I was wrong.

Bob Willet was putting a new washer on the tap when I arrived at school the next morning. He broke off to greet me.

'Never had this bother when I was at school here. Just had buckets of water.'

'There were buckets when I came,' I told him. 'And a fine old nuisance they were. Trying to keep the flies out was enough for me.'

'Arthur Coggs put a frog in one once,' he reminisced.

'He would.'

'Did you know there's a toad as lives up Mr Mawne's?'

'Have you seen it?'

'Dozens of times. Mr Mawne's put two pieces of slate lodged by his front door to make a little home for him. But he's not there now.'

'What, the toad? Is he hibernating?'

'No, no. Mr Mawne. He's in Ireland for a week or two,

seeing his relations. I'm doing the greenhouse while he's gone.'

'I hadn't heard.'

'You will,' said Bob, as he departed.

'Henry Mawne is away at the moment,' said the vicar when he came to take prayers. 'He asked me to keep it quiet, as it doesn't do to advertise the fact that the house is empty these days.'

'Isn't his housekeeper there?'

'No. She's having a break too.'

Mrs Pringle arrived later to wash up.

'So Mr Mawne's away in Ireland. I wouldn't want to have that crossing in this weather.'

Mr Lamb at the Post Office was more forthcoming still.

'Mr Mawne flew from Bristol. Don't take more than a few minutes to get to Cork. We'll miss him around for the next fortnight.'

Alice Willet, Jane Winter and Mrs Richards all wanted to know if I had heard that Mr Mawne had gone to Ireland.

So much for keeping things quiet in a village.

That same evening John Jenkins rang.

'Have you ever been to Rousham?' he enquired.

'Never. Where is it?'

'It's between Bicester and Chipping Norton. North of Oxford. A lovely place, and not far to go. I rang to see if you would care to go to a concert there.'

'How lovely! When?'

'It's rather short notice. Next Wednesday? I'd pick you up about six. The concert begins at seven thirty. It's in aid of the RSPB.'

'Oh! I suppose Henry might be there.'

'He's away in Ireland.'

'Of course. I had forgotten.'

We gossiped for a little about this and that, and he rang off.

Now what, I wondered, would one wear on a February night to a charity concert in an old house?

Something warm, I decided, and went to bed.

Mrs Pringle was just finishing her Wednesday chores when I got home that afternoon.

'I've done out under your stairs,' she announced, 'and not before time. There was a spider in there as big as a crab.'

'Good heavens!'

'And that ironing board of yours fell down again and hit my leg something cruel. You want to put that thing somewhere else.'

'But where? I have thought about it.'

'If it was my contraption I'd put it in the garage.'

Actually, I thought, that's not a bad idea.

'I'll put on the kettle,' I said, 'and I'll run you home a mite early. I'm out this evening.'

'Ah yes!' she said smugly. 'Out with Mr Jenkins, I hear. You'll have to see Mr Mawne don't get jealous.'

I pretended that I had not heard above the noise of the water running into the kettle, but my heart sank. I supposed it was all over the neighbourhood that I was pursuing a lone widower, if not two.

We drank our tea, and kept the subjects to such harmless topics as the ever-present influenza, the exorbitant price of seed potatoes, how much a Caxley decorator had asked for doing out the village hall, and so on.

John Jenkins was only mentioned again, as I drove her back to Fairacre.

'He's a nice-looking man,' said Mrs Pringle. 'He reminds me of the rent-collector as used to come regular to my auntie's in Caxley. Very civil he always was, and my auntie never failed to say what a pleasure it was to hand over the rent money every week.'

I made an appreciative noise.

'We was all surprised when he was took away for murdering his poor wife. Done it with a common meat cleaver too.'

Mrs Pringle sounded aggrieved, as though such a good-looking civil man could at least have picked a worthier weapon, such as a cavalry sword, for the job.

Driving back I hoped that John Jenkins, who looked so like the rent-collector, did not have the same murderous urgings.

Too late now to worry about it anyway, I decided, as I looked out suitable raiment for the outing.

It was a lovely evening. It was still light enough to see the countryside as we drove north, and the air was balmy.

John was an easy companion, and we had plenty to talk about. He obviously enjoyed music, played the flute, and was wondering if the Caxley orchestra would welcome him next season.

It was dusk when we arrived at Rousham, but the bulk of the house against the sunset glow looked interesting, and I said so.

'It is. We'll come again in the summer. It's the garden here that is the main attraction. It was laid out by William Kent early in the eighteenth century, and is pretty well unchanged. He had a lot to do with the house too. It's one of my favourite places. We'll make a definite date, as soon as it opens.'

The concert took place in the hall, and was just the sort

of music I like, a quartet playing melodious pieces of Schubert, Mozart and Haydn, a delight to the ear and enabling one to let the mind drift happily.

At the interval we ate delicious snippets of this and that with plenty of smoked salmon and prawns and luscious pâtés around, and red and white wine flowing copiously.

Some of us went outside and stood on the steps, for the night was pleasantly warm. The stars were out, and a light breeze rustled William Kent's ancient trees.

As we returned we met two Caxley friends, Gerard Baker and his wife Miriam. As Miss Quinn, she had lived for a time in Fairacre, and was a good friend of mine. Introductions were made, and Miriam and I caught up with local gossip, leaving the men behind.

'I hear you are retiring.'

I told her why. She was sympathetic and sensible.

'You won't regret it. As you know I go back occasionally to help out if Barney wants me, but as time passes, I really don't want to leave all my little domestic ploys.'

I said I could well understand that. I did not imagine that my life would suddenly become empty.

She laughed and agreed. 'It won't be, I assure you,' she said, as we made our way back to our chairs. '"Nature abhors a vacuum", as my old science teacher taught us.'

A tag to remember, I thought, as the music began again.

March, which is reputed to come in like a lion and go out like a lamb, was doing the thing in reverse.

Not that anyone complained. The gentle weather, which had been so much appreciated on the Rousham evening, continued to bless us, and the influenza and other patients returned in a straggle to their duties at Fairacre school.

I took them for a shorter nature walk than usual one afternoon, in deference to their debilitated condition. We

found catkins, of course, which had been fluttering in the hazel hedges for several weeks, but also some real harbingers of spring in the shape of coltsfoot, violets and one or two early primroses.

Joseph Coggs found a blackbird's nest, and we all had a quick peep, but hurried off as the male bird kept up an outraged squawking from a nearby holly tree, and we did not want his bright-eyed mate to desert the eggs.

'Soon be Easter,' said Ernest. 'My mum said Mr Mawne's going to have an egg hunt.'

This sounded odd to me. After all, Henry is a keen ornithologist, and an egg hunt sounded wrong. I must have looked puzzled.

'*Chocolate* eggs,' explained Ernest. 'All over the garden, and then a lantern show in the village hall.'

'That's very kind of Mr Mawne,' I said. This was the first I had heard that he was back in Fairacre. 'You will be going to both, I suppose?'

Ernest sighed. 'Well, my mum said you can't just collect the chocolate eggs and not go on to the lecture, so I suppose I'll have to go.'

Well done, mum, I thought!

As we passed the churchyard there was the sound of a spade at work. We looked over the wall to see Bob Willet digging at the bottom of a grave. He looked pink and cheerful.

'You lot playing truant again?' he asked, straightening up from his labours.

'Look! Two primroses!' shouted Patrick.

'And six violets!' called one of the Bennett boys.

'And we know where there's a blackbird sitting,' said Joseph.

'I can do better'n that,' replied Bob Willet. 'There was a grass snake sunning itself on my compost heap midday.'

'Can we go and see it?'

'He scarpered when he saw me. But it shows the spring's come. You'll have to look out for frogs' spawn before long.'

We waved him goodbye and returned with our treasures to the school.

This, I thought with a pang, would be the last time I should see the nature table decked with the bounty of spring. Where should I be when it came again?

I shook myself out of this melancholy mood.

Busy as ever, no doubt, for didn't Nature abhor a vacuum?

Amy rang me that evening to tell me about the plans for our Easter break in Shropshire.

'James has found a very nice country hotel, not far from Bridgnorth. The only snag is that we shall have to be there over the Easter weekend. It's the only time he can see the business man, evidently. He's abroad most of the time, but is nipping over to see his mother in Shrewsbury for the holiday weekend.'

'It's fine by me, Amy. I'm looking forward to it.'

'So am I. We'll pick you up on Good Friday morning then, and come back on Monday afternoon. Suit you?'

'Perfectly.'

'And did you enjoy the concert at Rousham?'

'How did you know about that?'

'I met Miriam and Gerard in Caxley. They said you were there.'

Was *anything* private, I wondered sourly?

'With that handsome John Jenkins,' continued Amy.

'That is quite correct,' I replied.

'Oh, good!' said Amy, with unnecessary enthusiasm. 'See you on Good Friday morning then, if not before.'

She rang off, and I went to close the kitchen window. The wind had sprung up, and squally rain showers were on the way, according to the radio weather man.

It was almost dark when I heard someone knocking at

the front door. Normally people come to my back door, usually calling out as they come.

I opened the door to find John Jenkins there, with a book in his hand.

'Come in out of this wind,' I said.

'I thought you might like to look at this. There's a nice account of Rousham in it.'

It was a handsome volume dealing with country houses and I said that I should enjoy reading it.

I rather hoped that he would depart. His car was at the gate, and I imagined that he was on his way elsewhere. However, he lingered, and I invited him to sit down, and offered coffee. The children's marking would have to wait.

While the kettle boiled I rummaged in a very superior square biscuit tin, a Christmas present, and wondered why the lids of square biscuit tins never go on properly first time. Almost as frustrating, I thought, pouring boiling water on to the coffee, as those child-proof medicine containers where you have to align two arrows in order to prise off the lid. So useful in the middle of a dark night. And anyway, a child could undo the thing with far more ease than I could.

John was well settled into an armchair, but leapt up politely as I entered.

He seemed very much at ease and admired the cottage. I told him how lucky I had been to inherit it.

'You must come and see mine,' he said. 'Are you busy next week?'

I told him that the end of term was looming up, and perhaps I might be invited during the Easter holidays?

He brought out a pocket diary immediately, and my heart sank at such efficiency. I could see that there would be no escape.

The Thursday or Friday after Easter was fixed for me to take tea at his house, and half an hour later he left.

By now, the rain was lashing down. In the light from the porch it slanted in silver rods across the wind-tossed shrubs.

He ran down the wet path, raised his hand in farewell, and a moment later the car moved off.

Thankfully, I removed the tray and took out my neglected school work.

I was just getting down to the correction of such sentences as, 'My granny never had none neither,' when I heard someone at the front door again.

John must have forgotten something. I put aside my papers, and made my way, cursing silently, to the door.

When I opened it, the light fell upon a wispy figure drenched to the skin, with dripping hair and frightened eyes.

'You'd better come in,' I said, following Minnie Pringle into the kitchen.

CHAPTER 9

Minnie Pringle's Problems

Minnie Pringle stood as close as she could to the kitchen heater and dripped steadily from hair, hands and hem-line. If she had just emerged from a river, she could not have been more thoroughly soaked.

'I saw your light,' she said, as if that explained everything.

'I'll get you a towel and something to put on,' I told her. 'Strip off and dump your things in the sink.'

I left her shivering and fumbling with buttons, and went to find underclothes and dressing-gown. When I returned she was sitting on the rush matting on the kitchen floor.

Her back was towards me as she struggled to pull off a wet stocking, and I felt a pang of pity at the sight of her boniness. She might have been a twelve-year-old child, rather than the mother of several children, and pregnant with yet another.

Her normally red hair was now darkly plastered to her head, and dripped down upon her bent back. I noticed dark marks on the shoulders and stick-like upper arms. Could they be bruises? Had Ern really attacked her?

I put the towel round her, and the fresh clothes on the back of the kitchen chair.

'Rub yourself down well,' I said, 'and get dressed. I'm going to make some coffee for us both.'

To the accompaniment of sniffs behind me as Minnie set about her toilet, I busied myself preparing a ham sandwich for my guest. The sink was slowly filling up with sodden garments as we worked, and my head was buzzing with conjectures.

What could have happened? Why had she come to me? Usually, in times of domestic crisis she went to her mother at Springbourne or to her aunt Mrs Pringle at Fairacre. Why me this time?

And what on earth was I to do about her? Obviously, she would have to stay the night, and as luck would have it, the spare bed was made up. As soon as I had made the coffee I would fill a hot-water bottle, but the first thing was to get this poor drowned rat dry, and sitting by my fire with a hot drink.

Within ten minutes we were studying each other before the blazing hearth in my sitting-room. Minnie's teeth still chattered, but she looked pinker than on her arrival, and her hair blazed as brightly as the fire.

I began a little questioning as she grew more relaxed.

'I run off. Ern was real rough this time,' she volunteered.

'But what about the children?'

'My mum's got 'em.'

'Couldn't you have stayed with them?'

She considered this for a moment. 'She never wanted me. She said to go back to Ern. She said my place was with him, but I ain't going back. He knocked me about terrible this time.'

It sounded as though 'being knocked about' was a regular and accepted part of Minnie's marital condition. This time, obviously, Ern had gone beyond the limits of matrimonial behaviour.

'Did you come straight here?'

She looked shocked. 'Oh no! I never wanted to push meself in, like. I went to Auntie's.'

'Mrs Pringle?'

'That's right. But it's her Mothers' Union night, and there wasn't no one there. Uncle Fred was out somewhere too. It was all dark. So I come on here.'

This meant that she had been out in the downpour for the best part of two hours, roaming at least five or six miles in the darkness. I think I was more appalled than she was. This poor little pregnant waif really raised some problems, as well as pity.

She was obviously physically exhausted, although she seemed as usual mentally. She was also ravenously hungry, and I returned to the kitchen to refill her cup and to make a second sandwich. I was seriously perturbed about the possibility of a miscarriage.

My medical skills are sketchy at the best of times, and coping with anything in the gynaecological line would certainly be beyond me. I resolutely put such a possibility from my mind, as I carved ham.

But someone really should be told where she was. I imagined that Ern, poor husband though he was, should be informed, but I knew there was no telephone in Minnie's house. Nor was there in her mother's, nor at Mrs Pringle's.

Minnie was dozing when I returned, but roused herself and attacked the second sandwich with energy.

Half an hour later she was asleep in my spare bed. I washed out the threadbare clothes in the sink, draped them on the clothes horse in front of the fire, and tottered to bed myself.

It was some time before I fell asleep. How to help Minnie was my main concern. It did not seem right to bother her doctor. Ern had been visited by the police before, and I wondered if I should ask for their help again. They had enough to worry them, I decided, with real crime at its present rate, without concerning themselves with this type of domestic upset.

On the other hand, it was obviously unthinkable to send Minnie back to Ern's vicious attacks. In the end, I decided that I must consult Mrs Pringle as soon as I saw her next morning, and meanwhile Minnie must have the sanctuary of my cottage.

*

It dawned on me in the morning that this was Wednesday, and Mrs Pringle would be doing her domestic duties at my home. She and Minnie could get together about future plans during the afternoon.

I left Minnie in bed with a tray of breakfast and strict instructions to stay indoors until her aunt arrived. She seemed to understand, and I set off for school.

'So that's where she got to!' exclaimed Mrs Pringle when I unfolded my tale. 'Ern was at his wits' end when he turned up at his mother's.'

'At his mother's?' I echoed, thoroughly bewildered. How on earth could Mrs Pringle have met Ern's mother anyway, during the rainstorm which had kept most of us indoors last evening?

'We had a real big service of the Mothers' Union at Caxley parish church. Beautiful singing, and the sausage rolls afterwards fairly melted in your mouth.'

'And Ern's mother was there?'

'Yes. She's always been a good member in the Caxley branch. Never misses a meeting, despite the shop.'

I was beginning to get lost again, but Mrs Pringle explained that Ern's mother, when a girl, had been in good service south of Caxley, and had been left a sizeable amount of money by her appreciative employer. This she had wisely invested some years ago in a little corner shop which continued to thrive.

Ern hoped to inherit it eventually, but had proved such an unsatisfactory son to his upright widowed mother, that she was having second thoughts.

'She told Ern so straight. She's always kept a good hold on Ern, and don't hesitate to put him right when he does wrong.'

'Will he take notice of her?'

'That he will!' said Mrs Pringle grimly. 'She give him a

taste of her tongue last night evidently, and she's going over tonight to sort things out. I told her I'd do the same with Minnie when she turned up.'

I was much relieved, and said so. I also told her that I had wondered who to turn to for help.

'Ern's mother and I can cope with this, don't you worry,' she said, heaving herself from the front desk where she had rested her bulk. 'I said to Ern's mother, "Well, here we are at a Mothers' Union meeting, and us mothers should stand together." I know our Minnie isn't much of a mother, but she is one after all.'

She plodded off to the lobby, and I heard the sound of children entering.

I returned to my own duties with feelings of unusual gratitude to my old adversary.

When I arrived again at my Beech Green home, I found that Mrs Pringle had ironed Minnie's outfit, and the kettle was ready for our cups of tea.

Minnie looked much healthier after her night's sleep, and remarkably clean in her newly laundered clothes. I looked out a scarlet cardigan, destined originally for the next jumble sale, to augment her flimsy attire, and though it clashed horribly with her sandy hair, this was no time to worry about sartorial detail, I felt.

Mrs Pringle had obviously given the girl the promised 'talking to', and our drive back to Fairacre was unusually silent. It was a relief to drop them, and to return to the peace of my own home, and the papers I had neglected the evening before.

What, I wondered, as I prised Pussi-luv from the tin for Tibby's supper, would happen when Ern and Minnie met again?

*

The end of term was not far off, and I seemed to have done very little. The children were always somewhat under par at this time of year. Illness had kept several away. The weather had not helped, and we all looked forward to a warm spring and summer to refresh us in body and spirit.

There was one particular event in the future which gave us all some cheer. Henry Mawne had suggested another trip to the Cotswold falconry, and then a visit, that same day, to the Cotswold Wildlife Park near Burford.

Now that our numbers had risen, thanks to the arrival of the two new families, it would be necessary to hire a single-decker bus, and this meant that we could also take several parents who would act as assistants to Mrs Richards and me.

Our earlier visit to the falconry had been paid for by Henry Mawne, and very grateful we were to him. On this occasion, it was only because he knew the staff well that we were able to visit privately and have the complete attention of the people there.

Henry and I worked out the cost per child or adult, and the result was relayed to the children. Of course, they all wanted to go. I sent a note to each household explaining the conditions, time and price, and the response was almost unanimous.

The only children who were not on the list were the three Cotton children. I was surprised at this. Alice had been the keenest child to come when the outing was first mooted, and the two boys seemed equally excited at the idea. Even the Coggs' children were coming, paid for, I suspected, by the vicar. It was puzzling.

Perhaps the Cotton parents did not approve of outings, even educational ones, during school hours? Perhaps their children were travel-sick? Perhaps the family was short of money? Whatever the reason, I did not feel that I could enquire too closely, although I was sorry that the three children would not be among those going.

It was Mrs Pringle who threw some light on the affair.

'Mr Lamb's in a bit of a taking about them Cottons. Don't like to be hard on a family, but he's given 'em a lot of credit, and they don't seem to be making much effort to pay their debts.'

I made no comment. It was easy for Mrs Pringle – or anyone else in the village, for that matter – to start a hefty scandal with the words, 'Miss Read was saying'. You get remarkably canny when you live in a village and 'Least said, soonest mended' is the best motto.

Nevertheless, this snippet, whether true or not, gave me plenty to think about, and I became more alert to the problems of the Cotton children in my care.

About a week before the great day out, Henry arrived at school one afternoon in a state of anxiety.

'Can we fit in one more on the bus?'

I assured him that we could.

'It's my wife's cousin. A nice enough woman, but never gives one any notice. Rang up last night to say she was coming over from Ireland and would stay indefinitely. It's thrown my housekeeper into a panic, I can tell you.'

I could well believe it. Anyone proposing to stay indefinitely, when uninvited anyway, must pose a few household problems.

'You don't think she means to stay *permanently* when she says *indefinitely*?'

'Heaven alone knows! She is what one calls fey. All rather Celtic-twilight and gauzy scarves round the head. Very clever though. Paints very well, and helps at the Abbey Theatre sometimes. But quite unpredictable.' He sighed gustily. 'Anyway, that's one day arranged. I must try to think up further entertainment.'

'Would you like to bring her to tea one day? A Saturday or Sunday would suit me best.'

His face lit up. 'Wonderful! I know she'd like that. I've told her all about you, and she is very keen to meet you.'

'I'll ring you when I get home,' I promised, 'and we'll arrange something.'

He departed looking positively jaunty.

And what, I wondered, had he said to this Irish lady when he had told her 'all about me'?

I looked forward to our meeting with considerable interest, but touched with a little trepidation.

To my surprise, Mrs Pringle returned my ancient red cardigan which I thought I had given to Minnie on that much-disturbed night.

It was freshly laundered, and looked so spruce I seriously thought of keeping it for myself after all.

'Our Minnie,' said Mrs Pringle, 'has settled down again quite nice with Ern, thanks to his mum.'

'I expect you helped too,' I said magnanimously, 'by talking to Minnie.'

'Hardly. Goes in one ear and out the other, with that girl. Nothing between her ears to stop any advice staying in her head. No, give credit where it's due, Ern's mother was the one what settled things.'

'How did she manage that?'

'She told him she was changing her will the minute she heard about any more upsets. He's banking on getting his hands on that shop of hers, and her savings. That really shook him, she said.'

I said that covetousness occasionally had its advantages.

'Mind you,' went on Mrs Pringle, ignoring my comment, 'she's made him go to the doctor too.'

'What's the matter with him?'

Mrs Pringle buttoned up her mouth, and I guessed that I should be denied full knowledge of Ern's visit to the doctor.

'It's not the sort of thing a single lady like you should know about,' she said primly. 'It's to do with Married Life and a Man's Urges.'

'In that case,' I responded, 'I'm sure you are right to say little. But did he really see the doctor?'

Mrs Pringle looked affronted. 'Ern's mother would never had said he did, if he didn't have,' she stated flatly. This sounded the sort of sentence with which I continually grappled, but I did not propose to go into that now.

'Ern's mother is the soul of truth. Lives by the Ten Commandments and signed the pledge too. If she said Ern went to the doctor, then he done just that.'

I apologised for my doubts.

'No offence meant and none taken,' she said graciously. 'Anyway the top and bottom of it is that Minnie shouldn't be put in the family way again, after the present little stranger comes to light.'

'I'm glad to hear it. She has quite enough children as it is.'

Mrs Pringle began to move towards the door.

'Well, we'll just have to see,' she replied gloomily. 'You can't take anything Minnie does for granted. After all, Ern isn't the only man in her life. It makes you think, don't it? You be thankful you're single, Miss Read.'

'I am,' I told her.

The proposed tea party took place on the following Sunday, and Amy had come over to help with my entertaining.

James was away on yet another business trip, and Amy said that she could not wait to meet a fey Irishwoman in gauze scarves.

In actual fact, Deirdre Lynch was dressed in a particularly smart purple outfit with amethysts to match, and Amy and I looked positively dowdy in contrast.

Henry was in buoyant spirits, and inclined to be rather facetious.

'I told you what a ray of sunshine Miss Read has been,' he said to Deirdre. 'I don't know what I should have done without her to guide me through the darkness.'

She smiled vaguely, not appearing to hear half that was said, and I wondered if she were deaf perhaps.

She contributed little to the conversation, until Amy mentioned some Irish friends. Evidently they were neighbours, and our visitor became more animated.

'Not that I go out much now,' she said. 'So many little upsets, you know. Our local pub was bombed last week, and four people blown up.'

Some little upset, was my private thought!

'That's why I am beginning to wonder about coming to live over here.'

Henry, startled, dropped a piece of cake on the floor, and bent to retrieve it. His face was pink when he returned to an upright position, but whether with shock or stooping, it was impossible to say.

'What! Permanently?' he spluttered.

'It seems a good idea. I have lots of friends here – you included, Henry dear – and I think a cottage just like this one would be a perfect place to live.'

Henry began to look very unhappy, and champed his cake moodily.

'I thought I could stay with you while I looked around,' continued Deirdre. She turned to me.

'Do you know of anything?'

'Not at the moment.'

Amy came to the rescue with her usual aplomb. 'Why not get *The Caxley Chronicle* while you are over here? Always lots of houses for sale. And we've some very reliable estate agents in this area. I'm sure you would find something.'

Henry choked, and gave a malevolent look in Amy's direction.

'I don't think it will be convenient for you to stay with me,' he said, when he had regained his breath. 'I'm particularly busy over Easter. This egg hunt, you know, for the children. You are giving me a hand with that, aren't you?'

He turned an appealing face to me. I felt a twinge of guilt.

'We are going away together,' put in Amy quickly. 'We shall be in Shropshire for a few days over the Easter weekend.'

Henry looked stricken. 'But I was *relying* on you,' he wailed. 'I don't think I can manage without your help.'

Deirdre looked smug. 'I shall be there to help, Henry. I don't plan to return to Ireland for some time yet.'

'More tea?' I enquired brightly.

'I believe a robin is looking for a nesting place in my garden,' said Amy, backing me up in my rescue attempt.

Henry continued to look furious. 'Too early,' he said tersely.

When they had departed, Amy lit a cigarette, and sank back on the sofa with a sigh.

'Well, what a to-do. That man is heavily smitten with you, my love, and you'll have to do something about it. If I know anything about these affairs, our Deirdre has got her eye on him, and he knows it. You'll have to come to his rescue. You could do much worse. He's a very nice fellow, I've always thought, and absolutely devoted to you.'

'Oh, shut up, Amy!' I snapped. 'Henry must fight his own battles. I'm not taking him on.'

Amy laughed so heartily that I was forced to join in.

'Let's get out the map and plan our route to Bridgnorth,' she suggested. 'It's time you had a break, I can see.'

'Hear, hear!' I agreed warmly.

Two days before we broke up for the Easter holidays, the trip to the Cotswolds took place in perfect weather.

The stone villages glowed warmly in the spring sunshine and every now and then we crossed the River Windrush, with the willows drooping freshly green branches above it.

Most of the children were already acquainted with the birds of prey and their attendants and all were greeted as old friends. There was no shortage of volunteers to offer arms as perches to the great birds as they showed off their capabilities.

The Cotswold Wildlife Park was enjoyed with equal enthusiasm by the children, but my pleasure was somewhat marred by Henry's behaviour.

As soon as we took our places in the bus, Henry sat beside me. Deirdre sat in the seat behind, and occasionally leant forward to speak to him. He was not very forthcoming to Deirdre's comments, but talked brightly to me, virtually ignoring his visitor.

At the first opportunity, I changed my place, making sure that I was adequately hemmed in by children. When we stopped, however, to go round the falconry or the park, Henry appeared at my side. So, I noticed, did Deirdre.

I escaped every now and again, excusing myself saying

that the children needed attention. It was all rather irritating, and done, I felt sure, to annoy Deirdre in which, I was glad to see, he did not succeed.

She stayed close to Henry throughout, and on this occasion was actually wearing one of the gauzy scarves draped attractively round her head. I was getting rather fond of Deirdre, I decided, looking across the eagles' enclosure where I had found temporary sanctuary.

She was obviously good-tempered, impervious to Henry's rudeness, and implacably intent on winning him with her charms.

And good luck to her, I thought. Perhaps, by the time I returned from my break with Amy and James, she would have succeeded.

What a relief that would be!

CHAPTER 10

Romantic Complications

I was particularly glad to welcome the Easter holidays. Although I could not complain of anything definite about my health, and managed, I thought, to perform my duties as well as ever, I was conscious of being a little below par.

For one thing, I did not sleep as soundly as I had before my strokes, and I tired more quickly if I undertook gardening or furniture shifting. However, I still enjoyed my meals and my walks around the fields and lanes of Fairacre and Beech Green, and reckoned that I was in pretty good shape.

Nevertheless, it would be good to get away. When one is at home there are innumerable little jobs waiting to be done, and out of sight would be out of mind, thank goodness. The bookshelves that needed a thorough cleaning, the curtain linings that needed shortening, the refrigerator that needed defrosting and the bathroom tap that dripped steadily could all be left behind while I kicked up my heels with Amy.

And besides these domestic annoyances there were more personal irritants. Henry Mawne was one, Minnie Pringle's unsatisfactory marriage was another. The unexplained tension among the Cottons was another. It would be a real relief to leave all these problems behind me for a day or two.

On the last day of term Mrs Pringle dropped a plate on the lobby floor, and was unusually upset by this misfortune.

'There! That's the third,' she exclaimed crossly. 'Yesterday it was a pudding basin, and before I come along here today the handle of one of my best cups come away in my hand.'

She stooped to retrieve the pieces.

'My aunt gave it to me years ago,' she went on, red in the face from her exertions. 'A beautiful tea set it was too, though the teapot lid went to glory years ago, and there's only four cups left, but you have to expect that with a teaset over the years.'

I said that there was no need to worry about the school plate. I would re-imburse the kitchen department and explain the matter.

She looked a little more cheerful. 'Well, there's an end to it now, I daresay, as the three's done.'

'The three?'

'Everything always goes in threes. Like three blind mice, and three-in-one-and-one-in-three.'

I felt that mice and the Trinity were in strange juxtaposition in this theory, but forbore to comment.

'Like your strokes,' she continued. 'You've had two, and I'll wager – if I were a betting woman that is – that you'll get a third.'

'Well, really —' I began indignantly, but was ignored.

'Always in *threes*,' repeated the old harpy. 'It was the third as took off my Uncle Ebeneezer in the end. You want to watch out.'

She was out of the door before I could think of a suitable response.

As usual, she had had the last word.

That evening, as I was busy ironing some clothes before

packing them for the holiday, a shadow fell across the ironing board, and there was John Jenkins making his way to the back door.

'Oh, I see you're busy,' he exclaimed.

'Nothing urgent,' I assured him. 'Do come in.'

We went through to the sitting-room, and John settled down as though he intended to stay some time.

He refused tea, coffee, sherry and whisky, and looked about him very happily.

'I was just passing, you know, and I realised I wasn't sure what date we'd fixed for you to see my cottage. What about this weekend?'

I explained that I should be away.

'Pity. I've invited Henry and his girlfriend to supper. He seems in a bit of a tizzy about his visitor. I thought she seemed rather a good sort.'

'So did I.'

He appeared surprised. 'Did you now? I think Henry felt you might be upset. He said as much to me. Out of Deirdre's hearing, of course.'

I began to feel my usual irritation with Henry's behaviour, but managed to answer equably. 'I've no idea why Henry should imagine that I mind at all,' I said.

'He's very fond of you,' said John. 'Understandably.'

He looked at me with such a strange expression on his face that I felt alarm overtaking my irritation. Not *another* suitor? How delighted Amy would be!

'I'm sorry about this weekend,' I replied briskly. 'Could we arrange another day? I'll get my diary.'

I had left it upstairs, and although I was glad of a few minutes' respite from John's company, I was not best pleased to discover Tibby stretched out asleep on the eiderdown with a headless mouse alongside.

I snatched up my diary, left the two to get on with it,

and returned to find John leaning on the mantelpiece in a dejected manner.

'I could come on Thursday or Friday of next week,' I offered. He appeared to rally slightly.

'Not Thursday. I'm expecting a new fellow to start on the garden that day, and I ought to oversee him.'

'You're lucky! How did you get him? Jobbing gardeners are thin on the ground these days.'

'I put a postcard in Fairacre Post Office. This man called the same day.'

'Do I know him?'

'He's called Arthur Coggs.'

'Oh lor'! Our Arthur!'

'So you know him?'

'Everyone knows Arthur round here. You'll have to watch him if he does turn up, which I doubt. He's the local ne'er-do-well.'

John looked grim. I found it preferable to the amorous glance he had earlier given me.

'I didn't think he looked very prepossessing, I must admit, but I thought I'd give him a try.'

'Why not?'

John sat down again, just as I had thought he was about to go.

'This is where you are such a help,' he remarked. 'You seem to know everybody.'

'Well, I ought to. I taught most of them over the years.'

'I suppose it is just being a newcomer in such a tight little community, but I must admit that I feel very lonely at times. The complete outsider.'

'You'll soon make lots of friends,' I said bracingly. 'What about Friday then?'

I held up my diary.

'Friday. That will be fine.'

He stood up, and held out his hand, which I obligingly took to shake, but was dismayed to find that he did not relinquish mine.

'You were my first friend here,' he said. 'I shall never forget it.'

I thought that I could smell scorching coming from the kitchen. For pity's sake, had I left the iron switched on? I could not tug the poor fellow willy-nilly along to see, but I wished he would let go of my hand of his own volition.

'John,' I said very kindly, I hope, 'I'm as pleased as you are to be friends, and I look forward to seeing the cottage on Friday week.'

At that he let go of my hand and gave me a wonderful smile. No doubt about it, he was a very handsome man.

I let him out of the front door. I certainly felt affectionate towards John Jenkins and wanted to see him again.

Meanwhile, the matters in my kitchen and bedroom needed more immediate attention, and any tender emotions must take second place.

It was good to be heading north-west to Shropshire on the afternoon of Good Friday.

We skirted most towns, but the few that we went through seemed busy.

Amy was rather censorious. 'In my young days,' she said, 'everything shut down on Good Friday. Even the level crossing near our home was closed.'

'You're thinking of footpaths,' James told her.

Amy wrinkled her brow. 'Well, perhaps I was,' she conceded, 'but the point is that Good Friday was really *observed*. Now you can pop into any shop for a pound of tea or a quarter of lamb's liver whenever you like.'

'The other way round,' commented James, jamming on the brakes to let a pheasant stroll haughtily across the road. 'You'd never buy a *pound* of tea at a time!'

'And talking of tea,' said Amy, quite unruffled, 'let's stop soon and have a cup somewhere.'

On this, we were all in agreement.

The hotel, when we arrived at around six o'clock, was all we had hoped. It was a solidly built house which had once been a Victorian vicarage, with a pleasant grassy garden and mature trees. The coach house and stables had been turned into attractive rooms, and other additions, such as a large sun room, blended well with the original building.

James dropped us off in Bridgnorth the next day while he visited his business friend, and Amy and I pottered about shopping, and found the funicular railway which descended from the town centre down the steep drop to the side of the River Severn.

We spent the day exploring until James picked us up again as arranged, at about six, in a car park near by.

'I feel as though I've been on the beach all day,' said Amy happily. 'All blown about in the freshest of fresh air.'

It was later that evening when James enquired after the new families at Fairacre, and I had a chance to tell him about the odd behaviour of Mrs Cotton.

He looked grave. 'I can't understand this. There should be no shortage of money. The Trust is very generous, and the whole point of the exercise is to give the children a happy home with the usual little treats such as your school outing.'

'I know. That's what's so odd. They don't live extravagantly, and I don't think he's a betting man. He certainly doesn't waste his money at the pub. Bob Willet told me that.'

'Bob Willet? Is he the local tippler?'

'Far from it! You're mixing him up with Arthur Coggs. Bob is an upright and God-fearing teetotaller, and Mrs Willet keeps him that way. He is also my chief informant on village affairs.'

'So what's his opinion?'

'He's as puzzled as I am, I think, though I haven't really discussed the matter much with him.'

James rubbed his chin thoughtfully. 'I'll call one day soon,' he promised. He must have seen my look of alarm. 'Don't worry. You won't be mentioned. It'll be a casual dropping-in to see how things are going. It's quite usual for a member of the board to keep a friendly eye on such matters.'

I went to bed with mixed feelings. Was I being meddlesome in the Cotton family's affairs? Should I have told James about my fears which were possibly groundless?

On the other hand, it was good to have James's support, and if there were troubles in that household he was the ideal man to put them right.

I did not worry for long. Good Shropshire air ensured that I slept soundly for eight hours.

We returned by a different route, travelling through the border country between England and Wales, more beautiful than ever with the trees decked in their spring finery. Here and there the wild cherries were in early bloom, reminding me of Housman's poem:

> *Loveliest of trees, the cherry now*
> *Is hung with bloom along the bough,*
> *And stands about the woodland ride*
> *Wearing white for Eastertide.*

In my Beech Green garden the daffodils were beginning to break, and there was the scent of spring everywhere.

The cottage was clean from Mrs Pringle's ministrations, and Tibby greeted me with unusual enthusiasm.

Altogether, it was good to be back, and the thought of almost a fortnight of the school holidays still stretching before me was an added bonus.

It was odd to realise that this holiday was the last one before a term. At the end of the summer term I should be at the outset of my retirement.

I contemplated the matter. Did it alarm me? Did I feel apprehensive about changing my way of life for – who knows? Twenty years of pleasing myself? Of going where I wanted when I wanted? Should I get fed up with my own company? Should I feel that life was aimless without the discipline and structure of a school year which had shaped everything for me for so long?

I had now had several months to get used to the idea, and it was a considerable relief to find that I now looked forward with enormous pleasure to the years ahead.

On Friday afternoon I put on my new cardigan suit and set off to have tea with John Jenkins.

On my way I saw my first butterfly of the season and noticed that the hawthorn hedges were beginning to break into leaf. Lambs skittered about Hundred Acre field on my left, and the sun was warm. I felt in high spirits.

John's cottage stood back from the narrow road we all call Pig Lane. It must have once been built of brick and flint, as mine is, and so many local cottages are. But some earlier inhabitant had lime-washed it, and the effect was very fresh and pleasing, although the purists might regret the concealment of interesting native brickwork.

It was somewhat larger than mine, and John had added an elegant conservatory at the rear. This led from his sitting-room, and gave a feeling of light and space.

Upstairs there were three bedrooms, larger and loftier than my own, and certainly lighter. I congratulated him on having found such an attractive place.

'My friends say it's really too big, but I need at least one spare bedroom for visitors, and in any case I'm used to big houses. I was brought up in a vast Victorian villa complete with a basement and attics. We must have had over sixty stairs.'

I followed him into the kitchen, and was impressed with the competence with which he dealt with setting out the tray and coping with the kettle and teapot, and all the other trappings.

'I don't rise to making my own scones yet,' he said, offering me the dish when we had settled by the fire. 'I get these from Lamb at the Post Office.'

This reminded me of the postcard he had put up, and I enquired about Arthur.

'Well, he turned up. I set him to cutting back a patch of scrub at the end of the garden, and he seemed to make some headway. I think I'll give him a trial run.'

'Watch your tools then,' I warned him, 'or anything else he can put in his pocket. Our Arthur needs a lot of beer, and he has to make a bit of money on the side for that.'

He said that he would be vigilant, and went on to enquire about my holiday.

I waxed enthusiastic about Bridgnorth and the country around it, and told him about a veteran car museum that James had taken us to, and about the ancient but glittering Lagonda I had fallen for.

'That's the sort of thing I miss,' he said, when I had run out of breath. 'The companionship and the fun of shared outings.'

'But you have made friends here,' I said, 'and you know Henry from the old days.'

'A little of Henry's company goes a long way,' he said. 'He can be very tiresome at times.'

I felt sorry that I had mentioned Henry. I had no wish to make mischief, but surely the two men were not vying for my favours? It was an uncomfortable thought.

I was soon enlightened.

'It would be very kind of you to agree to accompany me now and again on a little expedition. You know that I relish your company, and I should appreciate it so much.'

One cannot very well say, 'As long as the relationship remains friendly and not romantic', but that was in my thoughts.

Aloud I said that I should enjoy an outing with him now and again, although the next term would keep me unusually busy while it lasted.

'But then you'll be retired,' he said eagerly, 'and have time on your hands. You are bound to feel a little lost – even lonely – when you first retire.'

I did not like to point out that I had never yet been lonely in my life as a single woman, that I enjoyed my own company, and that I was looking forward to many hours of solitude. He might feel that I was criticising his own recent feelings, and I did not want to appear censorious. Luckily, he turned to another subject.

'I'm thinking of getting a dog. I thought of the Caxley Dog Rescue place. Do you know anything about it?'

'Not personally, but I'll consult Bob Willet. He'll know.'

The Easter holidays flew by at their usual surprising speed, and I was left contemplating all those jobs I had been going to tackle, and had not.

The curtain linings still remained unshortened, and the bookshelves uncleaned, but the bath tap had had a new washer and the refrigerator had been defrosted. I told myself that half the jobs had been tackled, and that was a better record than some of my school-holiday schedules.

As was usual, the first day of term dawned sunny and clear, and I thought how lovely it would be to potter about in the garden with the birds fluttering about collecting food for their nestlings, and to enjoy the scent of spring flowers. However, duty called, and I set off to face my last term at Fairacre school.

Mrs Pringle's leg must have 'flared up' again, as I noticed that she was limping about her dusting routine, a sure sign of trouble. What dire happening was I to hear of now, I wondered?

'I'm off to the doctor this evening,' said Mrs Pringle. 'I was knocked down by that Arthur Coggs.'

'Good heavens! How was that?'

'I went out late last night to put a birthday card in Lamb's letter box to catch first post this morning. It's my Auntie Margaret's eightieth tomorrow, and I want her to know I've remembered her. I'm in her will.'

'So how did you meet Arthur?'

'He was stepping out – or rather, *falling out* – of the Beetle and Wedge, and he was in a real drunken state. He bumped into me, and it's a wonder I didn't fall to the ground and break a hip. What's more, he never said a word of apology! Jogged my bad leg something cruel.'

I rendered my sympathy.

'That Arthur Coggs has been too flush with money lately for his own good. I date it from when he started work at that friend of yours up Pig Lane. He must be paying him over the odds. Everyone's talking about it.'

I felt some alarm. Could John have left valuables about despite my warning? Perhaps I should make enquiries when I returned home? Or was this none of my business?

Ernest appeared at the door.

'Can I ring the bell, miss? You never said nothing about who could.'

Clearly John Jenkins' affairs must wait. School affairs now engulfed me, including my old enemy, the double negative.

As it happened, John rang me as soon as I returned home.

He had been invited to the book launch of a local writer and would I accompany him?

As it was the same evening as our Parents' Association meeting at the school I was obliged to decline, but I was sorry. It certainly sounded more fun. However, duty came first.

I decided to broach the subject of Arthur's temporary affluence.

'You haven't missed anything?'

'No. Though I haven't looked thoroughly. Should I?'

'It wouldn't be a bad idea. Do you keep any money about? It sounded as though he had paper money.'

'Hang on. I'll have a quick look.'

I waited, stroking Tibby, who was impatient for a snack.

John sounded breathless when he returned. 'You're right! Two ten-pound notes missing from my desk drawer. I keep a hundred stashed there for any emergency.'

'When did you look last?'

'Can't say. I notice them, of course, when I go to get stamps and so on from the drawer, but if it looks undisturbed I naturally think the hundred is still there. What a fool I am! I should have thought of this.'

He sounded very put out, as well he might be.

'But does Arthur ever come inside your house?'

'I've shown him where the lavatory is in case he needs it.'

'And he'd pass the desk?'

'No, but the door is always open into the sitting-room. The desk's in full view of the hall.'

'Unlocked?'

'Not now it won't be,' he said grimly. 'I shall tackle him about it, but I don't know if it's a police affair. I should have been more careful.'

I felt very sorry for him. 'Cheer up!' I said. 'At least you know more about our Arthur Coggs.'

He gave a snort of disgust. 'And about myself too, alas!'

PART THREE

SUMMER TERM

CHAPTER 11

Something Unexpected

The first week of my last term as a school mistress was one of unbroken sunshine unusual for April.

The early mornings were particularly idyllic. In my garden the daffodils flourished their golden trumpets, and sturdy double tulips glowed in a stone trough by my front door. The lilac bushes bore pyramids of blue-grey buds, ready to burst into fragrant bloom, and everywhere the small birds darted feverishly in their search for food for their young.

The drive along the leafy lane to Fairacre was equally enchanting. The blackthorn bushes were a froth of white blossom which spilled into the road with every gust of wind, strewing the surface with petal-confetti. Lambs gambolled in the fields, larks sang above and it was almost too much to ask to go into school on such mornings.

I comforted myself with the exquisite thought that by next spring time I should be able to revel freely in all this feverish excitement of flora and fauna, untouched by the stern finger of duty pointing me to a bleaker path.

Now that the end of my professional life was so near I looked forward to freedom with ever-increasing pleasure. I even began to wonder why I had not given up years ago.

'Because you would have starved,' rebuked my sensible half.

'But think of the fun you've missed,' pointed out my frivolous half.

'Never mind,' I told myself, swinging the car into the school playground. 'It's all waiting for me at the end of term.'

One such blissful morning I was on playground duty when Eve Umbleditch emerged from my old home and joined me.

'What a day!' she said, turning her face up to the cloudless sky.

'Too good to work,' I agreed.

'Not for much longer, though. I came to ask you to supper one evening soon.'

I said I should love to come.

'Now that Andrew's a better sleeper, we feel we can do a little evening entertaining. What about next Wednesday?'

I promised to confirm this when I got home to my diary, and found it was then time to usher my charges back to school.

Later that day I rang Eve to say how much I looked forward to the party at Fairacre school house, as it once was, in my time.

'Good! We've asked John Jenkins as well. He was at the same school as Horace. Isn't it a small world?'

I agreed that it was indeed.

'And the Bakers. Gerard and Miriam,' continued Eve. 'Just the six of us. Anyway, as you know only too well, the dining-room won't hold any more.'

'It's the perfect number,' I assured her.

'I expect John will bring you,' she added. 'Unless you like to pick him up as you pass Pig Lane.'

'We'll fix something,' I promised, and rang off.

Almost immediately it rang again. It was John Jenkins.

'I hear we've been invited to the Umbleditches. What time shall I call for you?'

'Well, actually I had thought of picking you up, as I shall be coming your way.'

'No, no! Wouldn't hear of it. *I* shall collect *you*. It will make my day to have you to myself for a little time.'

'That's kind of you. Shall we say six thirty here?'

And so it was settled.

I pottered about the garden doing a little perfunctory weeding until it grew dark, and I went indoors.

My thoughts turned upon this new friend John Jenkins. There was no deluding myself. The man was getting remarkably attentive, and I should have to make up my mind what to do about it.

Here he was, in the same vulnerable state as Henry Mawne, a lone man obviously in need of companionship. Was I willing to supply it?

Occasionally, yes, was my reply to this self-posed query, but not on any permanent basis. He was an attractive man, he could offer a woman good company, protection and a comfortable home, and many a lone female, I felt sure, would be happy to consider marriage. However, I was not.

As Amy had so often pointed out, I was far too fond of my own company. Further, she was wont to add, I was very selfish, and it would do me good to have to consider someone else in my life. Look how much richer her own life was, she would say, married to James!

I forbore on these occasions to remind her of her unhappiness when James was away, presumably on business but, I guessed, with some dalliance with other ladies thrown in. Amy was no fool, and knew better than I did, I suspected, about such matters, but she was rock-bottom loyal, and never breathed a word about her doubts.

She was probably right about my selfishness, but what was wrong with that? I coped with my own worries as well as my own pleasures, without embroiling anyone else in my affairs. I gave help to others whenever I could, as in the case of poor distracted Minnie, and I suppose I could have done a great deal more if I had joined such excellent bodies as the Red Cross or the Samaritans, but I was never one for joining things, and in any case my spare time was limited.

No, the fact of the matter was that single life suited me admirably, and now that I was in my comfortable middle age I was decidedly set in my ways and would very much dislike sharing my home with someone else. There was a lot to be said for a lone existence, and I recalled a remark of Katherine Mansfield's when she said, 'If you find a hair in your honey, at least you know it's your own.'

I only hoped that John Jenkins' ardour would cool, and that Deirdre would be successful in capturing my other, rather less troublesome, admirer.

One could quite see the attractions of the monastic life, I thought, prising Pussi-luv out of the tin.

Promptly at six thirty on the following Wednesday, John's car arrived. He must have spent hours polishing it. It gleamed from nose to tail, and put my own shabby runabout to shame.

The evening was overcast but warm, and the heady scents of spring were all around.

John was cheerful, and not too embarrassingly solicitous, and my spirits rose as we approached my old home.

'Do you miss it?' he asked as we drew up.

'Not really. I think I prefer the cottage at Beech Green. For one thing, it is full of happy memories of Dolly Clare, and it is my own. This was only lent to me for the duration of my working life. I was always very conscious of that.'

'You are like me. I like to feel settled.'

Luckily, at this juncture, Horace appeared and greeted us. Soon the two men were reminiscing about their old school and the idiosyncrasies of some of the staff they remembered.

It was good to see Miriam and Gerard again. He was in the throes of producing a television series about diarists, and we all gave him conflicting and confused ideas about the people he should put in. I plumped for Parson Woodforde and Francis Kilvert. Miriam said John Evelyn was absolutely essential. Eve said that Gerard could do a whole series on Samuel Pepys alone, and we all got extremely excited about the project and bombarded poor Gerard with our ideas.

He bore it all very well, and when we had run out of breath, said mildly that he was not going to use any of those diarists but some unknown Dorset individuals he had come across when reading about various seventeenth-century writers.

John, with considerable aplomb, changed the subject to gardening while we got over our disappointments and paid more attention to our excellent roast lamb and redcurrant jelly. It was salutory to remember, I told myself, that writers and other creative artists do not relish other people's ideas. They usually have more than enough of their own, and well-meant suggestions only add to the burden of their already over-stocked minds.

Miriam and I were taken to see Andrew asleep upstairs, in my old spare bedroom, once we had finished at the table. He looked so rosy and angelic, with dark crescents of eyelashes against his velvety cheeks, that it was difficult to believe that I had seen him that morning roaring his head off, in a paroxysm of infant rage, when I had been on playground duty.

The rain had swept in whilst we were enjoying ourselves

and by the time we drove back to Beech Green the roads
were awash, hard rain spun silver coins on the tarmac and
the windscreen wipers were working overtime.

We passed the end of Pig Lane, and we soon approached
my cottage.

'Stay there,' commanded John, as we drew up, 'and I'll
get an umbrella from the boot.'

Huddled together we made a dash for the front door,
John holding the umbrella over me while I found the key.

'You must come in,' I said.

'Thank you,' he replied, scattering showers of raindrops
as he closed the umbrella.

'Coffee?' I asked, as he divested himself of his coat.

'How nice.'

I proceeded to the kitchen to do my duties. Frankly, I
should have preferred to go to straight to bed, rather than
sit making polite conversation, but I reminded myself of
the fact that I had been fetched and carried, and protected
from the downpour.

The fire was low, but I put on some small logs, much to
Tibby's satisfaction, and we sipped our coffee companionably.

'I hope I'm not keeping you from your bed.'

'Not at all,' I said politely, stifling a yawn.

'It's wonderful to be here. So marvellously *cosy*. The fire,
you know, and the cat, and you just sitting there.'

I wondered if he would prefer me to stand on my head,
or leap about the room in a lively polka, but was too tired
to do anything but smile.

'This is what I miss,' he said earnestly. 'The companionship, the sharing of things.'

Not again, I prayed silently. I was really too sleepy to listen
sympathetically to any man's description of his loneliness.

He put his cup and saucer very carefully in the hearth, a

move which I viewed with some apprehension. If this was a prelude to a proposal of marriage I must be on my guard. I felt such a longing for my bed that I might well accept him simply to terminate the evening's proceedings, and how should I feel in the morning?

He rose from his armchair and came to sit on a footstool very close to me. The light from the table lamp shone on his silvery hair. He really was an extremely handsome man.

'I'm sure you know how I feel about you,' he began, speaking quickly. 'It began when I first saw you. I had a premonition that we were destined to mean a great deal to each other. Do you feel that too?'

He looked so earnest, and his blue eyes were so pleading that I could quite see how easily I could agree.

'Well, I must say,' I began weakly, but was interrupted, rather rudely I thought, by my hand being snatched up and squeezed somewhat painfully. Aunt Clara's garnet ring was always rather small, and it was now being ground into my finger.

'Don't put me off,' he begged. 'Don't turn me down. You mean so much to me, and I couldn't bear it if you said "No". Say you'll think about it, if you need time. But what I dearly want to hear is that you would marry me.'

It was all said in such a rush, blurted out so urgently that there was no mistaking the sincerity of the offer. I was deeply touched, and withdrew my mangled hand as unobtrusively as I could.

'Dear John,' I began.

'You will?' he cried, attempting to retrieve my hand again. 'You'll have me? Oh, I can't tell you —'

'I didn't say that,' I pointed out. Was I never to get a word in edgeways?

He checked suddenly, and began to look crestfallen.

'Do have your coffee while it's hot,' I said. 'I was about to say, John dear, that I am truly fond of you, and it's wonderful for me to receive a proposal at my age. Let me think it over, may I?'

He sighed, and sat more upright on the footstool. I fetched his coffee and gave it to him.

'I suppose I shall have to be content with "truly fond", but I beg you to take pity on me. I'd do anything for you. We could move to wherever you fancied. Go abroad if you like. To France, say. I've a little cottage there. I'm not a rich man, but we shouldn't want for anything, and I do most dearly love you.'

'I know that. It touches me deeply.'

He put down the coffee cup again. It was still almost full. He stood up, and put his arms round me.

'Say you'll think about it. Say you'll tell me quickly. I shan't have an easy minute until I know. And please, *please* say "Yes".'

He kissed me very gently and made for the door. Outside the rain lashed down more fiercely than ever, and I handed him the umbrella which was still glistening with raindrops.

'I'll ring you tomorrow,' I promised, as he ran down the path.

Within a minute he was off, with a valedictory toot of the horn, and I put the cups and saucers in the sink, and put the fireguard round the ashes of the logs, and put myself, at long last, between the sheets.

What a day! I felt exhausted with all this emotion.

I had plenty to think about the next morning. I looked at myself in the looking-glass and wondered why anyone should want to marry me.

Certainly my hair was still thick and had very little grey in it, and I had always been fortunate enough to have a good skin, but otherwise I was humdrum enough in all conscience.

It was very flattering, though, to receive a proposal of marriage in one's late fifties, and I was duly elated in a moderate and middle-aged way. Perhaps, I thought, with some deflation, John had already asked more attractive women and they had turned him down?

Not with that silvery hair and those devastating blue eyes, I decided. He would make a most decorative adjunct to anyone's household, and no doubt be quite useful too in little manly things like changing electric light bulbs and washers on taps.

But did I want him? The answer was definitely 'No'! A pity, but there it was, and the really wretched thing was that I must tell him so in the kindest possible way.

I drove to school rehearsing different ways of turning down a nice man's proposal of marriage. They all seemed pretty brutal, and I was glad to reach school and to be confronted by my exuberant pupils.

Mrs Richards did not appear, and I took the entire school for prayers in my classroom. It was a quarter past nine when she arrived, full of apologies. Her car was being repaired. Wayne's van would not start. She had been obliged to go to catch the bus, and promised to tell me more at playtime.

Meanwhile, she hastened to her own duties, and I to mine. Every now and again, the awful fact of the impending telephone call I must make plunged me into gloom.

Mrs Pringle, arriving with clean tea towels, commented on my looks. 'Proper peaky again. You want to watch you don't have another funny turn,' she told me.

I said that I felt quite well. I could have said that if I were to have any more funny turns, it was not much good setting out to watch them, but I was in no mood to cross swords with Mrs Pringle in my present debilitated condition, and let it pass.

At playtime Mrs Richards enlarged on her early morning difficulties as we sipped our coffee.

'There I was by the bus stop when Alan came along and gave me a lift. I've known him for years. He was sweet on me at one time, but I was only eighteen and he was quite old, about thirty.'

I thought of John Jenkins, who must be in his sixties. No doubt Mrs Richards would consider him in his dotage. Perhaps he was? A dispiriting thought.

'He was a proper pest,' she went on, 'and I asked my mum to choke him off. She told him I was about to be engaged to Wayne, and I was furious with her.'

'Why?'

'Well, I'd only been out once or twice with Wayne, and I didn't want him to think that I was running after him. I mean, I knew I could never take to Alan. You always know, don't you?'

I agreed fervently that indeed one did always know.

'But I was quite keen on Wayne, and I thought people would tittle-tattle and he'd be frightened off. It was stupid of my mum to say that, wasn't it?'

'I must get out to the playground,' I said, 'before murder is done.'

Out in the fresh air, with the rooks wheeling about the trees, and the children rushing around being aeroplanes or trains, I felt much better.

On the whole, I thought that my assistant had been jolly lucky to have a mother to take her part. If only I had someone to 'choke off' my poor old John!

Well, it would have to be me, and perhaps that was all for the best, I decided, as we returned to the classroom.

It was almost five o'clock when I returned home, as I had been waylaid by a parent who was worried about her child's asthma and wanted to know if PE lessons upset him.

It seemed sensible to fortify myself with a cup of tea before tackling my difficult task. It was a bright afternoon and no doubt John was either in his garden or even farther afield. Would it be better to wait until it became dark, I wondered? He would be much more likely to be near the telephone then.

On the other hand, I wanted to get the job over. Besides, if I rang after six o'clock he might think I had waited for the cheap rate period, and I should appear parsimonious as well as callous. How difficult life is!

I finished my tea, took a deep breath, and rang John's

number. He must have been standing by the telephone, for it only gave two rings.

'Thank God it's you,' he said. 'I've been snatching up the phone all day, and had the laundry, the vicar, George Annett, and some idiot trying to get Venezuela. I've been dying for you to ring.'

'Well, I was at school,' I said weakly.

'Of course! I'd forgotten that.'

'I've only just got in.'

'You poor darling. You must be whacked. You need a cup of tea.'

I did not like to say that I had just had one. It seemed so heartless, especially as he had obviously had a distracting day.

'About last night,' I began, and wondered how to go on. Should I ask him if he remembered asking me to marry him? Should I say that I had been thinking of his kind offer? Should I say that I was feeling terrible? This last was true enough anyway.

Luckily, John took over the initiative.

'You've decided? Is it "Yes" or "No"? Please say it's "Yes"! I can't tell you how much it means to me.'

'John, it has to be "No", I fear.'

There was a strange sound at the other end. A sigh? A sob? A laugh?

He sounded calm when he spoke again.

'I was afraid it would be so. But at least you haven't asked me to be "just a good friend" because I'm a dam' sight more than that.'

'I know, John, and I'm sorry to have to refuse.'

'Well, there it is. No harm done, and I give you fair warning that I shall try again.'

'Please, John —' I said in alarm.

'Don't worry, I shan't pester you, but I'm not giving up.'

'Oh dear!'

'Will you come to a concert with me at Oxford next month?'

'Thank you. I should like that.'

'There's a nice girl! And wear that blue thing you had on last night. It was so pretty.'

He rang off before I could say any more.

Last night? Was it only *last night* that all this had blown up? Thank heaven he had taken it so well. My knees were knocking together after my ordeal, and I tottered into the garden to recover.

It was over anyway, and having staved off his first proposal I felt sure that I could cope with any more to come. Anyway, it would be nice to go to a concert with him later on.

What was it he had said? 'That *blue* thing, that looked so pretty.'

I had always thought it was *green*. Ah well!

CHAPTER 12

Romantic Speculations in Fairacre

Bob Willet was busy doing something to the school gate when I drove into the playground the next morning.

'Dropped a bit,' he explained. 'Them dratted kids swings on it.'

'I know. I've told them not to dozens of times.'

'You wants to give 'em a clip round the earhole.'

'I agree, but I'd probably lose my job these days.'

'Mind you,' went on Mr Willet fairly, 'most gates drop a bit. I had to do Mr Mawne's last week.'

'How is he?'

'Chipper. Very chipper indeed. His lady visitor's gone back to Ireland.'

'He'll be relieved.'

'But she's coming back! It seems she's gone back to put her house on the market.'

'So she is going to settle here after all?'

'Looks like it. And settled in with Mr Mawne if she gets half a chance.'

'Oh dear!'

He gave me a swift look, and I wondered if he expected to see disappointment in my countenance. Or perhaps relief?

'She's a very nice woman,' I said. 'I liked her.'

'But ain't she related to Mr Mawne? I was going to look up the Table of Infinity in my prayer book, but I trimmed the privet hedge instead.'

'She's no relation of Henry's. It was Mrs Mawne who was her cousin.'

Bob Willet looked slightly dejected, and hit the gate a thwacking blow with his hammer.

'Well, I suppose that's fair enough,' he said, 'but I'd sooner see Mr Mawne looking nearer at hand for a good wife.'

At that moment Mrs Pringle arrived, her oil-cloth bag bulging.

'Brought you some early spinach,' she puffed. 'Do you good to get a bit of green down you.'

I expressed my thanks and we left Bob Willet to enter the lobby together.

It was a most generous present, and I could see that most of it would have to go in the freezer for another day.

'Fred put cloches over 'em,' explained Mrs Pringle. 'Brought 'em on a treat. I've given a bag to Minnie, though she says her kids won't eat greens. I said to tell them that thousands of poor children would be thankful for a nice plate of spinach. But you know Minnie. She won't say nothing.'

'And how is she? When's that baby due?'

I suddenly remembered that evening of lashing rain last March when Minnie had sought refuge with me. Surely, I had not seen her since then, and I wondered how her stormy marriage was faring.

'The baby? Oh, that came to nothing,' said Mrs Pringle in an off-hand manner.

She must have seen my astonishment.

'Minnie's always in a muddle with her dates and that, and she thought there was another little stranger on the way. All for the best there wasn't.'

I agreed. It was certainly for the best, both for Minnie and the little stranger, in the present circumstances.

'I hear Mr Mawne's lady has left him at last. She's got her eye on him, you know. Bob Willet told me she's going to come back again.'

'Well, it's a free country,' I said equably.

'Not when you go shopping in Caxley on market day,' said Mrs Pringle. 'Why, I paid nearly a pound for a piece of cheese, that hardly did Fred's supper.'

Her cheeks wobbled with outrage, and reminded me of a flustered turkey-cock.

But at least the subject was changed, and that was a great relief.

Arthur Coggs had appeared in the magistrates' court at Caxley, so the local paper said, on a number of charges of theft.

The chairman had deferred sentence as he said he felt sure that there were some deep-seated problems in Arthur's past, so that the bench needed an up-to-date report from the probation officer and one from a psychiatrist.

Mr Willet was scathing. 'Anyone in Fairacre could tell him what Arthur's deep-seated problem is. He won't work, that's all. And he likes his beer. Put the two together and our Arthur's going to be in trouble all his life.'

He was right of course.

'My old ma used to tell us that if you don't work you can expect to starve. No one tells kids that these days, and they grows up expecting everythin' for nothin'.'

Mrs Pringle joined in at this juncture.

'I blame the parents. Our Minnie's kids never goes to church, and they don't never learn the Ten Commandments. Why, we had to recite them to the vicar, didn't we, Bob?'

'That's right.'

'"Thou shalt not steal" was one of 'em. But Arthur Coggs don't remember that one. And he won't get punished, I'll lay.'

'Nobody don't,' agreed Bob Willet. 'Punishment's out! No wonder they grows up not knowing right from wrong.' He turned to me. 'You given 'em something to think about over that dropped gate?'

He blew out his moustache belligerently.

'Well, I haven't lashed about them with a horse-whip,' I said mildly, 'but I did give them a talking-to.'

Bob Willet and Mrs Pringle exchanged disgusted glances, and I thought it discreet to take my leave.

In Fairacre, as elsewhere, the older generation takes a poor view of those growing up, and I expect it was ever thus.

It was the loveliest May I could remember. My spirits were high, as I looked forward, with increasing excitement, to the end of term and my retirement.

I had no fears now about my health. In fact, I occasion-ally wondered if I had been over-anxious and given in my notice before time, but these doubts soon passed, and I revelled in the future before me.

The summer flowers began to adorn the classroom window-sills and my desk. Everything was early this year. The may buds were bursting on the hawthorn. Dandelions glowed on the grass verges, and the cottage gardens were gay with wall flowers, early pinks and irises.

Beside the massive brass inkstand, on my desk, a relic of a Victorian headmaster, stood an earthenware honey pot of equally ancient vintage, bearing a nosegay of clove pinks that scented the classroom with their spicy perfume.

One evening during this halcyon time of early summer, I had an unexpected visit from James, Amy's husband.

'I've been to see the Cottons,' he began, coming straight to the point. 'Have you been worrying about them?'

I had to admit that I had been a little perplexed about their finances but Bob Willet had heard that there was money owing on a Caxley clothing club.

'Well, I'm thankful to say we seem to have come to the bottom of things.'

It appeared that this was Mr Cotton's second marriage. His first wife had left him and had married again. By this first marriage they had had one daughter, now in her early twenties. She was a nurse at a large hospital in the north, and it was she who had caused the money problems.

'He's a very devoted father,' said James. 'We knew all about his matrimonial background when the Trust appointed him and the present Mrs Cotton to this post. The girl then was just about self-supporting, but she got into the clutches of an unscrupulous fellow who wheedled her savings from her, and then began to exert really menacing pressure. She turned to her father, who tried to extricate her from her troubles. He should have gone straight to the police, of course, but he was reluctant to get the daughter involved in court proceedings.'

'How did you find out?'

'I asked him what the trouble was. He seemed relieved to have someone to talk to. He's had a pretty awful time worrying about the present family, and letting the Trust down, and so on. Why he didn't tell us, I can't think. We'd have supported him and the girl. He's a jolly good father – one of our best.'

I marvelled, yet again, at James's ability to communicate with all sorts and conditions of men. It was not just his obvious charm and good looks. They were the outward expression of a true understanding of the other fellow's point of view, ready sympathy and a clear mind to sum up the problem and its handling.

'So how is the girl coping?'

'She's just become engaged to a young chap with his head screwed on. He's put the matter in the hands of the police, and luckily he is in a steady job, and they propose to marry this summer.'

'So it's a happy ending?'

'It looks like it. Mrs Cotton gave me a lovely kiss at the end of our little pow-wow.'

'I bet she did! Have a drink?'

'No. I'm driving; and I expect Amy has the grub waiting.'

I walked with him to the car. A blackbird was singing its heart out on a lilac bush.

'You've relieved my mind about the Cotton family,' I told him.

'That was the idea. Can't have your last few weeks at Fairacre clouded in any way.'

He gave me a farewell kiss which I found as satisfactory I imagine, as Mrs Cotton had, and off he went.

A day or two later, I encountered our vicar as I was coming back from Fairacre Post Office.

'What weather!' he enthused waving a hand and encompassing in the gesture the cottage gardens near at hand, the rooks wheeling round the church spire, and the hazy downs beyond.

'I know. Aren't we lucky?'

'I've just been to see Henry,' he told me. 'Have you seen him lately?'

'No. How is he?'

'Rather lonely, of course. I'm surprised he hasn't been to see you. Deirdre's away, you know.'

I said that I had heard.

Gerald Partridge began to look troubled, and stopped to flick non-existent dust from his shirt-front. I knew the signs. Our vicar was preparing to face a difficult few minutes.

'I'm just a little worried about him. He obviously misses his dear wife, and I should so like to see him settled happily.'

'We all should.'

He looked relieved.

'I know it is a long time ago,' he continued, 'soon after you came to Fairacre, but I know that we all hoped – wrongly, as it turned out – that you and Henry —' He faltered to a stop.

'I well remember it,' I told him, not wishing to be reminded of an embarrassing interlude.

'Of course, Henry was married already, but we did not know that,' he continued hastily. 'Now, of course, the poor fellow is permanently bereaved, and I must say I grieve for him.'

He began to move on again, and we approached the school gate. The playground was empty, and the hands of the church clock stood at four fifteen. The sun had moved round and was now streaming down on my car. It was going to be a hot drive home.

'I don't think I should worry too much about Henry,' I said. 'He has lots of good friends in Fairacre. Both of us, for instance.'

'That's true.'

The vicar began to look happier.

'And I'm sure he will find someone to look after him before long, and be happy again.'

'I do hope so. Of course, Deirdre is coming back soon, and they do seem —'

'Exactly,' I said firmly, and made for the car.

The vacancy caused by my impending departure had been advertised in the usual educational journals, and I remembered how I had applied so long ago. Then, of course, one of the greatest attractions for me had been the school house, providing handy accommodation so close to my duties. Now that the Umbleditches lived in my old home the new head teacher would have to look elsewhere for a house.

It should not be difficult to find somewhere, perhaps in Caxley itself, if not nearer at hand in one of the downland villages, for no doubt the new teacher would have a car.

I had not had one for some years after my appointment, and had not missed having private transport, for the buses then had been more frequent, and in any case, I trundled around on my bicycle then in those comparatively traffic-free country lanes. Now my successor could afford to live anywhere within a comfortable ten-, or even twenty-mile, radius of Fairacre school and still be in good time for morning assembly.

There had evidently been a number of applicants for the post, and towards the end of May they had been whittled down to four on the short list, two men and two women.

They were being called up for interview by the governors, and the meeting was to take place at the vicarage. I could visualise the scene, for I had often been invited to sit with the governors when a new assistant was being interviewed. On the present occasion, I should not attend.

The interviews were always held in the vicarage dining-room, an impressive Georgian room with a beautiful mahogany table. Gerald Partridge, as chairman of the governors, sat at the head, and there was ample room at each side for the applicants' papers, the governors' gloves, pens, diaries and other personal impedimenta, whilst the applicant's chair was placed in solitary state, at the far end, facing the chairman.

One of the most prominent features of the vicar's dining-room is a portrait of one of Gerald Partridge's ancestors. The old gentleman is holding a letter which our vicar is convinced was written by Charles II, rendering thanks to his forebear for services rendered to his king, when he was in exile, before the restoration of the monarchy.

The vicar is inordinately proud of this portrait, but I always found it rather depressing for the subject of the painting appears very cross, and no one could say that he was good looking. His descendant is certainly much more pleasant to behold.

As is customary, the four applicants had been invited to inspect the school before their interviews, and so I acted as hostess and general usher at this time.

I liked all four, and knew that I should be happy at the thought of any one of them taking my place next September. It would be interesting to see if a man was appointed, for in the past Fairacre had several headmasters over the years.

In those days, when the children stayed at the same school until they were fourteen, the bigger boys were often in need of fairly firm discipline as the great world loomed nearer. But since Fairacre school had been a junior primary school, for children from five to eleven years of age, for some years now, it had been usual to appoint a woman.

Which would it be this time, I wondered? And who, looking to the future, would follow George Annett at the larger school at Beech Green? There, I guessed, a headmaster would be appointed when George stood down, but for us, in Fairacre, it was anybody's guess.

The vicar had been kind enough to tell me the arrangements for the aftermath of the interviews. It had been decided to leave plenty of time for discussion by the governors after the interviews, and the applicants were each to be telephoned and given the decision during that evening.

'So much depends on getting the right person,' the vicar assured me. 'The applicants can make their way home, and know that they'll hear within a few hours, without having to sit all together while we come to a decision just after the meeting. I have always felt, too, that it is quite an ordeal for the lucky one to have to face his disappointed companions so soon after a trying time.'

'An ordeal for the others too,' I pointed out. 'I think this idea is perfect, and they can pour themselves a congratulatory – or commiserating – noggin, in the privacy of their own homes.'

'Just as we thought,' said the vicar, beaming.

I thought a good deal about my successor as I pottered about that evening. The head teacher of a village school holds an important place in the village hierarchy, as I knew to my cost.

I remembered Dolly Clare's accounts of the head teachers she had encountered during her lifetime.

She had started her school life in Caxley, but at the age of six the family had moved to Beech Green, and she had been entered on the register there a day or two after their arrival.

As a shy child, she had found the change upsetting. Luckily, the first person she came across at Beech Green school was Emily Davis, whose desk she shared on that first terrifying morning, and whose friendship started then and continued all their lives. In fact, as two old ladies, they had shared the cottage which was now my home, until Emily Davis had died tranquilly one night in the room which was now my spare bedroom.

The girls' first headmaster had been an energetic disciplinarian called Mr Finch, but on his retirement a new young man called Evan Waterman had taken his place.

Changes began immediately. He was a devout young man, inclining to such High Church practices as genuflection and much crossing of the breast, which alone alarmed his neighbours. He was also good-looking in a girlish way, and this too was cause for comment among the men.

The women were more tolerant, and the free-and-easy methods of teaching which had replaced Mr Finch's stern régime did not worry them unduly to begin with.

But later, it was apparent that such modern methods were too soon for most of the boys, and downright disobedience and mockery began to grow, until poor Evan Waterman was requested to find a post elsewhere.

Before his departure, Francis Clare, Dolly's thatcher father, had seen to it that Dolly was transferred to Fairacre school. Her dear friend Emily was also going there, and the two girls found themselves under the boisterous charge of Mr Wardle and his wife. Both demanded work of a high standard, but gave praise and encouragement under which their little school thrived.

It was from such accounts, as well as the reports in the ancient school log books, that one realised how much influence those earlier teachers had on their pupils, and for that matter, on the lives of all who dwelt with them in the villages.

I could only hope that I would be remembered with some affection, and that my successor would be as happy as I had been in charge of the school at Fairacre.

CHAPTER 13

Junketings

As an old hand at secret fundraising, I soon became conscious of the chink of coins being put into a screwtop honey jar in Mrs Richards' room.

I had seen this receptacle one morning when I had called to consult her about a letter from a parent, and it had been whisked so hastily into her desk drawer that I guessed that a leaving present for me was in the offing.

The vicar had broached the subject some weeks before and I had begged him not to present me with anything, unless perhaps a bunch of flowers, preferably from the village gardens.

But this, of course, fell on stony ground, and I could see that I was bound to receive something much more prestigious.

There was nothing for it but to submit with good grace, although I regretted this collecting of money when there was so much hardship in the village. Fairacre had suffered, along with the rest of the country, from the economic depression, for many of the fathers and mothers worked in Caxley at some of the new industries which had sprung up during the past twenty years. Quite a number had lost their jobs as the firms succumbed to bad times, and it worried me to think of money being spent on me at such a time.

However, I was realistic enough to know that I should

receive a leaving present, and I intended to accept it in the great-hearted spirit in which, I knew, it would be given.

The summer term had always been punctuated with such time-honoured events as Sports' Day, the Fête, and the Sunday school and choir outing. The last always took place on the first Saturday in July.

Before my time, as I had learnt from the vicar, and from the school log books, local schools closed for a fortnight for a fruit-picking holiday towards the end of June. At the end of that time when the families had usually earned some welcome extra money, a charabanc was hired and a day was spent by the sea.

In those days, this annual excursion to the sea was probably the only one and a great occasion it was.

Nowadays, when most families owned a car, or possibly two, the same excitement was not engendered by a day-trip to the seaside, but the first Saturday in July was still set aside for the outing and continued to be a highlight of the summer season. It would be my last in my capacity as head teacher, although no doubt I should be invited when I retired, just as Dolly Clare had been.

I contemplated my future with enormous pleasure. As far as one could tell, I should have the best of two worlds. I should be living in the same place, close to friends and neighbours with all that that implied. But I should also be free of constricting limits, such as the hours spent in school, and the necessity to prepare lessons or deal with official correspondence.

What was even more pleasurable now was the fact that my health seemed to have improved enormously since my decision to retire. Maybe the summer sunshine had something to do with it. Maybe the slackening of my duties had helped. Maybe the doctor's tablets and my early nights had something to do with this welcome feeling of good health.

Whatever the cause, I relished it after my alarms of the winter. It had certainly sobered me, and made me realize that robust health should never be taken for granted, but simply as a bonus.

It was clear that June was going to be as glorious as May, at least for the first few days.

Bob Willet, in his shirt sleeves at eight thirty in the morning, bore witness to the warmth of the day to come.

'That cousin of Mr Mawne's is back,' he volunteered.

'*Mrs* Mawne,' I corrected him.

He looked startled. 'She ain't that already, is she?'

'Who d'you mean?'

'That Deirdre. Never did get her surname. She ain't married him? You said "Mrs Mawne". That's quick work!'

I knew that this mistaken statement would be round the village in a flash if I did not put it straight at once. This I proceeded to do.

'I only meant that Deirdre is cousin to the late *Mrs* Mawne and not *Henry* Mawne. And as far as I know, they have no plans to marry.'

'Well, he looks ripe for it to my way of thinking.'

'I expect he's a little lonely.'

'And whose fault's that?' enquired Mr Willet, making off before I could think of a reply.

The annual fête took place in the vicar's garden, as usual, and despite ominous clouds at breakfast time, the weather remained dry and firm.

The event was to be opened by someone known as a 'television personality', and expectations ran high.

'I've got his autograph,' boasted Ernest on the Friday afternoon. 'I cut it out of the paper.'

'That's not a real autograph,' said Patrick. 'That's only

printed. You has to have the actual bit of paper what his hand rested on.'

He looked at me for support.

'Well, strictly speaking —' I began diplomatically, but was interrupted by the vicar appearing in a state of agitation.

'I fear that we are in for a disappointment. Our fête-opener is indisposed. I wonder who would step in at such short notice?'

'Couldn't you do it?'

He looked dismayed. 'I could, I suppose, but what a come-down for everyone.'

I thought otherwise, but said nothing.

'Do you think,' he said looking brighter, 'that our dear friend Basil Bradley would step in?'

Basil Bradley is a local novelist who writes historical novels with heroines in muslin frocks and ringlets, and heroes who fight duels on their behalf. The books sell in vast numbers, and everyone relishes a nice hour or two of escapism. Basil himself is modest and cheerful, and we are all very proud of him.

'If he's free I'm sure he'd come to the rescue,' I said.

He certainly did. The fête was duly opened with a short speech and many compliments to those who had helped to get it ready for general pleasure and the support of the Church Roof Fund, and we all set forth to enjoy ourselves.

The cake stall, as usual, was the first to be besieged and as Mrs Pringle was in charge this year there were very few goodies hidden behind the stall for favoured customers.

'Fair's fair!' she boomed, 'and those who comes first gets first pick. But it's all to be above board this year. *No* favourites!'

This stern dictum was surprisingly welcomed by her customers, and I wondered if the more easy-going earlier stall-holders would emulate her strict example in the years ahead.

I returned exhausted, and viewed my collection of articles bought, or won, at the kitchen table. I could eat the gingerbread, the lettuce and the eggs, but what about that rag doll and the highly scented bath salts, not to mention the Cyprus sherry and the pickled onions in a somewhat cloudy and dubious liquid?

'Give them to the next bazaar, of course,' I said aloud.

And Tibby gave an approving mew.

A day or two later Henry Mawne arrived at the school with a pile of bird magazines for our delectation.

'You weren't at the fête,' I said accusingly. 'You *never* miss the fête. What happened?'

He looked a little confused. 'I had to go to Heathrow to meet Deirdre. She's back for a short while.'

'Oh good! You'll have company.'

'Yes. You could say that, but I'm really giving her a hand over selling her place in Ireland.'

He sounded surprisingly business-like and important, and it dawned on me that usually his former wife had taken the decisions, which was probably one of the reasons why he missed her so much. Not that Henry lacked business sense. He has been in charge of the church funds for years, and the vicar relies on him for anything involving figures.

This was one of the reasons that Henry's absence from the fête perturbed me. Usually, the final figures are given to the parish an hour or so after the event has finished. Luckily, on this occasion, Mr Lamb from the Post Office had stepped into the breach.

Of course, I was intrigued to hear about Deirdre, and asked if she had found a cottage in our area. Or had she changed her plans?

'Well, no,' said Henry, looking a trifle hunted. 'She still hopes to find something. In fact, we looked at five or six before she went back to Ireland, but there was nothing that appealed to her.'

I recalled Bob Willet's words about Deirdre hoping to settle in with Henry himself, but naturally did not mention this.

'I hear you are going to the Oxford concert next week with John Jenkins,' he said. Was this carrying the attack into my own camp?

I said that I was.

'I wanted to ask you myself when the first notices went out, but my plans were so unsettled with Deirdre coming and going that I'm afraid I've missed the chance.'

At that moment I caught sight of John Todd about to stuff some sort of foliage – no doubt filched from the nature table – down the back of Joseph Coggs' shirt, and rushed to the rescue.

When I returned Henry was on his way out, waving a hand in farewell, and I was left to speculate.

What were his real feelings towards Deirdre? Was he becoming fonder of her, more protective, happier in her company? Or was she still the nuisance he seemed to find her earlier? And did she really want a house of her own, or were these delaying tactics until she had Henry – and his home – where she wanted?

And what about Henry's attitude to me? I felt somehow that it was changing. There was something a little malicious in the way he had mentioned John's invitation to the concert, and a hint of relief that he was out of the whole affair.

This, of course, was fine by me. I was obviously going to have more attention from my new friend than I really wanted, and it would be a relief to have dear old Henry engaged elsewhere.

I do my best to simplify life, but heaven alone knows it is uphill work sometimes.

On Saturday morning I went to Caxley to buy a new frock, or perhaps just a new blouse, to honour the concert with John.

I bumped into Amy, much to my delight, and we hastened to take coffee together. Naturally, she was very approving of my desire to improve my appearance and agog to hear about John.

'Now, don't throw away the chance of a happy future,' she began.

'I'm not. I'm looking forward to a wonderfully peaceful, *single* retirement.'

'Yes, yes, I know,' she said impatiently, 'but do think about this nice man. How disappointed he'll be if he is turned down. Why, he may even move elsewhere if he's badly hurt.'

'No chance of that,' I said, and rather rashly told her about his proposal.

Her surprise at this disclosure I found a trifle wounding. After all, why shouldn't I receive a proposal?

On the other hand, her frank dismay at my dismissal cheered me considerably.

'And you think he will ask you again? How can you be sure?'

'Well, he said he would. And I'm sure he's a man of his word.'

'Oh good,' she replied, sounding much relieved, and we went on to talk of James, and his skill at sorting out the Cottons' problems, and whether the enormous price I had just paid for a perfectly simply silk blouse was justified.

'Of course it is,' said Amy. 'Why, it may affect your whole future.'

'Amy,' I said, 'you are the most romantic woman I have ever met!'

'I wish I could say the same of you,' she retorted, as we parted.

The halcyon weather which we had enjoyed changed abruptly with a spectacular thunderstorm one June night.

The bedroom windows streamed with rain, and flashes of lightning lit up the countryside. The thunder shook the cottage, and Tibby scratched at my bedroom door, was admitted and dived for cover under the eiderdown.

Sleep was impossible, and it was almost four o'clock before the storm abated. I suppose I must have had a few hours' sleep, but when the alarm clock went off at seven I could have done with more.

But everything smelled wonderful after the rain. The clove pinks in the border gave out their spicy smell and the madonna lilies above them added to the morning's perfume.

The lane from Beech Green to Fairacre was still damp from the night's downpour, and steam was rising as the sun's strength grew. Small birds were busy foraging for insects which had ventured forth into the morning dampness, and larks were already up and away soaring into the blue above.

It was going to be a wonderful morning, but the weather man had warned us not to expect it to last, and sure enough, by mid-morning the clouds rolled in from the west, and by dinner time the rain was falling again.

'You're off to Oxford tonight, aren't you?' said Mrs Richards, as we dealt out school dinners.

I said that I was, and wondered yet again how she had acquired the news. Not from me, so presumably my date with John Jenkins was common knowledge. This did not surprise me after so many years of village life, but just *how* the rumours get about continues to flummox me.

I was home before four thirty in time to make myself a cup of tea before arraying myself in my new finery. John was to call for me at six and we were having a meal before the concert began.

I had invited him to eat at my house before we set off, but he was so quick to suggest a meal out that I was prompted to wonder if he did not like my cooking. However, it meant that I need not bother, and that was a welcome relief.

I think Amy would have been proud of my appearance, for the vastly expensive blouse was splendid, and went well with the older parts of the ensemble. Apart from the fact that I looked decidedly heavy-eyed from lack of sleep the previous night, I decided I was passable, even by Amy's standards.

The rain grew heavier as we set off, but we were both in good spirits as we neared Oxford. John had booked a table at an Italian restaurant near the concert hall, and we studied the menu. John predictably settled for a steak, but I ordered a delicious chicken breast stuffed with asparagus and ham.

As we waited for our food to arrive John said, 'Would you like today's proposal now, or as we go home?'

'Oh John! Must we have one at all?'

'Definitely. I'm working on the principle of water dripping on a stone. I think your heart is pretty flinty.'

'I deny it strongly. I take in stray cats and wounded birds, and always put spiders out of the window instead of squashing them.'

'But what about love-lorn middle-aged men?'

'I'm extremely kind to them and go to concerts with them.'

'So shall it be now or later?'

'Let's have it now.'

'"And get it over", I expect you to say! So, here goes. Is there any change in that stony heart?'

I smiled at him. Give him his due, he was a trier.

'Not really, John. I shouldn't bother any more if I were you.'

He shook his head but he was smiling too, as the waiter arrived with our food.

I thoroughly enjoyed our meal, the concert and John's company throughout the evening.

I liked him even more when he declined my invitation to have a drink when he dropped me at my door, gave me a kindly kiss, and drove off in good spirits.

A nice man, but not for me.

The vicar and his wife had been away for a few days, but on his return he called at the school to tell me of the governors' decision.

They had appointed one of the women, Miss Jane Summers, and I knew at once that the children, and their parents, would wholeheartedly approve.

If I had favoured any one of the four candidates it would have been this person. She was large and jolly, in her thirties, and looked as though she had enough energy and humour to cope with all the problems which would confront her.

Even Mrs Pringle grudgingly admitted that 'she looked a *motherly* sort', who would be a comfortable figure for the new babies to confront on their first school day.

'But how she'll get on with them little monsters of boys in your room,' she said gloomily, 'the Lord alone knows. They could do with the strap now and again. The state of my lobby floors this week is enough to break your heart.'

I said, not quite truthfully, that I felt sure that Miss Summers would be as anxious about the lobby floors as she was herself.

'Well, that'll make a nice change,' said the old harridan. 'When have *you* worried youself about them, I'd like to know!'

She made her way out with no hint of a limp. Any such little triumph does her bad leg a world of good.

Mr Willet was less censorious, but cautious in his approach to a new set of circumstances.

'I don't like changes, as well you know, and I daresay this new lady will do her best, and no doubt we'll all shake down together in good time. But I tell you straight, Miss

Read, you've been a treat to work for, and me and Alice'll be real sorry to see you go. You've been a proper headmistress, and you'll be missed.'

I only wished that Mrs Pringle had been present to hear such compliments, but she, of course, was in the lobby grieving over the floor.

Naturally, the news of the appointment went through the village with the speed of a bush fire, and I received a great many comments.

Mr Lamb said that he was sure the new head would be welcomed but, he added gallantly, no one could possibly take my place. He wished though that a man had been appointed, for some of those boys could do with a clip now and again, and women were a bit soft that way.

Alice Willet said she wished I'd change my mind and stay on. Mr Roberts, the farmer, said he liked the look of the new woman. He always thought fat women were better tempered. Nothing personal, mind you, and if you were a bit skinny it couldn't be helped, but give him a plump woman every time.

The two newcomers, Mrs Bennett and Mrs Cotton, were inclined to be tearful, which I found surprising. But they pointed out that they had only just got used to me, and my school ways, and there I was *gone*!

Eve and Horace Umbleditch said it was a pity their boy would not have the inestimable privilege of starting his school career under my guidance, and that Jane Summers, no matter how worthy and clever, could never be a patch on me. Nevertheless, they agreed that I was Doing the Right Thing and Horace was already counting the years to his own retirement.

It was all very flattering, and I was duly grateful for these unsolicited tributes. But why, I wondered, did it need my retirement to prompt these kindly compliments?

In future, I told myself, I should make a point of expressing my admiration and respect for any deserving person who crossed my path and was still hale enough to relish my remarks.

The vicar called to remind the children about the outing on the following Saturday, and then drew me aside in a conspirational manner.

'I have been asked to request you to make a list of things you would like as your leaving present, so that the committee could choose something that you really want.'

'Oh, but please, you know that I really don't —' I began, but was cut short.

'Just jot down a few ideas. The whole village wants to contribute, and we already have a vast sum, so let us know what you would like.'

I stammered my gratitude to his retreating back, and sat down feeling stunned.

What was 'a vast sum'?

Knowing our vicar's complete lack of financial under-standing I thought it might be anything from five pounds to five hundred. And in any case one could hardly ask him what 'a vast sum' was.

Here was a problem. I really had no idea what I wanted. I knew that I needed some new nail scissors, but it did not seem quite the thing to put on the list.

I decided to shelve the problem until I got home, and as soon as I had refreshed myself with tea I set to work.

But before I began, Amy arrived with a bunch of roses from her garden, and was greeted with even more delight than usual.

'They're gorgeous,' I cried, taking them from her. 'I'll put them in a vase.'

'They could really do with a rose bowl,' said Amy,

looking round hopefully. 'I'll do them for you. I don't care for your grip-and-drop-in arrangements.'

I refused to take umbrage.

'You shall have a choice of vases,' I told her. 'I've never had a rose bowl.'

As she arranged them in two vases, I told her about my problem. She immediately began to organize things, much to my relief.

'How much is this "vast sum"?'

'That's the snag. I've no idea, and I don't want them to spend a lot on me. They know that, but they won't listen.'

'Well, we shall just have to make a list with a good range of price. Anything in the kitchen line you'd like?'

'The back-door mat is pretty shabby.'

'That's not suitable for the list,' said Amy in a brisk manner. 'What about a new gadget? Have you got a food-mixer?'

'I don't want a food-mixer. I should have to wash it up, and I'd be bound to lose all the twiddly bits.'

'A microwave? A steam iron? A coffee-maker?'

'Ah! D'you mean like yours? With a lid that pushes down over the grounds?'

'Yes. A cafetière.'

'I'd like that.'

'Well, at least we've made a start,' said Amy, writing busily.

'Now,' she went on, fixing me with a sharp eye, 'we'll take it room by room. Anything needed in the dining-room?'

After some heavy thought I decided that a sauce boat and new table mats could go down.

'Sitting-room?' said Amy briskly. 'I should think you might ask for a silver rose bowl.'

'I'd never use it. Besides I'd have to polish it. Perhaps another table lamp might be useful, or a clock.'

'You'd better be careful about a clock,' advised Amy, 'or you'll get landed with a black marble job in the form of a Greek temple like those that dominated our grandparents' mantelpieces.'

'I could stipulate a small brass carriage clock,' I suggested.

'Excellent,' approved Amy. 'Now for upstairs. What's wanted there?'

'I really need a new face flannel,' I said thoughtfully.

Amy threw down her pen in exasperation. 'You can't ask for a *face flannel*,' she protested.

'I know I can't. But you did ask me.'

She retrieved her pen.

'What about a hand-held shower?'

'Too messy. I'd sooner get in the tub.'

'Anything in the bedroom?'

'Oh, Amy, I can't be bothered any more! Let's have a turn in the garden.'

It was bliss out there, fresh and scented under a pale blue sky. We felt better at once.

'Tell you what,' said Amy, 'you could do with a nice plain teak garden seat, to replace that poor decrepit thing over there. Or a bird bath. Or even a nesting box or two.'

'The seat sounds rather expensive, but the others could go down.'

'Put the seat down too. This "vast sum" might well run to it.'

'Perhaps a small one,' I said weakening. 'A two-seater, say.'

Amy was looking round in a contemplative manner.

'Of course, if it really is "a vast sum" you could rethatch the cottage, or buy a new car. Haven't you any idea of how much this "vast sum" might be?'

I told her that the vicar's idea of a 'vast sum' could be anything around a hundred pounds.

'It's so difficult,' agreed Amy. 'You see, if James used that expression he would be talking about several millions.'

'Well, it won't be that, I'm thankful to say,' I told her. 'Let's go in and add those garden ideas to the list.'

We did that, refreshed ourselves with a glass of sherry, and I saw her on her way.

At least I had a list of sorts to offer the vicar, thanks to Amy's firm direction.

What should we do without our friends?

CHAPTER 14

The Outing

The day of the outing dawned still and bright, and we gathered at eight thirty sharp, as directed by the vicar, outside the Post Office at Fairacre.

The bus was already there and we scrambled aboard. Joseph Coggs elected to sit by me, and was kind enough to offer me an unwrapped mint humbug, rather fluffy from his pocket, but I explained that it was a little too early in the day for me to eat sweets, and he nodded cheerfully and ate it himself.

To my surprise, I saw that Henry and Deirdre were approaching and were soon settled across the gangway. Henry was looking very relaxed in a striped blazer, and Deirdre, true to form, had arrived with a gauzy blue scarf round her head, but this was removed when they had settled in their seats.

Henry, of course, as the vicar's right-hand man, had sometimes accompanied us on the annual outing, but I had not expected to see him this time as I knew that Deirdre would be at his house.

We exchanged chit-chat as we bowled along, and I thought that Deirdre seemed rather more animated than usual. Perhaps Henry's presence was stimulating.

I remembered the last time Henry, Deirdre and I had taken a bus trip together to the falconry, and how embarrassing I had found Henry's attentions to me, and his marked coolness towards his guest. It was a relief to have him less tiresome, but I was glad too to have Joseph Coggs ensconced at my side.

How well I remembered an earlier trip to the seaside resort of Barrisford, for which we were bound again this morning. As usual, after an outing, I had suggested to the children, during the following week, that they might draw a picture of something that they had enjoyed during that day.

Joseph had come up with the picture of a small man who, he insisted, was the Old Man of the Sea and had a palace on the sea bed beyond the end of Barrisford pier. He had stuck to his story adamantly, although we found out later that he had encountered one of the midget acrobats who were appearing that week in an end-of-pier show.

As far as I knew, Joseph still believed the story which had been told him, and even now, I surmised, he might be hoping to encounter him again.

Barrisford remained the most popular choice for our annual outing. Sometimes we had changed our destination and had visited Longleat and its animals, Bournemouth with its variety of entertainment and other renowned resorts on the south coast. But somehow we always returned to Barrisford, to its shining sands, its quiet respectability, and above all, to tea at Bunce's, the famous restaurant on the esplanade where Mr Edward Bunce himself waited upon us with never-failing courtesy.

Barrisford, we all agreed, was the *real* place to go for an outing.

Most of the party dispersed to the sands, but Deirdre made a point of joining me and suggested that we took ourselves

to Bunce's for a refreshing cup of coffee. Henry waxed enthusiastic.

When we were settled at a table overlooking the bay, I enquired how the house-hunting was getting on.

'We looked at two yesterday,' said Henry. 'Quite possible, I thought.'

'I didn't,' said Deirdre. 'They were poky.'

'Most cottages are,' I agreed, 'but that has its advantages. Less to heat, less to clean, and usually pretty snug.'

'One was near Springbourne,' went on Henry, ignoring his companion's dislike of the topic, 'on the hill there. Lovely views.'

'Not a house in sight,' said Deirdre with disgust. 'One would go melancholy mad.'

The coffee arrived at this moment and the subject of

houses was dropped until a little later when Deirdre had departed to the ladies' room and Henry and I were alone.

'I fear that Deirdre wants somewhere with bigger rooms. She's got used to living in my house, you know, and I think it has influenced her choice overduly.'

I thought of Henry's magnificent rooms in part of the Queen Anne house which had been old Miss Parr's when I first went to Fairacre. It would be hard to find such elegance in the small houses Deirdre was inspecting.

Henry sighed, and put his hand on mine by the coffee pot.

'If only things had been different,' he said.

I looked at him squarely. 'But they aren't, Henry, and never have been. At least on my side.'

'I had hoped,' he began, 'when I first came —'

'Henry, I don't care to think about that time. You meant nothing to me, except in a friendly way, and you know what a bundle of trouble village gossip put us to.'

He removed his hand, and stood up to welcome back Deirdre who had removed the gauzy scarf and looked, to my eyes at least, very attractive.

'Now I shall see you two settled,' said Henry, 'and then I'm off for a swim. Nothing like salt water!'

I was about to say, 'Probably laced with sewage', but felt it was kinder to remain silent. Henry had had quite enough chastening for one day, I decided.

Deirdre and I sat in the shelter of a rock and watched our fellow villagers disporting themselves on land and sea.

Henry was being splashed vigorously by three or four of my schoolchildren, but was giving as much as he was getting, amidst shrieks of delight.

'I'm very fond of Henry,' remarked Deirdre languidly. 'What do you think of him?'

'He's always been a good friend. Not only to me. Everyone in the village likes him.'

Deirdre gazed out to sea. Henry's head was now bobbing in the foreground.

'He's very fond of you. My cousin, you know, never really appreciated Henry. In fact, she stayed with me in Ireland for nearly two years, she was so fed up with him.'

I remained silent. I well remembered Henry's time alone when Fairacre supposed that he was a bachelor or widower, and well qualified to marry a single school teacher.

'She was horribly bossy,' said Deirdre. 'Henry never had a say in anything. He needed *kindness*, and I think that's why he was attracted to you.'

I was startled into speech. I had not thought of *kindness* as one of my more obvious virtues.

'I can assure you that I had no idea that Henry was attracted to me at that time. I must admit there was some village gossip, but one ignores that.'

'Well, it was largely that which brought his wife back to him. She may not have wanted him herself, but she did not intend to part with him. I was quite relieved to see her go.'

She looked out to sea again. Henry seemed to have vanished.

'Poor Henry,' she sighed. 'He has had a sad life. I think it is time he was shown some affection and consideration, don't you?'

'We can all do with that,' I assured her.

She turned her eyes from the sea, and looked steadily at me. 'When you retire, will you be lonely?'

'Not for a moment,' I said, knowing full well what prompted this solicitude on my behalf.

'I'm so glad we had this little talk,' she said, rising and dusting sand from her skirt. 'It makes things much easier for me.'

'Good luck with your house-hunting, and all your other projects,' I said, as we set off for a companionable saunter along the famous sands.

Tea at Bunce's was the highlight of the afternoon, and at six thirty we were all aboard again, wind-blown and sun-burnt, bound for Fairacre.

I was dropped off in Beech Green, only a few yards from my home, and waved farewell to my fellow passengers, as the bus moved off.

Deirdre gave me a broad smile and, I could have sworn, a wink at the same time.

Mightily content, I turned for home.

On Monday morning, Mrs Pringle limped heavily towards me and I feared the worst.

'I've got that dratted Basil all next week,' she greeted me, 'and I wondered if he could come up here. Next term he starts at Beech Green, and welcome they are to him, and no mistake.'

'Is Minnie ill?'

'She's got a little job up at Springbourne Manor. Just for next week.'

I was surprised to hear it. Minnie is well known for her complete lack of common sense, and has no idea how to tackle housework. I asked what she was being called upon to do at such a well-run establishment.

'They're cleaning out the stables. Some talk of them being turned into houses, and they've got two great skips up there to throw all the rubbish in. She's helping to fill 'em up.'

It seemed the sort of thing she might manage, but I wondered how many objects, later needed, would be the victims of Minnie's activity.

'But isn't the work rather heavy for Minnie?'

Mrs Pringle's countenance became even more gloomy than usual.

'The fact is they need the money. Them kids eats like oxen.'

I began to fear that all this was a preliminary to asking me to supply work for Minnie.

I was right.

'I don't suppose you could give her a couple of hours, now and again?'

'Mrs Pringle,' I began bravely, 'you know as well as I do that Minnie is absolutely hopeless in the house.'

The old curmudgeon had the grace to look abashed at this straight speaking.

'I was thinking about your brights. If she was to come, say, once a month, when I was there of a Wednesday, I could keep an eye on her and see she got out the Brasso and not the stuff to clean the oven. She couldn't do much harm cleaning brass and copper. Particularly your things.'

I did not care for this slur on my property, but overlooked it in the face of this larger menace.

'We could try it, I suppose,' I said weakly, 'but not just yet.'

'Mrs Partridge is having her to scrub out the back kitchen, and the old dairy and wash house, on a Wednesday morning. She's to have her dinner there too.'

Not for the first time, I saw Mrs Partridge as a true Christian, and a worthy wife for our vicar. In the face of such nobility of character, I began to review my own skimpy offering of help.

'She can start after the end of term,' I told Mrs Pringle.

And knew that I should regret it.

A week or two later, the school Sports' Day took place, and everyone prayed for the same sort of halcyon weather which had blessed our trip to Barrisford.

Mr Roberts, the local farmer, always lets us use the field

next to our school for our Sports' Day. He removes his house cow, who normally grazes there, and supplies stakes and rope to fence off the course itself.

Mr Willet, a few of the bigger boys and I usually spend an hour or so, on the evening before, getting the field ready for competitors, parents and other visitors.

The main task is roping off the sports area, and stamping down the largest of the molehills. The grass is tussocky in places, and any professional runner would blench at the hazards of racing on such terrain, but we are made of sterner stuff in Fairacre and cope with these little difficulties without complaint.

Sadly, the weather was far from perfect. A boisterous wind blew hair and skirts, and even threatened to overturn the blackboard on which Mrs Richards recorded the results. Chairs and benches had been brought from the school and village hall by Mr Roberts' tractor and trailer, and hardy parents and friends of the school bravely sat by the dividing rope, with the collars of their coats turned up against the breeze.

But at least the rain held off, and the infants stole the show with their sack race, seconded only by the parents' race which was won by our newcomer to the village, Mrs Bennett, amidst great enthusiasm.

It was half-past four when all was over. The chairs were piled upon the waiting trailer, the blackboard and easel manhandled back to their rightful place, and Mr Willet remained surveying the stakes and rope with a mallet in his hand.

Clouds were piling up in the west as children and parents departed, and I urged Bob Willet to leave his duties until tomorrow.

'Mr Roberts said as much,' I informed him. 'There's nothing there to hinder anyone overnight.'

'Then I'll be getting home,' he said, and departed.

I went back to the empty schoolroom to collect a few more of the belongings which had accumulated there over the years and which I was gradually transferring to my home or, more often, to the school dustbin.

There was no one in the building. Mrs Pringle had finished her ministrations and gone. Mrs Richards was halfway to Caxley to prepare Wayne's evening meal. The only sound was the measured tick-tock of the great clock on the wall, and I sat at my desk relishing the silence.

How many head teachers had sat here before me during the long life of this little school? Had I wished, I could have reached down to the bottom drawer of the desk at which I now sat, and lifted out the three great log books which recorded all that had gone before.

The opening entry had been made in 1880 by the first headmistress. She had been helped by her sister who was in charge of the babies' class. Ever since its opening the school had been a two-teacher establishment, as it was today. Sometimes a headmaster ruled, sometimes a headmistress, and very soon yet another headmistress would follow in my footsteps and be, I sincerely hoped, as happy as I had been.

This modest and shabby little building must have seen remembered by thousands of country people over its long history. Soldiers in the Boer War, the Great War of 1914–18, and the war which overshadowed our own lifetime had come from this classroom, had heard the clock tick as I did now, and had memories, no doubt, in those far-off and perilous times of a small and peaceful place where the rooks wheeled about the church spire and the scent of honeysuckle wafted in from the vicarage garden hard by.

Many former pupils had died overseas, for there was a strong attraction from America and from New Zealand where several families had emigrated at the turn of the century. But many pupils lay close by their school, in the churchyard of St Patrick's, among their old friends. And on the walls of the nave and chancel were many lists, poignantly long for such a tiny village, of those who had perished in battle.

Very soon Jane Summers would be sitting here, heiress, as I had been, to this little kingdom which wielded unknown power to influence so many future lives.

It was a sobering, but strangely uplifting thought, to know that one was just a link in a long chain:

> *. . . a poor player,*
> *That struts and frets his hour upon the stage,*
> *And then is heard no more.*

St Patrick's clock began to strike six. I gathered up my belongings and went outside towards the car.

As I was locking the school door I suddenly remembered an occasion when I had returned towards the end of summer holiday, and had found the gossamer threads of a spider across the closed door jamb. It was at a time when we had feared that Fairacre school would have to close because of falling numbers, and I had had the chill feeling that soon the signs of neglect and desertion would engulf the little place.

Cobwebs, dead leaves, the musty smell of an abandoned building would be its lot, and I had been shaken with sudden sadness.

Now I locked up with a braver heart. Thanks to the Trust's efforts and the two new families in our midst, that cloud had been lifted from us, and Jane Summers, and her successors, could look forward to continuing the tradition of our little school.

CHAPTER 15

Farewell to Fairacre School

The last day of any term is usually greeted with unalloyed joy and relief, by pupils and teachers alike.

This was no exception when I splashed happily in the bath tub, but as I sat at the breakfast table, looking out into a pearly quiet garden, a little shiver of apprehension cooled the glow of anticipation.

I was not worried about the larger issues of my retirement. Any doubts about the wisdom of my move had been sorted out and I had come to terms with my future plans.

What worried me now was the immediate programme of the day. There would be some emotional hurdles to overcome, and I felt some dread about my ability to cope with them.

For a start, the vicar had insisted on coming to take morning assembly, when no doubt he would make reference to my departure. Should I be mentioned in the prayers? I could certainly do with some support from church quarters, and any other for that matter, but would the vicar discourse too enthusiastically on my merits, if any, and his hopes for my future?

And then there was the presentation to face in the afternoon. The secret of what form it would take had been well kept, and I had no idea of what was going to be given to me.

I knew that I must make a speech of thanks, and had already planned that it would be short, sincere and simple. The most awful fear was that I might break down and weep. I shuddered at the thought.

Mrs Richards, I felt sure, would shed a few tears, as she was easily moved, confessing that a brass band or flags waving 'set her off'. I had already determined to see that she was placed well out of range of my vision, in case I wept in sympathy.

Oh dear, I thought, as I cleared away the breakfast things, how I *hate* publicity! My heart sank at the thought of all those people – no matter how well known and kindly disposed – and I remembered the fuss my poor mother had to face, years earlier, when I was forced to go to a party.

It was useless to point out that my friends would be there, that people would not have invited me if they did not want my company. The stark fact remained that I should have to be properly dressed, be particularly polite and, worst of all, act as though I were really enjoying myself.

Well, I told myself, searching for the car keys, I coped then, and I supposed that I could cope today.

Time alone would tell.

Mrs Richards was in school when I arrived and looked a little tearful already, much to my alarm. She was leafing through *Hymns Ancient and Modern*.

'I'm trying to find something suitable,' she said. 'You know, something really memorable.'

'Well, keep off "Abide With Me," and "Lead Kindly Light", I beg of you. What about "Praise my Soul"?'

'But that seems so *heartless*, as though we're glad to see you go, which we aren't.'

She began to look even more woebegone.

'I've got a soft spot for "Ye Holy Angels Bright" and I don't think it's too difficult to play.'

She began to turn the pages.

'If you really want that, then you should have the choice this morning,' she said, more cheerfully, and I left her to strum a few chords whilst I unlocked my desk.

Mrs Pringle, when she arrived, was almost smiling. No doubt with relief at seeing me on duty for the last time, was my uncharitable thought, but I was soon enlightened.

'I had a notice from the office. Wages are going up. Not much, mind you, but every little helps.'

I gave her my congratulations.

'It's no more than it should be by rights. That office can have no idea of what's wanted, trying to keep this place decent. Why, the stoves alone are one woman's work, and those everlasting boots all over the lobby floors, day in and day out —'

She was forced to take breath.

'You know it's been appreciated,' I said, feeling that I could afford to be magnanimous on my last morning.

'It's all right for *some*,' continued Mrs Pringle. 'Come tomorrow they'll be free of all this. Plenty of time to take it easy while the drudgery goes on and on for others.'

'Time for the bell,' I said briskly, and Mrs Pringle limped painfully out of sight.

Mrs Richards and I exchanged meaningful glances as Ernest burst into the room to ring the school bell.

The vicar, I was relieved to see, was much as usual, rather absent-minded and vague, and certainly entirely free from embarrassing emotion.

He always came on the last day of term, but had he forgotten that it was my very last day at Fairacre school? I need not have worried.

In the final prayer he mentioned 'servants who had served for many years with grace and unfailing cheerfulness', which I presumed referred to my endeavours, in the kindest possible way, and also to 'the hope that such servants, and in particular our own dear school teacher, should enjoy the bounty of a long and happy retirement', which I silently endorsed.

'I shall see you again at two o'clock,' he said, as he departed, and I chided myself for thinking that he would forget any of his duties. I should have known better after all these years.

There was a general air of excitement about the classroom that morning, and I knew that the secret they had so faithfully kept was contributing to it.

The atmosphere was not conducive to mental work, and in any case, most of the exercise books and text books were already neatly packed away ready for Jane Summers' over-seeing next term. We confined ourselves, in the usual end-of-term way, to paper games such as the old favourites, 'How many words can you make from CONSTANTINOPLE?', and 'How many boys' and girls' names can you think of beginning with S?'

More worldly children need videos and computers, but in Fairacre we still enjoy pencils and paper, I am glad to say.

I noticed that the lobby was unusually fragrant when I saw the children out at playtime. A chair, draped with a tea towel, screened what I guessed was a mammoth bunch of flowers, and I could smell lilies, roses, pinks, honeysuckle, a mixture of delicious scents. I diverted my eyes from the screen as I saw the children through the door, and was equally virtuous when I returned for my morning coffee.

The dinner lady brought us shepherd's pie with young carrots and calabrese, with pink blancmange for our pudding. The latter is a great favourite with the children as it is decorated with blobs of white stuff which the children call cream, but which I find unidentifiable.

She also presented me with a box of chocolates, kissed me warmly and said she would miss me. I began to feel dangerously tearful, but responded with equal warmth.

How nice to think that I should be missed!

By two o'clock there was a throng in the school playground, and luckily the sun shone and the boisterous downland wind was not in evidence.

A few chairs had been put here and there for those in need, but I was relieved to see that most visitors would be expected to stand. At least it showed that the proceedings would be brief.

A large object, draped in one of Mr Roberts' tarpaulins, stood in a prominent position. It could be a refectory table or a chest of drawers, but I secretly hoped it might prove to be a garden seat, although I had been appalled at the price shown in a gardening catalogue I had looked at. This had been *after* I had given the list to the vicar, and I had had a few bad moments about it.

It was a very large alien object in our playground, but I did my best to ignore it.

St Patrick's church clock struck two o'clock, and a few moments later the vicar clapped his hands for silence, and the ceremony began.

During the vicar's opening address, I had time to study the visitors. Among them Mr Willet stood to one side, and I was touched to see that he was in his best blue serge suit. Mrs Pringle too, was formally dressed and wearing a navy blue straw hat with a duck's wing spread along its ample brim, a real go-to-meetings hat, and its presence today I counted as a great honour.

The younger mothers, of course, were hatless and pretty in their summer frocks. Half a dozen toddlers roamed about, and I thought, with a pang, that I should not be teaching them when their time came. It was little sharp pin-pricks such as this that periodically jerked me into reality.

Someone from the county education office then said some more kind things, and Mrs Bennett, representing the parents and very shy about it, added her tribute.

The moment had arrived for the vicar, helped by Bob Willet, to throw off the tarpaulin covering the mysterious object, and this they did with a great flourish, displaying a magnificent garden seat to the admiration of us all.

It was overwhelmingly generous, and I began to wonder if I should be able to get through my carefully rehearsed speech without breaking down.

I stood up, took a deep breath and began my speech. To my horror I found that my voice was shaky, and that I had a painful lump in my throat. At the same moment I caught sight of Mrs Richards' face, streaming with tears. I began to wonder if I should soon be in the same state.

At this dreadful moment, a large Labrador puppy rushed across the playground, much to the indignation and dismay of my audience.

The vicar nobly attempted to grab the animal, but it romped towards the crowd, delighted to find so many playmates.

Voices rose.

'That's the pub's!'

'Always loose, that dog!'

'Those new people at the Beetle and Wedge have no idea!'

'Catch his collar, Ernest!'

'It's too bad. Miss Read's last day too!'

The puppy bounded about, resisting all attempts at capture. The children were even more excited and vociferous than their elders, and increased the animal's antics.

At last Bob Willet grabbed its tail, and then its collar, and dragged it into the school lobby and shut the door.

By this time I had collected myself, blown my nose, and was beginning to feel amusement rather than trepidation. I was able to go on with my speech, despite a background of yelps, whines and howls from the lobby. I sat down to a storm of applause.

The vicar was full of apologies which he shouted in my ear against even more prolonged clapping, and the meeting ended in general surging of all present, as we went to inspect my lovely present, and to greet each other.

Mr Roberts produced a length of binder twine from his pocket.

'I always carry a bit about me,' was his comment, and he went to secure the puppy and return it to the pub.

'I'm coming straight back,' he told me, 'to take your seat over to your place in the pick-up. Don't you hurry yourself. Bob's giving me a hand, and he knows just where to put it in your garden.'

'One moment,' said the vicar, 'we want a photograph of Miss Read on the seat, with all the school around her. Mr Lamb has brought his camera with him.'

We settled ourselves on my new possession. I sat in the middle and there was room for two squashed children on each side.

Mrs Richards stood behind me. While Mr Lamb fiddled importantly with the camera, she leant over and said with some agitation, 'Little Betty was supposed to be giving you a bouquet, but we dare not go into the lobby because of the dog. Can we present it after this?'

'Of course. How kind you all are!'

'Ready?' shouted Mr Lamb.

We all smiled, and John Todd held up two fingers in what I hoped was the V sign, as the camera clicked.

'Just another for good luck,' said Mr Lamb, and I was able to tell John Todd to put his hands away before the next click.

The vicar, who had been apprised of the bouquet incident, now requested everyone to wait, and the youngest child in the school emerged from the lobby carrying a bunch of flowers nearly as big as herself.

There was renewed clapping. I made a second speech of thanks, and very slowly some of the crowd began to drift homeward.

I went to collect my things from indoors. Mrs Pringle was surveying the lobby floor with a doom-laden face.

'As if it ain't bad enough with *children*, let alone *dogs*.'

It was a fitting farewell, I thought, as I collected my belongings.

I was home before the garden seat arrived, and was just about to put on the kettle when Amy arrived.

'I thought you might be feeling a bit low,' she said. 'It must have been a daunting day for you.'

'To be honest,' I said, 'it really hasn't sunk in yet. Such a lot happened.' I told her about the speeches and the presents and the dog and the photographs, and we agreed that a cup of tea was absolutely essential after all that.

Amy went out to her car as I set the tray, and returned with a pot containing a rose bush.

'It's one of the "Peace" variety called something like "Hope" or "Happy Future", but I seem to have lost the label.'

'It's heavenly,' I said, 'and marks the occasion perfectly.'

Mr Roberts and Bob arrived as we were pouring out, but having deposited the seat where my shabby old one once stood, they refused to join us, saying that they were now off to Springbourne to help with the cricket sight screen which was in a poor way.

'I'm not saying "goodbye",' Mr Roberts said, pecking my cheek. 'You'll be turning up in Fairacre again like a bad penny, I'll bet.'

'And I'll see you tomorrow,' added Bob, eyeing Amy's present. 'I'll put that in proper. I can see it's a beauty. I'll bring young Joe Coggs with me to hold it steady.'

We waved them goodbye, and returned to our tea cups.

'By the way,' said Amy, 'I hope you'll keep the last week of September free.'

'What's happening?'

'James is off to Florence for a conference. He'll be closeted in meetings all the time, so I hope you'll keep me company and we'll go sightseeing.'

'Perfect. But only if we go Dutch.'

'We'll see about that nearer the time,' said Amy. 'But what about the immediate future? I don't want you moping about regretting your decision.'

'I promise you I shan't do that. I've got the Annetts to tea tomorrow, and I'm going to Rousham with John next week, to see the garden.'

'Oh, I'm so glad! Perhaps he'll propose again.'

'I've no doubt about it. It's a regular occurrence.'

'So there's hope for you yet,' exclaimed Amy, looking so excited that I had not the heart to disappoint her.

*

It was when I was in bed that night that I began to think.

How kind everybody had been, overwhelming me with gifts and compliments! It had been a wonderful day, and I should never forget it, the culmination of many years of teaching in a village school.

To many it would seem a dull life, virtually untouched by great national events, and simple to the point of being humdrum.

But I had been happy in it. The day-to-day activities in what Oliver Goldsmith called 'the vale of obscurity' suited me and would provide me with many memories as, I felt sure, it would provide a lifetime of memories for the hundreds of children who had shared Fairacre school with me.

I thought of all those teachers who had preceded me, and who had made their contribution to the school.

Lying there, in Dolly Clare's bedroom, I remembered with affection her particular contribution to those who knew her. She had set an example of serenity and gentleness, and above all of bravery in adversity.

Nevertheless, I had done my best. I had been happy, and had encouraged the children to find happiness in the downland about them.

Perhaps that would be my small contribution to the history of Fairacre, making children aware of the wonders about them.

I found it a fitting epitaph.

CHAPTER 16

Afterwards

It is exactly two months since my last school day, and I have had time to get used to retirement.

The children are back at school, and I see them in the playground at Beech Green school as I saunter, in a leisurely way, to my local shop. At Fairacre, no doubt, there is the same shouting, rushing about and general mayhem, but now I am spared that.

Jane Summers has been to tea, and I can see that we are going to be good friends. She is cheerful, sensible, fond of her little flock, and I think that Fairacre school is lucky to have her to guide its fortunes.

Two more children have been added to the roll, and it looks as if the school faces a steady future.

Mrs Pringle continues to visit me on Wednesday afternoons, occasionally threatening to give the place a 'good bottoming' as it now gets even dirtier than before, as I am in it so much. Minnie has been twice, and I have seen her aunt settle her firmly at the kitchen table with the correct cleaning materials and my pieces of copper and brass. So far, no real damage has been done, although she was about to attack my gold wristwatch with Brasso when I had foolishly left it on the windowsill.

I enjoyed my second visit to Rousham with John, and we have had several jaunts together elsewhere. So far I have received seven proposals of marriage, and together we have brought the art of offer-and-polite-decline to a very high standard.

In a week or so I go to Florence with Amy and James, and relish seeing that lovely city in September sunshine. The thought of being on holiday, and permanent holiday at that, will add spice to this adventure.

Bob Willet is a regular visitor, occasionally bringing Joseph Coggs as his assistant. He told me last time that Arthur Coggs has been given a spell of probation for his recent offences. The Caxley magistrates had been much impressed by the psychiatric report which found Arthur 'deeply disturbed'.

'And so am I,' stated Bob Willet grimly, 'when I know Arthur's loose again.'

The two new families, housed by the Trust, are now firmly settled into our village ways, and the younger members will soon be among the pupils of Fairacre school.

But the most exciting news is that Henry Mawne has married Deirdre at a quiet ceremony in Ireland, and that he will be bringing his new wife back to Fairacre to live.

'We all thought he would,' was Mrs Pringle's comment.

Sitting on my spanking new garden seat, among the late flowers of summer, I think of all that happened during my last year at school.

I had known illness and fear, been obliged to make far-reaching decisions, which I now knew were the right ones, after the initial panic.

I had played my part in the hotchpotch of festivals, fêtes, outings, quarrels and friendships which make up the stuff of village life. New friends, as well as old ones, had enriched my days, and I had the ineffable satisfaction of knowing that Fairacre school would continue to flourish.

As for Fairacre itself, for me it will always remain, as T.S. Eliot put it:

The still point of the turning world.

A PEACEFUL RETIREMENT

with illustrations by Andrew Dodds

To the happy memory
of Beryl, Edie, Anthea, Laura and my sister Lil,
whose lives enriched my own

Contents

1   A New Start

WHEN I retired, after many years as headmistress of Fairacre School, I received a great deal of advice.

The vicar, the Reverend Gerald Partridge, was particularly concerned.

'You must take care of your health. You have had to take early retirement because of these recent weaknesses, and you must call in the doctor if you are in any way worried.'

My assistant, Mrs Richards, was equally anxious about my welfare, and urged me to cook a substantial midday meal.

'I've seen so many women living alone who make do with a boiled egg, or even just a cup of tea and a biscuit. In the end, of course, they just fade away.'

Mr Willet, who is general caretaker at the school, as well as verger and sexton at the church, and right-hand man to us all at Fairacre, told me not to attempt any heavy digging in my garden at Beech Green. He would be along to see the vegetables planted, he assured me, and there was no need to try to help with the plans he had in mind.

Mrs Pringle, the morose school cleaner with whom I had skirmished for years, ran true to form.

'I'll be along on Wednesdays as usual,' she informed me,

'and don't try taking that great heavy vacuum cleaner upstairs. That way my auntie Elsie met her death. Not that she died outright, mind you. She lingered for weeks.'

It was the vicar again who had the last word, leaning into the car window, and saying earnestly:

'Everyone hopes that you will have a *really peaceful retirement*.'

I promised him that that was my firm intention too.

It had been a bitter blow to me when I had been obliged to retire a few years before my forty years of teaching were up. But once I had made up my mind I began to look forward to an easier way of life, and had comforted myself with all sorts of future plans when I should have the leisure to enjoy them.

I continued to look ahead joyfully, but I must admit that during the first day or two of that particular summer holiday, the beginning of my retirement, those words of advice, so kindly meant, gave me food for thought.

It seemed plain to me that the four people who had advised me so earnestly, really had a pretty poor view of my capabilities.

The vicar obviously considered that I was now a tottering invalid and incapable of looking after my own health.

Mrs Richards, who should have known better, seemed to think that I should neglect my digestion, sinking to scoffing the odd biscuit, and never making use of my cooking equipment.

I was rather hurt about this. I like cooking, and enjoy the fruits of my labours. What's more, I enjoy cooking for friends, and Mrs Richards had frequently had a meal at my house. Why should she imagine that one so fond of her food would suddenly give up?

As for Mr Willet, it was plain that he deplored my horti-cultural efforts, and was practically warning me off my own plot. What cheek!

Mrs Pringle's attack caused me no surprise. The threat of coming as usual every Wednesday 'to bottom me', as she so elegantly puts her ministrations, was expected, and her warn-ing against lifting heavy objects, such as the vacuum cleaner, was only a request to keep from meddling with her equipment and damaging it.

Well, I thought, if the rest of Fairacre shared my advisers' opinions then it was a poor look-out for the future. I began to wonder if I should make early application for a place in an old people's home, but at that moment the telephone rang, and it was my old friend Amy's cheerful voice on the line.

*

Amy and I first met many years ago at a teachers' training college in Cambridge. We took to each other at once, although Amy, even then at the age of eighteen, had a worldly elegance which none of us could match. But with it she also had plenty of common sense, a kindly disposition and a great sense of humour. She was generally popular among the students of her own sex, and much sought after by the male undergraduates at Cambridge University.

We kept up our contacts when we were out in the world, and although Amy married within two years of our leaving college the friendship remained solid, and survived the union of James and Amy.

'What are you up to?' queried Amy.

I told her about my gloomy thoughts after receiving advice from old friends.

'Pooh!' said Amy. 'Pish-Tush, and all that! My advice is positive, not negative. Just you set to and enjoy your freedom. It's time you kicked up your heels, and did something exciting.'

'Good! I will!'

'Which reminds me. James has made the final arrangements for our week and a bit in Florence, at the end of September. It's all buttoned up. Air tickets, hotel and all that. I'll pop over one day soon and tell you more, and we can begin to make plans about what we girls are going to do while James is at his boring old conference.'

I was excited at the prospect. Amy had mentioned it earlier, but now this wonderful holiday was in sight.

I burbled my thanks and said I should look forward to seeing her at any time, as I was now a Free Woman.

I put down the receiver feeling considerably elated. A fig for my advisers!

*

Those first two or three weeks of my retirement were blissful. We were enjoying a spell of fair weather that summer, and downland is at its best then.

The garden was at its most colourful and fragrant. In the flower borders the pinks and cottage carnations scented the air during the day, and some tobacco plants added their own aroma as dusk fell. Mr Willet had experimented with a wigwam of bamboo sticks which was covered in sweet peas of all colours, and it was a joy to take my ease on my new garden seat, Fairacre's farewell present on my retirement, and to relish the delights about me.

I was filled with first-day's-holiday zeal, and washed and ironed curtains and bedspreads, rejoicing in the summer breezes which kept them billowing on the clothes-line. I turned out drawers and discovered enough rubbish to stock a dozen jumble stalls. This latter activity was accompanied by a commentary of self-accusation. Why did I buy that dreadful peacock-blue jumper? It was a colour I never wore. What on earth possessed me to spend good money on a mohair stole? I remember that the only time I wore it, to a Caxley concert, it had slithered from my shoulders half a dozen times, and had been retrieved by as many fellow listeners. It had so embarrassed me that it had been relegated to the bottom drawer with other jumble fodder such as too-small gloves, too-large petticoats and a variety of Christmas presents which I should never use.

It was a salutary task. I must take myself in hand, I told myself severely, and be much more selective in my shopping. After all, my income would be greatly reduced, and I must be more prudent.

Nevertheless, the feeling of achievement as I contemplated the tidy drawers did me a world of good, and added to my general contentment.

Of course, my domestic euphoria was dampened by the weekly visits of Mrs Pringle who enjoyed pointing out my shortcomings as she puffed about her duties on Wednesday afternoons. However, I was quite used to the old curmudgeon's strictures, and she brought me news of my Fairacre friends, which was most welcome.

I was particularly interested to hear how my old friend Henry Mawne was getting on with his new wife Deirdre. He had first come to Fairacre alone, and the village had been quite sure that he was a respectable bachelor, and it had been intrigued and delighted when he became most attentive to me. I did not share the general excitement, and found him rather a nuisance.

Fairacre's hopes of two middle-aged people tying the knot in the parish church of St Patrick's were abruptly shattered when Henry's wife reappeared. She had been staying with relatives in Ireland after the marriage had suffered a temporary set-back. My relief had been great.

The three of us became good friends and I was sad when she died. The new Mrs Mawne was one of her Irish relatives, and seemed to be generally approved of by the residents of Fairacre. But not, of course, by Mrs Pringle.

'For one thing,' she said, as we sipped tea, 'she talks funny. I don't take in one word in four.'

'I rather like that Irish brogue.'

My remark was ignored.

'And she's fair upset Bob Willet with all her fancy ideas for the garden.'

'What ideas?'

'A camomile lawn for one. Bob was fair taken aback by that. Takes years to settle he told her, and what was wrong with the grass lawn as had been there for years?'

'Will Bob do it?'

'Not likely. And she wanted Alice Willet to go up every evening and cook the evening meals. That didn't suit Bob nor Alice, as you can guess.'

I felt sorry for poor old Henry if his wife really was putting her foot in it so readily. However, one learns over the years to take Mrs Pringle's news with a pinch of salt, and I looked forward to hearing more from less rancorous sources.

'It's a great pity,' said Mrs Pringle, heaving herself upright ready for further onslaughts on my property, 'as he didn't look nearer home for a second wife. You'd have made him a good wife. Apart from the housework, of course.'

I was roused to protest.

'You know perfectly well that Mr Mawne and I had no sort of understanding. I certainly had no thoughts of entangling the man.'

The old harridan was quite unabashed.

'Which reminds me,' she said, 'how is your new friend Mr Jenkins getting on?'

I ignored the question, but she had scored a hit, and knew it.

John Jenkins was one of the problems I should have to face in my retirement. He was a most attractive middle-aged widower who had come to live in Beech Green quite close to my cottage.

We had become good friends, and shared a great many interests. We both liked walking, visiting splendid houses and gardens, attending plays and concerts, and enjoyed each other's company.

He had been lonely, I think, when he first arrived in Beech Green, and glad of my company. I was still busy at Fairacre school, and my time at home was pretty full with the usual woman's chores of cooking, laundering, writing letters and entertaining.

At times I found his presence tiresome. He was plainly at a loose end. I was not, but I tried to be a good neighbour and companion within my limits.

The awkward thing was that John soon wanted more of my time, and asked me to marry him. I refused, as kindly as I could.

However, he was not in the least dismayed, and continued to propose to me with admirable tenacity. But I was equally adamant, and a permanent, if uneasy, truce prevailed.

Amy, of course, was all in favour of marriage for me. Ever since her own union with James she has urged me to enter the state of matrimony, and produced a string of possible suitors over the years. I have been grateful to Amy for her well-meant endeavours on my behalf, but I have also been irritated. Time and time again, I have explained to my old friend that I am really quite happy as a spinster, but Amy simply cannot believe it.

'But you must be so lonely,' she protested one day. 'You come home from school to an empty house, so quiet you can hear the clock tick, no human voice! It must be almost frightening.'

'I don't,' I told her. 'I find it absolute bliss after the fuss and bustle of school. And I may not come back to human voices, but Tibby keeps up a pretty strong yowling until I put down her dinner plate.'

Amy was not impressed, and her attempts to provide me with a husband have continued unabated over the years.

This question of loneliness interests me. I remember when I made the move from Fairacre school house to my present home which dear Dolly Clare left me, that I had a brief moment when I wondered if I should really be at ease on my own.

At the school house I had been much nearer my neighbours, and in any case, the children and their parents were much in evidence around me. Certainly, at holiday times I had found the place much quieter, but this had pleased me.

After the move to Beech Green, and my passing doubts about loneliness, I found my new surroundings entirely satisfactory, and when I informed Amy that I was really and honestly not *lonely*, it was the plain truth.

I think perhaps those of us who have lived in a solitary state are lucky in that they have filled their time with a diversity of interests and friends. It is the married couples who suffer far more when their partner goes, for they have shared a life together, and it is shattered by the loss of half one's existence. Life for the one who is left can never be quite the same again.

I feel it would be heartless to share this thought with Amy. She is positive that she is the lucky one to be married, and I am to be pitied.

But I wonder . . .

I had taken very little notice of Mrs Pringle's strictures about Deirdre Mawne. I was so accustomed to her disparaging remarks about all and sundry that the Mawnes' marital affairs were dismissed from my mind.

However, when Bob Willet mentioned the matter, in his usual thoughtful and kindly manner, I began to take more notice.

He spoke about Mrs Mawne's invitation to Alice, his wife, to take a permanent job as their cook every evening at the Mawnes' house to provide dinner on a regular basis, weekends included.

'She offered to pay well,' said Bob fairly, 'but that's not the point. I'm not having Alice turning out in all weathers, and after dark too, best part of the year, to do a job as Mrs Mawne can quite well do herself. It's asking too much.'

I agreed.

'I don't know how they go on in Ireland,' continued Bob, putting four lumps of sugar in his mug and stirring briskly, 'but I should hope the folk there don't kowtow to the likes of Mrs Mawne. She won't find no slave labour in Fairacre. We ain't standing for her high and mighty ways, I can tell you.'

'She'll soon learn,' I said comfortingly.

'I'm not so sure. She's upset Mr Lamb at the village shop keeping him waiting for his money. She says she's always paid her bills monthly, but that's a long time for him to wait for the cash, and half the time he has to remind her because she's let it run on. People don't like having to do that. He's in a proper tizzy.'

Bob Willet himself was getting quite pink in the face as his account went on.

'And she's making trouble with the vicar,' he continued. 'Strode up the aisle to sit in the front pew where old Miss Parr always sat for years. She says that pew belongs to whoever has the house, which they do now, as you know, but no one ever took that pew after Miss Parr died. Mr Mawne always sat three rows back ever since he came to Fairacre.'

I rose to put my mug in the sink, hoping to bring this unhappy recital to a close. I had never seen the usually imperturbable Bob Willet so incensed.

'I'm sure it will all blow over,' I said hopefully. 'Henry Mawne knows all about village ways. He'll explain things to her.'

'If you ask me,' he said, putting his mug beside mine in the sink, and preparing to return to the garden, 'he's scared stiff of her.'

I heard him trundling out the lawn mower. He was singing *Onward Christian Soldiers*, which seemed, I thought, to suit his present martial mood.

I rinsed the mugs, feeling relieved that I no longer lived close to the Mawnes and their troubles. With any luck, I told myself, I should hear no more of the subject.

I should have known better.

The weather continued to be calm and sunny, and I pottered about my garden and the lanes of Beech Green in a state of blissful enjoyment. The thought that I need never go to school again filled me with satisfaction which, in a way, rather

surprised me for I had never disliked my job, and had certainly wondered if I should miss the hurly-burly of school life after so many years.

However, this halcyon period suited me admirably and I seemed to notice things which had escaped me before. I took to picking a few wild flowers from the banks and hedgerows on my daily strolls. I marvelled at the exquisite symmetry of the pale mauve scabious flowers and the darker knapweed that grow so prolifically in these parts.

There was a patch of toadflax just outside the wall of Beech Green's churchyard, and I enjoyed these miniature snap-dragons with their orange and yellow flowers, and the spiky leaves which set off their beauty so vividly.

It was one of these mornings, when I was mooning happily with a nosegay of wild flowers in my hand, that John Jenkins drew up alongside in his car and invited me to coffee. I accepted willingly and climbed in.

'You realize you are breaking the law, madam,' he said with mock severity, nodding at my flowers.

'It's all in the cause of botanical knowledge,' I told him. 'Have you been to Caxley?'

Our local market town on the river Cax serves many villages around, and there are still many people who go every market day for their shopping, despite one or two out-of-town supermarkets.

'Yes, I had to see my solicitor. Luckily he has a car park for clients at the rear of his office, otherwise I'd still be driving round and round the town looking for a parking place.'

'People shouldn't have cars,' I said.

'You mean *other people* shouldn't have cars,' he countered, turning into his drive.

Ten minutes later we were drinking proper coffee, expertly made, which put me to shame as I usually gave him instant.

'This luscious brew makes me feel guilty and weak,' I told him.

'Good,' he replied briskly. 'This might be a propitious time to suggest that you marry me. I promise to make the coffee in the years ahead.'

'No go,' I told him, 'but the coffee offer might have done the trick this time. By the way, I've been asked to take charge of the Sunday School here.'

'Oh dear, has George started already? I told him not to bother you.'

I felt slightly piqued by this. That John should institute himself as my protector was really a bit much. Anyone would think we were already married, and that I was incapable of looking after my own affairs.

'Well, George is not the only one, of course, to rush to enlist my invaluable services. But never fear! I realized that I should be pestered to join all sorts of things when I retired and I am determined to be firm.'

'I'm glad to hear it. Let me know if anyone starts to bully you, and I'll see them off.'

I put down my cup carefully. Mellowed though I was by his excellent coffee, I was not going to stand for this knight-to-the-rescue attitude.

'John,' I began, 'I'm not ungrateful, and you are one of the first people I should turn to in trouble, but I must point out that I have managed my own affairs – not very competently perhaps, but I've got by – for a good many years, and I am not going to start asking for help now. Unless, of course,' I added hastily, 'I am absolutely desperate.'

'What a prickly old besom you are,' commented John pleasantly, refilling my cup with a steady hand. 'You remind me of a hedgehog.'

I laughed.

'I like hedgehogs,' I told him.

'I like this one,' he assured me.

We drank from our replenished cups in relaxed and companionable silence.

2 Ponderings

THE EXPECTED rush of invitations to join this and that quickened its pace during early September, and I was asked to bestow my time and ability upon diverse activities, from arranging the flowers in Beech Green church to judging the entries of those local Brownies who were aspiring to a literary badge to wear on their sleeves.

The first invitation I turned down as politely as I could. I am one of the grasp-and-drop-in brigade of flower arrangers, and anything on a large pedestal involving great lumps of Oasis and hidden strings would be beyond me.

The Brownies could be undertaken in my own home and in my own time, and as hardly any of the little girls seemed to have literary aspirations, preferring very sensibly to opt for cooking or knitting, my judicial skills would not be over-worked. I took on this little chore with great pleasure.

I had the chance to be a secretary, a treasurer, a general adviser, a part-time librarian, a prison visitor, a baby-minder and a regular contributor to our local radio station.

'I can't think how they all got on without me,' I confessed to Amy one sunny September afternoon, as we sat in my garden.

'They must be jolly hard up,' said Amy. I thought this rather hurtful, but said nothing. 'I mean, your flower arrangements are pathetic, and I can't see you bringing any comfort to prisoners. You'd probably frighten the life out of them.'

'Well, I've turned those down anyway. I have put my services at the disposal of the hospital drivers.'

Amy looked alarmed.

'Not *ambulance* work surely? You know how you hate blood.'

'No, no. Of course not. I'm not qualified for anything like that. I've just offered to run people to hospital for treatment. George Annett asked me, and I'd turned down so many of his pleas to help at the church here, that I felt I had to say "Yes" to something.'

'It's always so difficult to refuse friends,' agreed Amy. 'My father always said: "Never do business with family or friends," and it was good advice.'

'Well, this isn't exactly *business*,' I began, but Amy interrupted me, with a wave of her long ivory cigarette-holder.

'Near enough. You're taking on responsibilities, and they'll be watching you to see if you can cope or not. Just be cautious, dear, that's all I'm advising.'

She spotted a butterfly on the lavender, and sauntered over to inspect it. I followed her.

'Stick to just one or two projects,' she continued. 'You are a bit like this creature, flitting here and there rather aimlessly.'

'Thank you, Amy! That's quite enough of your advice for one day! Still, it's nice to be compared to a butterfly. The last animal was a hedgehog.'

'And I bet that was dear John Jenkins' description,' said Amy shrewdly.

When Amy had gone I pondered on her words. I was feeling

rather bad about the Annetts. They were both old friends, and Isobel had been my assistant teacher at Fairacre school before she married George, the headmaster of Beech Green school.

My retirement, which brought me geographically so much closer to them, had made me more vulnerable to the demands on my time, as I had told Amy, from all those clubs, and so on, at Beech Green.

To my dismay, George Annett was among the most pressing in his demands, chiefly on behalf of his church.

He had been organist there for years, and at Fairacre's St Patrick's too. He was a zealous supporter of the church at Beech Green, and I was not surprised when he first made attempts to secure my services in one or more activities. But I did not want to commit myself. I might live now in the parish of Beech Green, I told him, but my inclinations and loyalties were towards the vicar and church at Fairacre.

'But you could do both,' he protested vehemently. 'There's no reason why you shouldn't attend Fairacre *and* Beech Green. The church is universal, after all.'

He was growing quite pink in his excitement, and Isobel intervened.

'She knows her own affairs best, George,' she said quietly. 'Don't *pester* her.'

He laughed, but I could see that he would return to the fray before long.

I spoke to Isobel privately, saying that I was sorry to be so adamant, but that I was conscious of having only a certain amount of time and energy, and I was determined to ration these precious commodities so that I could continue to enjoy an independent and healthy retirement.

She was understanding, but George, when Isobel was absent, I noticed, continued to solicit my help in various church affairs, so that, as I had told Amy, I had agreed to do some hospital-driving.

A sop to Cerberus, I told myself.

The day after Amy's visit I had to go to the doctor's surgery to check that all was well.

Since the alarming couple of strokes which had made me decide to retire a year or so earlier than I had intended, I had been given some tablets, which I did my best to remember to take, and otherwise pursued my ordinary way of life, except for a three-monthly check which my zealous doctor insisted on.

It was a perfect September morning, far too lovely to spend in a doctor's waiting-room. I had collected three pearly mushrooms from my lawn at breakfast time, and had great plans for an egg, bacon and mushroom supper.

The ancient plum tree was heavy with fruit which would soon have to be picked if the birds were not to rob me. A late crop of spinach, Bob Willet's pride and joy, was doing splendidly in the vegetable patch, and some fine bronze onions, their tops bent over neatly, were maturing in the sunshine.

As I drove to the surgery I passed a covey of young partridges running along the edge of the road. They rose with a whirring of wings above the hedge to take cover in Hundred Acre Field beyond.

Once, I thought, that great field would probably have been golden with stubble from the newly cut corn, and the partridges would have found all the food they wanted there. Nowadays, the field was ploughed and sown within days of the crop being harvested, and the partridges had to look desperately for their erstwhile natural fodder.

There were seven or eight people waiting when I arrived,

but no one I knew, which was a pity. I went to the small pile of magazines and wondered if an ancient *Horse and Hound* would be more to my taste than *Just Seventeen*. The only other periodical available was *Autocar*. Obviously, someone had been having a good sort-out of the usual women's magazines. I opted for *Autocar*, but it was heavy going for one ignorant of the combustion engine, and I welcomed the approach of a chubby toddler who left her mother and an older woman to greet me.

'Hello. How old are you?'

'Older than you are,' I said diplomatically, as all attention was now focused on us. 'And how old are *you*?' I asked, turning the tables neatly.

'Three. I shall be four next. Then five. Have you got a mummy?'

'Not now. I once had one.'

She returned to her mother and patted her knee.

'This is my mummy, and this is my granny.'

She banged the older woman's knee and beamed at me.

I smiled, and they smiled back.

Not content with this civility, the child proceeded to introduce everyone in turn, despite the mother's protests, and it was amusing to note the reaction of the embarrassed company.

The two men present simply ignored the introduction, studying their magazines with undue concentration. The women were more obliging.

A handsome, middle-aged woman, in the sort of knitted suit I am always seeking in vain, inclined her head towards the child's relatives and said: 'How do you do!' very clearly and politely. The others smiled nervously and looked apprehensive. Perhaps they thought that the child would drag them across the room for greater intimacies. Certainly, she looked determined enough to do so, but a head appeared round the door, and the grandmother, mother and child were summoned into the presence. Relief flooded the waiting room.

My routine took only a few minutes, and I found that I was getting quite blasé about that contraption that doctors wrap round your upper arm and blow up. At one time I was sure that I should be suffocated, although reason told me that my air passages were some distance from the point of operation. But as I had now survived several of these unpleasant ministrations, I was positively carefree when the band tightened. An old campaigner, I boasted silently to myself.

'Are you keeping busy?' he enquired, when the tests were over. 'You don't feel lonely or unwanted?'

'Fat chance of that,' I assured him, remembering all those requests for my time and attention.

'Oh, good,' he said, rather doubtfully, I thought. 'So many people find retirement a bit sad, you know.'

'Not me,' I replied firmly.

That evening John Jenkins rang. Could I help him?

'In what way?' I asked guardedly. With such a persistent suitor one needed to stay alert. One slip of the tongue and I might find myself committed to matrimony.

'Well, it's like this. I have an aged uncle, ninety-something, who is now in a nursing home near Winchester, and he wants to see me. I've said I'll take him out to lunch. Would you come too and give me moral support?'

'Of course. I'd love to.'

'It won't be easy. He's stone deaf, and always was pretty crabby, but he was good to my family when we had hard times. He paid my school fees for a couple of years, my mother told me, and I'd like to see the old boy again.'

'When are you thinking of going?'

'Next Tuesday, if you're free.'

A hasty study of the diary showed only the entry 'AMY?' and I knew that she would be delighted to postpone whatever we had provisionally planned if it meant any furtherance of romance for me, so I said I should look forward to the trip to the nursing home.

'Marvellous! What an angel you are! I warn you that you will be as hoarse as a crow and utterly exhausted after a couple of hours with Uncle Sam.'

'I'll cope,' I said.

'I'll bring you back to my house for a refreshing cup of Earl Grey and a slice of your favourite Battenburg cake.'

'Balmoral, isn't it? It got its name changed during the war.'

'Really? How erudite you are. Anyway, we always called it "window cake" in our youth, so you can take your pick. You do still like it?' he added anxiously.

'I do indeed,' I told him, and rang off. Now, what to wear when one visited a very old gentleman in a nursing home?

By Tuesday the weather had changed. The sky was dark with racing clouds rushing from the Bristol Channel to East Anglia.

I had put on a light-weight jersey dress with long sleeves, but brought a good thick cardigan with me. The fashion magazines are constantly telling their readers that: 'Cardigans are *out*', but not in Beech Green, I should like to tell them.

The windscreen wipers were active all the way, but it was warm in the car, and John and I enjoyed a lively conversation about the merits of nursing homes we had known, and which we should choose when the time came. Although the topic was a solemn one, we became mildly hilarious over our choice, and the journey passed happily.

Uncle Sam's nursing home lay half a mile from the road, and was an imposing building of Palladian design, set among well-tended gardens ablaze with dahlias and Michaelmas daisies. There were several white garden seats at strategic points, but these were dripping with raindrops as we emerged from the car, and naturally were unoccupied.

John's uncle was waiting for us in the hall. He was an imposing figure, tall and upright despite his ninety-odd years, and with a loud booming voice. He shook my hand with enormous vigour when we were introduced and offered us drinks which we declined.

'Let's get straight off to your local,' suggested John. I think he felt ill at ease in this very hot building with one or two occupants passing by on their walking frames or sticks.

We helped the old gentleman into an enormous raincoat, found his stick, cap and scarf and ushered him down the three steps to the car. Luckily the rain was ceasing.

As Uncle Sam and John were in the front, I could relax at the back and let their conversation take over. I began to understand why John had warned me about the old man's deafness. If John spoke, his uncle boomed: 'What? What?' and John was obliged to shout back. Uncle Sam himself spoke with a voice which would have carried across the Albert Hall. I began to wish I had brought some cotton-wool with me to stuff in my ears.

The bar of Uncle Sam's choice was warm and welcoming. He plumped for whisky and soda, and John and I sipped sherry. After studying menus so large that they really needed a lectern to support them, we all decided to have 'Today's Special', which was roast turkey with all the trimmings, and sat back with our duty done to enjoy each other's company.

I said that I was most impressed with the nursing home, and was he well looked after?

'Too dam' well,' he bawled. 'Blasted nurses always watching you. Go through the drawers to see if you've got a bottle there.'

'And have you?' said John.

'What? What? Don't mumble, boy.'

'Do they find a bottle?' yelled John.

'No need to shout, I'm not deaf. It's just that you young people mumble so these days. Yes, sometimes nursie finds a bottle. Friends bring me one from time to time. I'm allowed a drop sometimes.'

He fingered his empty glass, but John did not respond. A

waiter appeared to summon us to the dining room, and we went in.

It was only half full and I remembered Amy telling me that: 'Lunch these days is really a non-event, except at business conferences.' Perhaps she was right, I thought, looking about me.

A middle-aged couple were at the next table and I recognized them as people I had met at a fund-raising party in Caxley. He was a minister at one of the town's churches. Baptist, if I remembered rightly. They looked briefly at us, but obviously did not recognize me. I was rather relieved, and hoped that Uncle Sam's remarks, delivered fortissimo, would not disconcert them.

'You thinking of marrying young John here?' he boomed.

'No indeed,' I said.

'Not yet, but later,' John said, at the same time. We exchanged amused glances.

'You don't want to get entangled with our family,' he continued, attacking his asparagus soup with relish. 'Hard drinkers, and womanizers too.'

I was conscious of the attention of the minister and his wife.

'That's not true,' said John.

'What? What? Speak up, boy. Why, my brother Ernest got through two bottles of rum a day, and three wives. No, I tell a lie. *Four* wives, counting that flibbertigibbet that called herself a masseuse, and out-lived him.'

I noticed that the minister had cleared his plate rather quickly, and was asking the waiter for the sweet list. His face was somewhat flushed, although his glass had only been filled from the Perrier bottle on the table.

'Are there many other residents at the nursing home?' I enquired loudly.

'Forty, I believe. Don't see a lot of them. Mostly old women. Want to play cards for pennies, and I like high stakes myself. Always was a betting man, specially on the horses.'

Our turkey arrived and about half a dozen dishes with various vegetables, gravy and cranberry sauce. At the next table a waiter was setting plates of trifle before our neighbours.

'No, I shouldn't marry John here,' continued Uncle Sam. 'Not a good choice. Besides drink and women, there's a lot of nasty diseases in our family. That cousin of ours, lived near Portsmouth. Naval chap, remember him?'

He turned to John. He had dropped a large dollop of cranberry sauce down his shirt and I wondered if I should do some repair work.

'I don't think I knew a naval cousin,' said John.

'What? What? You must remember him. He was always picking up some foul disease abroad. Had rows of bottles on his wash stand. Can't think of his name, at the moment.'

The minister at the next table beckoned the waiter over.

'We will have coffee in the drawing-room,' he said firmly. 'Pray bring the bill there.'

He helped his wife from the chair, and they passed with dignity into the adjoining room.

If ever backs could register disapproval, theirs did. Frankly, I should have liked to join them.

Uncle Sam tackled apple pie and cream while John and I, replete and exhausted, watched him. John insisted on having coffee at the table, no doubt mindful of the minister and his wife recovering in the next room.

By the time our meal was over, there was a watery spell of

sunshine, and John suggested a drive before taking the old gentleman back to the nursing home.

'Splendid idea! Let's go and look at the race-course. It's years since I saw it.'

And so we drove some miles to the windy downs. By now Uncle Sam was quieter, content to watch the countryside and the trees beginning already to show signs of autumn.

There was a wide grass verge overlooking the race course, and here he insisted on getting out. He was very unsteady on his feet, but he seemed pleased to stand there, supported by John and me, while he relished the view before him.

The sun was out now, and great clouds threw their scurrying shadows across the grass. We all breathed deeply the exhilarating downland air, but it was chilly, and we soon returned to the car.

I think that secretly Uncle Sam was content to get back to the warmth and safety of the nursing home. He was beginning to look tired, and although he begged us, at the top of his voice, to stay for the rest of the day, we excused ourselves and made our farewells.

He shook hands energetically with John and took me into his arms to implant a very messy wet kiss on both cheeks. I was rather touched at such exuberance in a ninety-year-old.

A nurse appeared and took his arm.

'Now, Mr Jenkins, you've had a lovely outing and now it's time for your blood pressure pill.'

We watched the pair making for the lift, and then turned away.

'What a darling,' I said.

'I could do with a blood pressure pill myself,' observed John. 'What about you?'

'I think that cup of tea is more my mark,' I told him, as we pointed the car towards Beech Green.

*

We were quiet on the way home, not only because we were tired, but I think we were both dwelling on the problems of old age. The home was lovely, even luxurious, and the staff obviously dedicated and efficient. And yet it was sad.

I remembered the white hair, the frail limbs, the shaking heads, the walking frames and the distant bells ringing for help.

It was good to reach John's house, and to see that tea was already set out on a low table by the fireplace.

Soon he appeared with the teapot and the promised Battenburg cake, and we began to be more cheerful.

He insisted on running me home, and gave me a farewell

kiss as he drew up at my gate. It was, I noticed, much more acceptable than his uncle's.

'Thank you, my darling, for being such a support today. I suppose you couldn't make that a permanent part of your life?'

'Not really,' I said as kindly as I could, as I climbed out of the car. 'But thank you all the same for the nice thought, and the outing, and that perfect tea.'

He drove off looking, I thought, remarkably cheerful for an oft-rejected suitor.

3 Italian Interlude

THE LONG-AWAITED visit to Florence with Amy and James lay only three days ahead, and I had packed and unpacked my case at least five times to include or reject some item or other of my luggage.

Should I need a swimsuit? Unlikely, I decided, removing it. On the other hand, the pool was supposed to be a major attraction of the hotel. Perhaps? I put it back.

This sort of wavering went on for several days, and was most exhausting. I know that seasoned travellers simply pop in their essentials in twenty minutes flat, but I am not a seasoned traveller and, in any case, I like to be prepared for any eventuality. Air travel has made things worse for people like me. I might have been all right in Victorian times with a string of bearers humping a dozen or so pieces of my baggage on their heads. How simple it would have been to shout: 'Hey, could you put this hip bath on the last man's back?'

The evening before our departure I checked the case yet again, and also the contents of my small hand-case and handbag.

Domestic arrangements such as leaving keys and enough food for the cat – actually enough for three cats – had been made with kind Isobel Annett, who had also promised to report any such mishaps as burglary, fire or flood to the appropriate authority in my absence.

Mrs Pringle had insisted on coming for her usual Wednesday cleaning session, although I had begged her to have that day off.

'I won't hear of it,' she informed me. 'Miss one week in a place like yours, and there would be too much to cope with come the next Wednesday.'

I pointed out that there would be nobody in the house to make it dirty.

'What about that cat, traipsing in and out with mud on all four paws? What about any rats or mice he might see fit to bring and let lie *rotting* on the carpet? Then there's flies and wasps at this time of the year, not to mention birds as fly down the chimney.'

I gave in before this picture of my home as a teeming menagerie. As usual, Mrs P. had triumphed.

I had decided to go to bed early. We were to start for the airport at the civilized hour of 9 a.m., but I felt it wise to have a good night.

At half-past eight, as the sunset turned everything to gold, someone rapped at the front door.

On opening it, I saw to my dismay, that it was Henry Mawne, and he was looking singularly unhappy.

'Do come in, Henry,' I said. I should like to have added: 'But don't stay long,' but common civility restrained me.

He settled down in an armchair as though intending to stay for hours, and accepted whisky and water with a wan smile.

'Anything wrong, Henry?' I enquired. I hoped my tone was sympathetic. I was really trying to hurry the visit along so that I could get to bed early.

'*Everything*!' sighed Henry.

This did not bode well for my early-bed plans, but I made suitably dismayed noises.

'It's Deidre, she's pushed off.'

So the rumours had been right, I thought. In a village they usually are, but what could be done?

'She's bound to come back,' I said.

'I don't want her back,' replied Henry petulantly. He sounded like a four-year-old rejecting rice pudding.

'What went wrong?' It was best to get on with the story, I felt.

'*Everything*,' said Henry again. 'I should never have married her.'

He cast me a look so maudlin that I felt some alarm. For pity's sake, I thought, let me be spared another man needing my attention! I have neither the looks nor the temperament to set up as a *femme fatale*, so it did seem rather tough to have silly old Henry making sheep's eyes, especially when I needed a little peace.

'She's a very selfish woman,' said Henry. 'She never thinks about my side of things. Take breakfast, for instance.'

Should I be up in time to get mine, I wondered?

'I like a cooked one, bacon, eggs, sausage, you know what I mean. Deidre has a couple of slices of that straw bread with marmalade. I don't mind her having it, but why shouldn't I have what I want?'

'Do you cook it?'

He looked flabbergasted.

'Of course not. Old Mrs Collins always cooked it when I lived alone, before she started the housework. And that's another thing. She cut down Mrs Collins' hours, so she comes from ten until twelve.'

'Well, I expect she can manage with less help,' I said diplomatically. 'Your house always looks immaculate.'

'And she spends money like water,' continued Henry, swirling the contents of his glass moodily. 'Ordered a revolving summer house the other day. I put a stop to that, I can tell you. That's what really brought things to a head.'

'I'm sorry about this, Henry,' I said briskly, 'but there's really nothing that I can do. You and Deidre must sort it out. You've both got plenty of sense.'

'I wondered if you could speak to her for me? I've got her phone number.'

What a nerve, I thought!

'Henry, I shouldn't dream of coming between husband and

wife. In any case, I'm going away tomorrow.'

'Oh dear, that's most upsetting. I was relying on you.'

I began to get really cross. The selfishness of the man!

'I'm off to Florence, first thing.'

'How lovely! And such a short flight!'

He settled back in his chair, and held up his empty glass questioningly.

I took it and put it firmly on the table. Henry looked surprised.

'I'm certainly looking forward to the break,' I told him, 'but I've some packing to do now, and I'm going to turn you out.'

He rose reluctantly.

'I'm sorry if I've held you up.' He sounded huffy. 'You see, you are always the first person I think of when I'm in trouble. You mean so much to me.'

'Thank you, Henry, but this time things are different. You must get in touch with Deidre as soon as possible, and get her back. I'm sure you will be able to put things right between you.'

I opened the front door, and Henry paused. For one moment, I feared he was about to kiss me, but he thought better of it.

'Well, I hope you enjoy Florence,' he said wistfully. 'I wish I were coming with you.'

He set off down the path, his back registering the fact that he was a broken and misunderstood man.

I waved cheerfully as he unlocked his car, and then closed my door with great relief.

Come with me indeed! It would be good to be free of him for a blessed week.

Prompt as ever, James arrived in the car the next morning, and carried my case down the path while I locked up.

I bade farewell to Tibby who was too busy washing an elegantly outstretched leg to respond, and followed James to the car.

It was a blissfully sunny morning. The early mist had cleared, and the sun shone from a pale blue sky. All three of us were in great spirits.

We had no difficulty in getting to the airport and, having left the car in the long-term car park, James coped with all the necessary formalities, while we two pampered women went to see what the bookstall had to offer.

The magazine section displayed rows of journals most of them with covers showing bosoms and bottoms in highly uncomfortable attitudes. Some of the ladies were embellished with chains and whips, and the males adopted aggressive attitudes, unless they were entwined in passionate embraces with nubile females.

Amy studied the display with distaste.

'I really cannot fathom today's hysterical obsession with sex,' she remarked. 'One would think it was an entirely new activity.'

She selected *Homes and Gardens*, and I contented myself with the *Daily Telegraph* so that I could tackle the crosswords.

James joined us and surveyed the matter on offer.

'Good grief!' was his comment. 'I thought people grew out of that by fifteen. Where's the *Financial Times*?'

'Is the plane going to be on time?' asked Amy as we turned away.

'Only forty-five minutes late,' said James.

'Not bad at all,' replied Amy indulgently. 'What about a cup of coffee?'

My first impression of Florence was of all-pervading golden warmth. The buildings, the walls, the pavements, and the already changing colour of the trees from green to gold, gave the lovely city an ambience which enfolded one immediately.

Our hotel was in the oldest part of the city, not far from the Duomo, Florence's cathedral called so prettily Santa Maria del Fiore. The magnificent dome could be glimpsed, it seemed, from every quarter of Florence.

The hotel had once been the property of a wealthy Florentine family. The taxi driver whirled round the innumerable corners into ever more narrowing streets and at last pulled up with a flourish at an imposing doorway.

'I'm thankful I shan't have to do much driving in this place,' remarked James, as we alighted.

The taxi driver grinned.

'One way! Always one way!' He held up a nicotine-stained finger to add point, and then went to help James unload.

It was cool inside the building in contrast to the heat of the streets. The thick walls and small windows had been built to keep out the weather and had done so now for three centuries.

James and Amy were escorted into their room first, and I was ushered down a corridor to an attractive single room which overlooked the little garden.

It was an unremarkable patch, consisting mainly of some rough grass and shrubs, but my eye was immediately caught by the happenings in an adjoining garden.

A long clothes-line was almost filled with flapping white sheets, and two nuns were engrossed in unpegging them and folding them very tidily and exactly. They held the corners with their arms spread wide and then advanced towards each other, as if treading some stately dance, to fold the sheets in halves, then into quarters until there was a snowy oblong which they put on a mounting pile on the grass.

In contrast to their measured ritual of folding, and their solemn black habits and veils, their faces were animated. They smiled and gossiped as they worked. It was a happy harmony of mind and body, and a joy to watch.

We were more than ready for our evening meal when the time came, and the food was delicious, a precursor of all those we enjoyed at the hotel.

Later, we took a walk round the nearest streets, mainly for James to find the way from the front of the hotel to its car park at the rear.

Although he himself would have very little time for exploring, he had hired a small Fiat, to be delivered in the morning, so that Amy and I could do so.

'Do you know,' he exclaimed when he met us later at the hotel, 'it is exactly three-quarters of a mile from the front door to the hotel car park.'

'It can't be!' protested Amy. 'It's only at the end of the garden.'

'One way streets,' replied James, holding up a finger just as the taxi driver had done. 'Always one way!'

James was picked up each morning at nine o'clock. Two other men who were attending the conference were already in the car when it arrived, and we knew we should not see James again, most days, until the evening.

Amy and I found each day falling into a very pleasant pattern. After James' departure to work, we took a stroll to one of the famous places we had been looking forward to visiting for so long.

We soon discovered that there was enough to relish in the Duomo, Santa Croce and the Uffizi, to keep us engrossed for years rather than our meagre allotment of days available. But we wandered about these lovely buildings, and many others, for about two hours each morning when, satiated with art and history, we would sit in one of the piazzas and refresh ourselves with coffee.

After that we would return to the hotel, shopping on the way at a remarkable cheese shop. Here, it seemed, all the cheeses of the world were displayed. While we waited, and wondered at the riches around us, we looked at a line which ran across one wall of the whitewashed shop. It was only a few inches from the ceiling and marked how high the water had reached during devastating floods some years earlier. The proprietor told us about this with much hand-waving and eye-rolling, and although we had no words in common we had no doubt about the horrors the citizens of Florence had endured.

We purchased warm rolls nearby and delicious downy peaches, and thus equipped for a picnic lunch we went to fetch the car.

We made for the hills usually, visiting a cousin of Amy's mother's in Fiesole on one occasion, but falling in love with Vallombrosa we often pointed the car to that delectable spot which was just as leafy on those golden September afternoons as Milton described it so long ago in *Paradise Lost*.

> *Thick as Autumnal Leaves that strow the Brooks*
> *In Vallombrosa, where th'Etrurian shades*
> *High overarch't embow'r . . .*

Under the arching trees which sheltered us from the noonday sun, we sat in companionable silence enjoying the quietness around us and the bread and cheese in our laps.

Later, bemused with Italian sunshine and beauty, we would head back to the hotel. Amy negotiated the one-way maze of streets to bring us successfully to the garage at the back of the hotel.

We walked through the shady and shaggy garden into the dim coolness, there to refresh ourselves with tea, before bathing and changing and settling down to await James's return from his labours.

I think I grew closer to Amy in those few magical days than at any other time in our long friendship. It may have been because we were alone together, in a foreign place, for most of the day, without the sort of interruption that occurs in one's home. No callers, no telephone ringing, no cooking pot needing attention, no intrusive animals interrupting our conversation or our quiet meditation.

We hardly spoke about home, although I did tell her one day, in the quiet shade of Vallombrosa, about Henry's unwelcome visit on the eve of our departure.

I was surprised at her reaction. Normally, when she hears that any man has visited me or taken me out, Amy responds with much enthusiasm, imagining that at last romance has entered my bleak spinster's life.

This time, however, she was unusually censorious of Henry's behaviour.

'Henry Mawne,' she began severely, 'has made his bed and must lie on it.'

'You sound like my mother,' I protested.

'Your mother had plenty of sense,' replied Amy. 'Really, Henry should know better than try to engage your sympathy.'

'He didn't.'

'He's chosen *two* wives,' went on Amy, 'and doesn't seem to have made either very happy. I can't feel sorry for him, and I hope you aren't.'

I reassured her on this point.

'It'll all blow over,' I said, 'once Deidre comes back.'

'But suppose she doesn't?'

'I think she will,' I said slowly.

'You don't sound very sure about it,' commented Amy. 'I should nip any advances of Henry's in the bud. I shouldn't like to see you with a broken heart.'

'A flinty old heart like mine doesn't crack very easily,' I said, and at that moment James appeared, looking remarkably buoyant for one who had been engaged in high-powered discussions on international trade and finance.

The time passed in a golden haze. Florence was still basking in the sunlight, like a contented cat, as we went by taxi to the airport.

Our luggage had grown since our arrival, as Amy and I had succumbed to temptation and bought soft Italian leather handbags, wallets and purses and a pair of glamorous shoes apiece. The range of beautiful silk scarves, which we had also acquired, would be so useful for Christmas presents we told each other, but I had no doubt that we should see them being worn by ourselves in the future.

It was raining when we alighted from the plane, and people were striding about in dripping raincoats. I was surprised to feel that somehow this was absolutely right. It was home-like, familiar and reassuring. Even the smell of wet tarmac and petrol fumes was welcoming.

James dropped me at my door, propping my luggage in the porch and promising to ring during the evening. I tried to thank him, but he brushed aside my endeavours with a great hug and a kiss.

Tibby, asleep on the stairs, opened a bleary eye, closed it again and went back to sleep.

In the kitchen a piece of paper, anchored to the table by the flour-dredger, was covered in Mrs Pringle's handwriting. It said:

Am out of Brasso. Washer gone on cold bath tap. Mouse come out from under the stairs. And went back.

See you Wednesday. M.P.

I was home all right.

4   Home Again

IT WAS good to be back.
I relished the cool air, the green countryside, my own
goods and chattels, and best of all my comfortable bed.

In those first few days of my return, I realized how much
my habitual surroundings meant to me. I looked anew upon
morning dew on the lawn, on the yellowing poplar leaves fluttering and turning in the autumn sunshine, and the bright
beads of bryony, red, orange and green, strung along the
hedgerows. I had returned with fresh eyes.

I had also returned much stronger in body. The sunshine,
the lovely food and the warm companionship of dear Amy
and James had relaxed earlier tensions, and I had thrived in
these perfect conditions.

But, even more important, was the nourishment of spirit
which would sustain me for months, and probably years, to
come. Constantly, as I went about my everyday duties, cleaning, cooking, gardening and the like, pictures came to mind; a
glimpse of nuns folding washing, a sunlit alley, a barrowload
of peaches under a striped awning, Donatello's David with his
girlish hat and curls, or the plumes of water flashing from the
fountains of Florence.

These exhilarating memories and hundreds more would, I knew, *'flash upon the inward eye'* for the rest of my life.

Mrs Pringle, when she came on Wednesday, commented on my improved appearance.

'Done you a power of good,' she informed me. 'I said to Alice Willet before you set off: "She's aged a lot since those funny turns. You could never had said she was *good-looking*, but she used to look *healthy*, but even that's gone."'

'Thanks,' I said.

'Funny how people's looks change. Mr Mawne now, he looks a real wreck since his wife left him.'

'Isn't she back yet?' I asked, feeling some alarm.

'We all reckon she's gone for good,' replied Mrs Pringle, with much satisfaction. 'He's not an easy man to live with. Still got a bit of that military business about him. He used to criticize his wife something dreadful.'

'The bedroom windows could do with a clean,' I said pointedly.

Mrs Pringle went to fetch appropriate cloths, and made her way upstairs. Her limp was unusually pronounced and her breathing unusually heavy, but I ignored these signs of umbrage and went out into the garden.

I found Mrs Pringle's news irritating. Should I have to put up with Henry's unwelcome visits? Surely he would have the sense to realize that his marital affairs were no business of mine. I was genuinely sorry for him, but saw only too well what a nuisance he could be.

And what about John Jenkins? I remembered, with misgiving, his offer to see off anyone who molested me. The thought of two middle-aged men coming to blows over a middle-aged spinster – not even good-looking – was too silly to contemplate, and I resolutely set to and attacked a riot of chickweed in the flower border.

A few days after my return from Florence I peeled September from the various calendars around the cottage and faced October. About time I sent off those Christmas parcels to New Zealand and Australia, I thought, with my annual shock.

Usually, I miss the last surface mail date, and have to cudgel my brains for something light enough to be sent by air mail. My overseas friends must be heartily sick of silk scarves and compact discs. This year I would be in time, I promised myself, and send boxes of soap, or books, or even delicacies such as Carlsbad plums.

Thus full of good intentions and armed with a shopping list, I drove into Caxley one morning and parked behind the town's premier store.

I visited the hosiery department first to stock up for the months ahead. There was so much choice it was formidable. Having made sure that I was looking at 'TIGHTS' and not 'STOCKINGS', the first hazard, I then had to find my way among the 'DENIERS'. After that, already wilting, I had to decide on 'COLOUR'. Why do hosiery manufacturers give their wares such extraordinary names? Who can tell what one can expect from 'Carribbean Sand' or 'Summer Haze'? A few leave a minute square of mica showing the contents, but short of taking the box to the door and using a magnifying glass whilst there, it is really impossible to judge.

However, I plumped for three pairs of 'Spring Hare' and three of 'Autumn Night' and then went to inspect the boxes of soap for my distant friends.

I must say, the display was magnificent and I selected six fragrant boxes for presents and for myself.

Smug with my success I chattered away to the obliging assistant about catching the surface mail for Christmas. She looked up from her wrapping with dismay.

'But they will weigh so much,' she protested. 'Why don't you buy something like handkerchiefs or scarves?'

It was rather deflating, but I rallied well.

'They've all had hankies and scarves,' I assured her. 'Besides, I shall feel really efficient catching the right post this year.'

The weather now changed. It grew chilly in the evenings and Tibby and I enjoyed a log fire.

It was sad to see summer fading. The trees had turned to varying shades of gold, and the flowers in the border were looking jaded. Soon we should get frosts which would dull their bright colours, and start the fall of leaves.

But there were compensations. My cottage was particularly snug under its thatch in cold weather. The walls were thick, the windows small by comparison with modern houses, but those men who had built it so long ago knew what downland weather could be in these exposed parts, and designed their habitations accordingly.

One October afternoon Bob Willet decided to have a bonfire of all the dead weeds, hedge clippings and some rotten wood from an ailing plum tree which he had pruned, I thought, with an unnecessarily heavy hand.

'Do that ol' tree a world of good,' he told me as I watched the smoke rising. He had a great pile of debris standing at the side of the incinerator, and forked loads into it with great vigour.

'What's the news?' I asked him. 'And where's Joe today?'

Joseph Coggs, one of my erstwhile pupils, often accompanies Bob when he comes gardening. I had made a round of gingerbread that morning with Joe in mind, but I had no doubt that Bob Willet would make inroads into my confection with the same energy that he was showing with the tending of the bonfire.

'Maud Pringle's leg's bad again on account of Miss Summers' telling her the stoves might have to be lit early.'

'Oh, that's old hat!' I said. 'Nothing new to report?'

He gave me a swift look.

'Nothing about Mrs Mawne so far. Mr Mawne goes about lookin' a bit hang-dog, but Mr Lamb said he'd squared up the account at the shop, so he's relieved, I can tell you.'

'She's bound to come back,' I said, with as much conviction as I could muster.

Bob threw a fresh forkful on to the crackling blaze. There was a pungent smell of burning ivy leaves and dried grass.

'It's a real whiff of autumn,' I said, trying to change the subject. But Bob was not to be deflected.

'They say she's sweet on some chap in Ireland. A cousin or something. I must say, there seem to be a rare lot of cousins in Ireland. I wonder why that is?'

'Well, the population's fairly small,' I said weakly, 'and they seem to have large families, so I suppose there would be a good many cousins.'

I was more shocked than I wanted Bob Willet to know about the possibility of Deidre settling for good in Ireland. Surely Henry would have enough spunk to go and fetch his wife back?

'And young Joe's been to a practice match in Caxley this afternoon. Some junior football league he was rabbiting on about. I can't see him being picked, but I give him the bus fare and wished him luck.'

'Good for you,' I said, glad to get away from the Mawnes' troubles. 'You'll have to eat his share of the gingerbread.'

'You bet I'll do that,' said Bob heartily, and threw on another forkload.

As with all village rumours, once you have heard it from one source you can be sure of hearing it from a dozen more.

It was Gerald Partridge, vicar of Fairacre, who was my next informant. He had called to give me the parish magazine and seemed content to sit and chat.

'Henry is not himself, you know,' he said sadly. 'Seems to take no interest in the church accounts or anything else at the moment. There's some talk of Deidre having an attachment at her old home. I sincerely hope it is only rumour. It would break Henry's heart to lose a second wife.'

'What's gone wrong do you think?'

The vicar looked troubled.

'Something the lawyers call "incompatability of temperament", I suspect. She's very vague in her outlook to everything, and it upsets Henry who is really a very downright sort of person.'

Tibby chose this moment to leap upon the vicar's knees. Gerald Partridge began to stroke the animal in an absentminded manner.

'Primarily, I think it's money,' he went on. 'Henry is not a rich man, and I suspect that Deidre thought that he was when she married him.'

'I must admit that I always thought that he was comfortably off.'

'He has a pension, and he has that large house Miss Parr left him. He gets a certain amount from renting out part of it, as you know, but the place really needs refurbishing, and Henry showed me some estimates for repairing the roof and rewiring the whole place, and I must say that I was appalled. I forget how much it was – I have no head for figures – but there were a great many noughts. It was quite as frightening as some of the estimates we get in for work on the church.'

'I shouldn't have thought Deidre was extravagant,' I said, remembering her somewhat dowdy clothes and the complete lack of entertaining which had been a source of complaint from other ladies in the parish.

'She bets,' said the vicar. 'On horses.'

'I'd no idea she went to the races.'

'She doesn't. She sits by the telephone and watches the races on TV, or reads the racing news in the paper. I believe a lot of people do it.'

'Well, I must say it sounds more comfortable,' I replied. The vicar looked unhappy, and rose to his feet, tipping the outraged cat on to the hearthrug.

At the door he paused.

'Poor Henry! Do be particularly nice to him, my dear, he is under great stress.'

Mrs Pringle also told me about Henry Mawne's afflictions, but with less Christian forbearance.

'They're man and wife and should keep them only unto each other like the Prayer Book says. I know she's no right to carry on in Ireland with this cousin of hers, but what's Mr Mawne been up to letting her go like that? He should be looking after her, for better or worse, like he vowed to do.'

There was no point in arguing with Mrs Pringle when she was in this militant mood, and I cravenly retreated to the garden on this occasion.

George and Isobel Annett both enquired about Henry's predicament and asked if it were true that his wife had left him.

When John Jenkins rang up that evening I was quite prepared to cut short any discussion of Henry's affairs, of which I was heartily sick.

To my surprise he made no mention of Henry, but simply told me that Uncle Sam had died suddenly, and the funeral was next week.

It was a shock. Although he was obviously frail, and I remembered vividly helping John to support the old man against the downland wind, he had seemed so alert, so energetic, and game for years to come.

'I am truly sorry, John. He was a dear, and I'm glad I met him. We had a lovely day together, didn't we?'

'You made that day for him.'

He hesitated and then said:

'I don't know how you feel about funerals. This will be a very muted affair as he had no close relatives, but –'

'I should like to come if you would like me to,' I broke in, and I heard him sigh.

'I should like it very much.'

'When is it?'

'Next Thursday at eleven. I'll pick you up soon after nine, if you really mean it.'

'Of course I do. I'll be ready.'

I put the telephone down. How nice not to hear about Henry Mawne. But how sad to think that I should not see that indomitable old man again.

As I undressed that night I thought of all the advice I had been given about my retirement.

All my friends had pointed out that I was bound to be lonely. I should wonder what to do with the empty hours before me. I should miss the hubbub of school life, the children, the companionship and so on.

In the diary, before coming upstairs, I had made a note of Uncle Sam's funeral and had observed that every day in that week, and the next, had some event to which I was committed.

Fat chance of being lonely, I thought a trifle bitterly. I had imagined myself drowsing on my new garden seat, and studying the birds and flowers around me in a blissful solitude. So far, that had been a forlorn hope. Far from being lonely I seem to have had a procession of visitors beating a path to my door like someone or other (Thoreau, was it?), who had the same trouble, and for some reason I connected with a mousetrap. I reminded myself to look up *mousetrap* in the *Oxford Book of Quotations* in the morning.

The telephone too was a mixed blessing. While it was a pleasure to hear one's friends, it always seemed to ring when one was getting down to the crossword. I recalled Amy's concern about my loneliness when I retired.

'Do *join* things,' she urged me. 'Go on nice outings with the National Trust. Caxley branch gets up some super trips, and you'd meet lots of like-minded people. And there are very good concerts and lectures at the Corn Exchange, and no end of coach parties going up to the Royal Academy exhibitions or the Barbican or the South Bank. There's no need to *vegetate*.'

Amy, and all the other well-intentioned friends, took it for granted that I should long for a plethora of people and excitements. As I climbed into bed I was reminded of a remark of Toddy's in *Helen's Babies*.

Does anyone these days read that remarkable book published at the turn of the century, decribing the traumas of a bachelor uncle left in charge of his two young nephews?

The conversation has turned to presents. Budge, the elder boy, wants everything from a goat-carriage to a catapult. Toddy, aged three, says he only wants a chocolate cigar.

'Nothing else?' asks his indulgent uncle. 'Why only a chocolate cigar?'

'Can't be bothered with lots of things,' is the sagacious reply.

I decide that I have a lot in common with Toddy, as I turn my face into the pillow.

The weather was as sad as the occasion when we set out on Thursday morning for the funeral. Rain lashed the car, the roads were awash, and every vehicle seemed to throw up a few yards of heavy spray. We spoke little on the journey. John was concentrating on his driving, and I was feeling tired and sad.

We drove straight to the church which was some half a mile from the nursing home. A verger in a black cassock showed us into a front pew. There were very few people in the other pews, but I noticed the matron of the nursing home and one or two elderly people with her, whom I guessed were friends and fellow-residents of Uncle Sam's.

His coffin lay in the aisle in the middle of the sparse congregation. It bore a simple cross of white lilies, no doubt, I thought, a tribute from the little gathering across the aisle.

It was bitterly cold, with that marrow-chilling dampness which is peculiar to old churches. I felt anxious for the old people nearby, and glad that I had put on a full-length winter coat.

The organ began to play, and the officiating priest entered with one attendant, and as we rose I noticed for the first time two magnificent flower arrangements flanking the altar. They were composed of yellow carnations shading from cream to deep bronze and formed a glowing background to the black robe of the clergyman.

The service was simple but moving. After the blessing we moved slowly outside, and talked in the shelter of the porch to the other mourners.

The rain still lashed across the countryside. The yew trees dripped, the grass in the churchyard was flattened in a cruel wind, and a vase of dahlias on one of the graves blew over, scattering vivid petals to the wind.

The undertakers had driven Uncle Sam's remains to the crematorium. Cars arrived to collect his old friends and return them to their luncheons, and John and I sought the shelter of his car.

'We need something to keep out the cold,' said John. 'Would you have any objection to eating at the place we did before, with Uncle Sam? It's nearby and we liked it, didn't we?'

I said it would be perfect, and we set off.

'Nice service,' I said. 'Cheerful, but dignified. And the flowers were lovely.'

'The nursing home did the lilies,' said John, 'so I plumped for the carnations for each side of the altar. They looked pretty good I thought.'

'Splendid,' I told him.

'Well, the old boy was a great carnation grower in his heyday, and always had some beauties in his greenhouse. "Must have one for my buttonhole each day," he used to say, "and some for a bouquet for any lady that takes my fancy."'

We had to run from the car into the shelter of the bar, where a log fire, a real one with flames, welcomed us.

'What's yours?' asked John, helping me off with my wet coat. 'And don't say orange juice! It's too dam' cold. Have something stronger today.'

And so I did.

We were due at the crematorium, for our final farewell to Sam, at two o'clock. There were even fewer people present, although the good matron was there with two or three of the hardiest residents, who must have forgone their afternoon rest to see the last of their old friend.

The service was conducted by the same young clergyman. I was much impressed by his beautiful voice and the kindness of his manner when talking to us after the ceremony.

'He'd make a splendid bishop later on,' I told John, as we drove home. 'I must make a note of his name, and look out for his progress in years to come.'

'Let's hope you're right,' said John, 'and by the way, I have news for you. I'm off to Portugal next week.'

'Lucky you! Or is it just business?'

'No, pleasure. Golf, in fact. I ran across an old school friend in town a month or two ago, and he and his brother own a villa out there.'

'It sounds marvellous.'

'They're both married with children, and they go out in turns during the school holidays. He reckons it works out quite cheaply, and they all love the country. What's more, there's a first-class golf-course nearby.'

'I didn't know you played.'

'I haven't for years, but I'm quite looking forward to it.'

'Is this villa in the Algarve?'

'No, somewhere on the west coast near Estoril. They let the villa when they're not using it, I gather. Quite a sound investment so far, Bill said.'

'It sounds so.'

By now we were close to Beech Green, and I invited John to tea. We were both tired, and I was still feeling cold. I asked John if he felt the same.

'Just a bit,' he admitted. 'Shall I light your fire?'

He got on with the job while I busied myself with the kettle and some cake.

'This is more like it,' said John when I had poured out, and the fire was burning nicely.

'A holiday will do you good,' I assured him. 'I felt fine after that week in Florence. You didn't say how long you would be away in this super villa.'

'Just the week, but I might think of taking it again if it's as splendid as Bill says.'

He looked at me speculatively.

'I thought perhaps it might be just the thing for our honeymoon one day.'

'Well, you think about it, John dear,' I said kindly, 'but count me out. More tea?'

5   The Invalid

As time passed, the pattern of my days fell into a pleasant order.

I still woke up about seven, but allowed myself the luxury of staying in bed a little longer than in my working days.

When teaching I had a rough and ready timetable of early morning routine, getting downstairs about twenty to eight, dressed for the day, and ready to feed Tibby inside and the birds outside, take in the milk, collect my school work together, eat my breakfast and clear it away, and then set off for Fairacre.

Nowadays I lingered over my toilet, Tibby's, the birds' and my breakfast, and relished the arrival of the post and paper, both of which had usually arrived, in my working days, after my departure.

I thoroughly enjoyed this easing of pressure, and when I thought of school it was usually with the happy feeling that I had no need to be there. But I still found myself looking at the clock and thinking: 'Now they should be doing arithmetic,' or 'I wonder if it's fine enough for the children to play outside at Fairacre?'

Sometimes too, on my walks, I would see something

interesting, a spray of blackberries, some hazelnuts or a particularly fascinating fungus, and would think how well it would look on the classroom nature table.

But these were only passing reminders of schooldays, and I was very content with my new and idler life.

About once a week I drove to Fairacre, chiefly to buy stamps and to purchase groceries from Mr Lamb's shop, as I had done for so many years. Always I returned with up-to-date gossip as well as my bag of groceries, so that I felt in touch with all the goings-on in Fairacre.

I was careful not to mention Henry Mawne's troubles, but Mr Lamb soon told me that Henry had gone to Ireland and no one knew when he proposed to be back.

A fresh piece of news was that Joe Coggs' mother had found a part-time job in Caxley, filling the shelves in one of the supermarkets. Mr Lamb hoped that the extra money would help to pay off some of the debts which were still outstanding at his own modest establishment.

After depositing my shopping in the car on this particular afternoon, I took a walk about the village I knew so well. There were signs of autumn everywhere. The horse-chestnut tree outside the Post Office was shedding green prickly fruits which split open on impact with the ground to disclose the glossy nuts within. Conker time was here again, and Jane Summers would have to cope with the clash of conker strings at playtime.

I went as far as the bend in the lane from which I could see Fairacre school, but went no further. It was very quiet. The children were probably listening to a story.

I did not propose to call. Once one has left a post, I think it wiser to stay away. Too often I have heard friends telling hor-

rific stories of former heads dropping in, far too frequently, to give advice or simply to see what is going on in their former domain. Nothing can be more annoying, and I intended to wait until invited to return to Fairacre school.

I liked Jane Summers. She had been to tea with me at Beech Green, and I had been invited to her house in Caxley. I suspected that I would be invited to Fairacre school's Christmas party with all the other friends of the school, and that would be an enormous pleasure.

Meanwhile, I stood and looked at the quiet little building which had been the hub of my life. As I watched, a little girl came out of the infants' room outer door, and dashed across the playground to the stone wall. Here she paused, unaware of my watching eyes, snatched a garment from the top and returned to the classroom, skipping cheerfully as she went.

I could imagine the preliminaries to this trip. Mrs Richards, probably reading a story, would see the upraised hand.

'What is it?'

'I bin and left my cardigan out the back.'

'Then go and fetch it. And be quick.'

And so the delighted escape into the playground, the retrieving of the garment, and the obedient return to the rest of the story, after the refreshing break.

It was a heartening glimpse. Obviously, things continued much as usual at Fairacre school.

Mrs Pringle told me more about the ongoing saga of Henry Mawne and his troubles.

'Do you know, he *flew* to Ireland? Costs a mint of money to fly there. Most people go on a boat, Ireland being an island. That's why it's called *Ireland*, I suppose.'

She paused, looking at me for confirmation. I felt unequal to making any explanation, and she continued her narrative.

'Alice Willet was up there when Mrs Mawne rang up. She was on that telephone for the best part of twenty minutes, and this at *midday*! No waiting for cheap-rate time. No wonder they're short of money.'

'I believe it's raining,' I said, looking out of the window.

Mrs Pringle brushed aside this pathetic attempt to change the subject, and she continued remorselessly.

'Give him his due he did pay Alice at the end of the morning, and told her not to bother to call until he sent word. He went off that afternoon to Bristol, I think it was.'

She picked up a saucepan from the draining board and scrutinized it closely.

'What's been in here?'

'Only milk.'

'I'd best give it a proper do. Have you had a go at it?'

'Yes. Just before you came. What's wrong with it?'

'It's dirty. Give you germane poisoning, as like as not.'

Mrs Pringle's use of 'germane' instead of, I imagine, 'pto-maine', so intrigued me that my annoyance vanished. So often she gets a word half right, which makes it all the more potent. For instance, I have heard her refer to the slight stroke I suffered as 'Miss Read's inability', instead of 'her disability'.

However, with her opinion of my capabilities, perhaps 'inability' is nearer the mark.

As I drove her home after her ministrations, she told me a little more about Mrs Coggs' new duties at the supermarket.

'She has to be there from four till seven, so Joe gets the meal.'

'Can't that wretched Arthur get the children's meal? Don't tell me he's in work.'

'No. He's inside again. Shoplifting this time. Fairacre's quite peaceful without him.'

'Do you mean that Joe actually cooks a meal, or does his mother leave things ready?'

I had visions of overturned boiling saucepans, frying-pans on fire, and the Coggs children being rushed to Caxley hospital.

'You know how they live,' said Mrs Pringle sourly. 'She leaves a loaf of bread out and the jam pot, and that's it. Though I did hear as Joe heated up a tin of soup for 'em one cold day. He forgot to turn off the gas, but luckily their neighbour looked in, so all was well.'

I did not find this very reassuring, and returned home after depositing my companion, with grave misgivings about the safety of the junior members of the Coggs family during their mother's working hours.

But what could I do about it? Mighty little, I told myself sadly, turning into my drive.

*

I spent that evening at Amy's. James was away and she asked me to keep her company.

We sat watching a very old film in what someone once called 'nostalgic black and white' and thoroughly enjoyed it.

'I wonder why,' commented Amy at one stage when the heroine was crying copiously, 'women in films never have a handkerchief and have to be given one by the leading man? I suppose the film-makers think it is touching, but does any woman go out without a handkerchief? I doubt it.'

'You told me once,' I reminded her, 'of two sisters who used to go out with one hanky between them, frequently asking: "Have you got *the handkerchief*?"'

'That's absolutely true,' Amy assured me. 'By the way, I heard from Lucy Colegate. She's got her sister staying with her. She's just lost her husband.'

'What, Lucy? She's always losing husbands.'

'Now, don't be catty, dear. I know you and Lucy don't see eye to eye, but I quite like her. And it's the sister who has lost the husband. Lucy says she's quite numb with grief.'

'Poor woman. It must be absolutely devastating to lose one's other half. Like having a leg off. An awful amputation.'

Amy nodded.

'I can't bear to think how I'd feel if James died. As you say, I suppose one would just feel half a person.'

'Only for a time surely,' I comforted her. It was unusual to see Amy in such a sad mood. Perhaps the black and white weepie we had been watching had something to do with it. In the garden too the rain was tossing the trees in a dismal fashion.

'Time the Great Healer, and all that?' queried Amy.

'That's right. After a bit you would be bound to start again, getting interested in all sorts of things, doing a bit of travelling, visiting friends. And so on,' I ended weakly.

'Maybe,' said Amy, not sounding very sure. 'I suppose one would just have to find comfort in Little Things, as the agony aunts tell us in the women's magazines.'

'Such as?'

'Well, one suggestion was that you should read all the old love letters. Personally, I can't imagine any more upsetting activity, but I suppose some women might be comforted.'

'Have you still got James' love letters?'

'No. I threw them away years ago. We were moving all over the place, and the less luggage one had the better.'

I felt that this was the robust response which one expected of Amy.

'I think Little Things like *no snoring*,' said Amy, becoming more animated, 'might be some comfort. And not having any shirts to iron. I must say that I should find that of considerable consolation in the midst of my sorrow.'

'You are a very flippant woman,' I said severely.

'And a hungry one,' said Amy rising. 'It's all this emotion. Come and have some supper in the kitchen.'

So we did.

John Jenkins had rung me before his departure to Portugal, and had also sent a pretty view of some gardens in Estoril with the sea in the background, of that peculiarly hard blue which all seaside postcards seem to show, whether of the Isle of Wight or Amalfi.

He was expected back on Saturday, and the final line of his postcard read:

'Will ring when I return. Love, John.'

The last two words, I felt sure, had been read with great

interest by the Beech Green postman, but I was not particularly perturbed.

I half expected a telephone call during Saturday evening,
but guessed that his flight might have been held up. No doubt
I should hear tomorrow, I thought, as I went to bed.

But Sunday brought no call, and I assumed that he had
stayed on in Portugal. It did occur to me in the early evening
that I might ring his home, but George and Isobel Annett
called in after evensong, and I thought no more of the matter.

On Monday morning I needed extra milk, and walked along
to the obliging Beech Green shop to buy a pint. There were
several people there, including Jessie, surname unknown to
me, who was John's domestic help.

'Poor Mr Jenkins,' she said to me, as I stood waiting to pay
for my milk. 'Isn't it a shame?'

Of course, by this time I had John in a Portuguese hospital
with multiple injuries, and unable to speak a word of the
language. Alternatively, he could be in the wreckage of an
aeroplane at sea, with the rest of his fellow passengers.

'The doctor's with him now,' continued Jessie, hoisting
an enormous hold-all from the floor. 'I shall look in later
on.'

'But what's the matter? What's happened?'

'He was ill on the flight and went straight to bed on Saturday
night. Been there ever since.'

She staggered out with her burden, and I left soon after.

Within half an hour, I walked into John's house bearing a
few things which I thought might be acceptable to an invalid.

The doctor had gone, and the place was very quiet. I called
up the stairs.

'Come up,' said a weak voice.

He sat in bed looking thoroughly wretched, propped against

his pillows. I was secretly shocked at his appearance. His smile, however, was welcoming.

'I'm so sorry I didn't ring, but we were held up for hours at the airport. It was two o'clock in the morning when I crawled into this bed, and I've been here ever since.'

'What is it? Shouldn't you be in hospital?'

'I didn't ring the doctor until this morning. Can't worry the poor devil on a Sunday.'

I thought privately that this was being far too altruistic. If I had been as ill as John obviously was, I should have got the doctor whatever the day of the week. This patient was obviously of far nobler stuff than I was.

'What did he say it was?'

'Some bug which affects you rather like the malaria one. High temperature, shaking, nausea, all that.'

'When did it start? In Portugal?'

'I felt lousy on the plane. Some fly had bitten me earlier in the day, and it itched like mad. Doctor seems to think that started it. Anyway by the time I got home I was only fit for bed and quarts of water.'

'What can I do?'

'Nothing. Just stay and talk. Jessie is coming in every morning and evening, and she takes my sheets and pyjamas. I get soaked every few hours. With *sweat*, I hasten to add.'

I remembered Jessie's burden and felt guilty.

'I could wash some things for you.'

'I can't think what the neighbours would say if they saw my pyjamas blowing on your washing line.'

'To hell with the neighbours!'

John laughed. It was a wheezy laugh, and a weak one, but good to hear.

'That's my girl! But don't worry. Jessie's got a tumble drier, and she's taken everything at the moment.'

'Can I get you a drink?'

I made for a jug of orange juice standing nearby, but he grimaced.

'What I'd really like is a great mug of tea,' he said.

I went to get it, and when I returned he was lying back with his eyes shut. It was alarming, and he must have sensed my concern for he sat up again and spoke cheerfully.

'You could do something for me if you happen to be going to Caxley today.'

'I'm definitely going to Caxley today.'

'Well, could you get my prescription made up? And dare I ask you to buy me some more pyjamas? I'm running out of them pretty fast.'

'Of course. What size?'

He told me, and added:

'Three pairs, I should think. Any sort.'

I studied the pair he was wearing. They were the traditional blue and white striped things, probably made of winceyette. They reminded me of my father's night attire.

'Like those?'

'Not necessarily. Thinner, I think. I've got some polka-dot ones which Jessie's just taken away. It's a pity you didn't come when I was wearing them. I look like Noel Coward.'

'I'll take your word for it. I think I'd better get drip-dry ones to save Jessie some work.'

We sipped our tea in companionable silence for a few minutes. I felt very uneasy about him.

'Did the doctor mention hospital? I don't like the idea of you being alone. What about a nurse?'

'If you're offering, I can't think of anything nicer.'

'I'm the world's worst nurse,' I told him.

'This bug I've got gives you a pretty foul time for a week or two, but according to the quack it runs a predictable course and all one can do is to sweat it out and drink pints of liquid. The temperature drops after a bit, and apart from feeling like a wet rag one survives eventually.'

'But should you be alone? What about getting to the loo or having to fetch something from downstairs?'

'My dear love, and I mean that,' he said, suddenly earnest. 'I can get to the loo. I've even had a shower or two. I'm not eating, and the doc says that's OK as long as I *drink*. So I'm quite all right, and there's not a thing I need. Except your company, of course.'

I collected the mugs and stood looking at him.

'If Jessie's coming night and morning, I'll come and get your liquid lunch each day, and see what you need.'

He had a telephone by the bed, and I nodded to it.

'And *any* time, do ring. I'll come like a shot. You know that.'

'Suppose it is in the middle of the night? What would the neighbours say?' he laughed.

'You know what I think about the neighbours! Now I'm off to Caxley. Anything else you want?'

'You know what I want.'

I bent to give him a farewell kiss. His forehead was wet with sweat.

'You're terribly *dank*!'

'That's a fine thing to say to an invalid. You make me sound like a dungeon.'

'What you need,' I told him, 'is a few hours' sleep.'

'Maybe you're right.'

He was already slipping down the bed as I departed on my mission to Caxley.

*

I parked behind the same shop where I had recently bought
tights and boxes of soap.

The men's department was virtually unknown to me, and
seemed very quiet and austere compared with the toiletries and
haberdashery departments I usually frequented.

There was only one other customer in there, a man
absorbed in turning over piles of pants and discussing with
the shop assistant the merits of various weights of garment.

An elderly man hurried to serve me. He had a pink and
white face, white hair and moustache, and half-glasses. He reminded me of an old gentleman who used to keep our local
sweet shop when I was a child.

I explained my needs, and he held before me an oblong package wrapped in shiny cellophane, just as the sweet-shop owner

had been wont to hold out a flat dish of Everton toffee, complete with a small hammer for breaking it up, so many years ago.

He slipped the contents out of the bag and displayed the pyjama jacket. It was of some satin-like crimson material with black frogging across it. It reminded me of the sort of costume a Ruritanian prince used to wear in musical comedies in the 1920s. I could not see John in this confection.

'I think something *quieter*,' I said. He turned to the shelves and added three more packets to the first.

These were certainly more normal, the sort of uninspired garment sported that morning by the invalid. They also looked as though they would take hours to dry, even in Jessie's tumble drier.

'Have you got any non-iron pyjamas?' I asked, turning over the heavy ones before me.

'Hello,' said someone beside me. It was my former assistant at Fairacre school, Mrs Richards.

'What are you doing playing truant on a Monday?' I said, secretly rather taken aback in the midst of my male shopping.

'Half term,' she said succinctly.

'Of course. My goodness, it'll soon be November.'

She was eyeing the pile of pyjamas with considerable interest. I supposed resignedly that news of my purchases would soon be known to Fairacre. Ah, well!

'Getting Christmas presents already?' she hazarded.

'That's right,' I lied.

'Now these,' said my assistant returning, 'are our usual nylon sort. We sell a lot of these, particularly for summer wear.'

I looked at them. They were cold and slippery. They looked as though they would be horribly chilly for a feverish body. Possibly *dank* too after an hour's wear, I decided.

'Well, I'll leave you to it,' said Mrs Richards. 'I'm looking for a larger belt for Wayne.'

'You feed him too well,' I responded, before turning back to my task.

'Or these,' added my nice old gentleman, drawing out some light-weight pyjamas in a rather nice grey and white Paisley pattern. They felt warm but thin.

'A very nice crêpe,' enthused the man. 'Just come in. Fully washable, drip-dry and thoroughly approved by the medical profession.'

That clinched it.

'I'll take three pairs,' I said, getting out my cheque book.

6   Back To School

THE PATIENT made steady progress. Jessie went in morning and evening, and I cooked his midday meal, such as it was. For the first few days he only wanted liquids, but quite soon came the great day when he clamoured for bacon and eggs.

He had lost weight and tired easily, but the fever had gone after a week or two, and the doctor pronounced him fit soon after that.

I ceased my regular midday ministrations when he insisted that he could cope again, and perhaps it was as well that I was able to do so, for I had a surprising telephone call from the local education office one foggy November morning.

'Miss Read?'

'Speaking.'

'Francis Hannen here.'

He was the local education officer, a cheerful fellow who had held the post for a couple of years now. What could he want?

'We wondered if you could help us out.'

'In what way?'

'Miss Summers has been smitten with the prevailing flu

bug, but it has given her acute laryngitis, and she is speechless.'

'Poor soul! What an affliction for a school mistress.'

'It is indeed. Well, we've rung one or two ex-teachers on our list, but they are either in the same boat, or away, and I hardly liked to bother you when you are so recently retired, but –'

His voice faded away.

'How long for?'

'The doctor insists on a week, maybe longer.'

I mentally checked my engagements for the week. It was Friday today. That would give me time over the weekend to collect my wits and a few teaching aids. John Jenkins was now able to cope without help from me, and only a shopping trip with Amy lay ahead on Tuesday.

'Of course I'll stand in.'

There was a gusty sigh.

'Marvellous! Miss Summers will be so relieved. Her sister is with her at the moment, so I'll ring and tell her straight away. A thousand thanks. I'm sure the children will be thrilled to have you back.'

I was not so sure about it, but with mutual well-wishing we rang off.

Over the weekend I did a certain amount of telephoning myself. First, of course, to Miss Summers' house where I had news of the invalid from her sister.

'She seems a little better. Temperature down a trifle, and the throat not so sore, but not a sound comes from her. The house is remarkably quiet, and I find myself whispering to Jane. It's quite uncanny.'

Then to Amy to postpone the shopping trip, and then to Mr Lamb at Fairacre asking him to pass a message to Mrs Pringle about her usual Wednesday visit.

That evening she rang me, obviously delighted to be among the first with my dramatic news.

'It'll be quite like old times,' she said with such gusto that it sounded welcoming. This was a pleasant surprise, until she added:

'I'll come a bit earlier each morning while you're at the school. There's always more to clear up.'

'Thank you, Mrs Pringle,' I replied, hoping it sounded as sarcastic as I meant it to be, but she was not abashed.

'And I'll be at your place as usual Wednesday afternoon, catching the Caxley.'

'The Caxley' in this instance meant the Caxley bus. Sometimes 'The Caxley' means the *Caxley Chronicle*, as in 'I read it in the *Caxley*, so I know it's true.' The local inhabitants of these parts are loyal readers.

I also rang John to tell him where I would be the following week. There was no need to of course, I told myself, but it seemed the civil thing to do after our extra close ties recently.

He sounded aggrieved.

'Surely you're not tying yourself up with *teaching*, all over again?' His voice was querulous. 'I hoped I could bob in now and again, now that I'm back on my feet.'

I bit back the sharp retort I should like to have made, and as I put down the receiver reminded myself that he was still convalescent.

Men, I thought disgustedly, are selfish to the core.

I set out on Monday morning with mixed feelings. Part of me welcomed this return to my old pastures, but I also felt remarkably nervous.

Several children were already running about in the playground, and they rushed to the car as I got out.

'You going to teach us again?'

'Just for a week,' I replied.

'Will Miss Summers be back then?'

'Is she really ill?'

'Is she in hospital?'

'She learns us lovely.'

'Lovelily,' I said automatically, lifting my case from the car. 'Beautifully, I mean.'

I was back sure enough.

The familiar school smell greeted me as I crossed the threshold, accompanied by my vociferous companions. It was a compound of coke fumes from the welcome tortoise stoves, disinfectant, which Mrs Pringle puts in the water to wash the lobby floor, and the general odour of an old building. It was wonderfully exhilarating, and I felt at home at once. I was surprised not to see Mrs Pringle, but a note on my desk explained all.

'Off to Caxley on the early bus. See you dinner time.'
    M. Pringle

Mrs Richards had not yet arrived. I banished the children to the playground, while I surveyed my old surroundings.

Basically, it was much as usual, but there were several innovations. For one thing, the ancient long desk that had stood at the side of the room for many years, had now gone. It had been a useful piece of furniture. The children put their lunch packets and fruit in season there, plums and apples from their gardens, or blackberries and hazelnuts collected on the way to school.

Toys, books and other treasures from home rested there, and at this time of year long strings of conkers festooned its battered top. I missed it. It was a relic of the past.

There was a very efficient-looking shelf of nature pamphlets which was new to me, and the framed pictures had been changed from such old friends as *The Light of the World* by Holman Hunt (so useful as a mirror with its dark background) and *The Angelus*, to modern prints of the French Impressionists. I had to admit that they added lightness and charm to the walls, and remembered that the office had urged us to take advantage of the service of supplying pictures which could be borrowed for a month or more.

I unlocked the desk and took out the register. Something seemed strange about the desk, and then I realized that the ancient Victorian inkstand with its two cut-glass ink-wells, one for blue ink and one for red, was no longer in place.

The heavy object, with its great curved brass handle, had vanished, and although I had never used the thing, relying, as no doubt Jane Summers did, on two fountain pens for the marking of the register, I felt a pang of loss.

At that moment Mrs Richards arrived and greeted me with a smacking kiss. Half a dozen children who had come in with her, despite my express order for them to stay outside, were entranced by this display of affection.

The great wall clock, mercifully still in its accustomed place, stood at ten to nine. Joseph Coggs burst into the room and stood transfixed. A slow smile spread across his gypsy face and he took a deep happy breath.

'Can I ring the bell?' he said, as he had said so often to me.

I nodded assent. School had begun.

By the time the dinner lady arrived bearing shepherd's pie and cabbage, with bright yellow trifle for pudding, I felt that I had been back for weeks.

The dinner lady was as welcoming as the children had been,

and even Mrs Pringle, when she arrived to wash up, managed a small smile.

'Got Fred in bed again,' she announced. 'Same old chest trouble, wheezing like a harmonium. I popped in to get his subscription made up at Boots.'

I expressed my sympathy with the invalid, and told her about Jane Summers' progress.

'Well, I only hope she don't try to get back too soon. Mind you, she's bound to be worried with someone else muddling along. She's very tidy herself. Everything in apple-pie order here *now*.'

I did not care for the emphasis on the last word, but said nothing.

'You looked in the map cupboard?' she enquired. 'It's a sight for sore eyes. All them maps tidied up neat and labelled, and none of that mess of raffia and old plimsolls as used to be there encouraging the mice.'

'Good!' I said briskly, and walked away before I received any more broadsides. Reluctantly Mrs Pringle returned to her labours, and I set about preparing for the afternoon's work.

Driving home soon after four o'clock, I was alarmed at the tiredness which overcame me. I put the car away and put on the kettle. I lit the fire, and was thankful to sit in my comfortable armchair a few minutes later and to sip my steaming tea.

I reviewed the day. It had been interesting to see the changes my successor had made. She was certainly efficient and up to date, and from the remarks of the children she was obviously well liked. I liked her myself, appreciating her brisk cheerfulness and energy. It seemed that even Mrs Pringle approved, and that certainly was something.

This glimpse into my old world had done a great deal to confirm that I had been right to go when I did. It was plain that I just did not have the physical strength needed for sustained and energetic teaching. And what about my mental attitude, I wondered? Was I really forward-looking? Did I relish going on refresher courses, studying new methods of teaching various subjects, or even attending local educational meetings? The honest answer was a resounding 'No', and had been for more years than I cared to contemplate.

Not that I had been completely inactive, I consoled myself, but I had to admit that I had never been thrilled with the idea of leaving my fireside on a bleak winter's evening to listen to someone telling me how to improve my methods of teaching reading, for instance. In most cases, I well remember, the advice was 'to let the child come to reading when ready' and 'to provide reading matter well within the child's comprehension.'

I could think of a number of erstwhile pupils who would *never* have been ready to come to reading without coercion on my part, and a great many more whose reading matter would have been only comics if left to their own devices. Years of teaching had shown me that for every child who takes to reading like a duck to water and needs no help at all, there are half a dozen or so who need sustained daily teaching in the art, and a very hard slog it is for teacher and pupil alike.

I had done my duty for all those years to the best of my ability, and with many failings, but the pupils now there were getting a better education than I had been able to give them in the year or two before I left. I went to wash my tea cup, full of goodwill to Jane Summers and her little flock.

The next day the vicar called at the school and took prayers. Afterwards he told the children how lucky they were to have me back with them. Especially, he added, as I had not been too well myself.

This, I knew, would be related by my pupils to their parents with dramatic effect, so that Fairacre would assume that I was at death's door, and in no shape to take over from Jane Summers, even temporarily. However, there was nothing I could do about it but smile at the kindly vicar, and thank him for coming.

The second day passed more easily than the first, and I had time to notice how well the new families had settled. A Housing Trust, of which Amy's husband James was one of the directors, now owned several new houses in Fairacre, and the children of primary school age were now pupils at Fairacre school. The coming of these children had solved a problem which had beset the village for some years.

As numbers fell it had looked as if the school would have to close. The village, and I in particular, owed a great deal to the

Trust and the families they sponsored. Fairacre school looked safe for years to come.

It was such a mild afternoon for November that I decided to take the children for a nature walk, and Mrs Richards joined us with the infants' class.

It was quite like old times tripping along the village street towards the downs. I was really indulging myself, for I had always enjoyed these excursions from the confines of the classroom, and it did one's heart good to see the boisterous spirits of the children as they relished their freedom in the bracing downland air.

Of course, there was not the same natural bounty to be had as a nature walk in the summer. Then we would return with such treasures as brier roses, honeysuckle or cranesbill. We might even find an empty nest whose function was now past, and convey its miracle of woven grass, moss and feathers to the nature table at school.

Nevertheless, there was still treasure to be found such as berries from the wayfaring-tree and hips and haws. Someone found a snail's shell, another found a flint broken in half so that a granular silicic deposit glittered in the light.

We toiled up the grassy slopes until we were high above the village. It was too wet to sit on the grass, but we stood for a few minutes to get our breath back, and to admire the view spread out below us.

There was not much activity to be seen in Fairacre. Washing was blowing in some gardens. Mr Roberts' Friesian cows made a moving pattern of black and white as they grazed, and a red tractor moved up and down a nearby field as bright as a ladybird.

We returned to the village carrying our gleanings. John Todd had discovered a Coca-Cola tin among the natural beauties, and was prevailed upon to deposit it in the bin provided outside the Post Office, which he did under protest. The rest of the garnering was displayed on the nature table, and very attractive it looked.

By common consent I read a story from *The Heroes* by Charles Kingsley, which Jane Summers, I was told, had just started with them, and all was delightfully peaceful.

I was conscious of more attention being given to the newly decorated nature table than Theseus's exploits, but who could blame them?

That afternoon I arrived home in much better shape. Downland air and exercise? Or simply getting back into my old groove? It was impossible to say.

On Wednesday afternoon I arrived home in time to share a pot of tea with Mrs Pringle before running her home. As always, the place was immaculate. Mrs Pringle was a first-class worker, and it was worth putting up with her tales of woe.

After getting up to date with the state of her ulcerated leg (no better, and the doctor worse than useless), we proceeded to the reaction of the inhabitants of Fairacre to my present duties at the school.

'Great shame about Miss Summers everyone agrees. She was getting them children on a real treat. *And* they had to behave!'

I agreed that all seemed to be going swimmingly.

'Mr Lamb reckons that she's as good as a headmaster. Keeps them down to work. None of this skiving off for so-called nature walks.'

I ignored this side-swipe by offering the plate of scones.

'Not for me. I'm losing weight.'

I looked at the clock, and Mrs Pringle took the hint, rising with much effort and going to fetch her coat.

'Well, at least it's only for a week we all tell each other. Can't do much harm in that time.'

On the way home, she changed the subject of my inadequacies to the troubles of her niece Minnie Pringle, who lived at nearby Springbourne with a most unsatisfactory husband, named Ern, and a gaggle of unkempt children.

'She's looking for another cleaning job. Ern's keeping her short of money.'

I was instantly on my guard. I have suffered from Minnie's domestic methods on several occasions.

'Why is Ern keeping her short?'

'Hard up, I suppose,' said Mrs Pringle. 'I told her flat that she's not to worry you. Lord knows there's enough to do in your place each week, but I can cope without her muddling about.'

'Thank you, Mrs Pringle,' I said humbly.

Bob Willet appeared one evening that week, bearing some fine eating apples.

'They're good keepers,' he assured me. 'Lovely flavour.'

I complimented him on such fine specimens, but he halted me in mid-flow of thanks and admiration.

'They're my neighbour's. New chap's just moved in. Nice enough, but don't know a thing about gardening. A townee, you see.'

'He'll learn, I expect.'

Bob looked gloomy, and puffed out his walrus moustache in a great sigh.

'I doubt it. Do you know he's bin and dug up a great patch by the back door for what he calls "a car-port". It was the only bit of ground there as grew a decent onion. Enough to break your heart. I told him so when the cement-mixer arrived. D'you know what he said?'

'What?'

'He said there was plenty of onions in the shops! The shops!' added Bob in disgust.

'He may learn.'

'Never! He just don't have no interest in living things. He drives up to London every day. I'm fair sorry for him really. I offered to prune his fruit trees when the time comes. He was polite, and all that, but it's plain he don't care a button for them fine old apples he's got there. Fred Pringle's granny used to get first prize at the Horticultural Show every year with them russets. Still, to speak fair, he did say he'd advise me about investing my money.'

Bob gave an ironic laugh.

'I told him there was not much hope of that. Funny thing is

though, I can't help liking the chap. He's so strange, you know. Like a foreigner.'

He departed soon after, leaving me to ponder on his words.

'Like a foreigner' Bob had said, and, of course, he was. Bob Willet was a countryman as had all his forbears been. If you plucked Bob from his green garden and dropped him in the arid wastes of a city he would wither as surely as a plant in the same circumstances.

I remember him once saying to me: 'When I gets twizzled up inside, I goes down to the vegetable plot and earths up the celery.'

It was this close affinity with the land that gave him his strength and sanity. That's what people missed in the vast urban places where most had to live and work.

It went against Bob's grain to see that cement laid over the best onion bed in Fairacre. It flew in the face of nature, and in his bones Bob rebelled.

Of course, even in my time things had changed in Fairacre and Beech Green. Almost every household now had a car, if not two. Ease of travel meant that the breadwinner could leave his renovated country cottage and take the nearby motorway to work, leaving the village practically deserted during the day.

When I first took up my headship at Fairacre school the village was an agricultural settlement, as it had been for centuries. The majority of the people worked for the three or four farmers and landowners as farm labourers, carters, ploughmen, shepherds and so on. There were still one or two farm horses in regular use.

Over the years farming had changed. A farmer with only

two or three men could cope with the work, thanks to modern machinery and the change in farming methods.

The cottages were bought by strangers and refurbished. These were the people who were commuters, arriving home too late, and probably too tired, to do much gardening or to take an interest in village affairs.

No wonder Bob Willet looked upon them as strangers. But how good to know that he 'couldn't help liking the chap!'

I was still thinking about the changes to village life as I chopped up Tibby's supper. Soon all the old people who remembered that way of life would be gone, and what a pity it was that so much valuable social history will have vanished.

Perhaps everyone should keep a diary, I thought, putting down the saucer, or even keep the monthly parish magazine for future generations to study.

I recalled the tales that Dolly Clare had told me about her way of life as a child in this very cottage that I had inherited. Tales of mammoth washdays, fetching water from the well, clear-starching and goffering irons. Stories about gleaning, grinding the corn, using flails to separate the chaff from the grain, about country remedies and the use of herbs. Why had I not written it all down?

Alice Willet, Bob and Mrs Pringle too often dropped a remark which gave a fascinating glimpse of life as it had been so recently, and which was now gone.

Perhaps I should start myself? Or better still, get a tape recorder and get Bob and the other old people to record their memories. Maybe I would start a diary of my own as well in the New Year. After all, what pleasure I had enjoyed from reading other people's diaries, Francis Kilvert's, for example, or dear Parson Woodforde whose diary lay on my bedside table and took me into rural Norfolk in the eighteenth century whenever I cared to accompany him.

Well, I must think about it, and also urge others to keep a diary. What success would I have in my encouragement of others, I wondered?

I recalled that I had once urged Bob to write down his memories, and his reply had been: 'I've no fist for writing. It's only the gentry as has the time and the learning to put pen to paper.'

Nevertheless, I could try again, and a tape recorder could be my ally.

Full of such plans for the future, I went early to bed and slept soundly.

7 Disturbances

I HAD KEPT in touch with Jane Summers throughout my time at school. Her sister had answered for the first few days, but on the Thursday Jane spoke herself.

She sounded hoarse, but very cheerful, and said that she had been pronounced fit for work on Monday. She was profuse in her thanks before we rang off.

I was mightily relieved to know that I should not be needed. It had been an interesting break, but I should be glad to return to my peaceful retirement.

But was it peaceful, I asked myself? I remembered the pipe-dreams I had indulged in when I said farewell to Fairacre, the leisurely walks, the lounging on my new seat in the garden, the settling down to read in the afternoon at a time when I should normally have been teaching. Somehow such bliss had been interrupted by events.

I pondered on the problems of John Jenkins and Henry Mawne which had arisen, and those presented by Mrs Pringle every Wednesday, and possibly Minnie Pringle in the future. I remembered George Annett's increasing pressure to help with church activities, and even dear old Amy's well-meant efforts to marry me off. It dawned on me suddenly that almost all my worries came from *people*. Left alone I should be much more content in my retirement.

I looked through the window at the November scene. A few chaffinches foraged below the bird table. Two rooks squabbled over a bread crust. Otherwise all was silent and peaceful.

The bare branches of the copper beech and lime trees dripped gently after the night's rain. The grey trunks, so reminiscent of an elephant's hide, were streaked with moisture. Nothing moved, nothing could be heard.

Here was peace indeed, I told myself. If only people would leave me quite alone to relish my solitude then I should certainly enjoy that peaceful retirement which so many kind souls had wished for me.

> *Where every prospect pleases*
> *And only man is vile.*

Whoever wrote that knew his onions, I thought, turning from the window.

*

On Friday I said farewell to Fairacre school with a light heart. The vicar had called first thing to take prayers as usual and to thank me for my efforts during the week. He was so genuinely sorry to see me go that I felt quite guilty.

'But you will come again?' he pleaded earnestly. 'Should anything like this crop up again, I mean?'

I pointed out that it was the office's decision, and that I had only been asked this time because the flu bug had cut down the number of local supply teachers.

'Of course, of course, I do realize that, but it is so pleasant to see you here when I call in. Will you be coming to the Christmas festivities?'

I said that I hoped to be invited, and he left slightly comforted.

The children were refreshingly off-hand about my departure, saying how nice it would be to see Miss Summers again, and go on with the story she was telling them 'out of her head' about a Roman soldier who used to live in a camp up on the downs.

This was the first I had heard of Jane Summers' imaginative skills and I was full of admiration for her, and very conscious of my own limitations.

I did my best by leaving the sweet-tin replenished to the top, and by leaving a handsome pink cyclamen for their headmistress as a welcome-back present.

Driving home I felt that I had done my poor best for the week, but trusted that now I could resume my leisurely existence.

During the evening John Jenkins rang sounding his usual cheerful self.

'I've been given a brace of pheasants, just right for cooking. Come and help me eat one of them on Sunday.'

I said that I should be delighted, and was he roasting them?

'No, no,' he said, sounding rather pleased with himself. 'I'm cooking them in a casserole with apple. I warn you, it's the first time I've tried the recipe. Are you still on?'

I assured him that I was and promised to be there just after noon.

Obviously he was now back to normal, and relishing one of his favourite hobbies. He was an adventurous cook, and I admired his willingness to experiment. I was still thinking how good it would be to see him again, when someone knocked at the door, and on opening it, I was surprised to see George Annett.

'Hello! Do come in.'

'Mustn't stop. I'm supposed to be in Caxley.'

This was typical of George Annett. He never seemed to stay in one place for long, but flitted from here to there like a bird on the wing. A restless fellow, I had always thought, but on this occasion he actually sat down, and I took an armchair opposite him.

He began to rummage in a large envelope, and took out a small pamphlet.

'Now, this,' he said in a schoolmasterish way, 'is the pamphlet we leave in Beech Green church for visitors to peruse. They are supposed to buy it, but more often than not they simply walk around the church with it, noting the things mentioned, and then dump it back on the table. And pretty grubby some of these get, I can tell you.'

I agreed that such conduct was highly reprehensible, but wondered privately what I was being asked to do about it.

I soon learned.

'The thing is that this little history is now rather out of date, and I wondered if you could possibly find time to up-date it. Now you've retired, I mean. I expect you find time rather heavy on your hands and it's the sort of thing you'd do so well. Have a look anyway. For instance, some of the memorial tablets are not mentioned, and the new stained-glass window should have a note. I'd give you a hand of course, when I have a spare minute.'

He glanced at the clock, gave a cry, and leapt to his feet.

'Must fly. Shall I leave it on the table?'

Within two minutes he had gone.

Peace came surging back as I resumed my seat and had a preliminary look at the pamphlet. So this was the great work I was supposed to rejuvenate! Now I was retired, as George had said, with 'Time heavy on my hands' (a chance would be a fine thing!), here was something to console me.

I studied it more closely. Penned originally by a hand long dead, it was a dispiriting account of the church's attractions. The print was small, the paragraphs immensely long and the style pedantic. I wondered who could have been the author. I told myself that I must be particularly careful to keep my opinions to myself. It was bound to have been the work of some aunt, uncle or grandparent of a neighbour in Beech Green. No doubt any alteration of mine would be construed as vandalizing Holy Writ, but I agreed with George Annett that a new edition was needed.

The first thing to do, I decided, was to scrap the very poor photograph on the front. It must have been taken on a foggy day one winter's afternoon some fifty or more years ago, for it was indistinct and the trees, which now towered above the roof, were shown as mere saplings in the picture. Perhaps a nice bold wood-cut, or a really artistic modern photograph would liven things up?

At this juncture the telephone rang again, and it was Amy enquiring if I were still alive after a week's teaching.

'Just about,' I told her, and added that it had brought home to me the wisdom of retiring when I did.

She expressed her sympathy.

'What I really rang about was a recipe for gooseberry fool. Have you got such a thing? I seem to have half a dozen bottles of gooseberries in my store cupboard, and I thought I'd have a stab at gooseberry fool. The only thing is I believe you have to make a proper egg custard and I'm not sure if one uses the whites.'

'Don't burden yourself with egg-yolks, double saucepans and all that lark,' I told her. 'You'll have a sink full of dirty crocks and probably the custard won't have thickened. I'll post you my recipe unless you're coming over, but just use dear old Bird's custard and add plenty of cream.'

'Thanks for the tip,' said Amy. 'I'll pop over tomorrow evening if that suits you.'

'Perfectly.'

'And who were you buying three pairs of pyjamas for?'

'Never end your sentence with a preposition,' I countered, playing for time.

Now how on earth could Amy, at Bent, ten miles away, have heard of my purchases? I had half expected to have a comment or two from my Fairacre friends, but obviously Mrs Richards' momentary interest in the shop had passed, and she had made no comments. I was, as always, intrigued by this dissemination of knowledge.

'Don't be so pedantic,' said Amy. 'There's such a thing as common usage these days.'

'I bought them for John when he was ill,' I said. 'But how on earth did you know?'

'Charlie, who helps us in the garden when it suits him, was buying his winter pants at the same time.'

I remembered the only other customer in the men's department who had seemed totally absorbed in choosing his winter underwear. Ah well! That was explained.

'And how is John?' she went on.

'Fine now. He's giving me Sunday lunch. Pheasant cooked with apples.'

'Lovely!' enthused Amy, but whether she was so delighted at the thought of pheasant cooked with apples or my approaching visit to John Jenkins, was anyone's guess.

'See you tomorrow then,' she cried, and rang off.

Sunday dawned so bright and fair it might have been May rather than November. Only the bare trees outlined against a tender blue sky, and the shagginess of the lawn showed the true time of year. But the air was warm, the birds sang, and there was even a drowsy bumble-bee trying to get in at the window.

My spirits rose to match the sparkling day as, dressed in my best and bearing a pot of honey for my host's delectation, I set out for John's house.

The congregation of Beech Green church was just emerging from the porch. Someone raised a hand to me, and I tooted the horn in reply, edging out to turn away from all these good folk as I went towards my old parish.

I wondered why I felt so remarkably buoyant. Was it just the weather? Was I feeling devil-may-care because I had skipped church that morning? Was it because I knew that my new suit was unusually becoming? Or was it, I wondered with some misgiving, that I was going to see John Jenkins?

I hoped it was not this last reason. Much as I enjoyed John's

company I had no intention of accepting him as a suitor although he had offered marriage often enough, heaven alone knew. I had lost count of the times he had proposed and been kindly, I hoped, rejected by me. No, I decided, turning into John's drive, it was just a happy amalgamation of all those factors that contributed to my well-being. I should continue to enjoy that happy state.

The most delicious aroma was wafting from John's kitchen, the honey was warmly received, and within five minutes we were sipping sherry in John's sunlit sitting room.

He was looking remarkably fit, and confirmed that he had now completely recovered from what he described as 'the Portuguese Peril'.

'And what have you been up to, besides deserting me for Fairacre school?'

I told him about George Annett's church pamphlet, and he was all in favour of a new edition.

'Nothing more off-putting than a dreary photo and small print,' he agreed. 'An aunt of mine tried to get me interested in *Lorna Doone* when I was about ten, and gave me a horrible edition with those shiny sepia pictures which look as though they have been executed in weak cocoa. It put me off for life.'

'Like double columns down the page,' I added, 'beloved of Victorian editors.'

'I'd better prod the bird,' said John, making for the kitchen. 'Come and give me your advice.'

I followed him to the oven and watched him raise the casserole lid. Everything smelt wonderful, but we agreed that the lid should now be removed so that the bird could brown.

We returned to our sherry and the conversation turned to the subject of recording the memories of the older generation.

'And ourselves,' added John. 'We're knocking on, and I don't suppose there are many of us left who can remember the Schneider Trophy air race, or even the Abdication.'

'That was quite something,' I agreed. 'The children used to sing: "*Hark the herald angels sing, Mrs Simpson's pinched our King*".'

'I like that,' said John delighted. 'I was in Kenya then, and feelings ran high.'

He put down his glass.

'Which reminds me,' he went on, 'if you really want to go on with this recording business, I have a tape recorder I can lend you. I bought it when I came back from Kenya. Do borrow it.'

I expressed my thanks, but wondered if I should ever get down to embarking on this worthy project.

'Perhaps keeping a diary would help,' I pondered. 'But I suppose it would be best to start that next January.'

'It sounds to me,' said John firmly, 'as if you are pro-crastinating. My father's motto was: "Do it now", which I found a little daunting at the time, but I can see the point now.'

'I suppose I'm beginning to get a reaction from my week's teaching,' I said. 'I have a feeling that my life might get a bit aimless.'

'Make me your aim,' suggested John. 'Think how rich and full your life would be married to me.'

'Is that today's proposal?'

'Of course. Or would you prefer a more passionate one after the pheasant?'

'I reckon that pheasant will be done,' I replied. 'Shall we investigate?'

It was, and very soon we settled down to enjoy the tasty meat. The fluffy apple in which the bird had been resting was deliciously flavoured with its juices and with the red wine which had been added. John had also cooked pears in red wine, explaining that as he had opened a bottle of good claret to moisten the pheasant dish, he felt it should be used up.

I complimented him on such exemplary domestic economy. He certainly was a very capable man, I thought, watching him prepare coffee. Really, one could quite see his attractions as a husband. But not for me, of course.

It was while we were enjoying our coffee that the telephone rang. Whoever it was at the other end must have been in full spate, for John's answers were sparse.

'No bother at all,' he said at last. 'I'll be there at three, without fail. See you then.'

'Henry,' he said. 'Ringing up from Ireland. I'm picking him up on Wednesday at Bristol airport.'

'With Deidre?'

'He didn't say. He sounded rather flustered, and kept

apologizing. I don't know why. I told him I'd meet him if he decided to come home at any time.'

'I do hope they've made it up. Poor old Henry is a bit lost on his own.'

'Well, don't take pity on him if he is. It's his own fault. There are far more deserving cases of lone men nearer home, you know. Would you like to hear more about one of them, or have a walk round the garden?'

'I think,' I said, putting down my empty coffee cup, 'I could do with a walk round the garden after that delicious meal.'

'Ah well!' said John, rising. 'There'll be another time, no doubt.'

'I was afraid of that,' I told him, laughing.

I drove home from John's feeling remarkably well in body, but disturbed in spirit. There was really no reason, I told myself, why I should concern myself about Henry Mawne. He and Deidre were quite old and experienced enough to know what they were doing, so why should I bother?

To be honest, I knew the answer. I just did not want the added complication of Henry's intrusion into my own life. Over the years he had caused me embarrassment and annoyance, and now with John to further complicate matters, I just prayed that Deidre would be accompanying her husband back to a settled life in Fairacre.

Another thought was niggling too. John's offer of his tape recorder had brought to the fore this nebulous idea of writing a book, or booklet, or perhaps a series of articles for the *Caxley Chronicle* based on the recordings I might be successful in wheedling from my older friends.

I had told John that I had felt somewhat restless after my week's work at Fairacre. This was true, but was it only transient? Did I really want to work again? I certainly did not intend to give up the delight of staying day-long in my own beloved cottage, and going out to some place of business.

Perhaps this little job of George Annett's would help me to settle things? It would be a feeler, keep me busy and interested, and it would not be too demanding mentally. After all, I had appeared several times in the columns of our local paper. I had a slight but happy relationship with the present editor, and felt sure that he would take any of the local memories I was envisaging for future subject matter. Of course, if I really got a lot of material I might make a whole book and post the type-scripts to the Oxford University Press or any other respected publisher.

Yes, I told myself, as I swung into my drive, the little pamphlet's up-dating should give me some idea of what I really wanted to do in retirement. I felt rather more settled in my mind as I unlocked the door and made my way into the sitting-room.

Here chaos confronted me. A starling had fallen down the chimney, and now dashed itself dementedly against the window-pane. I let it out and surveyed the wreckage.

The hearth was thick with soot. The carpet had a good sprinkling too, and my newly laundered loose covers on the sofa and chairs bore black claw marks and a light film of soot.

I went upstairs to take off my finery donned for the lunch party, enveloped myself in an overall, and went to fetch the vacuum cleaner, dustpan and brush, and a bucket of hot water and scrubbing brush.

The problems of future authorship, and those pertaining to Henry Mawne's troubles, were shelved.

I had enough of my own.

8 Christmas

PREDICTABLY ENOUGH November slipped quietly into December, and I had my annual shock on visiting Caxley to find that the shop windows were bedizened with Christmas trappings, and that there were men on tall ladders and a sort of fork-lift affair getting ready to string Christmas decorations across the High Street.

This year in particular I seemed to be unprepared. The fact that I had sent my overseas gifts off in good time had engendered a smugness which had insulated me against the stark truth that the bulk of my shopping had yet to be done.

An added factor was that for the first time I had had no Christmas preparations in school to keep me on my toes.

There was no time on that day to start Christmas shopping, and in any case I had not yet made a list of recipients and the right presents for them. I comforted myself with the thought that I had at least got all my cards in the cupboard upstairs, thanks to the RNLI and RSPB catalogues which had arrived on a scorching July day.

No doubt even that forethought would not be completely successful when the time came to write the cards. Usually, I had to scurry to Mr Lamb in Fairacre shop for a further dozen

of rather less superior articles. Any of my friends with sur-
names beginning with W, Y or Z were doomed to have cards
with lots of sparkle on them and unnecessary couplets of
doggerel inside.

It was Mr Lamb who first told me the news about Henry
Mawne. He had arrived home without his wife, and had said
little about her.

'There's talk of him selling the house,' said Mr Lamb,
adding two tins of Pussi-luv to the little heap of my purchases
on the counter.

'Oh, I hope he won't,' I cried. 'It's been in his family for so
long. I remember his aunt, Miss Parr, telling me about it.'

'Costs a mint of money to keep up, a place like that. They
say he might get something smaller in Ireland. Mind you, it's
not a good time to sell. No money about, and who wants a
great barn of a place like that?'

'Quite. I'm thankful I've only got a small cottage.'

'And a very nice one.' He looked at me speculatively.

'Now if you ever felt like selling,' he went on, 'I reckon
you'd soon find a buyer. I'd be interested myself, by the way, if
you ever decided to go into one of these flats attached to a
nursing home, for your last days as it were. I'm beginning to
think of retiring myself sometime. The shop's a great tie, and
the paperwork's something vicious.'

I was too stunned to reply, but paid my dues and left.

A short visit to Fairacre shop usually gave me food for
thought. I had plenty to mull over this time.

Did I really look so decrepit that my only option was a nursing home? Had I ever been foolish enough to say that I might
leave my cottage? I searched my mind, but had no recollection
of such a thing. In fact, I had always maintained that nothing
would induce me to leave Beech Green.

No, Mr Lamb, with his own retirement in mind, was simply putting out feelers, I told myself. But how aggravating it was, and what a cheek on his part!

My indignation continued for the time it took me to get home, and it was not until some time later that Henry Mawne's affairs crossed my mind.

Was there any truth in these rumours that his house might be for sale? Was he really contemplating going to Ireland? If so, did it mean that he was going to return to Deidre?

In any case, how did it affect me? To be honest, it would be a relief to have Henry Mawne out of my life. That was the over-riding fact, sad though I should be to see his fine old house in someone else's hands.

I began to feel a little sorry for him. Poor old man, he was getting on, and there seemed to be a lot of trouble ahead for him, one way or another.

Perhaps it would be simpler for him to give up his home and his wayward wife and just go into one of those nice flats attached to a nursing home, as recommended by Mr Lamb?

Who knows? I might meet him again there one day. It would be just like the gods to have the last laugh.

A day or two later, I found an invitation to a Christmas party at Fairacre school lying on the mat when I returned from a walk.

Jane Summers had probably dropped it through the letter-box on her way home to Caxley. I was sorry to have missed her, but was glad to see that she was prudently saving postage.

The invitation was written in a child's handwriting, and I put it in pride of place on the mantelpiece. That was one festivity I should look forward to attending.

Meanwhile I started to work on the church pamphlet. Basically, I decided, it provided useful facts about the building, but needed a few additions. For instance, a rather attractive stained-glass window in memory of twin sons killed in the First World War had no mention at all, which seemed a pity. The family was an ancient and honourable one whose seat had been at Beech Green for centuries. The last of the family had left in the fifties, and it was now a nursing home. (Perhaps it was this one Mr Lamb had in mind for me?)

There was also a fine Elizabethan tomb in the Lady Chapel, with rows of little kneeling children mourning their recumbent parents. This had been dismissed in the present leaflet with: 'The Motcombe tomb is to be found in the Lady Chapel.' I decided to give it more prominence in my version.

To this end I spent a happy morning in Caxley Library looking up the history of both families, and was surprised at how quickly the time passed whilst engaged on my simple researches.

Driving home I began to wonder if this sort of gentle activity was what I needed to fill my days in the future. I began to wax quite enthusiastic and wondered if a small book about local history would prove a worthwhile project. It could have maps in it, I thought delightedly. I like maps, and I imagined myself poring over old maps and new ones, and deciding how large an area I would cover, and what scale I should choose for reproducing them.

Caxley itself could provide a wealth of material for a volume of local history, but I decided that other people had done this before me, and in any case I had no intention of burdening myself with trips to the crowded streets of our market town to check facts and figures.

No, I shall concentrate on something simpler, Beech Green, say, or Fairacre. I remembered some of dear Miss Clare's memories of her thatcher father and his work, and of the way of life she had known as a child in the house which was now mine. If only I had written them down at the time!

Such pleasurable musings accompanied me as I went about my daily affairs. When at last I settled down one wet afternoon to write up my notes about the two families commemorated in my parish church, I began to have second thoughts.

This writing business was no joke. Both accounts were much too long. I did some serious cutting and editing, then began to wonder if my predecessor had discovered the same difficulty in describing the earlier tomb, which accounted for his terse advice to visit the Lady Chapel.

I put down my pen and went to make a pot of tea. I needed refreshment. Perhaps it would be better to devote my energies to recording people's memories, as I had first thought, and writing my own diary next year. I was beginning to realize that historical research and, worse still, writing up the results was uncommonly exhausting.

I had a chance to broach the subject of recording memories when Bob Willet arrived with Joe Coggs the next Saturday.

'We've come to split you up,' announced Bob.

I was not as alarmed as one might imagine. Translated it meant that he and Joe were about to divide some hefty clumps of perennials which had been worrying Bob for some time.

They went down the garden bearing forks and chatting cheerfully, while I went indoors to make some telephone calls.

I could hear them at their task. Bob was busy instructing his young assistant on the correct way to divide plants.

'You puts 'em back to back, boy. Back to back. Them forks.

Pretty deep. Put your foot on 'em, so's they gets well down. That's it. Now give 'em a heave like.'

I could hear the clinking of metal as the operation got under way, then a yell.

'Well, get your ruddy foot out o' the way, boy! You wants to watch out with tools.'

I hoped I should not be called upon to rush someone to hospital, and was relieved to hear no more yells, just Bob's homely burr as he continued his lesson.

Some time later, their labours over, we all sat down at the kitchen table with mugs of tea before us, and a fruit cake bought from the WI stall in the middle.

My two visitors did justice to it and Bob congratulated me.

'You always was a good hand at cake-making. My Alice said so.'

This was high praise indeed as Mrs Willet is a renowned cook. However, common honesty made me confess that I had not made this particular specimen.

I broached the subject of Bob's early memories, and drew some response.

'Well now, I don't really hold with raking up old times, but there's a lot I could tell you about Maud Pringle in her young days as'd make you sit up.'

The dangers of libel suddenly flashed before me. Perhaps old memories were not going to be as fragrant and rosy as I imagined.

'I wasn't thinking of *people* so much,' I began carefully, 'as different ways of farming, perhaps, or household methods which have changed.'

Bob looked happier.

'You can't do better than to talk to Alice. She remembers clear-starching and goffering irons and all that sort of laundry lark. She sometimes did a bit for old Miss Parr. She had white cambric knickers with hand-made crochet round the legs. They took a bit of laundering, I gather.'

I said I should love to hear Alice's reminiscences, and meant it.

'I could put you wise to old poaching methods,' said Bob meditatively. 'Josh Pringle, over at Springbourne, he was the real top-notcher at poaching. He'd be a help too, but I think he's in quod at the moment. He's as bad as our . . .'

Here he broke off, having recalled that young Joe was the son of the malefactor he had been about to mention.

'As I was saying,' he amended with a cough, 'Josh is as bad as the rest of them, but he'd remember a lot about poaching times, and dodging the police.'

I began to wonder if I had better abandon my plans for

enlightening future generations. Danger seemed to loom everywhere.

'Then there was that chap that worked for Mr Roberts' old dad,' went on Bob, now warming to the subject. 'Can't recall his name, but Alice'd know.'

'What about him?'

'He hung himself in the big barn.'

This did not seem to me to be a very fruitful subject for my project. Dramatic, no doubt, but too abrupt an ending.

'What about the clothes you wore as a child? Or the games you played?' I said, trying to steer the conversation in the right direction.

'Ah! You'd have to ask my Alice about that,' said Bob rising.

I said I would.

When they had departed, Bob with a message to Alice to ask if I might call to have a word with her about my literary hopes and Joe with the remains of the WI cake, I decided to ring John Jenkins.

I told him about my conversation with Bob Willet and my plan to visit Alice. Would it be convenient to borrow the tape recorder after I had seen her?

'Have it now,' urged John. 'I never use the thing, and if you've got it handy you may get on with the job.'

It sounded as though he doubted my ability to go ahead with the project.

'I'll bring it over straight away,' he said briskly, 'and show you how it works.'

He was with me in twenty minutes. I was relieved to see that the equipment was reassuringly simple, just a small oblong box which, I hoped, even I could manage.

'I think this plan of yours is ideal,' he said when he saw that I had mastered the intricacies of switching on and off. 'It's the sort of thing you can do in your own time, and there must be masses of material.'

'If it's suitable,' I commented, and told him about Bob Willet's memories of Mrs Pringle's youthful escapades and Josh Pringle's brushes with the law. He was much amused.

'Yes, I can see that a certain amount of editing will be necessary.'

He was silent for a moment and then added: 'You could tackle another local subject, I suppose. I mean some historical event like the Civil War. There were a couple of splendid battles around Caxley, and one of the Beech Green families played a distinguished part.'

This I knew from the church pamphlet I was altering, but I expressed my doubts about my ability to do justice to such a theme.

'I never know,' I mused, 'which side I should have supported.'

'As Sellar and Yeatman said in *1066 and All That*, the Royalists were Wrong but Wromantic, and the Cromwellians were Right but Repulsive.'

'Exactly. On the whole I think I'd have been a Royalist. Their hats were prettier.'

'So it's no-go with a historical dissertation?'

'Definitely not. I'll try my more modest efforts.'

I looked at the clock.

'Heavens! It's half past seven. You must be hungry.'

I mentally reviewed the state of my larder. A well-run pantry should surely have a joint of cold gammon ready for such emergencies. Mine did not.

'I could give you scrambled eggs,' I ventured.

'My favourite dish,' John said gallantly. 'You do the eggs and I'll do the toast.'

And so we ended the evening at the kitchen table, and were very merry.

The next time I saw Bob Willet he brought a message from his wife.

'Alice says could you put off this interview lark until after Christmas? What with the shopping and all the parties she's helping at, she can't see her way clear to think about old times.'

I said I quite understood and I would try my luck in the New Year.

In a way I was relieved. I too had a good many things to do before Christmas, and it would give me time to collect my thoughts about the proposed work.

'You're putting it off,' said Amy accusingly, when I told her.

'I know that, but the world seems to have managed without my literary efforts so far, and I reckon another few months won't make much difference.'

Meanwhile, much relieved, I finished my Christmas cards, decorated a Christmas tree for the window-sill, and looked forward to the party at Fairacre school.

Fog descended overnight, and the last day of term when the party was to take place, was so shrouded in impenetrable veils of mist that it seemed unlikely to clear.

Everything was uncannily still. Not a breath of wind stirred the branches or rustled the dead leaves which still spangled the flower beds.

There were no birds to be seen, and no sound of animal life anywhere.

There was something eerie about this grey silent world. One

could easily imagine the fears that plagued travellers abroad in such weather. It was not only the fear of evil-doers, the robbers, the men who snatched bodies from graves, the boys who picked pockets, but the feeling of something mysterious and all-pervading which made a man quake.

By midday, however, the fog had lifted slightly. It was possible to see my garden gate and the trees dimly across the road. No sun penetrated the gloom, but at least the drive to Fairacre would not be hazardous.

I wore my new suit and set off happily. This would be my first Christmas party as a visitor, and I looked forward to seeing all my Fairacre friends.

I was not disappointed. There were the Willets, the Lambs, Mrs Pringle with her husband Fred in tow, and of course the vicar and Mrs Partridge and a host of others.

Jane Summers, resplendent in a scarlet two-piece, and Mrs Richards in an elegant navy blue frock greeted us warmly, and I had a chance to admire the look of my old quarters in their festive adornment.

I was glad to see that the infants' end of the building still had paper chains stretched across it. The partition between the two classrooms had been pushed back to throw the two into one, and Miss Summers' end was decorated in a much more artistic way than ever it was in my time.

Here were no paper chains, but lovely garlands of fresh evergreen, cypress, ivy and holly. The splendid Christmas tree was glittering with hand-made decorations in silver and gold, and the traditional pile of presents wrapped in pink for girls, and blue for boys lay at its base.

I was pleased too to see that Mrs Willet had made yet another of her mammoth Christmas cakes, exquisitely iced and decorated with candles.

The vicar gave his usual kindly speech of welcome, and we were all very polite at first, but gradually the noise grew as tea was enjoyed. We were waited on, as usual, by the children and it was good to see how happy and healthy they looked.

The hubbub grew as we all moved about after tea, greeting friends and catching up with all the news.

'Mr Mawne hasn't turned up,' I heard Mrs Pringle say. 'But then I suppose he's got enough to think about.'

This was intriguing, but I was busy talking to Mr Roberts, the local farmer, and heard no more.

I had not noticed Henry's absence, but now I came to think of it, it was strange that he had not appeared. As a good friend of Fairacre school he had always been invited, and I felt sure that Jane Summers would have made a point of sending him an invitation. Perhaps he had another engagement, or was not well, or had returned again to Ireland? Who could tell? In any case, it was none of my business, I told myself.

People began to move off. The fog was thickening, and it was plain that we should have another black night.

I was sorry to leave my old haunts, and said goodbye to my successor and Mrs Richards with real regret. It was sad to leave the Christmas warmth and splendour for the cold murkiness outside, but I drove slowly home through the treacherous fog glowing with the aftermath of good food and good company.

Two days later, I set off for Dorset to spend Christmas with my cousin Ruth. I stayed with her until New Year's Day and returned wondering if I should be strong-minded enough to make the first entry in my new diary, as I had planned to do.

Years before, Amy had presented me with a large diary, and I had done my best to put a few meagre jottings into it through the months.

This time my new diary was a present from John, who was obviously going to see that I kept my nose to the grindstone.

I had every intention of doing my best. Over the years I have had so much pleasure from other people's diaries and I was interested to read recently that some psychiatrists recommend the activity. The theory, so I gathered, was that everyone needed 'a speech friend' with whom the small details of everyday living could be discussed. I promised myself that this diary would be my 'speech friend', and just as the great diarists of the past, Kilvert, Woodforde, Evelyn and Pepys, had put down their thoughts, so would I, in my small corner at Beech Green.

I recalled Virginia Woolf's comment on Parson Woodforde's diary-keeping: 'Perhaps it was the desire for intimacy.

When James Woodforde opened one of his neat manuscript books he entered into conversation with a second James Woodforde. The two friends said much that all the world might hear, but they had a few secrets which they shared with each other only.'

Even in the eighteenth century, it seemed, a 'speech friend' was a comfort. I too knew what it was to guard my tongue in a small community. In my diary I could relax and chatter away without any restraint or fear of gossiping tongues.

The day after my return, I took out John's handsome present, and with some excitement, laced with some trepidation, I made my first entry.

How long, I wondered, would I keep it up? Time alone would tell.

9 Problems Old and New

ONE BLEAK Wednesday afternoon in January Mrs Pringle arrived with news of Henry Mawne. I confess that I was eager to hear it, for I had not seen him for weeks, and the rumours about him were many and various.

The vicar, who had called to see me soon after Christmas, was sad and bewildered by Henry's circumstances, but seemed to know nothing of his plans.

Mr Lamb at Fairacre shop, my most reliable informant, was equally reticent.

'Well, I suppose you've heard about Mr Mawne,' began Mrs Pringle, as she hung up her coat and donned a cretonne overall.

'Not a word,' I told her.

'That's a surprise. I said to Bob Willet that if you didn't know then nobody did.'

I found this assumption that Henry Mawne would confide in me distinctly annoying, but said nothing.

'My cousin in Caxley said the house was going up for sale. It'll be in the *Caxley* this week.'

'But if it hasn't been advertised yet, how does your cousin know?'

'She works at the estate agent's office,' replied Mrs Pringle. I decided not to pursue that aspect of the news.

'I'm sorry to hear it. Henry will miss the place, I'm sure, and he has done marvels with the garden.'

'Well, he'll have to try his hand at gardening in Ireland, so I hear. They say he's going to get that new wife of his to see reason.'

I was unusually disturbed by this news, but tried to hide my feelings.

'Must be upsetting for you,' observed Mrs Pringle, eyeing me shrewdly. 'You and him have been through a lot together over the years. Want the windows done upstairs? I thought they were a disgrace last week.'

I gave my assent to the cleaning of the disgraceful upstairs windows, and went into the kitchen to ponder on this news.

It was maddening, of course, to have Mrs Pringle pitying me for what she enjoyed thinking of as my broken heart. My chief feeling towards Henry was irritation, and always had been. Nevertheless, he had many good points, and was an old friend. I was going to miss him.

But my chief concern was for Henry himself. His house and garden had always been dear to him, and to part with it now would be a terrible blow. Was it wise to throw away the pleasant life he had made for himself in Fairacre, to pursue an unpredictable future and a stormy marriage overseas?

I hoped he had found someone to advise him. No doubt his solicitor would have pointed out the pros and cons, and he must have many old friends with whom he could discuss his problems. I sincerely hoped that these troubles would soon be resolved for him, and that whatever the future held it would be happy.

Poor old Henry, I thought sadly! Well, at least he was

worrying this out on his own, as far as one could see. In the old days he had often brought his troubles to me, and I could not help feeling relieved that it seemed I was to be spared from any involvement in his present worries.

I should have known better.

Over our cups of tea, Mrs Pringle broached the subject of my work on old memories.

'I hear as you're having Alice Willet recorded,' she said, with some hauteur. 'Is it for the BBC?'

'Good lord, no!' I began to explain my modest aims, but she still looked offended. Could she be jealous of a tape recorder?

'I hoped you might tell me about some of your early memories too,' I said, doing my best to placate the lady. 'It needn't be recorded, of course. I could just make a few notes if you'd prefer it.'

'If Alice Willet's going to speak into one of those contraptions then I will too,' she said. 'I reckon my memory's as good as hers any day.'

'That would be fine by me,' I said hastily. 'I'd better see Alice first as I've mentioned it to her, and then I should love to hear your reminiscences.'

She looked somewhat mollified, accepted a piece of shortbread graciously, and things were back to normal.

As I drove her back to Fairacre, Mrs Pringle dropped her second bombshell.

'It's about Minnie,' she began, as the village came in sight.

'You know I don't want her to work for me,' I said firmly.

'I know that. And I don't want her messing up the work I do for you, I can assure you. It's quite bad enough getting your place clean without Minnie under my feet.'

My relief was short-lived.

'No, it was about something quite different.'

'What?'

'Bert.'

'Bert?' I squeaked in horror. 'What on earth is Bert to me?'

Bert is the most persistent of Minnie's admirers and the subject of many domestic rows in Minnie's home. Ern, her husband, is understandably jealous of Bert, and the police have often been called to break up a fight between the two men.

'Minnie wondered,' said Mrs Pringle, as I stopped at her gate, 'if you'd have a word with Bert and tell him to stop worrying her.'

'But, Mrs Pringle,' I expostulated, 'why me? I am certainly not going to do anything of the sort. Minnie's affairs are her own, and if she can't choke off Bert, with Ern's help, then she must call the police.'

'Ah well!' sighed Mrs Pringle, collecting her belongings. 'I told Minnie you'd say no, but she's got such an opinion of you. She says you could frighten Bert off with just one of your looks, but I told her how it would be. Still, I kept my word. I did mention it, didn't I, like I promised Minnie?'

'You did indeed,' I said, still seething. 'And now you must tell her that I absolutely refuse to have anything to do with the matter.'

Driving back I pondered on Minnie's touching faith in my disciplinary powers. Did I really have such a basilisk glare? It would have been nice to think I had, but it had certainly never worked on Mrs Pringle herself.

Galvanized into action by Mrs Pringle's remarks about Alice Willet's recorded efforts, I got in touch with my first contributor and arranged to bring to bring my tape recorder to her home one afternoon in the next week.

Making a date to suit us both was far from easy. Alice said that Monday afternoon was devoted to ironing, Tuesday was her Bright Hour afternoon, Wednesday she had to go to Springbourne manor house to shorten some curtains, Thursday, of course, was always out as it is Caxley market day, and would Friday be any good?

As Friday afternoon was the only day of that week when I too was engaged, we embarked on a long and complicated discussion about my calling on her after depositing Mrs Pringle on the Wednesday.

'Well, I think it could be done,' she said doubtfully. 'I'll be back from Springbourne by four, and Bob can have cold pilchards for his tea when he gets in.'

We left it at that, and I wondered how high-powered business men worked out their arrangements with clients abroad and their overseas flights, when Mrs Willet and I had such difficulty in finding an hour together in our comparatively tranquil lives.

But was it tranquil? I still wondered about that peaceful retirement I was supposed to be enjoying. Honesty pointed out that I really was having an easier time, but it was far more hazardous than I had envisaged.

There was the problem of dear old John Jenkins, for instance. There was this business of Henry Mawne, whose troubles, I felt in my bones, would one day be brought to my door.

Mrs Pringle was always with me as an irritant, rather like 'the running sore of Europe' one used to hear about in history lessons long ago. Turkey, was it, or France? No, if I remembered rightly 'France's bugbear was a strong and united Germany', so it must have been Turkey that was the 'running sore'.

And then, of course, there was Minnie Pringle, I thought, returning to my list of problems after my historical diversion. It was bad enough having to be on guard against giving her a job in the house in a weak moment, with the train of domestic catastrophes that would entail. Worse still was this new complication of being expected to mediate between Ern and Bert.

'Never come between husband and wife,' had been one of my mother's maxims, along with 'Lazy people take the most pains,' and 'Least said soonest mended.'

I certainly did not intend to become involved in Minnie's matrimonial affairs. Or her extra-marital affairs for that matter.

On the following Wednesday afternoon I duly arrived at Mrs Willet's with my borrowed tape recorder.

Mrs Pringle had eyed it somewhat scornfully as I put it on the back seat, and given a dismissive snort, which I ignored.

Alice Willet had prepared a tray with two teacups and an iced sponge cake large enough to feed a family.

I put the recorder on the table as we refreshed ourselves and assured Alice that I should not switch it on until she gave me permission.

Following Bob's mention of laundry work in her youth I started by asking her to tell me what she remembered. I was surprised at her fluency and memory for detail, and after two minutes switched on with her permission.

From descriptions of the sorting of linen, cotton and similar materials from the woollen ones (no man-made fibres in Mrs Willet's youth), she went on to starching, the use of the blue-bag, turning the heavy mangle by hand, and all the processes that followed.

Within ten minutes I had a wonderful amount of material on laundry work, and she went on, without prompting, to the mending of the freshly ironed clothes and household linen that needed repair.

'Would you like a rest now?' I enquired, but Alice then embarked on the preparations needed in the kitchen before preparing a meal for 'upstairs'. This involved so many technical terms connected with the coal-fired stove, such as 'dampers', that I feared I should have to get expert advice before translating Alice's account for modern readers, and we decided to end our session.

I played it back when I got home, and congratulated myself – and Alice, of course – on having such a wonderful start.

I was still in a state of excitement when Amy called on her way home from Oxford.

'A very good thing that you've found an interest,' she said approvingly, 'but rather a *solitary* occupation, this writing business. I should feel much happier if you *joined things.*'

'But I do,' I protested. 'I belong to Fairacre and Beech Green WIs, and am always buzzing about going to concerts and lectures. And things,' I added rather lamely.

'But it seems so *aimless*,' said my old friend. 'I feel you need to use your mind more. What about politics?'

'What about it?'

'Wouldn't you like to take an active part in helping your local candidate?'

'Frankly, no. And I've had quite enough of meetings and committees and all the rest of 'em while I was teaching. Now I'm enjoying retirement, don't forget, and even so, I get called upon to do jobs I really don't want to do.'

'You did a very good one on updating the pamphlet about the church here,' said Amy generously. 'Isobel Annett told me at the last Choral Society practice.'

'It's with the printers now, I believe,' I said, rather mollified. 'I quite enjoyed that little exercise.'

'Well, you were always good at English at college, so perhaps this little dabbling in old memories will be fulfilling for you.'

'You sound like my doctor,' I observed. 'He doesn't think I'm fulfilled because I haven't had children.'

'You don't want to take any notice of doctors,' said Amy sturdily. 'They get such silly ideas of their importance always being kowtowed to by adoring nurses. It gives them ideas above their station.'

She rose to go.

'By the way, I've promised to raise funds for the Dogs for the Blind some time. I thought a cheese and wine evening perhaps. Makes a change from a coffee morning, and one gets more men if it's a cheese and wine do.'

'I'll come to that with much pleasure. Better still, I'll come over and help you get things ready.'

'Better still,' repeated Amy, 'bring that nice John Jenkins or Henry Mawne. Or both.'

'Not together,' I told her.

Mrs Pringle had heard all about my recording session with Alice Willet, but was pleased to see that the instrument was lying on the kitchen table to be put to use during a prolonged tea interval.

I noticed her smoothing her hair and adjusting her blouse, as I switched on, as if she were facing television cameras.

'Shall I tell you about how my old grandma met her end?' she enquired. 'She had a funny turn coming down the steps at Caxley station, and her legs was –'

'Perhaps something more general,' I broke in. 'About your schooldays in Caxley?'

'Well, they wasn't all that different to things today,' began Mrs Pringle, thwarted of the gruesome account of her grandmother's end. 'Still, I could tell you what I wore when I went to school.'

'Splendid,' I said encouragingly, and she was well away.

'Well, in winter I wore a good woollen vest next to the skin, then a starched cotton chemise, then a petticoat, blouse, woolly cardigan and a pinafore over the lot.'

'Knickers?' I suggested politely.

'Of course,' said Mrs Pringle, bridling. 'Fleecy lined with elastic at waist and legs. In summer I had cotton knickers as fastened on to my Liberty bodice.'

It was surprising how much useful material was obtained at this session. When I came to play it back that evening, I found not only Mrs Pringle's memories of her youthful garments, but some fascinating recollections of old country remedies.

'If we had a stye on the eye, my mum used to rub it with her wedding ring. Had to be pure gold, you see, or it never worked.'

Parson Woodforde, I recalled, writing on the same subject in 1791, had been advised to stroke his stye with the tail of a cat. It had to be a *black* cat, but fortunately he had one handy, and proceeded to stroke the stye with its tail. He found some immediate relief but four days later, he notes 'Eye much inflamed again, and painful,' so presumably the cat's tail was not wholly proficient.

I went to bed that night full of hope for my future project. The next move, I thought, would be to jot down as much as I could remember of dear Dolly Clare's reminiscences. That should give me another few pages, I thought happily, as I settled down to sleep.

My other literary project, the keeping of my personal diary, was not faring so well.

The last entry, for instance, read: 'Washed my new cardigan. It had gone out of shape and the sleeves are now far too long, dammit.' Not, I felt, the sort of thing to match the work of Pepys or Evelyn. It was all rather dispiriting, and the murky January days did not help.

We had a spell of dismal weather, so dark that the lights had to be on all day, and one realized how near the arctic circle our storm-girt island lay. I longed for spring, for sunlight, warmth and flowers.

On just such a gloomy afternoon I was glad to have a visit from John Jenkins, who had called to return a book.

He had also brought me a bowl of early hyacinths, just coming into flower. Nothing could have been more welcome, as I told him.

He enquired after my literary efforts and I brought him up to date, remarking upon my uninspired diary entries.

'Cheer up,' he said kindly, 'at least you're keeping your hand in, and it's your life you are noting, not Pepys' or Evelyn's.'

We sat eating toasted crumpets and sipping tea, and were enjoying each other's company when the telephone rang.

To my surprise, it was Henry. Could he come and see me soon? He'd like to talk things over with me. My heart sank. 'Come to tea tomorrow,' I said, as warmly as I could. 'What's it about?'

There followed a lengthy monologue about his present troubles, Deidre's absence, the possibility of leaving Fairacre, and a touch of sciatica, to add to things.

'But do you think I can help?' I asked doubtfully.

He said that he knew he had been a confounded nuisance in

the past, but he would dearly like a sensible woman's views on his present plight. He sounded sad, but genuinely troubled, and I said I should look forward to seeing him the next day.

'That was Henry,' I told John.

'That man's a menace,' he said, jumping up impatiently, and beginning to pace up and down the room. 'Shall I see him off for you?'

'Why?' I said, suddenly extremely angry.

He turned to look at me, and his face changed.

'I'm sorry,' he said contritely, 'I shouldn't have said that. It's no business of mine.'

'Quite!' I said, still seething.

'It's just that I didn't realize you were so fond of old Henry.'

'I am *not* so fond of old Henry,' I almost shouted, in my exasperation. 'Henry has annoyed me on many occasions, and I think I know his faults as well as you do. However, he's in real trouble and wants my advice, for what it's worth. He's an old friend. He's always been generous to me and the school children. I shall do what I can for him.'

'You put me to shame,' said John. 'I'm sorry I've upset you. Perhaps I'd better go.'

'Oh, don't be a *chump*,' I said wearily. 'Sit down and have another cup of tea. We're not going to have a row about Henry.'

He resumed his seat. For the first time he looked thoroughly discomfited, and I liked him all the better for it.

'I should know better than to interfere in your private affairs,' he said. 'It's just that I'm so fond of you I hate to see you being bothered by anybody.'

'Point taken,' I replied lightly, and let him have the last crumpet.

10   Henry's Troubles

O F COURSE, I spent that night, the next morning and early afternoon pondering on the coming interview with Henry Mawne.

All that I had said to John during my outburst was quite true. Henry had been the source of much embarrassment to me over the years, but he was a decent man, I liked him, and I was very sorry for him at the moment.

On the other hand, all my mother's warnings about interfering in married couples' affairs, came back to me and, in any case, I certainly did not want to encourage Henry to come and pour out his heart whenever he felt inclined.

I thought he had aged a lot when he arrived, and soon supplied him with that panacea for all ills mental and physical, a cup of tea. It crossed my mind, as I handed it to him, that Amy would be delighted to know that I had company. My own unworthy thought was, should I ever have my house to myself?

He seemed unable to broach the subject of his unhappiness, and in the end I took the bull by the horns and said:

'Well, fire away, Henry. I am truly sorry about your present affairs. Can I help?'

'It really all depends on Deidre,' he began, crumbling a

piece of shortbread in a rather messy fashion, so that a goodly proportion was strewn on the hearth rug.

'She's still in Ireland, I suppose?'

'Yes, and likely to stay there. I don't blame her. She never really settled in Fairacre. But she is really being most difficult.'

I began to wonder if poor Deidre was going to be blamed for Henry's misfortunes in her absence. It rather complicated the issue for me as adviser.

'So what's the position?'

'She's determined to stay in Ireland, and I shall have to go there to live if I want to save the marriage.'

'And do you?'

Henry looked startled.

'Do I want to save my marriage?' he queried, sounding amazed at such a question. 'Of course I do! Deidre may be rather a handful at the moment, but I love her very much. Besides, we made a contract to keep to each other for better or worse, so long as we both should live. Can't go back on a promise like that!'

'Plenty do.'

'Maybe,' said Henry. 'I don't.'

At least one point was clear and I was not going to be called upon to come between husband and wife.

'Will you mind living in Ireland?'

'Not a bit. Lovely country, know quite a few people there, and the gardens do well.'

'So what's the problem between you both?'

'I suppose I tried too hard to get her to come back here. I really have put down roots in Fairacre, and I love the old house and garden. But she was so obstinate about it I lost my temper pretty often, and then she'd flit off to stay with friends and leave me "to stew in my own juice", as she used to say.'

'Have you been in touch since you've been back? Does she know you are willing to go back to Ireland?'

Henry looked doubtful.

'Well, I've written several times, but she doesn't read letters, and often doesn't answer the phone. I think I shall simply go back and tell her.'

'Have you got somewhere there to live?'

'That's the snag. She still owns – or rather rents – a tumble-down Irish cabin in County Mayo. We couldn't live there permanently, but I haven't enough cash to buy a suitable place until I've sold my own here. You know, I expect, that it's on the market?'

I said that I had heard. I did not like to say that I had been acquainted of this news long before the advertisement had appeared in the *Caxley Chronicle*, and from several informants, but Henry knew village ways as well as I did, so I kept quiet.

'What do you think I should do?' enquired Henry, looking helpless.

'You must tell Deidre what you have just told me, that you want a happy marriage and you are content to live in Ireland. Write and telephone as well, and if you don't hear from her you will have to get a go-between.'

'A go-between?' echoed Henry. 'One of those marriage guidance blokes, or counsellors, or whatever they call themselves? Not likely!'

He had turned quite pink with indignation, and I hastened to explain.

'No, no! I meant an old friend of you both whose judgement you valued. Or your solicitor. Someone like that who would explain things to Deidre if you hadn't been able to hear from her.'

Henry seemed relieved.

'Oh, our solicitor is just the chap over there. He was at

kindergarten with Deidre, and we go fishing together. Can't think why I never thought of him before.'

'But do try Deidre first,' I said hastily. 'And tell her you've put the house up for sale. It will show her you are really serious.'

'It's not going to be easy to sell. Wants a lot doing to it. Still, it's a nice place, and I'd like to see it go as a family house. Gerald Partridge seemed to think that some institution like Distressed Gentlefolk or Delinquent Boys might be interested.'

'Not to *share*, I trust. The Gentlefolk would soon be even more Distressed with Delinquent Boys under the same roof.'

Henry ignored my flippancy. He was looking at me with great solemnity.

'You wouldn't feel like going over to explain things to Deidre yourself, would you?'

'Definitely not!' I said firmly. 'Now, you write to Deidre this evening, and try to get her on the telephone, and if you haven't heard anything by early next week, then ring your solicitor and tell him to get on to Deidre urgently.'

'I suppose you're right,' agreed Henry, glancing at the clock. 'Well, I'd best get back. If I write tonight it should get the first post.'

He rose, and made for the door. There he turned.

'You are a dear girl,' he said. 'Helped me a lot.'

'Not really,' I said. 'You'd already worked it out.'

I opened the front door.

'See much of John Jenkins?' he said suddenly.

'Quite a bit.'

'Good! He's a thoroughly nice chap. He'd take good care of you. Always liked him.'

He strode off briskly to his car, and I returned to the fireside, pondering his comments on John.

Comparisons are odious, we all know, but in this instance

Henry appeared in a more favourable light than his old school friend who had spoken so disparagingly of him at our last encounter.

I carried the tea things to the kitchen, and returned with a dustpan and brush to clear up the remains of Henry's meal from the hearth rug.

I woke next morning with the comforting thought that there was absolutely nothing in the diary to upset my day, and also that it was the first of February, and surely Spring must come soon?

I promised myself a solitary walk in the woods nearby, and a leisurely potter in the garden sometime during the day. With any luck I might find that '*Peace came dripping slow*', as W. B. Yeats put it. It was high time it did, I thought.

It was wonderfully quiet in the little copse some hundred yards from my home. Only the rustle of dead leaves under my

feet and the throbbing of a wood pigeon's monotonous song above disturbed the silence.

I sat on a handy log and surveyed the scene. It was still a winter one, with bare trees and little foliage apart from two sturdy fir trees which must have provided welcome shelter to the birds during the storms.

But there were small signs of spring. The shafts of sunlight sloping through the trees provided some warmth, and near at hand the wild honeysuckle, which twined about the trunk of a young beech tree, was already showing a few tiny leaves, 'no bigger than a mouse's ear', as I had read somewhere.

On moving the dead leaves with my muddy boot, I unearthed the small shiny upsproutings of some bluebells which, in a few months' time, would be transforming the scene into a mist of blue and filling the wood with heady fragrance.

I picked a sprig of the honeysuckle to take home as a forerunner of spring, and half an hour later I put it in a glass specimen vase to stand beside John Jenkins' pink hyacinths, now at their best.

Much refreshed in spirit, I set about a pile of ironing which had been awaiting attention for far too long, and then resumed my outdoor wanderings around the garden.

It was showing hopeful signs of spring too. Already the early miniature irises, yellow and blue, were showing colour, and a viburnum had broken into leaf.

There was a good deal of bird activity in the hedges, and I guessed that nest-building had already begun. Altogether I had a delightfully refreshing day of solitude, and it was seven o'clock before the telephone rang. Luckily, it was Amy.

'Do you know,' I told her, 'you are the first person I have spoken to today.'

'Good heavens,' cried Amy, sounding shocked, 'how

dreadful for you! If only I'd known, I should have asked you here.'

I tried to explain that I had thoroughly enjoyed my day after rather a lot of visitors, but Amy could not understand it.

'I assure you, it's been like Paddington Station here the last few days,' I said, and told her about Henry's troubles.

'I think you've been very patient with him,' she said at last. 'He must be a rather silly man.'

'He's unhappy.'

'Well, I expect it's six of one and half a dozen of the other,' said Amy philosophically. 'They must sort it out together. You've done your bit admirably, I'd say.'

I felt quite flattered. Amy seldom praises me.

'It's about my proposed wine and cheese party,' she went on. 'The "Dogs for the Blind" do, I spoke about.'

'The children of Fairacre always called it "Blind Dogs",' I told her. 'They used to bring masses of silver paper for blind dogs. I can't think what they imagined the poor animals would do with it.'

'Didn't you explain?'

'Of course I did, but it went in one ear and out the other, I expect.'

'I know, I know,' said Amy sympathetically. 'Well, the point is that I must postpone the idea. James has a conference in Cyprus soon, and he wants me to go with him. I must say the thought of some sunshine attracts me, and as the dates I had thought of have already been snaffled by the local National Trust and the League of Pity, I'm bowing out until later in the year.'

'Fair enough. Count on me for help when the time comes.'

'Thank you, darling. And how's John Jenkins?'

'Very well,' I said guardedly.

'I gather he may be giving up his house in France,' said Amy.

'Friends of ours use the same agent over there. They know John slightly.'

'Oh? I hadn't heard anything about it.'

'Just a rumour, I expect,' said Amy lightly. 'You know how things get about.'

'I certainly do!' I said with conviction, and we rang off.

When Mrs Pringle arrived on Wednesday afternoon, it was obvious that she was bursting with news.

'You heard about our Minnie?' she asked. I felt my usual alarm at the mention of Minnie.

'Don't say she wants to call here,' I said.

'No, no! Nothing like that. But her Ern's run off.'

'Good heavens! It's usually the other way. Who with?'

Mrs Pringle bridled, and I felt that I had made a gaffe.

'With nobody! Just run off. Back to his ma, I expect. And he won't be welcomed there, that's for sure.'

I remembered Mrs Pringle telling me once of Ern's mother's high principles and her stern ways with malefactors, particularly those related to her.

'But surely she will send him back to Minnie?'

'That's the trouble. You see, Bert's moved in with her.'

Bert is one of Minnie's long-term admirers, and has caused more trouble than anyone in that storm-torn household.

'He must be mad!' I exclaimed.

A maudlin look came over Mrs Pringle's dour countenance.

'That's true. Mad with *love*!' she said, almost simpering.

There is a streak of sickly sentimentality in Mrs Pringle's otherwise flinty make-up, which never ceases to dumbfound me.

'But Bert must know he is making trouble,' I protested.

'He don't see it that way. He just wants to be with the woman he loves.'

I gave up. Minnie, Bert and Ern must get on with their own muddles. Let them stew in their own juice.

'Of course, if you'd like to have a word with Bert,' began Mrs Pringle, but I cut her short.

'No!' I said, fortissimo.

'In that case,' she replied, 'I'll Flash the bathroom.'

She made for the stairs. Her limp, I noticed, was marked.

Later that day Bob Willet cycled over from Fairacre, ostensibly to return a cookery book I had lent to Alice, but really, I guessed, because he needed company.

We sat by the fire with a glass of wine apiece, and Bob told me all the news.

'Heard about Minnie?'

I said I had.

'Don't blame Ern for slinging his hook, but that Bert wants his head seen to.'

I agreed.

'Mind you,' he went on, 'Bert is a useless article altogether. He's supposed to be a painter and decorator, but Mr Mawne had him in to do the doors and windows, and a proper pig's breakfast he made of it.'

I was secretly glad to hear of Henry, and rather hoped that Bob would tell me more.

'Bert with a paint brush,' continued Bob, 'was like a cow with a musket. I told Mr Mawne, on the quiet, to give him the sack. I could've done better myself, and I don't reckon to be a painter.'

He put down his glass and looked at the clock.

'Am I in your way?'

I reassured him on this point.

'Well, my Alice won't be back for an hour or so.'

I refilled his glass.

'Hey, watch it!' he protested. 'I'll be falling off my bike.'

'Well, you won't be breathalyzed.'

'That's true. Mr Mawne was the other night, but sober as a judge, so that was lucky. He still hasn't sold the house, you know.'

'So I gather.'

'It's not everyone's cup of tea.'

'Rather large, but someone might buy it as an investment.'

'Rather them than me,' said Bob stoutly, rising to his feet. 'I'd best be off before you gets me too tiddly.'

I watched him set off. He seemed as steady as ever on his ancient bicycle, and I returned to the fireside wondering once more about Henry Mawne's future.

11   A Fresh Idea

SIGNS OF spring grew thick and fast, lifting our spirits after January's gloom. The miniature yellow irises blazed in a sheltered corner, the first leaves of the bulbs were pushing through, and the horse-chestnut gleamed with sticky buds.

Two blackbirds were busy making a nest in the lilac bush near the gate, watched by Tibby with great interest.

But perhaps the most cheering sign was the lengthening days. I remembered Dolly Clare saying how she welcomed February, 'because you could have a walk in the light after tea'. From such little things does spring begin.

Some days after Bob Willet's visit, I had a telephone call from Henry Mawne. He sounded in his more usual, buoyant mood, and I felt relieved.

Evidently he had had some trouble in tracking down his elusive wife, but had taken my advice and got in touch with the solicitor friend who knew where she was staying at the time.

'Luckily, she answered the phone,' said Henry, 'and I must say was very sweet and helpful about everything. I'm flying over tomorrow, and that's why I'm ringing now. You were such a tower of strength, and I want to keep you in the picture.'

I must say that it was nice to hear that I had been a tower of strength. I must remember to tell Amy sometime, I decided.

'Did you mention the house?' I asked.

'Which one?'

'Yours, of course. Is there any other?'

'Oh! *My house* here, you mean? Yes, I told her it was up for sale. She was pleased about that.'

I thought he sounded a little hurt at Deidre's reaction.

'I do mind a bit about it, you know,' he said, as if he had guessed my thoughts. 'If I had the money to put it right, I

think I'd have gone on with my efforts to persuade Deidre to stay here.'

Privately, I thought it would have been banging his head against a brick wall, but I voiced my thoughts more kindly.

'Well, you tried, Henry, heaven knows, and you got nowhere by sticking to your guns like that. In fact, it may have made Deidre more decided, as it happened. I'm sure you are doing the right thing to put your marriage first.'

Whether he had been listening to my words of wisdom, I don't know, but his next remark was about another house.

'Deidre's been looking out for somewhere to live over there. That's why I was in a muddle when you mentioned a house. No hope yet, but property's not so expensive there, so with luck, the sale of the Fairacre one should provide something Deidre likes. And where she wants it, of course, which is the main object.'

'Well, good luck with it all, Henry,' I said, rather anxious to end the conversation, as Tibby had just walked in holding a writhing mouse.

'I'll be in touch from Ireland,' he assured me.

I put down the receiver to attend to more immediate problems. Tibby was not amused.

I had not seen John Jenkins since our little tiff about Henry's affairs, but he had rung once or twice, and I knew he was busy with something to do with Uncle Sam's affairs.

As a young man Uncle Sam had put money into some farming project in South America. It had not proved very lucrative, but now that he was dead there was a certain amount of clearing up to do, and the authorities over there were remarkably difficult to pin down, according to Uncle Sam's solicitor.

'As far as I can see,' John had told me, 'there will be nothing coming in from all these tedious negotiations but a hefty bill from the legal eagles on both sides of the Atlantic. I'm just letting them get on with it.'

He ended the conversation in the routine way by asking me to marry him. I expressed my usual appreciation of the honour he had done me and refused yet again.

Sometimes I wondered what he would do if I said 'Yes'.

But I did not intend to try it.

The wind got up on the night that Henry had rung me. The windows shuddered in the onslaught, and clouds scudded across the face of the full moon.

The winter-bare branches of the copper beech tree waved wildly this way and that, and the roaring of the gale made sleep impossible.

I went downstairs to make a cup of tea. It was the sort of night when roof tiles slid off, and chimney pots hurtled to the ground. I hoped that Henry's roof would stand up to the rigours of the wind, and was glad that I had a snug thatch to protect me.

It was quieter in the kitchen at the back of the house, and I sat at the table with my tea and hoped that the gale would blow itself out before poor old Henry set off.

At least he would be flying, and not have to face hours on that notoriously choppy crossing from England to Ireland.

But I was apprehensive for Henry's future, although it was really none of my business. My opinion of him had risen considerably since our talk about his problems. I thought that he was tackling them with wisdom, patience and courage. I only hoped that Deidre would continue to co-operate as she seemed to have done when Henry had at last tracked her down.

Although I liked Deidre, I suspected that her feelings and her loyalties were nowhere near as firmly rooted as Henry's. She was a light-weight. She was wayward and spoilt. Would she lead Henry a dance when she had him back, or would they be able to settle down, I wondered? Well, no good speculating, I told myself, draining my cup.

I went to bed again, and slept like the dead, oblivious of the raging storm around me.

The rough weather continued for several days, and when Mrs Pringle arrived the next Wednesday 'to bottom me', she was wind-blown and breathless.

'I was nearly flung to the ground waiting for the Caxley,' she told me. 'Tossed about like a leaf.'

I tried to envisage Mrs Pringle as a twelve-stone leaf, but failed.

'Plays my leg up real cruel,' she went on, 'and Fred's got his chest again.'

I bit back the query as to where Fred's chest had been, and helped her off with her coat.

'You'd better sit down,' I said, 'before making a start.'

She lowered herself heavily into a chair, and sighed.

'I told you about Ern, didn't I?'

I said that yes, indeed she had, and was everything settled now?

A look of intense satisfaction spread across her face.

'Thanks to Ern's mum, everything's fine.'

'Good,' I said, waiting expectantly.

'It's like this. As you know, Ern's mum has got a nice little corner shop in Caxley, and a flat above it. Savings too, she's got, so Ern thinks, and as he's the only child he reckons he'll come into it all.'

'And will he? I had an idea she had threatened to cut him out of her will some time ago because of his behaviour.'

'That's right. She did *threaten*, but never actually done it. But this time she took a stronger line. No sooner had he turned up, when she told him that he was to take her to Springbourne and she'd sort things out.'

'But Bert was there surely? Wasn't that rather rash?'

'You don't know Ern's mother. If ever there was a Christian soldier it was her. Right's right and wrong's wrong to her, and she told Ern he had duties as a husband and father, and he was just to get back home and do them.'

I began to feel the greatest respect for Ern's mother. If ever she decided to stand for Parliament, she would have my vote.

'Go on, what happened?'

'Well, knowing as that will of hers was going to be altered the very next morning, of course Ern had to take her back in the van. She took her husband's old gun with her too. Not loaded, of course, but she wasn't above giving Bert – or Ern, for that matter – a clump on the head with it.'

The kitchen clock ticked on as Mrs Pringle's narrative continued, but I decided the housework took second place this afternoon.

It appeared that as soon as the van pulled up and Ern's redoubtable mother emerged with the gun, Minnie Pringle set up the sort of hysterical screaming that engages the attention of all within earshot.

Consequently, interested neighbours appeared in their front gardens, or at open windows, the better to take part in the drama.

It was a swift victory. As the raiding party, Ern and his mother, stormed up the front path, Bert ignominiously burst

from the back door, leapt the privet hedge and ran across the field of turnips to take cover in a nearby wood.

Minnie, still yelling, opened the front door, two toddlers clinging to her skirt, to let in her husband and mother-in-law, who carried the gun pointing before her.

The onlookers had the exquisite pleasure of seeing Ern's mother prop the weapon by the umbrella stand with one hand and administer a sharp slap to Minnie's face with the other, before the front door was slammed shut, and the noise of the battle ceased.

'She told me,' said Mrs Pringle, 'that this was the last straw, and she told Minnie and Ern that if she heard another squeak out of them or out of Bert, her shop and the flat and her savings in the Caxley Building Society was all going to the Salvation Army. She's always been a great supporter of that, and Ern knows it.'

It seemed right to me that such a militant Christian should leave her resources to such a good cause, and said so.

'She will too,' said Mrs Pringle, struggling to her feet. 'I think she's settled their hash properly this time. Gave them a good fright.'

'What about Bert?'

'If my Minnie's got any sense, and mind you, she hasn't got much, as we well know, she'll keep Bert at bay, if he's silly enough to worry her again.'

She looked at the clock.

'Is that the time? Well, if you will keep me gossiping here, I shall just have to leave the brights till next Wednesday, and do the usual and leave it at that.'

I felt that the postponement of attention to the copper and brass objects in my establishment was a small price to pay for being brought up to date in the stormy history of Minnie's matrimonial affairs.

As we drove home after her labours, Mrs Pringle asked how my work on old memories was progressing, and I was obliged to tell her that I was not getting on very fast.

The project, I had to admit to myself, for some time now, was not very satisfactory.

Apart from Mrs Pringle's contribution and that of Mrs Willet, there were very few sources, I discovered.

I had jotted down those memories of Dolly Clare's which I could recall, but she would have supplied a wealth of material.

Dear old Doctor Martin who had been in practice when I first came to Fairacre, and Miss Parr who had lived at Henry Mawne's house in my early days, were dead.

The vicar had said that he would do his best to recall anything that might be of interest, but frankly, I did not think the material he could offer would be particularly interesting.

I discussed my problem with John, who had read all my efforts and given me much encouragement. He was also somewhat critical, so that I was alternately flattered and dismayed.

'I think this trivial sort of thing is getting you nowhere,' he announced. 'You say yourself that you'll never get enough useful material together to make a book. What else can you do with it?'

I told him that I had broached the possibility of an article or two in the *Caxley Chronicle* with the editor.

'And what did he say?'

'He was diplomatic, but decidedly daunting. He said they had masses of similar material, and suggested I might like to use some of my stuff for 'corner-fillers' on their 'Local Memories' page. You know, 'How Grandmother Cured her Chilblains' in two hundred and fifty words. I don't want that.'

'I should hope not.'

John looked at me steadily.

'You know you write extremely well. Forget this fiddling about and start a proper book.'

I looked at him in horror.

'A book? A novel, do you mean? I haven't a clue about thinking up a plot, to begin with!'

'You could do it,' he said decisively. 'That is if you really do want to carry on with this writing idea. What made you start anyway?'

I tried to explain about my restlessness after that week of teaching again at Fairacre school, and he listened patiently.

'I think that simply brought things to a head,' he said at last. 'You were full of euphoria when you first started retirement, revelling in having time to yourself and so on, and then this spell of teaching just made you realize that you needed something more from life than just mooning about in the fields and woods.'

'I don't care for that expression "mooning about"', I told him. 'You make me sound like some loony old witch.'

He ignored my interruption and continued.

'And you're right, of course. You're much too bright to find complete satisfaction in domestic matters.'

'Thank you,' I said, somewhat mollified.

'On the other hand,' he went on, now well away in analysing my problems, much to my amusement and some surprise, 'you're not the sort of person who wants to play bridge or golf, or join a lot of clubs where you meet hordes of people. That I can well understand.'

'So what do you suggest, dear Agony Uncle?'

'Well, you could marry me, and find enormous satisfaction in looking after me. It would be a very noble aim, and much appreciated.'

'Nothing doing, John.'

'So I feared. But that aside, I do think something like writing, which you could do in the solitude you like so much, might be just the thing for you.'

He looked so earnest that I got up and kissed the top of his head. He really had the most attractive silvery hair I had ever seen on a man.

'What's that for?' he asked, looking up.

'To thank you for all your kind concern, and as I was passing to put on the kettle, I gave you a friendly kiss.'

'You couldn't make it more passionate?'

'Not until we've had our coffee,' I told him, going into the kitchen.

After John had gone, I thought about his ideas for my future. I was much touched by his concern for my happiness, and wished I loved him enough to marry him. What a simple solution that would be!

His final words about my proposed literary career had been spoken as we walked down the path to his car.

'You know, I couldn't possibly write a novel,' I protested.

'No one asked you to. It was your crazy idea to write a novel. All I think is that you should write about something you know.'

'But I don't know anything.'

He stopped to unlock the car door, and then straightened up.

'You know all about being a village schoolmistress for years. You could start on that.'

He waved to George Annett who was wobbling by on his bicycle, and then got into the driving seat.

'I'll give you a word-processor for your birthday,' he promised, and drove away, leaving me to mull over all his plans for my future employment.

It was good of him to take so much interest, I thought, as I went about my affairs during the next few days, and I was intrigued by his insight into my character.

He was quite right about my dislike of joining things that would mean meeting lots of people. Amy was not nearly so perceptive, although she had known me far longer.

I remembered her horror when I had told her that I had been alone all day. To Amy solitude was anathema. To me it was vital, at least for part of my day. John had recognized that. He had also realized that domestic duties would not satisfy me. Of course, it might have been a polite way of excusing my house-keeping shortcomings. Perhaps he thought me a proper slut? Compared with his own immaculate house I supposed mine might look rather a mess, despite Mrs Pringle's weekly attentions. It was a chastening thought.

I decided to put aside all these problems. After all, I had come to terms now with my retirement. Despite John's assessment of my needs, I was slightly less restless than I had been after my unsettling week at Fairacre school, but maybe I did need some central interest which I could pursue at my own pace and in the quietness I preferred.

I would think about it. Thankfully my health seemed to be restored after what Mrs Pringle called 'my funny turn', actually a slight stroke.

I had good health, a dear little house and, even more precious, a host of friends.

These things spelt happiness.

12 Looking Ahead

HENRY MAWNE was as good as his word, and I had a long conversation with him one evening on the telephone.

He sounded happy and said that he and Deidre had been busy searching for a house that they both liked and could afford.

'Any luck?'

'Well, we've looked at everything from one-roomed cabins you wouldn't keep your chickens in, to crumbling castles, but I think we've whittled it down to a couple of farm houses. They've both got enough fields to keep horses for Deidre.'

'I'd no idea she wanted horses,' I said, somewhat shocked.

'Oh, everyone keeps horses in Ireland,' said Henry airily. 'Just as we keep an old bike in the garden shed.'

'And are prices high over there?'

'Less than ours, which is a good thing. And the great news is that the Caxley agent has had an offer for the Fairacre one.'

'Well, that's marvellous! Will you take it?'

'It's not the asking price, of course, but I hardly expected that. But it's a very fair offer and I shall certainly accept it.'

'Who is it?'

'No idea. The agent didn't say. I'll know before long, I expect.'

He asked after his Fairacre friends, told me that he would be writing to the vicar about a discrepancy he had found in the church accounts, and we rang off with mutual expressions of affection to all and sundry.

I was delighted to know that all was going well, and hoped to hear more about the purchaser of Henry's property when I met Mrs Pringle or Bob Willet or Mr Lamb in the near future.

To my surprise, Mrs Pringle knew nothing about it, but hinted darkly about *developers* who more than likely would raze Henry's home to the ground and put up a couple of dozen rabbit hutches on the site in which you couldn't swing a cat should you so wish.

Bob Willet was no more help, and Mr Lamb had heard it was 'some old gent who was now past driving and wanted to be within walking distance of the shop and the church and that.'

With these unsatisfactory snippets I had to be content, but knowing village life I felt that I should soon learn all.

Spring seemed lovelier than ever this year. The early daffodils had 'come before the swallow dared', and lit the garden with their brightness.

The growing warmth lured me into the garden, and all sorts of indoor duties such as turning out cupboards, sending loose covers to the cleaners and polishing the windows, simply went by the board.

One sunny morning I was busy weeding at the end of the garden, watched by Tibby lolling nearby, when I thought I heard somebody at the front door, and went to investigate.

I found John trying to stuff a large envelope through the letter-box.

'Hello,' I said. 'You'd better let me have that before my letter-box snaps your fingers off. What is it?'

'Open it and see,' he said.

'Well, come and sit in the garden,' I said, pulling off my muddy gloves.

We sat side by side on my new garden seat. I ripped open the envelope. Inside were two things. One was an exercise book, and the other a long box containing a splendid pen.

'John,' I exclaimed with delight, 'this is the pen the opera stars use in the advertisements.'

'And the top footballers,' added John.

I turned to the exercise book. It was one of those nice old-fashioned ones with multiplication tables on the back, and the useful rhyme about the days in each month.

'Heavens! How this takes me back,' I cried. 'How clever of you.'

'It's really to start you moving with that book of yours,' he confessed. 'I thought you'd be more at home with a pen and exercise book, and once you're well away I'll add the word processor.'

'I'll have a go,' I promised him. I began to feel quite excited at the prospect.

'Good girl!' he said, stretching out his long legs and turning his face to the sun.

'Let's go out for lunch,' he added. 'What about that nice pub we visited once when we were going to Stratford? The White Hart, or The Red Lion, or some coloured animal.'

'You don't mean The Blue Boar?'

'No. It was up on the downs. We went through Spring-bourne to it. They always do bubble-and-squeak.'

I racked my brain for more coloured-animal pubs which did bubble-and-squeak, but drew a blank.

'Do you mean The Woodman?'

'That's right. Let's go there.'

'I'd love to. Coffee first, or go now?'

He looked at his watch.

'Let's go now while the sun's out. We'll get a marvellous view from the top of the downs.'

The sun was high as we got out of the car, and walked on the springy turf to a handy five-barred gate nearby.

The view was indeed marvellous. The village of Fairacre could be seen below us to the left, and Springbourne to the right, two small settlements dwarfed by the great fields about them.

'That reminds me,' I said. 'I had a call from Henry a day or two ago.'

'How is the old boy?'

'He sounds more hopeful. Deidre is being co-operative at the moment and they are busy looking for a house. Thank goodness that after all this time he has had an offer for his Fairacre place.'

John's answer astounded me.

'I know. I made the offer.'

When I had got my breath back, I bombarded him with questions.

'But why? Why go to Henry's house when you have a much nicer one in Beech Green? Do you mean to leave that one?'

John turned round from the gate and leant his back on it. He looked amused.

'No, I do not intend to leave the house in Beech Green, at least for some time.'

'Well, that's a relief! I should miss you terribly. But why buy Henry's?'

'Come back to the car and I'll tell you. This downland air is very invigorating but a trifle parky, I find.'

'It's like this,' said John, as we trundled gently away towards bubble-and-squeak. 'I'm looking to the future. There's going to come a time when my staircase at the cottage is going to be a problem. It's steep and twisty. Added to that, I have to get out the car every time I need anything. In my old age I shall want a ground floor flat within walking distance of the village shop and the church, not to mention neighbours nearby.'

I suddenly remembered Mr Lamb's comment about 'the old gent who was past driving,' and began to laugh.

'What's the joke?'

I told him.

'Well, as you see, he's just about right,' was his comment.

I was still perplexed.

'But can you afford to run two homes, John? I believe Henry's place needs a lot doing to it.'

'It certainly does,' he agreed. 'But luckily I've sold my place in France. I've got past coping with the drive down, or even hanging about at airports. I'm now shortening all my lines of communication.'

By this time we had arrived at The Woodman, but we sat in the car outside to continue the story.

'Also I had the chance to sell my share of Uncle Sam's holding in that South American farming project. Some distant cousin, twenty-five times removed, has taken it on, which should bring me in something. When, heaven knows, but I'm keeping my fingers crossed.'

'You seem to have been very business-like, and I'm so relieved you are staying in Beech Green.'

'I shan't go until I'm absolutely decrepit, but I've always liked Fairacre more than Beech Green, and that house of Henry's is a gem. I shall enjoy doing it up. Besides, it's going to be my source of income in the future. I could make three first-class flats out of it and they should bring in quite a bit. I shall have a lovely ground floor one to share with you as soon as you say the word.'

I began to laugh.

'Is that today's proposal?'

'Of course. And I forgot to say that dear old Uncle Sam's effects have been sold at quite incredibly high prices, and I have the proceeds. So can I invite you to share a dish of bubble-and-squeak?'

'Indeed you can,' I assured him, as we emerged from the car.

There was plenty to think about in the next few days. I was much impressed by John's efficiency and the way he was facing the future.

If things worked out as he hoped then he would have a pleasant and rewarding time ahead putting Henry's house in order. He had asked me to help him with advice, and this I looked forward to doing. It was good to know that he had done his old schoolfellow a good turn when Henry had been in a difficult situation. Henry had always expressed his admiration of John to me, but it was John who had, until now, been somewhat dismissive and derogatory about Henry.

I did not like to think of myself as the woman in the case, but there was no doubt about it that once Deidre appeared again on the scene John's attitude had become less aggressive towards Henry.

In any case, they must get on with it, I thought, and maybe in the light of these new developments peace and harmony would be restored.

I had put John's exercise book on the dresser to remind me of my promise to him 'to have a go', but the days passed, and I found myself feeling more guilty daily.

If I were to take his advice and write my own memoirs as a village schoolmistress, I ought to think of a title, I told myself. This, of course, kept me from the dreaded moment of writing on the first blank page of my exercise book.

What about *Memories of a Village Schoolteacher*? Too dull, I decided. Or perhaps *Rooks Above the Playground*? Too fanciful, I thought. *Country Children*? *The Heart of the Village*? Somehow none seemed right.

I did actually sit down at the kitchen table one morning and open the exercise book. I sat staring at the virgin page in a state of gloom. Surely, all books should begin with an arresting opening which would lead the reader on to pursue the two or three hundred printed pages with rapture.

At that moment Amy had rung me, and I put the book back thankfully on the dresser.

She was delighted to hear about John's present and my future literary success, and promised to buy a dozen copies for Christmas presents.

Mrs Pringle, on Wednesday afternoon, was less enthusiastic. She picked up the book by its corner, as if it were something highly contagious, and asked what I was doing with it?

I said, with some hauteur, that I proposed to write in it one day. She sniffed, and limped away.

The book began to haunt me. To put it out of sight in a drawer seemed like admitting defeat, so it stayed on the dresser and gave me a twinge of conscience every time I passed it.

A week or two after our lunch at The Woodman, John picked it up and looked inside. I felt like a child caught with a spoon in the honey pot.

'My darling girl,' he cried, 'you haven't written one word!'

He looked so disappointed I could have wept. He brushed aside my feeble excuses with his customary kindness.

'Good lord!' he said briskly. 'Don't let it bother you. If I thought you would worry I shouldn't have given you the things. Put 'em in the dustbin, and forget all about it.'

He changed the subject by telling me that all was going ahead steadily with the purchase of his new house, and that he and Henry had had a long telephone conversation, to their mutual satisfaction. Better still, Deidre was being the perfect wife, and they had started their own negotiations for the farm-house of her choice.

'They hoped,' he added, 'to see us over there when they had got settled.'

As he went, he picked up the exercise book.

'Shall I dispose of it for you?' he asked. 'I'm not going to see you worrying about the wretched thing.'

'No!' I said with sudden strength. 'Leave it there. I may get inspired some time.'

It was obvious, I thought, as I waved him goodbye, that I was going to get involved in other people's affairs, as well as my own, during my peaceful retirement.

*

Three days later, I came in from 'mooning about the fields and woods' as John had once described my walks.

The early evening sunlight had fallen across the neglected exercise book, and seemed to exert a stronger influence than ever. I sat at the kitchen table, and opened it. I reviewed again the half dozen or so titles which had occurred to me over the weeks. Somehow they all seemed pretty trite, and I could not see hordes of eager readers flocking to the booksellers to buy it.

I turned resolutely from this dispiriting thought. After all, one did not need to have the title until the book was written. In fact, it would probably be best to see how it turned out before labelling it.

I picked up John's lovely pen. A vision of his disappointed face, as he had seen my empty exercise book, floated before me.

I pulled the book before me, refusing to be daunted by that virgin page, and all the others which followed it.

On the top line I wrote: CHAPTER ONE, and felt marvellous.

At last, I had made a start.

MISS READ OMNIBUSES

Fairacre

Thrush Green

Miss Read

'Evocative and captivating stories of village life'; 'the epitome of Englishness'; 'Her books avoid sentimentality and have an asperity like the tartness of a good apple'.

These are all comments that have been made about the novels of Miss Read. You might remember your mother reading them, or perhaps you have never come across them before? They are a world of enchantment, the perfect antidote to the crime and madness that take up so much of the shelving in a modern library.

There are two chief settings for Miss Read's stories – the Cotswold village of Thrush Green, and Fairacre nestling under the Berkshire Downs – and novels centred upon either appeared more or less alternately since the first, *Village School*, was published in 1955. Between that and the final book, *A Peaceful Retirement*, published in 1996, there are over forty titles. Any one of Miss Read's books can be read on its own without reference to the others, but a definite progression does emerge through the development of the characters, and life in these villages themselves.

Miss Read (alias Dora Saint) trained as a teacher and taught for several years in a large school in Middlesex. Shortly before the war, she married and moved to Wood Green just outside Witney in Oxfordshire, on the edge of the Cotswolds. This village was destined to become Thrush Green. After the war, the couple moved to a small village on the Downs, the inspiration behind Fairacre. Miss Read's literary career commenced with short articles and stories for *Punch*, *The Times Educational Supplement* and *The Lady*, and when the MD of Michael Joseph spotted one of these stories, the rest, as they say, is history.

Miss Read was published throughout her career by Michael Joseph Ltd in hardback and Penguin Books in paperback.